DUNAWAY'S CROSSING

Nancy Brandon

Published by Lake Union Publishing, Seattle

www.apub.com

Amazon, the Amazon logo, and Lake Union Publishing are trademarks of Amazon.com, Inc., or its affiliates.

ISBN-13: 9781477821251
ISBN-10: 1477821252

Cover design by The Book Designers

Library of Congress Control Number: 2014947631

Printed in the United States of America

DUNAWAY'S
CROSSING

For Stephen

Chapter 1

1918

"M iss Bea Dot! You all right? What happen to you?" California's husky voice penetrated the darkness, first as a tinny, distant sound, as if on the other end of a telephone line, but gradually growing clearer. No one ever had trouble hearing California. Bea Dot's mind cleared at the warmth and gentle pressure of her housekeeper's wide palm on her back.

"What Mr. Ben mad about this time?"

Bea Dot opened her eyes, disoriented at first by the close-up sight of the heart-pine floor. She shifted her gaze, and a piercing pain jabbed at her temple as she focused on California's shabby shoes and ashy brown shins. Pushing up from the floor, she stopped a few inches from it, wincing. "Please help me up, Cal," she said with a shaky, almost whimpering voice.

California knelt and slipped a tree limb of an arm under Bea Dot's back and cradled her head in a wide, calloused palm. "You got a nasty knot on your forehead," she said, rubbing her thumb against Bea Dot's dark brown curls. "I'll get you in bed and then call Dr. Arnold."

Bea Dot rested for a moment on her housekeeper's arm, hoping the headache would subside, tuning out the raspy voice as she tried to remember what she'd done this time to provoke her husband's ire.

"Always knew Mr. Ben was uglier than the devil. Meaner too." California talked on, unaware that Bea Dot only halfway listened. She leaned her throbbing head on California's shoulder, and the wooly braids brushed against her cheek. "Don't know why men think they got to hit they wives, 'specially in your condition. He never knocked you out before. Temper's getting worse."

Bea Dot touched her temple, ignoring California. She needed a bed, not commentary. With Cal's support, Bea Dot managed to rise. After pausing a moment to let a wave of nausea pass, the two women shuffled toward the bed, and Bea Dot kicked something that clinked like broken glass.

"Don't worry 'bout that, Miss Bea Dot. I'll get you a new frame."

Ben must have broken the picture of Bea Dot's mother. Was the damage deliberate, or just a casualty of his tirade? Suddenly all thoughts of Ben vanished as Bea Dot's midsection seized her like a boa constrictor taking hold of her body. She cried out as she doubled over and her legs collapsed.

"I got you, missy. I gone take good care a you."

The authority in California's voice did little to sooth Bea Dot. California scooped her up in strong arms and carried her to the bed, laying her down like an infant. Bea Dot pulled her knees to her chest and rolled on her side, the cramps burning and squeezing her insides. She clamped her eyes shut, and tears rolled across the bridge of her nose and onto the pillow. Her head pounded while the rest of her constricted in agony. When the muscles finally relaxed, a moist warmth between her legs shocked her eyes open, and she exhaled, feeling relief for the first time in her five-month marriage.

"You gone be all right," California crooned as she rubbed the back of Bea Dot's head.

Bea Dot reached behind her, clutching California's hand. "Call Dr. Arnold, Cal," she said. "Then please call my aunt Lavinia."

Bea Dot sat propped against her pillow, dark brown curls looping over her shoulders. From the teacup and saucer in front of her, the stink of beef broth steamed her nostrils. She curled her lip at the thought of sipping it. The afternoon August heat offered no breeze through the partially opened window. Why couldn't she have a nice glass of iced tea?

"You must keep up your strength," Aunt Lavinia and California told her each time either of them pushed the teacup closer to her face.

Aunt Lavinia sat in the maple rocker that used to belong to Bea Dot's mother. Resting on the floor next to it was a basket of fabric strips, which Aunt Lavinia rolled absently into white balls. "Dr. Arnold says you're young and strong," she said without looking up from her rolling. "I imagine you'll be pregnant again in no time."

Bea Dot wasn't worried about that.

California had swept up the broken glass. After placing the picture on the bureau, she had taken the dustpan out back to empty it. Now she'd returned to take away the pile of soiled linens and Bea Dot's bloody clothes. Aunt Lavinia rose and eased herself onto the edge of the bed, rubbing Bea Dot's arm consolingly as she spoke. "Darling, Dr. Arnold wants to know if you want to name the baby."

Bea Dot plunked the teacup and saucer on her side table. Beef broth sloshed out, and a brown stain spread on the crocheted doily. Why would she want to name a dead baby? She bit down on her thumbnail and whispered, "No." Then she turned her face to the window. A blue jay lit on the dogwood branch outside.

Aunt Lavinia turned to face California, then shook her head quickly. California nodded and left the room, her arms full of linens.

"Look at me," Aunt Lavinia said softly after turning back to her niece.

Reluctantly, Bea Dot faced her aunt and found love and urgency in the aged eyes. Bea Dot prepared for unsolicited advice. This time, though, numb from the day's ordeal, she didn't dread the conversation, but only wondered why Aunt Lavinia insisted on wearing her gray-blond hair in that insipid Gibson-girl bun.

"What set off Ben's temper, darling?" Aunt Lavinia asked in a low, grave voice. "Did you two argue?"

Bea Dot sighed and shook her head. The blue jay flew away. She wished she were it.

"Uncle David could speak to Ben's father," Aunt Lavinia suggested. "Maybe ask him to give Ben some marital advice. You're still newlyweds after all. Perhaps Ben has a misperception of what it means to be head of a household."

Bea Dot exhaled a snide chuckle. "Do you really believe that's the problem?" she asked. "A simple misunderstanding?"

Aunt Lavinia pressed her lips and straightened her spine, and Bea Dot regretted her stinging words, but she also knew Uncle David's intrusion would only exacerbate Ben's anger. After a few seconds, Aunt Lavinia leaned forward, her talcum scent blending with the odor of beef broth.

"I'm only trying to help," she said. "Your marriage can't continue this way. I never understood why you insisted on marrying Ben, but since you did—"

Thank goodness Dr. Arnold entered the room. A lock of gray hair fell over his forehead, and he had rolled his sleeves to his elbows. He approached the end of the bed, placing his black satchel at Bea Dot's feet and resting his white-haired arms over it.

"Thank you for coming, Doctor," Bea Dot said.

"You're welcome, dear. How are you feeling now?"

"Stronger."

"Glad to hear it. Now, I will tell Ben you need your rest for several days."

"All right." Bea Dot nodded. How much did he know? She suspiciously eyed Aunt Lavinia, who had returned to her chair, intent on rolling her bandages.

"Only your aunt and California can visit," Dr. Arnold explained, "but in a few days you should consider going someplace where you can, uh, get some fresh air, take your mind off your loss."

Bea Dot tensed as the doctor searched for polite words. She shifted accusing eyes to Aunt Lavinia as her cheeks heated in shame. Then she stared at her hands, too embarrassed to face Dr. Arnold.

"I'll check on you Thursday, but call me if you need me." He picked up his satchel and stepped toward the door.

"I'll see you out, Doctor." Aunt Lavinia stood and followed him.

Exhaling, Bea Dot reclined against her pillows, glad, finally, to be alone. She relaxed in the just-washed stiffness of the linens. Closing her eyes, she inhaled their off-the-line scent. The pain in her forehead had subsided to a dull ache. Maybe she could sleep.

Before she drifted off, a shuffle roused her again. Ben leaned against the doorframe, holding a folded newspaper, which showed only half the front-page headline: "President Wilson Calls . . ." Ben's pudgy pear shape and doughy skin belied his actual strength. Bea Dot always bit her tongue when friends observed how lucky she was to have married the second in command at Ferguson Shipping. What they didn't know was that the smallest provocation brought out her husband's demons, and her short marriage, Bea Dot had met them often. For now, it seemed, he had tucked them away.

"You lost the baby," he said, with neither regret nor contempt.

"Yes."

He nodded, then looked at the floor, shifting his weight from one shoe to the other. His height and girth filled the doorway.

"Can you have others?"

Bea Dot raised one eyebrow skeptically. He wanted more children? The thought of conceiving a child with him chilled her, but she willed herself not to shudder. "Dr. Arnold hasn't said one way or the other."

"We'll have to ask him."

"Yes, we will," Bea Dot replied calmly, knowing *we* wouldn't ask the doctor anything. Ben had been absent throughout Dr. Arnold's visit. Not that Bea Dot wanted him.

"Your head." Ben touched his left brow. "Does it hurt?"

"A bit." She lightly touched her temple.

"I hadn't realized how hard I hit you."

Was that an apology?

"Dr. Arnold says I'll be fine." Immediately Bea Dot wanted to kick herself for excusing his violence.

"Well, I'm glad you're all right," he said, still in his neutral tone. He'd have used the same tone with his employees at the office.

What else could she say to him? He offered no words of comfort. She hadn't expected any. The couple eyed each other for a beat. Then he said, "I just came from my parents' house."

So that's where he'd been.

"Mother and Father wish you well." He sounded like a business letter.

"Thank you," Bea Dot echoed in the same tone. "That's very kind of them."

"They asked how long your recovery would be. They're eager for a grandson, you know."

Of course. The precious grandson. She should have known where his priorities lay. The stilted conversation tired Bea Dot. How long would he stand there, barely pretending to care? "Dr. Arnold says I need rest," she said in what she hoped was a convincingly tired voice. "Perhaps I should try to sleep." She pulled the covers up to her chest.

"Yes, maybe you should," he replied as he turned to leave, but before walking away, he faced his wife again, this time with a slight, curious frown.

"Bea Dot, are you sorry you lost this baby?"

Was he that perceptive? Bea Dot surveyed the room, as if a suitable reply would present itself somehow.

"Don't say anything," he continued. "I'm not. I just want you to know I think this . . . ordeal . . . is for the best. I couldn't have stood raising another man's child."

Bea Dot sucked in a breath and held it. How long had he known? And how did he find out?

"Yes, I know, but your petrified look confirms it."

Bea Dot's face and neck burned with humiliation. "I'm sorry, Ben," she muttered as she examined the monogram on her sheet: BFB.

After a pause, he replied, "You'll be sorrier if you ever deceive me again."

Chapter 2

"Cough."

"Why?"

Ralph Coolidge sighed heavily as he pressed the stethoscope against Will Dunaway's back. At the touch of the cold disc, Will stiffened his spine, which pulled at his wound. He winced.

"Dammit, Will, don't be contrary. Just cough for me."

"It hurts, so I'd rather not. Why do you need to hear my lungs anyway? I have broken bones, not pneumonia."

Ralph stepped around the examining table and faced his patient, his downturned mouth revealing slight frustration. "Structurally, you're fine. You'll still feel some discomfort for a while because of that puncture wound and the compound fracture. Luckily, we got you home when we did, so I could set the bone correctly. But I want to listen to your lungs, so will you please cooperate?"

Guilt softened Will's attitude. After all, his friend had bent over backward to bring him home to Pineview. Still, Will had a busy afternoon and needed to get going. "Just tell me why, Ralph."

The physician frowned slightly, crossing his arms and leaning against the cabinet in the crowded examining room. "I'm checking all my patients as I see them. No need to panic," he began, and with that remark, Will felt a pellet of alarm, "but a bad influenza has sprouted up north and in a few army camps in the Midwest."

"Widespread panic?" Will exhaled and smiled. "Over the flu? I've had that dozens of times."

"Not this flu." Ralph shook his head. "It's a menace. It spreads quickly in densely populated areas, and it kills. That's one reason I wanted you out of that hospital tent at Camp Gordon."

Ralph returned to the examining table and stood behind Will, pressing the cold stethoscope under Will's shoulder blade. "Good thing Netta's father plays poker with Senator Hardwick. Without his influence, you might still be in France. Now, cough."

Will nodded, also thankful for his friend's family connections but still baffled as to how a country doctor attracted a wife from such a prestigious family. He coughed and pinched his face as a claw of pain grasped his right side. He'd be glad when he could move freely without the gripping reminder of the gruesome crash at Belleau Wood.

"Thank you," Ralph said, hanging the earpieces of his stethoscope around his neck. "Your lungs are as clear as spring water. You can put your shirt on now."

About time. As he dressed, Will watched Ralph write notes in a file. In the August humidity, the pages stuck to Ralph's hands as he wrote, and perspiration stained the shirt under his thick arms.

"How's the work coming along at your store? Open for business yet?" Ralph asked.

"Next week, maybe." Will had managed to pull his sleeve over his still bandaged arm, but buttoning the shirt one-handed challenged him. He worked slowly as he answered Ralph. "I'm on my way to the post office to talk to the master about a rural route."

Ralph whistled softly. "The farming families out there will love you. Terrence Taylor still helping you with the carpentry?"

"Helping's an understatement," Will said, exhaling a soft chuckle.

"Not much I can do with one hand." He had succeeded with three buttons and was working on the fourth.

"Come by next week." Ralph turned to face his patient, looking over his wire-rimmed spectacles. "We'll remove that bandage."

"I'll appreciate that." Will had managed the fourth button. Only one more to go.

Ralph closed his file and leaned forward with his next question. "How are you doing . . . you know . . . otherwise? Sleeping through the night? It's not unusual for returning soldiers to, well, suffer some emotional or psychological effects."

"I'm fine," he lied. Annoyance bubbled in Will's gut as he focused on the last button. No doubt he was glad to be home, but would everyone pry into his emotional state like this? He sensed Ralph's skeptical gaze. Still, he refused to meet the doctor's eye.

"Okay, then," Ralph relented. "I'll see you in a week."

"Thanks, Ralph."

Will exited the small office, which was adjacent to the Coolidge home. He untied his horse, Buster, from a nearby fig tree and led it to the front steps of the house. He still had to use a step or stool to climb into this saddle, but at least he could get around town now, instead of staying cooped up in the Coolidges' extra bedroom, bound by bandages and memories. Using the aid of the steps, Will lifted his leg into the stirrup and pushed himself over the saddle, the twinge of the exercise having subsided significantly over the past couple of weeks.

"Oh, Will Dunaway," a woman's voice came from behind him.

Will turned Buster so that he could face Ralph's wife, Netta. She held a napkin-covered plate in one hand and a glass of lemonade in the other. Beads of condensation dripped down the glass and over her fingers. Her usually long, slender face was puffed in her late pregnancy, and she leaned back slightly to accommodate her growing girth.

"Hello, Mrs. Coolidge." Will tipped his brown leather hat as he greeted her. "You look like a picture this morning."

Netta laughed shyly in response as she looked down at her white cotton smock. "Perhaps a picture of a hot-air balloon," she joked. "I'm sorry you have to see me this way. I was just taking Dr. Coolidge his lunch. I didn't realize he had a patient."

"He has no one now," Will replied. "We just finished our appointment. And you look lovely. If I may say so, your condition becomes you."

Netta blushed before saying good-bye and disappearing into her husband's office. Will started his horse down the double ruts of the Coolidges' long drive, wondering if he'd embarrassed Netta with his compliment. Coming from a refined Savannah household, she always impressed him as more polished and graceful than Pineview's other ladies—more nervous as well. With her large, wide-set eyes and long chin, she reminded Will in more ways than one of a deer.

He took his horse slowly into town, pulling to the side of the dirt road for motorcars. He made way for them more often these days. A few passengers called out to him, and he replied to their backs as they passed. On Depot Street, he tied his horse to a corner lamppost, away from the row of parked automobiles. Then in his typical long-legged gait, he ambled down the sidewalk, stopping here and there to reply to the townspeople's typical greetings:

"So glad you're home safely."

"You look so well."

"We'll have you to supper sometime soon."

"We're all so proud of you."

That last remark drove a stake right through him. Since when was killing American soldiers something for an ambulance driver to be proud of? Will felt not one bit heroic. However, he politely but hurriedly thanked the well-wishers and went on his way. As he passed the funeral home, its owner stepped outside with a broom. Will called to him without stopping.

"How goes it, Pritchett?"

"Rather slow these days, Dunaway." The undertaker swept his front stoop.

"Glad to hear it," Will replied as he passed by, and ambled down the sidewalk to the redbrick post office on the other end of the block. Inside, Will expected to find the young woman the postmaster recently hired. She had moved to Pineview from nearby Hawkinsville, and since starting her job, she greeted Will with an irksome flirtatious simper. To Will's relief, the postmaster stood at the window and, upon seeing him enter, immediately drew out some papers from a nearby drawer.

"Thanks for coming by. Here are those papers I mentioned." He placed them on the counter. "Just fill these out and sign them, and I'll send them to Atlanta."

Will moved to the end of the counter to fill in the blanks. When he finished, he returned the paperwork to the postmaster.

"Like I told you before," the postmaster said as he double-checked the forms, "we'd rather have someone with a motorcar deliver the mail out there. Makes delivery go faster, you know. Any chance you'll get one sometime soon?"

"Afraid not," Will said, shaking his head. "But to my knowledge, no one else is signing up for that rural route."

"You're right," the postmaster replied. "I'll take what I can get."

"Besides," Will said—as he usually did when someone suggested he purchase a car—"horses don't run out of gas, and they don't break down."

But the real reason was that the ambulance at Belleau Wood weighed on him like a lead jacket. He'd never forgive himself for killing his comrades, and he couldn't stand to be behind a wheel. He shivered at the sight of a gearshift, which tortured him with the memory of that broken rod piercing his side. Whenever a careless driver veered off a muddy clay road, Will winced at the recollection of moans from injured soldiers thrown atop each other in the back of the wrecked truck.

"Will? Did you hear me?"

"Sorry." Will snapped back to the present. "What did you say?"

"I said I'll let you know when I hear back from Atlanta. Here's a map for the meanwhile."

Will shoved the map in his rear pants pocket and left the post office. With no steps in sight for a boost, Will pulled himself into the saddle, the skin at his side pulling like a stretched canvas. Although he'd have a scar forever, he hoped the sensory evidence of his injury would soon disappear. He chucked Buster's sides again with his heels and led the horse out of town toward his new home.

The horse's slow gait made for a long but painless ride home. Under his wide-brimmed leather hat, Will's brown hair dampened in the Georgia heat. As the wide clay road led him through a pine forest, the August sun gave way to evergreen shade—and insects. Holding the reins close with his right hand, the one with the bandaged arm, he waved away deer flies with his other. Once out of the woods, Will continued past acres of cotton fields. The deer flies' torment abated as the sun resumed its oppression. Over the fields, Will gazed at the welcoming farmhouse where he'd grown up, now occupied by the Taylor family.

Summer had been good to the cotton crops, blessing farmers with early rains and no boll weevils. If those tiny crop destroyers stayed away another month or two, the Taylors would be set for the year. Maybe in a few years, if the store succeeded, he could buy back some of his father's property and grow cotton of his own.

Several miles later, Will's new home came into sight—a roadside wooden building, the main part grayed and weathered, but two sections on each side constructed of new yellow lumber. From underneath the front tin overhang, a lanky figure under a straw hat carried a toolbox and placed it next to the water pump. As Will approached the building, he waved his good arm and called, "How'd you do today, Terrence?"

The lanky figure turned toward Will, lifted the hat, and wiped his damp forehead with his forearm. Only fifteen years old, Terrence Taylor, the son of Will's neighbor to the east, already stood six feet tall. His sweaty blond hair drooped over his freckled forehead before he replaced the straw hat. Then he disappeared under the overhang, only to return a second later carrying a small wooden bench. He placed it on the ground, and Will steered his horse to it.

"Thanks." Will slid off the horse and onto the bench. He actually only needed the boost for getting into the saddle, but he appreciated Terrence's consideration. "So tell me," he repeated, "how'd you do today?"

"I finished," Terrence replied, smiling broadly with pride.

"You hung all those shelves?"

"Yes, sir, I did. She's all done." Terrence always referred to Will's remodeled building as *she*, something Will found silly. But when the young man offered to do cheap carpentry, Will asked no questions about vocabulary. "All she needs now is some dry goods to put on 'em," Terrence said.

"I've got some in the back room at Richardson's in town," Will replied. "More's on order. If I work straight through, I can open for business by Monday."

"Mama will be glad to hear that," Terrence said, shifting his weight to one foot.

"That baby hasn't come yet?"

"Nope, but she's moving slower and slower. It'll be any time now. With a baby in tow, she ain't gone be able to get into town."

"I should stock some baby goods, then," Will suggested.

"I'll ask her what she might need." Terrence then lifted his gaze to the truck approaching from the east, the same way Will had come. "Here comes my pop."

Will and Terrence watched the Ford truck approach and pull over next to them. Thaddeus Taylor, a bear of a man, pushed himself out of the driver's seat and lumbered over to where Will and Terrence stood. "Whatcha know, Will?"

"About ready for business, thanks to your son's help."

"Glad he's been some assistance to you." Thaddeus nodded to his son with a look of pride and said, "I come by to offer you a ride home. You ready?"

"Yes, sir," Terrence replied.

"Just a minute, Terrence," Will interjected. "I'll go inside and draft you a check."

Terrence shoved his toe into the red dirt. He eyed his father, as if for approval, before saying, "You ain't got to pay me, Will. Instead, could I fish in your lake some time or another?"

"Now, don't be silly, Terrence." With hands on hips, Will cocked his head at the boy and his father. "You worked too hard not to be paid. Besides, your land has almost a whole mile of lakefront. You have access to the water."

Terrence studied the ground again before glancing at Thaddeus. Putting two and two together, Will chastised his neighbor. "Did you put him up to this?"

"You ain't got to pay him, Will. We're happy to help out, help you get back on your feet again."

Will sighed. Why did the Taylors feel guilty about taking over the Dunaway property? He'd much rather see them take the land than some stranger.

"It was my father went broke before he died," Will said, "not me. I have money. Now I'm paying the boy. He's earned it." To Terrence, he said, "Wait here. I'll be right back."

Inside, the empty store smelled of sawdust. Will stepped behind the front counter, opened the drawer underneath, and pulled out his check binder. He wrote a draft to Terrence Taylor, ripped out the check, and took it outside, where he tucked it into Terrence's shirt pocket.

"Thank you, Will," Terrence said.

"Why don't you come to the house for dinner?" Thaddeus asked.

"I appreciate it, but I've got a lot of work to do if I want to open shop Monday. I'll eat a quick bite here."

"What, a can of sardines?"

"Nothing wrong with that. They're good for you," Will argued.

"Eliza's right, Will," Thaddeus chided. "You need to find yourself a good woman to take care of you."

Will bristled at the mention of marriage. People suggested that almost as much as purchasing a Model T. Amazing he didn't have more time on his hands with so many people minding his business for him.

"I'll cross that bridge when I come to it," he said. "Right now, I got my hands full with this store." Although he received war benefits, that modest income could never support a business. He'd sunk his small inheritance into the store. He needed it to thrive.

"If you're opening Monday, you'll need to give it a name," Terrence said.

Will lifted his eyebrows. He hadn't thought of that. "You got any ideas?"

Both Thaddeus and Terrence surveyed the building and grounds, as if the name would appear from behind a bush.

"You're at a corner," Thaddeus said. "How 'bout Will's Corner?"

"Hmm." Will shook his head with uncertainty. "That sounds more like a soda pop stand. What about something plain like Pineview General Store?"

"Nope," Terrence said. "You got to have your name in it somewhere." He stared at the crossroads that lay just beyond the building. After a pause, his face lit up. "This here's Dunaway's Crossing."

Chapter 3

Even as she kept to the shady side of Whitaker Street, sweat trickled between California's braids and tickled her scalp. Why hadn't Miss Bea Dot sent her to the stationer's early in the day? Thanks to Miss Lavinia's tongue, news of Miss Bea Dot's miscarriage had raced over the telephone lines. Now, even though Dr. Arnold ordered peace and quiet, the Ferguson household had been flooded with visitors bringing flowers, food, and sympathy. Now Miss Bea Dot had run out of paper for the thank-you notes, just when California was trying to cook dinner. A new box of stationery in hand, she hustled back, praying no motorcars stirred up the dust that stuck in her nostrils and throat.

As she crossed Jones Street, Forsyth Park's azaleas and oak trees appeared in the distance. Not much farther now, thank heavens. She just might be able to get back in time to iron the linens and polish the silver before the chicken was done. Lately she'd been trying as hard as Miss Bea Dot—maybe harder—to avoid Mr. Ben's fury, and nothing sparked his anger more than a late meal. Fortunately, during Miss Bea Dot's convalescence, Mr. Ben kept his temper on the back burner. But there was no telling when or what might turn that heat up.

As she approached Gaston Street, the rumble of an engine taunted her. "Nasty motorcars." She scowled, wondering about their appeal. True, they were fast, but they were also loud and expensive. She rolled her eyes at the amount Mr. Ben had paid for his new touring car. The racket grew louder, and Cal tensed her shoulders, anticipating a deposit of dust on her clothes and face. Maybe she could get back to work before another one of those machines drove by.

Holding her hand to her brow, she squinted against the afternoon sun. Ahead, Lavinia Barksdale, engrossed in a letter, sauntered along Gaston Street toward the same corner California approached. The car's rumble, now upon her, drowned California's voice when she called, "Morning, Miss Lavinia." Eyes still on her letter, Mrs. Barksdale stepped into the street to cross.

"Miss Lavinia!"

California grabbed Mrs. Barksdale's arm and pulled her back as the Dodge full of Savannah High School students whipped by, the passengers oblivious to the near miss. Lavinia yelped as California jerked her out of harm's way. Pages of her letter flew above her, then fluttered to the ground like leaves.

"What on earth!"

"Miss Lavinia, you almost got yourself killed. You got to watch where you going."

Dumbfounded, Mrs. Barksdale watched the car disappear around a distant corner while Cal chased after the scattered pages of the letter, picking up papers in one hand while clutching the package of stationery in the other. She handed a wrinkled wad of pages to the perplexed woman.

"Cal, thank you. I don't know what would have happened if you hadn't come along."

"Well, I do. And it would a been some kind a mess. You best put that letter away 'til you get where you going."

"Actually, I was on my way to see Bea Dot." Mrs. Barksdale folded the pages and stuffed them back into their envelope. "I have a letter from Netta, and I wanted to show her."

"Hmph. You were 'bout to go in the wrong direction and get flattened." Cal followed as Mrs. Barksdale crossed Gaston Street, this time keeping her eyes ahead of her. Almost single file, they walked toward the Ferguson house.

"How is my niece, Cal? Is she recovering?" Mrs. Barksdale asked over her shoulder.

California nodded gravely, more to herself than to the lady in front of her. "People been coming every day. They's got so much food in the house, Miss Bea Dot's asked me to take some home. Don't know why people think they got to bring food in a time a sorrow. Grieving people ain't hungry." At least black people weren't. When she lost her own baby all those years ago, sorrow made paste of the smallest morsel of food. For weeks her mama got nothing down her but broth and coffee.

"Poor child." Lavinia sucked her teeth and shook her graying blond head, her poufy bun an upside down mushroom of hair. "Considering how it happened, this loss must be even worse than any one of Netta's."

California knew better, but she chose her words carefully. "Seems more relieved than anything."

Mrs. Barksdale stopped and turned, shading her eyes as she looked into California's leathery face. "What do you mean?"

"Soon as Miss Bea Dot started showing, that's when Mr. Ben got ornery, scowling at her—and me—all the time." Cal's butterflies alit inside her stomach. Miss Bea Dot wouldn't like her divulging such personal information, but what else could she do? She felt partly responsible for her mistress's condition. And Miss Lavinia could help. "Nothing suited him, not that Miss Bea Dot tried very hard. Fact, she seemed to egg him on. Once I asked her should she be talking to him that way. She told me to mind my business. That was a week 'fore she lost the baby." Cal bit her lip, stopping herself before she revealed too much.

"Oh, Cal. I thought this recent episode was the first." Miss Lavinia put her hand to her mouth, which must have been open as wide as her blue eyes.

"No ma'am. 'Course, he never hit her when I'm around."

Mrs. Barksdale resumed walking. California followed close behind as she talked.

"But it's all different now, Miss Lavinia. Since the . . . accident, they act polite to each other, not like married folk. They more like two squabbling children whose parents made 'em be nice to each other."

"Well, I declare." Mrs. Barksdale held her hand to her chest as she frowned.

When she and California had reached the Ferguson home, they stopped on the sidewalk. Miss Lavinia thumbed the envelope she held as California tacitly prayed, *Stick your nose in her business. It's what you do best.*

"What can I do to help her?" She spoke more to the letter than to California, who was delighted her prayer had been answered.

"I been with Miss Bea Dot since she was a baby," she said. "I was about her age then too. All this time I ain't never seen her like this. She need a change."

Miss Lavinia sighed and turned her daughter's letter over in her hands. "You might be right. Maybe she could come stay with me and Mr. Barksdale for a while."

California looked to the heavens. White women could be so simple. "Miss Lavinia, she don't need to go up the street. She need to go away." Moving in with her aunt wouldn't solve Bea Dot's troubles, only bring on a new set of them.

"Or maybe she needs to go somewhere she's loved and needed. I think I know just the place." Miss Lavinia held her letter in one hand and tapped it on the palm of the other.

California watched Mrs. Barksdale ascend the steps to the front door before going round to the back. "Mm, mm," she muttered. "Thought she'd never think a sending Miss Bea Dot to Pineview."

The scent of roast chicken permeated the house as California situated the aunt and niece in the parlor with a pitcher of lemonade and two glasses filled with ice chips. Then she returned to her work. She should have ironed the linens first, but polishing the silver kept her in the kitchen close to the chicken—and within earshot of the ladies' conversation.

Miss Lavinia read her reorganized letter and told Bea Dot the news of her only daughter. "She's feeling fine, thank goodness, but to be on the safe side, she mostly stays home. She goes out only when absolutely necessary."

"Well, that makes sense," Bea Dot replied in a dull but polite voice. "After all she's been through, she has reason to feel gun shy, even this far along."

Like a silent participant in the conversation, Cal nodded. Three prior miscarriages justified Netta's caution.

"And Bea Dot," Miss Lavinia continued, "Netta is heartbroken to hear about your loss, just as we all are. She so wanted you to have children the same age."

Cal paused with the silverware as Bea Dot paused before replying. Why would Miss Lavinia say something like that? Miss Bea Dot hadn't heard from her cousin in almost a year. Then a knot formed in Cal's stomach. She felt partly to blame for that rift.

"Well, that is so sweet of her," Bea Dot finally replied. "Do tell her thank you for me."

"Why don't you write her yourself?" Aunt Lavinia suggested kindly.

California chuckled quietly at Miss Lavinia's remark before mumbling into the sugar spoon, "Might as well ask her to kiss Miss Netta feet."

"Maybe I will," Bea Dot replied.

Cal shook her head at her mistress's lie. At the same time, impatience grew in her gut. Miss Lavinia was taking too long to get to the point.

"Why don't you go to Pineview to visit Netta?" Miss Lavinia continued like a mind reader.

Cal heard Bea Dot cough and plunk her glass on the table. "Aunt Lavinia, I can't just pack up and go to Pineview."

"Why not?"

"Well, first of all, I haven't been invited."

"Oh, good heavens, Bea Dot." Exasperation rose in Miss Lavinia's voice. "You know that's just a formality. You know you're welcome at Netta's any time."

"No, Aunt Lavinia, I don't know that." This time Bea Dot's voice lost patience.

Another glass plunked down, and Cal hoped they weren't sloshing lemonade on the table. Those white circles were the devil to get out of the finish.

"You two are being downright silly," Aunt Lavinia said. "You are a nineteen-year-old married woman, and she is a twenty-nine-year-old mother-to-be. But the truth is that you're both behaving like children. It's well past time to bury the hatchet."

California pursed her lips and widened her eyes. She'd never heard Miss Lavinia raise her voice. She put the meat fork down and listened intently.

"We didn't just have a spat," Bea Dot protested. "Netta refused to come to my wedding. She was supposed to be my matron of honor."

"Now, be fair," Aunt Lavinia replied. "She didn't think you should marry Ben, and when she voiced her concerns, you told her not to attend." Bea Dot's aunt sighed before saying, "True, she crossed a line with her absence, but considering all that's happened, I can't help wishing you'd listened to her."

California stretched her face in surprise. Usually Miss Lavinia ignored the elephant in the room.

"I didn't have a choice," Bea Dot said.

"Why not?"

Cal's eyes popped open. Would Bea Dot tell?

At the young woman's stammer, Cal relaxed again and picked the meat fork back up. The sound of footsteps told her Lavinia had left her seat to join Bea Dot on the sofa. The woman's voice softened.

"Bea Dot, darling, you have no idea what it's like to have siblings. Netta was the closest thing you had to a sister. But as the oldest of three girls, I can assure you that precious as they are, sisters can also pester us worse than mosquitoes. That's what happened between you two. Netta only wanted what was best for you."

A long pause nagged at California. What was happening in there?

"You must know," Miss Lavinia continued, "Netta loves you. Truly. Why, she even named you."

"Oh, that's not true," Bea Dot protested. "I was named after my two grandmothers."

"Yes, Beatrice and Dorothy were your grandmothers, but Netta complained that Beatrice Dorothy was too stuffy, and she started calling you Bea Dot. You didn't know that?"

After a pause, Bea Dot said no.

California put a hand on her hip and huffed. She'd told Bea Dot that story dozens of times.

"A visit with Netta would be good for both of you. Staying at home so much, Netta could use a companion. And you would benefit from some time away from home."

"Oh, I'm fine."

"Don't hide your problems from me, young lady." Aunt Lavinia's voice grew urgent. "I saw that knot on your head. Dr. Arnold did too."

At Miss Lavinia's frank talk, Cal leaned toward the kitchen door, tempted to peek around it to see Bea Dot's face. Instead, she furiously rubbed the meat fork, which shone like a mirror from its five-minute buffing.

Bea Dot's silence provoked Aunt Lavinia's persistence. "Has he given you any more trouble, dear?"

"No, he hasn't," Bea Dot spoke up after a pause. "In fact, he's been the opposite—too polite, as if he just met me. At breakfast he says good morning and comments on the weather. Then he's off to the office. We eat dinner in complete silence. I live with a long-fused stick of dynamite, and I have no idea when the spark will reach the gunpowder."

California clutched the fork and buffing rag to her chest, smiling and thanking heaven. At last Bea Dot had admitted her fear.

"Then perhaps you should leave while you have the chance to do so," Aunt Lavinia advised.

"But even if I decide to go, Netta wouldn't want me there."

"Of course she would, dear. I'll write her immediately."

California sighed, smiled, and closed the silver chest. Now she could do the ironing with a lighter heart. Praise the Lord for Miss Lavinia getting Bea Dot out of this mess. Now Cal could stop beating herself up for getting Miss Bea Dot into it.

Chapter 4

Dearest cousin,
My heart breaks for you. Please know my prayers go with you
at this time of great loss. Having endured the same grief three
times before, I can tell you that occupying one's thoughts and
body with activity is the only way to get through this period
of mourning. Please come to Pineview, Bea Dot. The distance
from your home and the different surroundings will be good
for you in this sorrowful time. What's more, your presence
will be a great comfort to me during my confinement. I've
missed your company and would love to see you again. Let's
put the past behind us and be cousins again. Please say you
will come.

> *Much love,*
> *Netta*

There. Mother should be satisfied with such a gracious invitation. Not that Bea Dot would ever reply, or even read it. All Netta's
other letters had been met with complete silence.

But Netta did wish her cousin would accept the invitation. Poor thing. Netta always knew Ben Ferguson was an arrogant man, but she had no idea a monster lurked inside that pudgy physique. She shivered and placed her arm over her growing stomach at the thought of how Bea Dot had lost her baby. *If she'd only listened to me.*

"Miss Netta, here the mail." Lola's dark-brown hand contrasted sharply against the white envelopes she placed on Netta's desk.

"Already? Why didn't you tell me the mailman was here? I needed him to take this letter." Netta leaned back in her chair and slid her letter into an envelope. Then she fanned her face with it, praying silently for a thunderstorm. She didn't know how much longer she could tolerate this heat.

Lola widened her big brown eyes and shrugged. "I didn't speak to him, Miss Netta. I found the mail just a minute ago. He must of come while I was hanging the laundry."

Netta addressed the envelope and held it out to her maid. "This letter must get to Savannah as soon as possible."

"You want me to mail it on my way home this evening?"

Honestly, sometimes Lola could be thick as a brick.

"No, that's too late. It must go out today. Take this to the post office right away." Netta shifted in her chair. The heat rash on her backside pricked at her.

"Doc Coolidge ask for chicken salad for lunch." Lola's brow wrinkled in her sad, uncertain way when questioning Netta's decision. Netta hated that. "And I ain't shred the chicken yet."

"This letter must be on the train to Savannah today." Couldn't she just do as she was told? "You'll have to go now. You can shred the chicken when you get back."

"Yes'm." Lola put the letter in her apron pocket.

Netta flitted her hands toward her to shoo her out of the bedroom. "Go on, now, and hurry."

Lola would probably work in stony silence for the rest of the day. Too bad. Netta had too much to do to worry about her maid's feelings. She had a houseguest arriving soon and a nursery to be put together, not to mention all the baby clothes still to be made.

Netta stood and wiped the sweat from her face and neck before moving into the parlor, which was cooler because of the shade of an oak tree outside. She sat gingerly in her rocking chair so as not to irritate the heat rash and picked up the knitting from the basket on the floor. The back screen door slammed, and Netta lifted her shoulders in aggravation, certain Lola had banged the door deliberately. She shook her head. The best way to fight Lola's petulance was to ignore it.

After knitting a few minutes, she noticed she'd dropped a stitch. Swearing silently, she pulled on the yarn and watched her last few minutes' work disappear. And she still had a cap and booties to make. Maybe Bea Dot could help her prepare the layette.

Netta looked at the ceiling and sighed. *Stop pressuring yourself,* she thought, remembering Ralph's repeated advice. True, she should have started this work sooner. But Will Dunaway needed her help more. For three weeks he convalesced in the extra bedroom while she tended to that dreadful wound. She still shuddered at the thought of being impaled. During that time, she also listened with sympathetic agony to his cries in the night. If Will's nightmares came close to the realities of war, then the battlefront must be worse than she could ever imagine.

Now Will was healed, though, physically at least, and Netta tried not to panic with just a few weeks to prepare for her baby's arrival. She shook her fist as she realized she'd forgotten about the paint job. She must remember to ask Lola whether her husband, Jim Henry, could paint the nursery on Friday.

The front door opened, and Ralph entered, his face red and wet from perspiration, his shirt soaked with a wet V in the back. "Hello, dear," he said as he leaned to kiss the top of her head.

At the whiff of the sour smell of perspiration, Netta felt a pang of sympathy for her husband. He must be more miserable in the heat than she. She wrapped the loose yarn back into its ball. "Busy morning?"

"Not especially," he replied, putting his black leather satchel on the table near the door. "I had to drive out the lower river road to the Mashburns' place. That's always a long trip."

"Who's sick?"

"No one. The boy fell out of the loft, thought he'd broken his leg. But he's all right. Just sore." Ralph looked around the corner into the kitchen. "I'm starved. Where's that chicken salad? I've been thinking about it all morning." He wandered into the kitchen in search of lunch.

Netta smiled slightly at the way Ralph could shift his thoughts so easily from an injured boy to a cold chicken. When she first married him, his matter-of-fact talk about injury and illness could shock her. Now, after seeing him at work for several years, she better understood his perspective. Setting a broken bone to him was like trying to repair a rip in her favorite dress. They both hated the damage, but mending it was all in a day's work.

"Lola will make it as soon as she gets back." Netta slipped her knitting needle carefully back into the working stitches.

"Where's she off to in this heat?" Ralph asked, walking back into the parlor.

"To mail my letter to Bea Dot. The mailman came before I finished it."

"Couldn't she have waited until the sun went down some?"

Netta put the knitting in her lap and eyed her husband with a raised brow. "Well, I suppose she could've, but then again, why make her walk? I should have asked her to wait until you could drive her there in the car."

Ralph chuckled and sat on the footstool near the fireplace. His knees jutted up to his shoulders, making him look like a big spider. "I just meant that the mail doesn't go out until five o'clock."

Netta silently blessed Ralph, who was one of few people who appreciated her caustic sense of humor. She picked up her knitting again. "I know, but Lola might have gotten busy and forgot about it."

"Oh, has she been forgetful?"

Feeling sheepish, Netta paused her knitting needles. "No," she said slowly. "I suppose not."

Ralph slid off the stool and knelt in front of Netta, putting his hands on her round middle. They felt like two warming pads on her torso, and the baby stirred inside her.

"That's my little boy," Ralph said proudly.

"Or your little girl." Netta put her hand over one of Ralph's.

Ralph nodded, gazing at Netta's girth as if it were a beautiful wonder. He shifted his hand on her stomach to meet the infant's protruding foot or hand. "We hired Lola because she's the best at minding children."

"Of course." Netta nodded. "Only the best for our little angel." She rubbed her stomach lightly. After a moment, she asked, "What are you trying to say?"

Ralph looked up at her lovingly. "If we trust Lola with the most precious thing in our lives, shouldn't we be able to trust her with a letter?"

Netta exhaled and slumped in her rocker. She'd done it again. So determined to have things her way, she'd sent her housekeeper out in the noonday sun in the middle of a heat wave. If she kept up that attitude, Netta would lose Lola to Berma Daniel, who'd been trying to hire Lola away for weeks.

Ralph stood, and Netta gazed at his shoes, black patent leather dusted with red Georgia clay. He leaned forward and put his finger under Netta's chin, lifting her face so that she could meet his eyes. His damp black hair fell over his wide forehead.

"Point taken," she said.

He smiled at her and winked. Netta always felt like a bashful schoolgirl when he did that. She couldn't help smiling back.

The telephone rang in the hallway, and Ralph went to answer it. From his usual short inquiries, Netta could tell he was speaking to another patient. He hunched over the telephone stand as he listened to the caller, his broad back filling the doorway. The back of his hair spiked with wetness.

After hanging up the earpiece, Ralph returned to the parlor. "That was Will Dunaway."

Netta put her hand to her throat in alarm.

Sensing Netta's worry, Ralph quickly said, "He's fine. He called to tell me Eliza Taylor's in labor. Thought I should ride out and see her."

Netta smiled at Ralph's report. It was just like Will Dunaway to suggest such a thing—always looking out after his neighbors.

"Eliza's delivered all her own babies," Netta said, knitting her next row. "She's probably better at it than you are." She gave Ralph a teasing grin.

"You may be right." Ralph walked into the kitchen. He called to Netta from the other room. "But I'll ride out there just in case." The icebox door squeaked as he opened it. "Can I eat this chicken the way it is?"

"That's for your chicken salad," Netta called back, but the silence told her Ralph was already eating the bird. "Dear, let me at least make you a sandwich." She pushed against the armrests to rise from the rocking chair, but Ralph stuck his head in the doorway, a drumstick in his hand.

"Don't get up, honey. I'm halfway finished already." He disappeared into the kitchen again. In a few seconds Netta heard water running. Then Ralph returned, drying his hands on a dishtowel.

"I only ate a little bit. Lola can make chicken salad for supper."
He leaned down and kissed Netta's cheek again, leaving a slick of
chicken grease on her face. "I'll be out at the Taylors' place if anyone needs me." He grabbed his bag and was gone.

With two fingers, Netta touched the spot where he kissed her.
Then she grabbed the front of her smock and fluttered it, moving
air through her collar and down her chest. She peered out the window. Where was Lola?

She pushed herself out of her chair and shuffled into the
kitchen to clean up after her husband, but she discovered that
Ralph had put the chicken back into the icebox. With an endearing smile, she had wet a dishcloth to wipe down the kitchen table
when a knock interrupted her.

"Coming," she called as she waddled to the front door, wiping
her neck and forehead with the damp rag. She still held it when she
opened the door to find Mr. Bradley, who owned the drugstore.

"Morning, Mrs. Coolidge," he said. His brown hair was mat-
ted from the hat he now held in his hand. "I'm looking for the doc.
He's not in his office. Is he home?"

"No, he's not." Netta shook her head. "He's gone out to the
country to deliver a baby." Netta leaned on the doorframe, the
weight of her pregnancy tiring her back and legs. Her heat rash
burned, but she tried to ignore it as she faced the druggist.

"Oh, I see." Mr. Bradley turned away from the door and looked
disappointedly at the distance as if to see Ralph driving away.
Cicadas sang in the pine trees. "Then I suppose he'll be a long
while." He turned back to face Netta. "My wife's feeling sick, Mrs.
Coolidge. She came home from Macon yesterday with a headache,
and she's gotten worse ever since. It's not like her to take to the bed,
so I thought I'd fetch Dr. Coolidge to look after her."

"I'm sorry to hear that, and I hope she gets better soon," Netta
said. Poor Mr. Bradley looked so helpless. His wife must have been

feeling terrible to cause such a concerned expression. "There's no telephone at the Taylors' house, but I can call Dunaway's Crossing and ask Will to convey a message."

Mr. Bradley raised his eyebrows with a bit of hope. "Thank you, ma'am. I'm much obliged." He put on his hat and left.

As Netta closed the front door, the back screen door slammed again, making her flinch. She opened her mouth to reprimand Lola, but stopped, remembering Ralph's words. Netta shuffled back into the kitchen, where she found her maid putting on an apron.

"Thank you for running that errand for me, Lola."

Lola cocked her head with surprise in her eyes. "Yes, ma'am."

"Dr. Coolidge has already come and gone," Netta said. She thought she detected a glint in Lola's eyes that said "I told you so," but it disappeared as quickly as it came. "But he'd like to have chicken salad for supper."

"Yes, ma'am," Lola replied. "Can I get you anything?"

"Yes." Netta picked up a *Farmers' Almanac* and fanned her face with it. "If you could take the ice out of the icebox and put it here on the parlor floor, I'll just lie down on it for a spell."

A wide-eyed Lola stuck her head around the doorframe.

Netta laughed. "Could you just put some milk on ice chips for me, please? And maybe some toast and jam?"

Lola smiled. "Yes, ma'am."

"Just call me when it's ready." She started down the hallway toward the telephone. Thank goodness Will had installed a phone at the crossing. Ralph would be able to help more patients that way.

Chapter 5

Dear Netta,
Thank you for your letter and for your gracious invitation.
Unfortunately, I'm afraid I must decline. In your last weeks
of pregnancy, the last thing you need is a guest in your house.
I would be more of a hindrance than a help—

"Why'd you write that?"

"Good Lord," Bea Dot exclaimed as she jumped, scratching black ink across her notepaper. "You scared me to death, Cal." She tore the page of stationery into small pieces. "Why do you look over my shoulder like that? You know I hate it."

California placed a glass of iced water on Bea Dot's desk. Bea Dot picked it up immediately and held it against her cheek, then her chest. The water vibrated at the rapid thump of her heart, and the cool glass relieved her from the heavy, sticky midday air.

"I didn't sneak up on you," California fussed. "You asked for a glass a water. I can't help it if I see what you writing." She held out her wide hand, and Bea Dot placed the torn paper in it. "Why you ain't going to Pineview?"

Bea Dot rose and stood next to the open window. A breeze blew her shift against her body. The warm air was little relief, but moving air was better than nothing. California dropped the shreds of the letter into the wastepaper basket, then joined Bea Dot at the window.

"Why you ain't going, Miss Bea Dot?" This time her voice was softer, even maternal. She handed Bea Dot a fan, which she waved furiously in front of her face.

"The only reason Netta invited me is that Aunt Lavinia asked her to."

"Your aunt put the idea in her head, but Miss Netta a grown woman, and you know her. She make her own decisions. If she invited you, she want you to come. She said she miss you."

Bea Dot raised her eyes at California. "You read her letter to me?"

"Well, you left it on the desk yesterday." Cal avoided Bea Dot's eyes as she answered. "I couldn't help seeing it as I was dusting."

"You shouldn't have read it."

"Why you being so private now? I know everything about you." Cal's voice rose with petulance as she turned to face her mistress. "Go visit your cousin, Miss Bea Dot."

"Hmph." Bea Dot put her hand on her hip. "First thing she'll do is tell me I should have listened to her about marrying Ben. Always has to say 'I told you so.' And she'll have me knitting and sewing night and day. I can hear her now. 'You're doing the cross-stitch?'" Bea Dot mimicked her cousin's polite but bossy voice. "'Don't you think the chain stitch would be prettier?'"

California offered a knowing smile, then crossed her arms in front of her. "So you'd rather put up with Mr. Ben's bullying than Miss Netta's bossiness?"

Bea Dot studied California's face, the lips drawn tight, the wrinkles across the lifted forehead. She hated it when Cal was right.

"You got no good reason to stay, Miss Bea Dot, but you got lots a reasons to go."

Bea Dot sighed. "All right. I'll go."

California nodded. "That more like it." She pulled a dust rag out of her apron pocket and turned to leave the room. "You might as well call for a ticket on the morning train. Your trunk's all packed."

Bea Dot and Ben faced each other from opposite ends of the dining room table. The only sound in the room was the clinking of silver against china. Their eyes barely met, but instead focused on the baked flounder, cucumbers, and tomato slices. Throughout the meal, Bea Dot had been summoning the gumption to tell Ben she was leaving, but with each swallow, she lost her nerve. She glanced at his plate, almost empty. *It's now or never*, she told herself, then pulled Netta's letter out of her pocket and placed it on the damask tablecloth. "I've had a letter from Netta."

Ben stopped his fork in midair and eyed Bea Dot with surprise. "I saw no such letter in this afternoon's mail."

"Please don't misunderstand." Bea Dot's heart pounded at Ben's suspicion. Her temperature rose in anticipation of an outburst. "I didn't touch your mail. This letter came yesterday. It was special delivery, so the postman brought it to me in the morning while you were at the office." She held her breath, bracing for a reaction.

His shoulders relaxed, then Bea Dot's. Good. He believed her. He put his fork down, leaned back in his chair, and put his napkin on the table. "A special delivery, eh? Must be an important letter. You haven't heard from her in . . . How long has it been?"

"Well, it is important, actually." She picked up the envelope and turned it in her hands as she spoke. "Netta's expecting a baby, and she's entered her confinement. She'd like me to come to Pineview to help her." Bea Dot had kept her eyes on her hands, but she forced herself to meet Ben's gaze.

Skeptically he asked, "Help her do what?"

"Oh, you know," Bea Dot continued casually, her heart still

galloping in her chest, "prepare the nursery, make the layette. I'm sure she has some house chores she can't do on her own."

"She doesn't have a girl to do that for her?"

Bea Dot paused. His questions didn't surprise her, but she'd hoped he'd want her to go. "I don't know about that. She didn't explain in her letter."

"You've deceived me before," he said coolly, as if reading her mind. "How do I know you really intend to visit your cousin?"

"I have her letter here." She held it up.

"Let me see it," he said, holding his hand out.

Bea Dot rose and took the envelope to him, then returned to her seat, a knot growing in her stomach. Ben's inquiry made her feel like a criminal before a judge. She waited as he read the letter. What would she do if he said no? Leave anyway?

He put the letter down and eyed Bea Dot again, this time from under the hood of his brow. "My parents still expect me to have a son. We can't very well do that if you're off in Pine Needle."

"Pineview," Bea Dot corrected him. At the thought of conceiving a child with him, she pushed her plate aside. "Remember that Dr. Arnold advised me to take some time before having more children. Actually, he recommended that I get away for a while." She felt her pulse quicken again. Ben hated being corrected.

"So he did," he nodded. "When would you want to leave?"

Bea Dot almost deflated with relief. "In the morning."

"So soon? You have this trip all planned out, don't you?"

Bea Dot shrugged and attempted a smile. "No time like the present."

Ben pondered her request. Then he stood and said, "Two weeks. Then I'll expect you home. I'll not have people thinking you've run off and abandoned me."

He left her at the table, where she stayed a few minutes, unsure if she should feel insulted from his remark or relieved at his consent. She opted for feeling nothing and went to her room.

What Bea Dot loved most about her bedroom was the adjacent bathroom, which Ben had had installed for her as a wedding gift, before he knew about her deception. Especially during the sweltering summer, Bea Dot relished a soak in a cool bath. Some days she'd have to peel her clothes off before washing away the sweat, grime, and shame of her sham of a marriage. Since her miscarriage, Bea Dot's bathroom had become even more of a refuge. She reclined against the porcelain and wondered if Netta had indoor plumbing. Probably not, in such a small country town. Tonight's bath might be her last for a couple of weeks, so she stayed in the water until her fingers and toes pruned.

When she got out, she dusted herself with talcum powder and slipped into her seersucker robe, her drabbest but also her coolest. California must have packed her other one in the trunk sitting at the foot of her bed. Bea Dot sat at her dressing table, took the pins out of her dark, curly hair, and brushed it.

After a soft knock at the door, California poked her head into the room. "Miss Bea Dot?"

"Yes, Cal. Come in." Bea Dot met her gaze via the reflection in the mirror, then turned on the stool to face her.

Cal entered and stood towering over Bea Dot, holding a brown canvas sack. She'd removed her apron, so her fraying shirt and skirt revealed their age. Her brown boots, dull with miles of wear, must have taken her to Atlanta and back over the years. Bea Dot wondered if they had holes in the soles.

"'Less you got something else for me, I'll be going. My niece just come and say she need me home cause Matilda gone to see Miss Jubilee, who got the sick headache."

"I'm sorry to hear that, California. I hope she feels better soon."

"She always do. Well, I s'pose this good-bye for a spell. You have a good trip and say hello to Miss Netta for me."

"Thank you, Cal. I will, and I'll see you when I get home." Bea Dot smiled and joked, "You might enjoy having me gone for a while."

California chuckled and shook her head slowly. "I don't know, Miss Bea Dot. Mr. Ben ain't no cakewalk, but I'll look after him." She paused a beat, then added, "I sorry I got you in this mess, but I think this trip gone help both of you."

Bea Dot sighed and then stood and embraced California. "Oh, Cal. Nothing is your fault. You've always taken good care of me." She breathed in the odor of sweat, cooking, and dishwater. California had smelled that way as long as Bea Dot had known her.

"Child," California said, taking Bea Dot's shoulders and holding her at arm's length, "you done had your bath. Don't go hugging on me and getting dirty again."

Bea Dot nodded and smiled.

"You gone be fine. I'll see you when you get back."

"Bye, Cal." Bea Dot watched her close the door behind her. As she gave her hair a few more strokes with the brush, she ambled back to the dressing table. Her curly dark brown hair, fluffy from the brushing, hung behind her shoulders. *I look like the madwoman in the attic*, Bea Dot thought as she opened a drawer to find a nightgown. As she rummaged through the camisoles and shifts, a sound at the door startled her.

"Cal, I thought you went home."

"It's me."

Bea Dot's chest tightened as she turned to face Ben. He hadn't been in her bedroom since the day he knocked her down. Nerves humming, she stood and approached him, trying to keep him from coming farther into her refuge. "Did you call me? I didn't hear you."

He took another step forward so that he stood immediately in front of her. More than a head taller than she, he looked down at her with his hands clasped behind his back. His thick black eyebrows came together over his nose like a large caterpillar.

"No, I didn't call. I heard you in here, and I thought I'd come in."

The whiskey on his breath failed to cover the fish he'd eaten for supper. When he put his hands on Bea Dot's waist, she tensed, and his slight frown registered her reaction. She couldn't help herself, though, since the last time he'd touched her he'd been looking for a fight. He untied the sash of her robe, and Bea Dot took a step back. The robe fell open, and she clutched it again, her heart racing like a scared rabbit's.

"Easy," he said, as if talking to a skittish filly. He grabbed her arm, then pulled her to him again.

Bea Dot pushed against him, but he was too strong for her.

Fear's simmer escalated to a boil. "Ben," she urged him, "remember, Dr. Arnold said—"

"Hush," he said sharply before pressing his mouth to hers so hard that her lips hurt from mashing against her teeth. Disgust ignited inside her, as it had done before with forced, drunken kisses.

She wriggled away from his grasp, wiping her mouth with the back of her hand. "Ben, stop. Please."

He glared at her with the familiar dark wrath in his eyes, and his height increased as he inhaled with anger. Then he drew back his hand and swung it full force across her mouth.

She fell back and hit the dressing table before landing on the floor. Her hand mirror, brush, and cologne bottles toppled around her. Her face felt like it had exploded, and the taste of blood flooded her mouth. She tried to get her feet under her, but Ben was too fast. He yanked the robe off her shoulders, wrenching her arms still in their sleeves. Gripping her elbow with one hand, he tossed the robe to the side, then slung her over the bed.

Quickly she stood again and faced him. Her heartbeat pounded in her ears. "No, Ben," she tried to assert herself. "Don't do this."

But she knew he didn't hear her in his rage. He grabbed her hair again and yanked her to the bed, pushing her into it face-down. He held her there by the neck, pressing her face into the embroidery of the counterpane. She heard him unfasten his belt buckle with his free hand, so she gritted her teeth and tightened her muscles, ready for a lashing.

Instead, he pushed her legs apart with his. Then her flesh tore as pain ripped through her. She cried into the mattress and tried to press up with her palms, but Ben only pushed her neck harder, pressing her face so deep into the bed linens that she could hardly breathe. She grasped handfuls of fabric and ground her teeth with each excruciating thrust, not even relaxing when he finally shuddered and loosened his grip. She turned her head and sucked in air. The bedspread was wet with her tears, stained with the blood from her mouth. She kept her face turned from Ben as she listened to him fasten his trousers and leave the room.

When she could no longer hear his footsteps, she drew her knees to her chest and lay on her side as she wept, pain still pulsing through her. After a few minutes, she gathered the strength to stand, and she shuffled across the room and picked up the robe. She used it to catch the blood dripping down her leg.

Wincing with each step, she crept to her bathroom and turned the tub tap for a second time, numbly going through the all-too-familiar motions of the aftermath of forced sex. She watched the water fill the tub as she wiped tears from her cheeks, her legs still shaking, her backside still throbbing. Gingerly lowering herself into the tub, she reclined so that most of her weight rested on her spine, not her bottom. Part of her knew she should be heartbroken or horrified or shocked. Instead, all she could think of were practicalities. As heinous as Ben's brutality was, this rape had not hurt as much as the first one. And at least this one would not result in a baby.

Chapter 6

Only a handful of passengers scattered across the platform of Pineview's small train station, most of them country folk returning home, hugging loved ones who had come to greet them. A cluster of Girl Scouts in uniform waited for passengers to deboard, eyeing their prospects timidly, afraid to make their approach to sell Liberty Bonds. Will watched them skeptically. Every scout to save a soldier? Who came up with that slogan? It would take more than Girl Scouts to save the men he killed in France. He removed his wide-brimmed hat and ran his hand through his straight brown hair. Then he replaced the hat and turned for a full view of the platform.

Where was she? Ralph had said to look for a petite woman, well dressed with dark hair. In the last five minutes Will had seen no one fitting that description, and in this town, he'd expected her to stand out. Eyes still on the train, he stepped backward toward the ticket office when he felt a bump, then heard a sharp, high-pitched cry. He turned and cursed himself. "Oh, no. Ma'am, I am so sorry."

She sat on the cement platform, wearing a ruffled white shirt and a brown skirt. She'd drawn her knees to her chest and buried her forehead in them, so that he saw not her face but the top of her hat. He knelt beside her.

"How could I be so stupid?" He took her satchel, which lay beside her, and cupped her elbow with his palm. "Let me help you up."

She shook her head emphatically, holding up a white-gloved hand. "Let me take a moment," she said into her knees. Her back rose and fell a few times before she lifted her face and revealed tear-streaked cheeks. Immediately, she searched the pavement and found a small drawstring bag. She picked it up and withdrew a handkerchief.

"My God, I've hurt you," he said, still holding her elbow. "I'm so sorry." Will's neck and face burned with humiliation as well as the late summer heat. But his gut wrenched in confusion as well. Had he really bumped her hard enough to draw tears?

"Can I get you anything?" Stupid question. What could he possibly get her? What should he do? He couldn't let her sit on the hard pavement, but she didn't want to get up. A group of people had clustered around them, which exacerbated Will's embarrassment to full-fledged shame.

"No, no," the woman said, waving her small hand. "I'm fine, really." She blotted her cheeks with the handkerchief and then looked at Will with round dark eyes that pulled him in like a riptide. "I'm more surprised than hurt." A curled lock of dark brown hair escaped its pin and fell against her cheek. He almost had to step on his hand to keep from brushing it away himself. The lady tucked the lock behind her ear and offered him a weak smile.

Then Will noticed the monogram on her handkerchief—BFB—and with another bullet of embarrassment, he realized whom he had knocked down. "You're Mrs. Ferguson, aren't you? Netta Coolidge's cousin?"

She nodded and knit her brow. "How did you know?"

"I'm Will Dunaway, ma'am. Ralph Coolidge asked me to fetch you. He was called away unexpectedly to see a patient."

"I see," she replied. "Well, thank you for meeting me here."

Did he hear disappointment in her voice? Who could blame her? Ralph Coolidge couldn't have chosen a worse person for this job. He might as well have sent a goat to pick up his cousin. He reached for her arm to help her up. At first she flinched, and he recoiled in response. Then he said softly, "May I help you up?"

"Oh," she said with a quick nod, as if she finally understood his intent. "Of course." Still clutching her purse, she held up her arm, which he gripped at the wrist and elbow. She bore down on his grasp as she rose. Standing up, she came just to his shoulder. Will leaned forward to pick up her satchel, and as he did so, she took a step away from him. Was he that scary? He was trying his best to make amends.

She dabbed at her lip with the handkerchief, and only then did he notice the small cut at the edge of her mouth. Just when he thought he couldn't feel worse about knocking her down.

"You're bleeding," he said. "I'm so sorry. I'll get you some ice. Come, have a seat on the bench, and I'll go get it."

"No, no, Mr. Dunaway." She held up her hand reassuringly. "You didn't hurt me. This"—she pointed to her mouth—"happened before I came here. I had . . . an accident at home."

Will cocked his head in confusion. What kind of accident could a lady like her have to bust her own lip? Was she just saying that to make him feel better? Maybe she just wanted to be rid of him. Silently, he berated himself. He had quite the penchant for hurting people.

A porter wheeled a trunk on a luggage cart. "Mrs. Ferguson, where would you like me to take your baggage?"

"I'll take it from here." Will dug into his pocket for a coin. "Thank you." He tipped the porter and took the cart from him, placing the satchel on top of the trunk. "I'll come back for your baggage," he said to Mrs. Ferguson. "First, let me get you seated."

He held out his elbow, and she hesitated a beat before wrapping her thin, gloved fingers around it.

Will walked slowly, in case she was still sore from her fall. After two or three steps, though, he realized he had to slow his gait even more. Mrs. Ferguson wore one of those skirts bunched at the ankle. He'd seen a few around town. Women thought the skirts made them look dainty, but Will thought they made women look like closed umbrellas. Mrs. Ferguson scanned the grounds surrounding the train station. A few automobiles sat here and there on the grass, but none of them in the direction he led her.

"Which motorcar is yours, Mr. Dunaway?"

"I'm afraid I'll have to take you to the Coolidges' house in my wagon," he said, pointing to it with his free hand. "I have not followed the trend and bought myself one of those machines."

"Oh," she replied, and then fell silent, as if searching for something else to say. How backward she must have thought he was.

Still clutching his elbow, she virtually tiptoed to the end of the platform and leaned closely against him as she descended the steps. When they reached the wagon, Mrs. Ferguson's eyes widened at the height of its seat, which was level with the top of her head. In her skirt she'd never be able to step up or down.

"Wait one second, ma'am." Will left her side and pulled an empty crate from the wagon bed. Then he placed it on the ground beside her. "This should help."

"Thank you." As soon as she said it, Will's embarrassment returned. Surely she'd never had to use a crate to get into an old box wagon.

He held out his hand, and she grasped it for support and pulled up her skirt the few inches it would allow. With some effort, she managed to step onto the crate and hoist herself up. As she sat gingerly on the wooden seat, she winced, and Will winced with her at the reminder of his clumsy blunder.

"I'll just be a minute," he said after returning the crate to the wagon bed. Then, taking the steps two at a time, he returned to the baggage cart. He pushed the trunk and satchel to the platform steps and handed the satchel to Mrs. Ferguson, who placed it at her feet as he went back to get the trunk. He lifted it onto his shoulder and thanked heaven to feel only a small stitch at his side as he walked down the steps and to the wagon before lowering it on the bed. He situated it between a can of kerosene and a bag of oats. Other sundry crates stood guard at either side. After climbing into the seat himself, he took the reins and clucked his tongue while tapping Buster's rump with the leather straps. Slowly he drove Mrs. Ferguson through town.

"Have you visited Pineview before?" He hated small talk.

"No, it's my first visit," she said, more to her gloves than to him.

"Well, then," he said as he turned onto Pineview's main street, "this is Bay Street, although I don't know why we call it that. We're nowhere near the water." He laughed awkwardly, but she didn't join him. Then he pointed to his right. "And there's our bank, our pharmacy, our hardware store. Oh, and our newspaper office."

Mrs. Ferguson nodded as he pointed out Pineview's other landmarks, dotting his explanations with a polite "Oh, how nice" or "I see." She asked no questions. Why should she? What did Pineview have to interest a high-society lady from Savannah? Will felt like a stable boy trying to impress a princess.

Finally, after passing the Pineview Grain and Feed and a whitewashed Baptist church, to which Mrs. Ferguson reacted with "Oh, yes. How lovely," Will turned the wagon down a residential street lined with white clapboard houses adorned with green shutters and gingerbread. At the end of the street, on a larger lot with a long, rutted drive, stood a white house with a wraparound porch. A small addition to one side bore a sign, "Ralph Coolidge, MD." He drove the wagon to the front yard, then pulled on the reins with a quiet, "Whoa."

"Oh, my." Mrs. Ferguson's polite countenance gave way to one of genuine admiration at the sight of her cousin's home. "What a splendid front porch," she said as she rose slowly, holding on to the backrest for balance. She shifted her gaze toward the front steps. "But that's an odd place to put a rocking chair."

In the middle of the front walk a maple rocker waited with green and white cushions. "You're right," he replied. "Maybe your cousin wanted some fresh air? She's confined herself until the baby arrives."

"Yes, she told me that," Mrs. Ferguson said, still standing. Her skin had begun to pink in the late afternoon sun. "But with all those comfy chairs on the porch and that swing, I'd think she'd want to sit in one of them."

"Ma'am, I'm as puzzled as you are." Will shook his head. "Maybe we should ask her."

He stood to dismount the wagon and help Mrs. Ferguson down. But before he could put one foot on the ground, the screen door opened onto the porch, and Ralph Coolidge emerged, assuming a wide stance, hands on hips, at the top of the front steps. His loosened tie and rolled-up sleeves revealed an unusually busy day.

"Don't come any closer, Will." Ralph held up his palm like a patrol officer ordering someone to halt.

Perplexed, Will returned to his seat. He looked at Mrs. Ferguson, who remained standing, her forehead slightly furrowed. Thin locks of hair at her neck had dampened with perspiration. She glanced questioningly at Will and then waved at the porch.

"Hello, Bea Dot," Ralph called.

Bea Dot?

"I apologize for greeting you this way, but several folks are down with influenza this morning. I've been exposed, and I don't want to give it to you." Will nodded. This must be the influenza Ralph had mentioned to him before. He'd hoped it would never reach Pineview.

"Oh, dear." Bea Dot frowned and muttered before sitting back down. Will couldn't help noticing she gripped the seat edge and winced as she did so. The sight sent a bolt of shame through him.

"I know your trip was long," Ralph continued, "but I'm afraid I must extend it a bit more. I'm sorry, but I assure you it's for the best."

Bea Dot nodded uncertainly and replied, "Of course, Ralph. Whatever you say."

"Will, I must tend to more patients this evening," Ralph said. "I've got to try to contain this disease, and I can't spread the germ to Netta and Bea Dot. Could you take her out to the camp house? Lola drove Netta out there earlier."

"Of course. Anything else I can do?"

"Could you take Netta's chair out to her? It wouldn't fit in the motorcar."

"I'll do it." Will climbed down and approached the house to get the chair. As he neared the porch, Ralph quietly called his name.

"I'm sorry to ask so much of you," Ralph said quietly, "but I had no other choice. In her condition, Netta would be especially at risk if she caught this bug."

"No apologies, Ralph," Will said. "I'm going out that way anyway." He picked up the rocking chair.

"Don't say anything to the ladies, though. You know how Netta worries."

"Of course. I'm glad to help." Will carried the rocking chair to the wagon and lifted it into the back. As he tied it down, he snuck a peek at a bewildered Bea Dot, who dabbed at her forehead with her handkerchief.

"Bea Dot," Ralph called again. "I'm sorry for this inconvenience, but it'll only be for a day or two. Will, I'll be in touch."

Will kept his eyes on his rope, hoping Ralph was right. After tightening his knot, he returned to his place beside Bea Dot. On the porch, a nurse appeared behind the screen door, her voice barely audible. "Dr. Coolidge, you have another call."

Ralph turned to her and nodded, then faced the wagon one last time. "I must go. Thank you, Will. Bea Dot, I'll see you soon." He disappeared into the house.

Next to Will, Bea Dot sat biting her already injured lip and wrinkling her forehead. Will felt an unsettling twinge. Here she was having just arrived at this unknown place only to be sent with a stranger out to the country to avoid contagion. He could only imagine what she was thinking. He put a consoling hand on her forearm, and although she didn't jerk it away this time, he felt her muscles tighten. He pulled away at once.

"Don't worry," he said. "Ralph's a good doctor. Everything will be all right."

She nodded but didn't reply. Why should she believe him?

He turned the wagon around and steered it back down the long gravel drive.

Chapter 7

Bea Dot had stopped worrying about her hair an hour ago. Will Dunaway must have thought she was a fright. When Netta saw her, she'd surely go running in terror. Perspiration dribbled down her neck and back, her shirt clinging between the shoulder blades. Her poor handkerchief, now dingy from constant use, looked more like a tiny dust rag. Each time a drip of sweat touched her split lip, it stung like it had been swabbed with alcohol. Dabbing it brought little relief.

And poor Will Dunaway drove the wagon at a snail's pace just to keep from jostling her. Surely he wanted to get home, but on top of prolonging his day, she was letting him think he had knocked her down. Guilt pestered her, but biting her tongue about his misunderstanding was much easier than explaining she'd bumped into him and toppled over her own satchel. The truth wouldn't explain those god-awful tears, and she wouldn't dare reveal what sparked them. She'd tried to hold them back, but landing on her rump revived the pain from last night's heinous episode. Mr. Dunaway must have thought she was as helpless as a gray-haired old lady.

Perhaps she was.

Dingy, sweaty, exhausted from the extended train ride, and dying to get out of that cursed hobble skirt, Bea Dot felt more like a vagabond than a young lady visiting her cousin. The skirt, meant to hide the real reason she walked so slowly, turned out to be the worst idea of the day. She looked silly wearing it in this small Georgia town, especially in this heat.

My stars, this place is nothing but red clay and pine trees, she thought as she surveyed the environment from atop Will Dunaway's wagon. She flapped her handkerchief at a pesky horsefly, but it just came right back, buzzing about her head like a bad memory. Eventually the insect lit on her knee, but before she could wave it away, wham! Will Dunaway whacked it with his hat, making Bea Dot cry out in alarm.

With the hat's brim, he brushed the dead bug off her skirt, then placed the hat back on his head. Speechless, Bea Dot gaped at him, her eyes probably as big around as her open mouth. In a second or two, he noticed her incredulity, then turned bright red. "Oh, dirt! Forgive me, Mrs. Ferguson," he said, flustered. "I didn't mean to frighten you. I thought you'd like me to kill that horsefly."

"That's all right." Bea Dot composed herself and replied, "I am glad you killed it. I'm just surprised is all." *Scared to death* better described how she felt. Living with Ben Ferguson made her expect any blow to be directed at her. She took a deep breath, then exhaled to slow her pounding heart.

She dabbed at her upper lip and forehead again. Her damp handkerchief was almost useless, now turned orange-gray from the Georgia dust and constant handling.

The wagon continued down the red dirt road, the pine trees creeping by, the cicadas' song creating a crescendo from the woods. Bea Dot had just relaxed again when the wagon thumped into a pothole, jarring her on the hardwood seat and charging pain from her bottom up through her core. She gasped and covered her mouth with her hand, drawing deep breaths in an attempt to ease the pain. Her eyes burned, and she turned her head away, refusing to let Mr. Dunaway see her cry again. She begged the tears not to come.

"Mrs. Ferguson, are you all right?"

She nodded, inhaled deeply, then uttered a yes, which sounded more like a yelp. In a few moments, she'd gathered herself again, but her heart plummeted when she faced Mr. Dunaway, who looked like he'd shot his best friend.

"Of course you're sore from your fall," he said. "I should have thought of that. I'm sorry."

"Please," she said, holding up her hand (good heavens, her glove was dirty), "no more apologies, Mr. Dunaway. You've been nothing but attentive and generous with your time, and I only regret that I've taken up so much of your afternoon."

He sighed and pulled a bandana from his pocket, which he used to wipe the sweat from his neck. His skin had browned from frequent exposure to the sun, but his green eyes were kind and, thanks to Bea Dot, still full of worry.

"I'll feel much better if I can make you more comfortable," he said. He turned, as if the solution to his problem lay in the wagon bed. Then, spying Netta's rocking chair, his eyes widened. "I have an idea."

He drew the horse to a stop, climbed down from the driver's seat, and went to the tail of the wagon, where he climbed aboard. After shuffling around Bea Dot's trunk and the many crates, he shifted the rocker to the front of the bed, just behind the driver's seat. He tied it in place, then patted the gingham cushion. "You can't rock, but this chair will be much softer."

Bea Dot smiled at his ingenuity, surprised at his willingness to secure her comfort. She turned to step off the wagon, but he stopped her.

"Wait just a second. I'll help you."

In a moment, he was on the ground in front of her. Bea Dot eyed her skirt uncertainly, and he read her thoughts. "Will you permit me to lift you down?"

He held his hands up to her.

"How?"

"Put your hands on my shoulders," he said. "I'll take you by the waist—if you don't mind."

She hesitated a moment, her nerves buzzing, unsure of how to respond, unaccustomed to having a man ask permission to touch her. The idea provoked caution, even though the source of her hesitation was at home in Savannah.

Bending forward, she placed her hands on Mr. Dunaway's shoulders. He took her by the waist and lowered her to the ground, and as he did so, her cheek grazed against his stubbled whiskers. He smelled of sweat and leather. Through her light gloves and his plaid cotton shirt, his shoulder muscles rolled under her palms. Heat rose into her face, even though Mr. Dunaway had done nothing untoward.

He walked her to the back of the wagon, where he lifted her onto the bed. After carefully stepping around the trunk and the crates, Bea Dot sat in Netta's rocker, the cushion and backrest a welcome relief.

He'd climbed aboard the wagon as well, and as he took the reins, she said, "You're right. This is much better. Thank you, Mr. Dunaway."

He turned halfway to her as the horse started up again. "You'd do me a favor by calling me Will."

"Then you must call me Bea Dot," she replied.

"That's an unusual name," he said. After a tick, "I like it."

Bea Dot smiled. Ben had always said her name was too juvenile. "Mr. Dun—I mean Will—can you tell me about this camp house where we're going? Will Netta and I be camping?"

"It's a small log house down by a lake a few miles ahead," Will explained. "Ralph uses it as a fishing camp, but I'm guessing he's sent plenty of provisions to make it suitable for you two ladies."

A small log cabin. One room? Surely Ralph wouldn't send his wife to live in a house like that. Did the cabin at least have running water? Bea Dot bit her thumbnail. When she'd accepted Netta's invitation, she'd not packed for two weeks in the woods.

When her stomach growled, she put her hand on her middle. She hadn't eaten since early that morning before boarding the train. *Please, don't let Will hear my stomach grumble,* she prayed. She would just die if he felt he had to feed her as well as deliver her to Netta.

When the road curved, the wagon passed a large green field. Overlooking it in the distance stood a two-story house with four square columns. Lovely, but lonely.

"How long have we been traveling?" she asked.

"Almost an hour," he answered after peering at his watch.

"You're wearing a wristwatch," she said. "Isn't that what the army makes soldiers wear?"

He nodded. "That's right."

"Are you home from the war?" Some of Bea Dot's classmates had gone "over there," but they hadn't come back yet.

"Yes," Will answered without turning his head.

"And you're already home? I hope you weren't injured."

He paused while the cicadas sang another chorus. Then, "I mended."

Bea Dot had to lean forward to hear his reply, but there was no mistaking the reluctance in his voice. She'd never spoken to a Great War veteran, but she'd heard talk about the cold, mud-filled trenches and the machine guns' rapid fire. Battle in Europe sounded more brutal than anything she could imagine. She changed the subject.

"What's growing in those fields?"

"You've never seen a cotton field before?" Laughter laced his voice.

"That's cotton? I thought cotton was white."

"It is white, once the cotton bolls open," Will explained. "This crop's not ready to harvest yet."

Bea Dot watched the crops pass by, like rows of soldiers marching in a parade. "When will they be ready?"

"In another month or so. The cotton bolls will open, and then all these fields"—he stretched his arm out toward them—"will look blanketed with snow." He chuckled a moment before adding, "It's the only snow this part of the country ever sees."

Agricultural talk must have put Will at ease. He was in the best mood she'd seen him in all day, so she asked more questions about cotton, peanuts, tobacco, and other Georgia crops. He answered cheerfully and also told her about some of the farming families in the area. By the time the sun had lowered to the tip of the pine trees in the distance, Will seemed to have forgotten any previous mention of war. "Will, I do believe you have stumbled upon an excellent idea. Maybe every wagon should have a rocking chair in the back."

He laughed. "I'd pursue the idea further if the country weren't already running out to make Henry Ford wealthier. But if you like your seat, I'll make your cousin an offer on that rocker so that you can always ride comfortably with me."

"My friends in Savannah will be so jealous," she joked. After a pause, she asked, "Will we be at the camp house before dark?"

"Yes, but just before," he said. "Here's our turn."

He steered the wagon into a grove of pines. Bea Dot welcomed the shade and inhaled the scent of evergreen. The cicadas serenaded the two again as the wagon lumped along the two-rutted path. Thank heavens for Netta's chair. She could not have endured such a bumpy ride otherwise.

She touched her cheek, and her skin nipped back at her. *My face must be red as California's head rag*, she worried. Fortunately, when she dabbed her lip, the sting had dulled. She could only imagine how dirty her face was. From the looks of her gloves and handkerchief, she must have enough dust on her face to make her dark as California.

Eventually, the cart path rolled down a short hill. Through the pines and undergrowth the sun reflected on water, and through the foliage she noticed the water wasn't flowing like a river or stream.

"Is that a lake?" she asked from her rocking chair.

"Yes, we're getting close to the fishing camp now," he replied.

Eventually, the wagon came to a clearing, and the lake appeared in full view on her left, the water gently lapping on the grassy bank. To her right stood a small wooden house. Stacked bricks served as front steps as well as footings underneath. The walls were weathered and warped, the tin roof brown with rust. Next to it, a small boat rested upside down atop two wooden sawhorses. *Cabin* was too good a term for this structure. It was a shack. Bea Dot hoped to God she wouldn't have to stay in it more than two or three days.

"Here we are." Will pulled the horse to a stop, then climbed down from the wagon. Bea Dot stayed seated, staring at the shanty resembling those she'd seen in the Negro sections of Savannah. Will called to her from behind.

"Are you ready? I can help you down now."

"Oh," she said, tearing her eyes away from the camp house. "Yes, of course."

Holding the wagon's side for balance, she carefully picked her way around Will's cargo, but at the sound of a rip, she gasped and reached for her skirt. She'd caught one of the gathers in a nail poking out of a crate and ripped a three-inch hole in the front.

"Oh, jiminy," she said, frowning, wishing she could say something worse.

Will pulled his lips into his mouth, obviously stifling a laugh. "Pardon me for saying so," he said, "but that rip would be a real tragedy if it were in a more practical skirt. Now that you've torn it, I wish you'd let me cut that"—he gestured toward her ankles—"that business at the bottom of it. You'd be able to walk again."

Her stomach tightened at the thought of cutting up her skirt. But when she studied the raveled edges and realized no seamstress could work her magic to repair it, her shoulders sagged. "Oh, all right."

She shuffled to the end of the wagon as he bent over. When he straightened, he held up a hunting knife. Alarm cut through her as she hopped back.

"It's all right," he soothed her. "I'll only cut the skirt."

"You keep a knife in your boot?" Her shoulders relaxed again.

He shrugged. "You never know when it might come in handy."

"Isn't it uncomfortable?"

"I'd wager it's a sight more comfortable than that skirt." Palm up, he drew his fingers toward him as he spoke. "Now, if you'll allow me."

She stepped to the edge of the wagon, then pulled up the corner of her mouth and turned her gaze to the sky, unable to watch the destruction at her feet. Her skirt tugged downward, and a ripping noise made her cringe. "Oooh! I bought this skirt in Atlanta."

When the cutting ended, she studied Will's handiwork. The slit extended from just below her knees to the hem. Stray threads dangled here and there, and the brown weave had already begun to loosen. But the vent allowed air to cool her legs—what a relief. Will tucked his knife back in his boot. When he straightened again, he said, "Whatever you paid in Atlanta was too much."

"I'll have you know this skirt is the height of fashion." Bea Dot put her hands on her hips.

"Mm hmm. But now it makes more sense. Put your hands on my shoulders, and I'll let you down."

Bea Dot complied, and Will placed her on the ground the same way he had before. Absently, he kept his hands on her waist as he asked, "Still sore?"

"Not as much. Thank you." Still looking up at him, Bea Dot removed her hands from his shoulders and took a step back, still nervous around him but this time in a strange, thrilling way, as if she were committing a crime and enjoying it.

He smiled and nodded, then offered his arm. "Then let's go inside and see your cousin."

Chapter 8

L ola, be sure to remind Ralph to send out that rocking chair."

"Yes, ma'am." Lola put the Model T in gear, but Netta held on to the driver's-side door.

"And don't forget to ask Jim Henry to paint the nursery."

"I told you, Miss Netta, he planning to do that this Friday."

Netta sighed and wiped her damp forehead with the back of her hand. What else should she tell Lola before sending her off back to town?

"Miss Netta"—Lola patted her hand with a sympathetic look—"you gone be just fine. Mr. Will and your cousin gone be here shortly. But I got to go. Doc Coolidge need his motorcar back to go see sick folk."

Netta nodded in resignation and let go of the door. She stepped away from the automobile as Lola revved the engine and chugged the car toward the cart path and to the woods. Netta waved after her as she pulled away, but the housekeeper kept her face forward, having only just learned to drive that afternoon.

Netta walked into the cabin and smoothed the tattered blanket on one of the rickety cots. How was she supposed to sleep on that thing? She hated to question Ralph's judgment, but with her precarious condition, wasn't it more logical for Ralph to stay at the camp house and for her and Bea Dot to stay at home? But who was she to contradict the town doctor?

Netta's emotions played hopscotch all day, and currently, they'd landed in the frustration box. Earlier they'd landed in the fear box as Ralph rushed her and Lola into a packing frenzy and shooed them off to the camp house. When Netta arrived and surveyed the little shack, she hopped into the panic square at the thought of receiving Bea Dot and welcoming her guest in this one-room shanty. But the panic lasted only about an hour because Lola, with her insistence that she return to town, pushed Netta into the resentment square.

Left alone to make the cabin the least bit presentable, all the while unable to lift anything remotely heavy, Netta worked herself into such a dither that she couldn't think straight. Her heart pounded, and her underarms grew sticky with sweat. The best thing for her, under the circumstances, was to rest in her rocking chair, which she couldn't do because Ralph made her leave it, in the front yard of all places. The neighbors would surely think she'd gone batty.

Without the rocker, Netta decided to take a walk around the cabin to calm her nerves, and that helped a bit, but the stench of the outhouse and the harsh summer sunshine drove her back indoors. Finally, she sat on a straight-backed wooden chair, the one that wobbled the least, and took a few deep breaths.

She rubbed her rounded belly, a habit she'd developed over the past few months, a kind of tacit signal to her baby that all would be well. When she'd reached the three-month milestone, she wept for joy, with relief that she'd finally have that beautiful child of her dreams. Now, at seven and a half months, she found herself stuck in the middle of nowhere without even her husband, the only person she would trust to deliver her baby.

Netta held her feet up in front of her. The ride to the country and walk outside had exacerbated her swollen feet so that now the tops of them puffed like half-baked loaves out of her slippers, the only shoes she could still wear. Ralph always told her to put her feet up, but if she lay down on that cot, she might not be able to get up by herself. Instead, she pushed the other wooden chair around the table so that the two chairs faced each other. Then she rummaged through a box of housewares until she found her book, Baroness Orczy's *The Elusive Pimpernel*, a birthday gift from Ralph. Sitting in one chair with her feet in the other, she resolved to ignore the hard seat and focus on whether Chauvelin would succeed in tricking Sir Percy Blakeney in returning to France. She never fancied this kind of romantic fiction. She much preferred an Edith Wharton novel, but the closest library was twenty miles away in Hawkinsville, and its collection was sparse. Buying new books required a trip to Macon, which was impossible for her these days.

The swelling in her feet subsided a bit, but she doubted they'd ever look the same again. Apparently, the fluid in them had traveled to her bladder because she was about to pop. Of course, lately that need arose hourly. As she tensed her muscles and crossed her legs, her eyes widened in alarm. She could never use that putrid outhouse once, much less a dozen times a day. What would she do?

She tried to read more of the novel, but the building pressure inside her ruined her concentration. Still, she ignored the urgency in her bladder until her belly ached. Shutting her book, she whispered a curse on her husband, then pushed herself out of the chair, shuffled to the door, and waddled down the cement block steps. The sun had lowered itself in the sky, but the temperature had dropped little. That outhouse would be both stinky and stifling. She'd just have to hold her breath while she was in there.

As she neared the rickety wooden structure, its emanating odor withered her resolve. She stopped, considered the alternative for a moment, and then turned toward the lake, just down a slight embankment. At the sound of water lapping the edge, Netta thought she would wet herself, but she held on long enough to remove her underclothes and find a bush thick enough to squat behind. *It would be just my luck for Bea Dot to arrive at this moment*, she thought as she hiked up her skirt and held the fabric in her fist. With her other hand, she grasped the trunk of the bush for balance and squatted. She'd never felt such simultaneous relief and shame. Here she was, a graduate of St. Vincent's Academy, former secretary of the church-women's guild, and wife of Pineview's only physician, urinating out in the open into a country lake. Her mother would just die.

When she finished, she put her underclothes back on, and just before turning to go back to the camp house, she spied a large black turtle sitting on a nearby log, staring at her. She stuck her tongue out at it before trudging up the embankment, and then a frightening thought occurred to her. What if that turtle had been a snake? Weren't there water moccasins out here? What about alligators? She shivered at the thought and made her heavy legs push her up the embankment and into the house. No more outdoor business for her. She would just have to fashion herself a chamber pot and then ask Will Dunaway to phone Ralph. There had to be a better option than this shabby fishing camp.

She went back to the stiff wooden chairs, propped up her feet, and returned to *The Elusive Pimpernel*, taking short breaks to stretch her aching back and to light an oil lantern once the sun began to set.

"Where is my cousin Bea Dot?" she asked the bare walls. Then as if on cue, voices drifted through the open window, and she peered out to see Will Dunaway's wagon by the lake. Bea Dot stood on the back of the wagon while Will was doing something to the hem of her skirt. What on earth could they be doing? Then he took her by the waist and put her on the ground. He spoke to her briefly before she took his arm and walked with him to the house. They looked like a courting couple, except her hair was a mess, and what in the world happened to her skirt? She went to the open door, stopping at the top step.

"Hello! Bea Dot, dear, it's so good to see you!" Up close her cousin looked even more disheveled. Her hair was a rat nest underneath her hat, and her dirty face was streaked from drips of perspiration. "Will, thank you for bringing my cousin to me." She held her arms out to Bea Dot as the young woman slowly ascended the steps. Why did she walk so stiffly, as if she'd just gotten a lashing?

"Hello, Netta," she said with a tired smile. "It's good to finally be here." Bea Dot held her arms out, and Netta embraced her. Good heavens! She smelled like Will Dunaway's horse.

"Do come in. You must be exhausted."

Netta led Bea Dot into the camp house, and Netta's nervousness escalated as she saw Bea Dot's face fall at the sight of the two rickety cots, the wobbly table and chairs, and the wood stove in the corner.

"I know it's not much," Netta said as cheerily as she could. "But it'll just be for a few days, until Ralph can get that flu bug contained in town. Then we'll go back to my house. Oh, you'll love it, Bea Dot. It has such a beautiful porch."

"Yes, I saw it," Bea Dot said dully, not taking her eyes off the two cots. Then she turned to Netta and smiled politely. "I'm sure it's lovely on the inside as well."

"Excuse me, ladies." Will entered the cabin carrying Netta's rocker. Netta's heart leapt at the sight of it. At last a comfortable place to sit. He set it in the middle of the room. Though a small piece of furniture, it consumed the entire space. Will stood with hands on hips and surveyed the cabin, one eyebrow raised.

"Do you have everything you need here, Netta?" he asked.

Actually, what she needed was her own house. "Well," she replied uncertainly, "I think we have enough to get us by for the next few days."

"Hmm." He stepped over to the table and two chairs and peered into the two crates on the floor. "Is this all the food you brought?"

"Yes."

"How will you get more if you need it?"

"I was hoping you would help me with that." Netta smiled sheepishly.

Will frowned slightly and stepped to the door, looking out. After a pause, he returned. "Ralph didn't leave the Model T with you?"

"No, he said he needed it in town to call on patients." She knew he should have left that machine. Even Will thought so.

Will rubbed the back of his neck and looked out the door at the setting sun. Outside the world was turning gray. He exited the cabin and disappeared around its corner.

"Where is he going?" Bea Dot asked.

Netta shrugged. Then she asked, "How was your trip? Was the train on time?"

Bea Dot opened her mouth to answer, but Will reentered the house before she could speak.

"You hardly have any firewood out there. Did you know that?"

She hadn't given firewood any thought. She always had plenty at home. Ralph saw to that.

"And someone should dig you a fresh latrine. Smells like something fell in that one and died."

Netta curled her lip, and Bea Dot covered her mouth with her hand at the grotesque image.

"Netta, I know Ralph wants you to be safe, but staying at this camp house can't be the solution. Seems like he didn't think this plan through."

Hallelujah! Will was going to take them back to town!

Outside, crickets chirped, and the room had grown dark except for the oil lamp, which at least improved the look of Bea Dot's dirty face. Will scratched his head and thought a moment before continuing. "Well, I can't leave you two out here. I suppose you'll have to come with me."

"Back to town?" Netta asked, the pitch of her voice rising with hope.

"To Dunaway's Crossing," he replied.

Netta's heart sank a little. But at least Will's new trading post was better than this camp house.

"Where's that?" Bea Dot asked. From the worry on her face, Netta could tell Bea Dot loathed the idea of more travel.

"It's my place," Will explained. "Just on the other side of the lake. It won't take long to get there."

Netta pressed her palms together, but said nothing. It wasn't home, but Dunaway's Crossing was a sight better than this sorry shack. His new place might be rustic, but at least he had a telephone and access to the main road. She and Bea Dot could tolerate staying there for the short term until Ralph sent for them again. "Well, I suppose you're right," she said cautiously. "Can we take my rocking chair?"

"Certainly," he said. "If you'll pardon me a few minutes, I'll put your belongings in my wagon, and we'll be off."

Netta turned to Bea Dot with a triumphant smile. Bea Dot tried to return it, but she failed to conceal the fatigue in those dark eyes.

Chapter 9

Customers trickled in for now, but Bea Dot felt sure that once word spread of Will Dunaway's country store, a steady flow of clientele would run in and out his front door. He had stocked shelves with a variety of goods rural folk might need: cornmeal, molasses, salt, coffee, tobacco. She relished the store's scent of raw pine and fresh paint, which was why she'd decided to knit at the kitchen table with a view through the doorway of the shop. She much preferred helping Will behind the counter or arranging items on the shelves to the tedious knit two, purl two of making Netta's layette.

"Your stitches are so even." Bea Dot jumped as Netta's voice over her shoulder startled her like a tiny shock of static electricity. Her cousin circled the straight-backed chair and faced her. "That's going to be a precious receiving blanket."

She took the piece into her own pudgy hands to examine it more closely, and though Netta wore a smile of admiration, Bea Dot knew to expect a word of critique veiled in compliment.

"Oh, dear, you've dropped a stitch." Netta laced her voice in regret. "But at least it's on this top row. You can still fix it."

Oh, hooray! There's still hope for this blanket! Tacit sarcasm helped Bea Dot bite her tongue at her cousin's frequent criticisms.

Out loud, she said, "I'll just add a stitch at the end of this row."

"Yes, you could do that," Netta said before chewing on her lip, a telltale sign of disapproval. Bea Dot counted silently, wondering how long Netta would hesitate before suggesting a better solution. Poor Netta tried so hard to abandon her bossy perfectionism, but old habits died hard. "Then again, you could take out those few stitches and pull the dropped stitch over your right needle."

Pressing her lips, Bea Dot hid a smile. For a whopping seven seconds, Netta had held in her opinion. A new record for her. Bea Dot nodded, then put the blanket in the basket on the table. "My hands are getting sore," she lied. "I'll make fewer mistakes if I come back to this later."

"In the middle of a row?" Netta's incredulous blue eyes widened.

"It'll be all right." Bea Dot patted her cousin's shoulder.

"I'll just finish this row for you," Netta said, taking a seat across the table.

Bea Dot knew she would.

"I think I'll see if Will needs any help in the store," she said as she took a step in that direction.

"Oh, don't bother him, darling," Netta replied, already pulling out Bea Dot's stitches. Bea Dot tried not to be insulted by her cousin's presumptuous gesture. It was, after all, Netta's receiving blanket. But Bea Dot still felt a pang of resentment at how quickly her cousin took over her work.

"I'm not going to bother him." Bea Dot tried to dampen the edge in her voice. "I'm going to offer to help."

"That's sweet of you, dear, but I think we should try our best to stay out of his way." Netta spoke to the yellow yarn rather than to Bea Dot. Her pudgy fingers flew like hummingbirds around the knitting needles. "We've already crowded him out of his home. No need to interfere with his work."

Perplexed, Bea Dot leaned in the doorsill and watched Netta

knit. The temporary living arrangement was the very reason she wanted to help Will. She hadn't considered her gesture a nuisance. Five days ago, Will had driven the two women and all their belongings to his small home, which was attached to the back of his trading post. He'd given up his bedroom, even putting up an extra bed, before moving his own belongings into the storage room at the other end of the store. There, he slept on a pallet among the bags of grain and cans of coffee.

"But when I offer to help," Bea Dot explained, "he seems to appreciate it."

"Oh, Will wouldn't complain." Netta still spoke into her knitting. "He's too considerate to do that." She'd already finished a row and started another.

"But after all he's doing for us, I want to do something to reciprocate, to repay him for all his effort and his hospitality." What better way to do so than to help him get his new store organized? Weren't two hands better than one?

"That's a nice idea." Netta lifted her head to face Bea Dot. "Instead, why don't you make him a nice pound cake? I'm sure he'll love that."

"Right," Bea Dot replied uncertainly. "A pound cake." She backed out of the kitchen and shuffled through the store and to the back porch, still pondering Netta's suggestion. Now she didn't know whether to trust Will on the matter or her cousin. She didn't want to be a pest, but at the same time, how did Netta know how Will felt about her help? And what good would a pound cake do? Even if she had the ingredients to bake a cake, she lacked the skills to make one. All her life, California had done the cooking, the sewing, the housework. Bea Dot's cake would likely turn out heavy as lead, which would be fine if Will really needed a new doorstop. Inhaling deeply while pushing down her frustration, she sat on the porch's log bench and stared through the screen toward the lake.

Bea Dot found the water soothing, so different from the coast's tidal creeks and rivers. No incoming or outgoing tides, just the consistent gentle waves lapping on the bank. No stale marshland odor or honking seagulls, just the scent of pine, hardwood, and mud along with the hum of cicadas in the background.

On her first day at the crossing, she'd discovered this welcome respite from Netta's disguised disapproval. Whenever Netta failed to stifle her bossiness, Bea Dot turned to the lake, reminding herself that in spite of those irritating habits, Netta had invited Bea Dot to Pineview out of love and a desire to protect her from Ben's wrath.

The screen door creaked behind her. Will stepped onto the porch and sat next to her on the log bench. Gazing out on the water, he said softly, "Taking a break from your cousin?"

"Is it that obvious?" Bea Dot stiffened at the thought. Inside, her nerves hummed. "Does she know that's why I came out here?"

"I've seen her out here too." Will chuckled softly. "There's something about this lake." He stretched his legs out in front of him. "It eases the soul."

Bea Dot didn't feel at ease, though. "I mean no disrespect to Netta."

"I understand." Will held up his hand to stop her. "You two are cooped up here day and night." He shook his head twice. "Too much togetherness. You both try your best to get along, but sometimes you need to part ways."

"The last time we were together, we parted ways . . . well . . . it's been a long time since we've seen each other." Bea Dot sighed. No need to burden Will with her problems, although somehow she felt comfortable enough with him right now to do so.

"No need to explain." Will kept his eyes on the water. "It's no business of mine. But you're welcome to help out in the store as much as you'd like."

"Thank you." A pang of embarrassment stabbed at her. Had he heard her and Netta's conversation? She studied his tanned face as he gazed at the lake. His straight brown hair lopped just slightly over his forehead, even though he kept it cropped close above his ears and off his neck. To the side of his throat, a vein ran downward, throbbing rhythmically, as if beneath that calm exterior some troubling thoughts struggled to emerge.

"Actually, I came out here to ask if you'd be willing to mind the store tomorrow," he said.

"Of course." Bea Dot nodded enthusiastically, delighted at the chance to help him.

"I must go into town to pick up some orders. I may be gone awhile. I'll show you where the ledgers are and how to record information in them, but it shouldn't be too busy. Would you mind?"

"Certainly not," she said. "I'd be happy to."

"Thank you." He stood. "And if you'd like, I can send word home while I'm in town. Do you have a message for your husband?"

Bea Dot's heart skipped a beat, and a grip of caution seized her, a familiar tension she realized she hadn't felt since she'd arrived at the crossing. Maybe she should inform Ben of her whereabouts, but she felt safer keeping him in the dark. Besides, it was easier not to think about her problems at home. "I don't think so," she said. "But I'm sure Netta would like you to take a note to Ralph."

Will nodded. "All right. I'll ask her."

He went back into the house and left her there listening to the lapping lake and the song of the cicadas.

A thunderstorm brewed up during dinner. Bea Dot and Netta ate quietly by lamplight while listening to the wind and rain.

"I hope Will isn't on his way home in this storm," Bea Dot said, looking anxiously out the window.

"So do I," Netta replied, "but if I know Will Dunaway, he's probably stopped at a neighboring farmhouse until the storm passes. He's very resourceful."

Her cousin was right. In the short time Bea Dot had known Will, she'd witnessed several instances of his self-sufficiency. Still, she hated the thought of someone so kind being caught in the wind and rain.

"Are you finished?" she asked.

Netta nodded, and Bea Dot took up both plates and put them in the dishpan, then pumped some water into it before rubbing the dishrag over her plate.

"Don't you want to heat the water on the stove before washing with it?" Netta asked.

Bea Dot straightened her back and gritted her teeth, trying to summon more patience, but her supply had run low. She exhaled slowly, trying to release at least some irritation. "Netta," she said smoothly, "maybe you'd like to wash the dishes. Then you could make sure they get done right."

"What does that mean?" Netta asked, raising her eyebrows and straightening her back, which meant, *How dare you talk to me that way?*

"I mean exactly that," Bea Dot told her, dropping the dishrag in the pan. "I can't do anything to suit you."

"That's not true," Netta said, folding her napkin, then flattening it with her palms. Bea Dot could tell Netta was trying not to get flustered.

"Yes it is. Heat the water. And bake a pound cake. And tear out my stitches." Bea Dot's voice escalated. She couldn't help her next remark. "And not marry Ben."

Netta huffed. "Advice you clearly should have heeded."

Resentment fired into anger, and Bea Dot stomped to the back porch before she said something she'd regret. Outside, the rain had subsided and the evening had cooled. The pine trees bent in the wind, the needles whipping the air. The screen door creaked as Netta joined Bea Dot on the porch.

"I'm sorry," Netta said. "That was insensitive of me."

"Don't apologize." Bea Dot faced her cousin. "You were right—as usual." She hated admitting that.

Netta paused before answering. "I would rather have been wrong. It breaks my heart to see what he's done to you."

"To see? What do you mean?"

"The way you walked the day you arrived. And that cut on your lip. He'd . . . he'd thrashed you hadn't he?" Netta's face scrunched up as if uttering the thought caused her physical pain.

Netta didn't realize the half of it, but Bea Dot preferred that her cousin believe Ben had beaten her rather than know the truth. She turned her gaze toward the lake. The water rippled in the wind. "Yes."

"Oh, sweet Bea Dot." Netta's voice quaked, revealing tears on the offing. "Why didn't you tell me sooner? Ralph and I would have loved to have you come stay with us."

"How could I have known that?" Stung by her cousin's remark, Bea Dot faced Netta again. "You boycotted my wedding, and I never heard from you."

"What do you mean?" This time Netta frowned, hands on hips. "I sent you many letters of apology. You never wrote back."

"Really? When?"

"Here and there for the past several months. I also sent you a card on your birthday."

"I never got them," Bea Dot said, slowly shaking her head. She stopped as she realized why.

"None of them?" Netta asked.

"No."

"That's the strangest thing I ever heard. I can understand one letter getting lost in the mail, but all of them?"

"They didn't get lost, Netta. Ben took them." Bea Dot put her hands on her hips as her heartbeat sped at the thought. "That makes perfect sense now. He never wanted me to bring in the mail. He insisted on doing it himself. He hid your letters from me." That goat. Her chest burned with hatred for him.

"But why?"

"Because you didn't want me to marry him? Or just to spite me? I wouldn't put it past him. He despises almost everything about me." Then it hit her. Ben had suspected all along that she'd deceived him. If that were the case, did he know the whole truth? She shook the question away. How could he?

Netta's frown remained. "Then how did you get my last letter?"

"California met the postman at the door that day," Bea Dot recalled. "He happened to mention he had a letter for me, so she took it and gave it to me." Bea Dot remembered lying to Ben about the letter coming by special delivery, but she felt silly that she never wondered why she'd never received other letters before. Then again, no one would have written to her except Netta, and Bea Dot believed all along Netta hated her.

"Bless California's heart. Thanks to her, I have my Bea Dot back." She stepped over to Bea Dot and put one arm around her shoulder, her round stomach protruding in front of both of them. They watched the rain in silence for a few minutes. As each raindrop fell, it made a tiny pockmark in the water.

"Why did you marry him, Bea Dot? You seemed so determined to do so, but I never saw love in your eyes."

Bea Dot stepped away from her cousin. Thunder rumbled in the distance, and the wind chilled her. She rubbed her arms but couldn't warm them. How could she explain that dreadful decision? She couldn't dare tell her cousin the truth.

Netta persisted. "Bea Dot, did you have to get married?"

"Yes." At least she could answer that question honestly. But she silently begged Netta to stop probing.

"Did Ben force himself on you?" Suspicion rose in Netta's voice. "Is that what happened?"

"Can we not talk about this? What's done is done, right?" Bea Dot's muscles tightened like coils as Netta's inquiry ventured too far.

"Of course," Netta conceded. "Let's go inside. It's getting cold."

Bea Dot followed her cousin indoors, shaking off one last shiver as she reentered the warm house. A cold pan of dirty dishes awaited her, but the sound of the front door opening made her heart leap. Will was back.

"Hello!" Will shivered just inside the front door. When he removed his hat, water dribbled down the back of his damp flannel shirt. He shook his hair and shucked his waterlogged canvas jacket.

"Oh, Will, you're home. I'm so glad." From the back of the house, Netta approached him holding a kerosene lamp. "We were worried about you in this storm." Bea Dot followed in her shadow. Holding the lamp in front of her pale face, Netta looked haggard, almost ghostly. Bea Dot, a more welcome sight, rushed around her cousin, looked up at him, and smiled, making his heart thump.

"We thought you'd stopped somewhere to get out of the rain," Bea Dot said. The light of the lantern flickered in her dark-brown eyes.

"Bea Dot, can you pick up that wet coat?" Netta asked. "I can't bend over that far. Let's try to dry it in front of the stove."

Bea Dot's welcoming smile turned to an embarrassed one as she stooped to pick up the soggy jacket.

"No, Miss Bea Dot. I'll get that. You'll soak your dress." He crouched beside her. Will marveled at Bea Dot's ability to tolerate her cousin's constant instruction. Taking her elbow, he pulled her up gently as he rose, glad that she accepted his refusal of help. She was the only person these days who did so.

"Are you all right? We expected you before dark. And then this storm hit . . ."

Bea Dot's expression warmed his heart. She was different from everyone else in Pineview, who repeatedly asked that sorrowful "How are you," constantly reminding him of his war injury. Bea Dot knew nothing about his past troubles, so her concern simply stemmed from weather.

"I'm fine, just wet," he said, smiling, his hand still on her arm. He could have wrapped his hand around it. "I saw those clouds forming, but I didn't quite beat them here."

"If you had a motorcar, you'd have made it," Netta said. "Come in the kitchen where it's warm. You'll catch your death."

Will winced at Netta's remark. After what he'd seen in town today, he feared Netta's casual statement bore more significance than she realized. He let her lead him to the stove. The women had already eaten, but the room still smelled of roast chicken. Dirty plates sat in a half-full dishpan, and Will stifled a smile at the bits of food floating on the surface. Bea Dot must have been cleaning up. He found her lack of household skills endearing.

"Sit, sit," Netta told him, pushing him down into a chair. "Bea Dot, get Will a blanket." She fluttered her hands at her cousin as she sent her out of the room, and Will felt a pang of sympathy for Bea Dot. Netta took a plate off the shelf and spooned up a serving of the chicken potpie on the stove. "It's still warm," she said as she placed it in front of him. "You must be starved."

Bea Dot returned with a gray wool blanket. As she placed it over his shoulders, he caught a whiff of her talcum powder and a glimpse of the underside of her jaw. A large freckle lived just south of her ear. He wished he could touch it.

"Tell me about Ralph," Netta said, interjecting into his thoughts. She sat close to him at the table, leaning in with her questions. "Is he all right? Did he send me a note? Did he read mine? What did he say?"

"Netta, give the poor man a moment to eat." Bea Dot sat in the chair opposite him. Will took a bite of pie and closed his eyes at his first taste of the savory meat, thankful for another benefit of having quarreling cousins in the house.

"This is delicious," he said, digging in for another bite. "I hadn't realized how hungry I was."

He stood and took a glass from the cupboard, then dipped some water from the bucket next to the icebox. When he returned to the table, Bea Dot rested her chin in her hand and watched him eat. Though he kept his eyes on his food, he felt her gaze on him. He liked the feeling. He glanced at Netta and immediately turned back to his food. She almost bounced in her chair waiting to hear about her husband. How could he tell her he'd never spoken to Ralph? He scraped his plate, knowing it was rude, but trying to stall the conversation.

"There's plenty more," Bea Dot said.

Eyes still on Will, Netta picked up the plate, wordlessly handing it to Bea Dot, who rose to refill it. Before he could object, Netta asked, "How's Ralph, Will?"

He sighed and wiped his mouth with a used napkin lying between them. Maybe it was Bea Dot's. She put another full plate in front of him and sat again. Will savored the closeness of his petite, dark-haired guest, but he also dreaded the conversation with his friend's wife. He shifted in his seat nervously.

"Netta," he said softly, looking at his fork instead of her, "I didn't see Ralph. He wasn't at his office, so I slipped the letter under his door."

"I see." Netta stiffened her back and fiddled with a button on her sleeve. "You weren't able to go to the hospital?"

"That's the first place I went, actually." Will's heart sank in pity for her. She only wanted some assurance of her husband's well-being. Will put his hands in his lap as he continued to meet her gaze.

"He wasn't there?" Netta leaned in toward him.

"Yes, he was there, but I couldn't see him. A nurse turned me away at the door. No one is allowed in except Ralph, nurses, and patients. Ralph's orders."

"What do you mean? What about family members?"

Will shook his head. Bea Dot lifted her eyebrows, also waiting for an explanation. This time he chose his words carefully. He felt like he was on the witness stand.

"The flu's spread much faster than anyone expected," he explained. "Ralph's trying to contain the illness, so no one enters who isn't sick."

"Well, that makes no sense." Netta stood, her hand on her back, her large stomach knocking the table as she rose. She covered the pie plate with a cloth and placed it in the icebox. She picked up a napkin and twisted it in her hands. "Family members always help tend to sick patients. It's how the hospital manages with so few nurses."

"This time it's different." Will tried not to distress her any further. "This flu is worse than others. Ralph is just taking precautions."

"How bad is it?" Netta asked.

"Well," Will hesitated, "a few folks have died."

"From the flu?" Bea Dot frowned, her mouth opening into a small O.

"Like I said, this one's different."

"How many?" Netta asked.

"I don't know." It was the truth, but Will thought it best not to describe the black bows bedecking many of Pineview's front doors. "But I do know this." He came around the table and took Netta's hand. "Ralph is fine. He would get word to you if he weren't. We have a telephone, and if he were ill, he'd have called or had someone else call."

Netta nodded blankly and stared at Will's hand holding hers.

Bea Dot rose and put her hand on her cousin's shoulder. "He's probably home now reading your letter," she said.

Netta turned to her cousin with a faint look of hope.

Bea Dot nodded and continued, "Your letters are probably his one joy while you're away. Why don't you go write him another?"

Netta turned her eyes to Will for assurance.

He smiled at her, agreeing with Bea Dot. "It can go out in the morning's post."

Without a word, Netta turned and went into the bedroom.

In a few seconds, he heard a drawer open and a chair scrape the floor. He looked down at Bea Dot and whispered a relieved "Thank you."

Her eyes followed him as he returned to his seat and resumed his meal. This time, though, he felt not flattered, but uneasy by Bea Dot's gaze, as if he should feel guiltier with each bite.

"What are you not telling her?" she whispered. The corners of her mouth turned down in suspicion. "Is Ralph really all right?"

Will pushed his plate away, considering how much information he should give her.

"Be honest, Will."

"I have not lied to you." He frowned, trying to swallow indignation.

"No." Her tone softened. "But you're holding something back, something that might worry Netta. If her husband is in trouble, she ought to know." Her voice was still barely audible.

"As far as I know, he's fine." Will exhaled and put his palms up on the table. "No one at the hospital indicated otherwise, and if Pineview's only doctor were down with flu, I doubt that would be a secret."

Bea Dot's countenance relaxed—just a bit. "Then what are you afraid to tell us? We're not children, Will. We can take the truth."

"I don't doubt that *you* can," Will began. Something about the gravity in her voice told him she'd seen her share of hardship. "But in Netta's condition . . ." He gave up. If the situation didn't improve in Pineview, the women would find out anyway. "I just didn't see the need to give her all the details. I truly don't know how many people have died, but what I saw wasn't encouraging."

Bea Dot's eyes narrowed to chocolate quarter moons.

"Mr. Bradley from the pharmacy wasn't in. His clerk told me Mrs. Bradley died several days ago."

Bea Dot bit her bottom lip and frowned. After a pause, she said, "That's just one person."

"She's just the one I know." Will shook his head. "Mr. Bradley's clerk named some other people as well, and he said the school's only half-full these days."

Bea Dot exhaled and put her head in her hands.

"Anyway," Will continued, "I know Netta wants to hear from Ralph, but he's just too busy to stop what he's doing to write a letter. At the same time, I don't want to frighten her unnecessarily. Until we know more, we should hope for the best."

She raised her face and nodded, seeming to accept Will's reasoning, but he could tell she didn't entirely agree with it. But now she knew all he did, so if she felt Netta should have all the facts, she could give them to her.

Will swept up the last of the chicken pie on his plate and swallowed it quickly. Though the stove warmed him, his feet were cold in his wet boots. He'd have loved to take a hot bath, but with the women in the house, he'd have to wait until they were asleep.

"Thank you for dinner," he said, gathering his dish, fork, and cup and carrying them to the counter, putting them next to the dishpan instead of in it. He wrinkled his nose at the slick of grease floating atop the water. "I've taken too long with my supper, and now your dishwater's gone cold." He removed the dirty plates from the pan and carried it to the door to dump the water outside. Bea Dot rushed to him and opened the door. He'd tried not to embarrass her; still, her face and neck flushed.

"I'll heat another pot of water," she said.

Glad she played along, he nodded.

When he returned, Bea Dot was pumping water into a pot. He watched her as she lifted it and placed it on the stove. In the lamplight, a glimmer of perspiration shone over her lip. She wiped it off with her sleeve before she noticed him. She smiled and reached for the dishpan.

"Thank you," she said as she placed it on the countertop. She reached for the box of soap powder on the shelf. "The water will be hot in a few minutes. You should get out of those damp clothes," she said.

"You're right." He stepped toward the doorway to the store, then turned to view Bea Dot in the kitchen and Netta in the bedroom. Bea Dot poured too much soap into the dishpan. He smiled, then turned his eyes to Netta, who sat at a small table, writing a letter to Ralph, a slight frown of concern across her forehead. Will's gut flushed at the thought of Netta's worry for her husband. Then he turned his eyes back to Bea Dot and wondered why she had never mentioned her own husband back in Savannah.

Chapter 10

Bea Dot turned her back to the ledger and leaned on the counter to relieve her aching back and feet. With Will on his mail route, she hustled to assist the flux of customers. California always said, "All the nuts come out in the rain." That might have been true in Savannah, but in rural Georgia, everyone came out after the rain, like ants swarming to repair their damaged nest. She hadn't realized how much effort went into operating a store until she'd taken on the task herself. Now she admired Will's ability to recognize a need in this rural community and work hard to fill it. The customers who came to the crossing always asked after Will, and their questions spoke of the same admiration for him that she was developing.

She had sold out of coffee and was running low on kerosene. Will would have to make another trip to town to restock, and he'd just come home from Pineview yesterday. She'd mentioned once or twice already that a truck would make his work more efficient, but he'd rejected the suggestion soundly. She knew not to make it again.

Every person so far had tracked in red mud so that Will's beautiful pine floors looked just like the road outside. At first, Bea Dot occasionally swept up with irritation, but she eventually gave up that battle, hating the idea of the new planks quickly growing dull with wear.

She peered out the window at the rumble of an engine. Several motorcars had passed by, but none had stopped. Customers at the crossing typically arrived on foot or by horseback. Several folks came in asking to call in telegrams. Not knowing whether Will charged for those services, Bea Dot wrote down the messages for Will to call in when he returned. One family had just had a baby. Another—bless their hearts—had lost a son in France. Bea Dot's chest ached for the heartbroken man who left that message. A third family had canceled a trip to Atlanta. Bea Dot already knew why, but she listened to the woman's reasoning anyway. "My cousins wrote me and said they was leaving the city to get away from all the sickness. I'd of invited 'em to stay with me, but what if they brung the flu with 'em?"

So the outbreak wasn't isolated to Pineview. She and Netta had wondered. The cousins were dying for a newspaper, but Netta's was delivered to the house, and Will didn't subscribe. They depended on the sprinklings of news that walked through the door each day, and even those bits of information were speculative since many farming families had chosen not to go to town that week for market day.

If Atlanta had been hit, had the flu also affected Savannah? She picked up a pencil to jot down a telegram to Aunt Lavinia, but then she drew her hand to her mouth. What if Ben caught the disease? She shook the thought from her head, ashamed to be the kind of person to wish for someone else's—even Ben's—death.

The telephone rang again, interrupting Bea Dot's musings, so she pushed herself away from the counter and stepped on aching feet to the telephone stand. "Dunaway's Crossing," she answered into the mouthpiece.

"Bea Dot? Is that you?"

"Yes, yes it is." Bea Dot frowned, not recognizing the voice at first.

"It's Ralph calling, Bea Dot."

"Ralph, thank goodness. Are you well?" Her heart thumped with simultaneous relief and concern. "What is happening there? We keep hearing such dreadful stories."

Netta's face appeared in the bedroom door, and with her arm Bea Dot beckoned her to the phone. Netta waddled over, anticipation lighting her face. Bea Dot didn't even hear Ralph's answer to her questions because Netta grabbed the earpiece and pushed herself in front of the phone, edging Bea Dot out of her way.

"Ralph, oh darling, how are you? I've missed you so . . . Yes . . . I've tried to call, but I never get an answer."

Bea Dot stepped out to give Netta some privacy, understanding her cousin's urgency but also a little annoyed at being pushed aside. Maybe now Netta would stop chewing on her lip and sighing into her teacup. Still, she wished she'd been able to get more information from Ralph.

Bea Dot rubbed her lower back as she turned her face to the midday sun. The warmth, combined with the brisk breeze, refreshed her. Her feet still smarting, she stepped over to the log bench in front of the store. "Ooh," she said as she sat down. Leaning forward relieved her back even more. She stretched out her legs and put her hands on her knees, relishing the welcome ache in her lower back. If this position felt good, would touching her toes feel even better? Could she even do that? She crawled her fingers down her shins, over the hem of her skirt, and across her bootlaces until she clutched the tips of her feet. Across her back and down her hamstrings, the tension felt so good that she sat that way for a minute or so, examining a stinkbug inching its way into the shadow under the bench.

"Well, ain't you a nimble thang?"

"Whoop!" Bea Dot almost fell over as the husky voice caught her by surprise. She straightened and shielded her eyes as she looked up at a smiling man towering over her petite frame. At least six feet tall, he was as wide as Santa's doorway. With wiry blond hair and a beard to match, he looked exactly the way she'd envisioned Odysseus. His dialect, however, more resembled Huckleberry Finn.

"I didn't mean to scare you, ma'am. I just ain't never seen nobody grab they feet like that."

"It's quite all right." Bea Dot stood, her face burning, but not from the sun. Regaining her composure, she replied, "Can I help you?"

The man held out his hand, even though Bea Dot had not offered hers first. "Thaddeus Taylor. I live in the house on the neighboring property. You Miss Netta's cousin?"

"Yes, I'm Bea Dot Ferguson." She took his hand, which completely covered hers.

"Pleased to meecha. Will told me y'all was staying here." He put his hands on his hips and surveyed the area.

"I'm minding the store for Will while he's delivering mail," Bea Dot explained. "Do you need anything?"

"Oh, naw, not today." He waved his big paw like he was swatting away a bee. "Just thought I'd stop by and see how y'all's doing. I ain't seen the store since it got up and running. My son Terrence, you know, helped put in the shelving and what not."

"No, I didn't know that," Bea Dot replied. "Do come in and see. Netta is talking to her husband on the telephone."

He nodded as he followed her through the door. Netta was just hanging up the earpiece. "How's things in town?" he asked.

"I suppose you should ask my cousin," Bea Dot said, smiling at Netta, who had just hung up the earpiece. "She has the latest word from Pineview."

Netta stepped away from the telephone, offering a polite countenance and voice. Still, Bea Dot could tell Ralph had said something to worry her. Netta balled a handkerchief in her fist.

"Why, Thaddeus Taylor, how are you?" she asked. "How is that
new baby of yours?" She leaned on the store's front counter with
one hand and put the other behind her back.

"Doing well, Miss Netta, and the baby's fine. Little boy. Named
Troy."

"What a nice, strong name," Netta said with a faint smile. "Do
tell Eliza I'll look forward to meeting him as soon as I can."

"I'll do that," Thaddeus said.

"Now, if you'll excuse me, I must go lie down." Netta turned
to leave with a stoop in her shoulders.

"Netta, do you feel well?" Bea Dot called after her. "Can I
bring you anything?" Did Ralph have bad news? The phone call
should have perked Netta up.

Netta held her hand up in refusal as she slowly disappeared
into the bedroom.

"She's close to her time," Thaddeus said, almost as if he needed
to apologize for her. "Bet she's as tired as a coal man in January."

"I suppose so." Bea Dot shook her head in sympathy.

"Well, I'll be going," Thaddeus said, turning to the door. "Let
you women have some quiet. Tell Will his store looks mighty fine.
Mighty fine."

Just as Bea Dot said good-bye to Thaddeus, two customers
arrived. One needed cornmeal; the other asked for mousetraps of all
things. Bea Dot couldn't help him with that but assured him she'd
ask Will to bring some from Pineview on his next trip. Eager to see
about Netta, Bea Dot almost pushed the customers out of the store.

In the bedroom, Netta sat solemn-faced as she rocked slowly
and stared out the window onto the lake. Before Ralph's call, she'd

been anxious and nervous, telling Bea Dot how to arrange items on the shelves and sweep the floor. Now she was deflated.

"Tell me about your telephone call." Bea Dot sat on the end of one bed. She watched Netta's back as she rocked. Netta remained quiet for so long that Bea Dot wondered if she'd heard the question.

"Netta?"

Netta shook her head slowly. "Mrs. Bradley died last week," she said quietly. "She was in my sewing circle."

"I'm so sorry." Bea Dot's heart plunged into her stomach. She could have told Netta about that last night.

"Before we came out here, Mr. Bradley came to the house looking for Ralph. He told me Ina was sick, but I thought she'd had a bad cold. If I had only known, I would have sent for Ralph right away."

"You can't blame yourself for that," Bea Dot said. "How could you have known the flu would be so severe?"

Netta kept rocking.

"And Edith Gentry died too. She was the organist at our church. Now her husband is in the hospital." Netta turned toward Bea Dot as much as her body would let her. "I thought Ralph was calling us to come home." Her eyes pooled, and her face pinked. "He was calling to tell me not to worry if I don't hear from him for a while. He has so little time for telephone calls." A brief sob escaped from her lips. Bea Dot took the handkerchief from the nightstand and handed it to her cousin.

"But he's all right, isn't he?" A flash of frustration shot through Bea Dot. Why did Ralph tell Netta all that bad news?

Netta nodded as she cried into her hanky. Then she took a deep breath and blew her nose. Another minute went by before she spoke again.

"I'm so silly," she said. "All this time I was worried about him getting enough to eat and getting enough rest." She huffed a cynical laugh. "I actually thought Ralph had sent us out here because I was so cautious about the baby." She rubbed her round belly. "It never occurred to me that he was afraid for our lives."

"I'm sure he didn't want to alarm you."

"Bea Dot, what if Ralph gets sick himself?" Netta's chin quivered. "I don't know what I'd do without him." She wrapped her arms around her middle as if she were lifting a huge ball. "I can't raise this baby by myself."

Panic simmered behind Netta's eyes, and Bea Dot kneeled next to Netta's rocker and clutched her hands.

"Stop thinking like that," she said with as much authority as she could muster. "Ralph is counting on you to be brave. He's doing everything he can to protect himself." At least she hoped he was. "All of that effort will be for naught if you drive yourself to an early labor with all this worrying."

Netta straightened, to Bea Dot's relief. Thank goodness she'd struck a chord.

"You're right." Netta inhaled, then sighed. "I must pull myself together and stop behaving like a scared child. Ralph deserves better."

"That's the right attitude." Bea Dot tucked a wayward blond lock behind Netta's ear. Then she rose, her knees creaking from kneeling on the hardwood floor. "Maybe you should lie down for a little while."

"I have this layette to finish," she replied, shaking her head. "Then I must write to Ralph. A letter from me will do him good."

Bea Dot smiled, hoping Netta realized the blessings of a husband who returned her love. She sighed and shuffled to the back porch, where she lowered herself heavily into one of Will's rocking chairs, as if she'd absorbed all the weight of Netta's fears. What if Ralph took sick? What then? And even if he stayed well, how long would this outbreak last? What about all the people coming in and out of the store? Could they bring influenza to the crossing? Would

Netta give birth out here in the country? Would Bea Dot have to deliver the baby?

After urging Netta to stop worrying about what-ifs, Bea Dot couldn't help imagining them herself. A chilly breeze whisked through the pines, and Bea Dot shivered. The lake had lost its calming effect. Instead of the soothing laps of the waves, she heard only the repeated rhythmic sound, *black, black, black.*

Unable to listen anymore, she returned indoors, back to the storefront. She sorted the telegrams to be called in—the canceled trip, the death announcement. She let them drop to the table.

She wanted Will to come home.

Chapter 11

"This old coat wrapped round me tight as Dick's hat band," Cal muttered into her chest. She shrugged and lowered her head against the October wind. The gusts blew through the tattered wool coat, and the front of her skirt pushed through her legs, giving her the appearance of wearing pants. "This chill come up sudden, like God say, 'Summer over! Here come fall.'"

Daylight dimmed as she hustled up Jones Street, hoping to reach the Barksdale home before dinner. Mr. David hated to be interrupted while he ate.

"God, don't take my Matilda," she muttered on her way. "I done lost my baby. Done lost my mama. Even Miss Bea Dot gone away. All I got now is my Tilda and her two girls. Don't take 'em now."

Ahead, lights shone in the Barksdales' dining room, and Cal's heart sped with worry. *Maybe Penny still setting the table*, she thought as she jogged to the yard and around to the back door. She took the steps two at a time and pulled the screen door open to knock, but the wind blew the handle out of her hand and slammed the door against the jamb. Before California could open it again, Penny pushed it wide. "Why in the world Mr. Ferguson send you out this time a day?"

Penny stood aside, allowing California into the Barksdales' warm kitchen, which smelled like cooked onion. Cal shook off the temptation of the fireplace. "He didn't, Penny. I come to see Mr. Barksdale. He eating dinner yet?"

"Just sit down." Penny gave a quick nod.

California's heart sank as she shifted her weight from one foot to the other. Should she ask Penny to interrupt him?

"What's wrong with you, Cal? You look like you stepped in ants."

California's eyes burned as she tried to hold back tears, but her throat went tight and her chin warbled. Penny wrinkled her brow, took California's arm, and led her to the fireplace, pushing down on Cal's arm so she'd sit in the maple rocker. California couldn't speak without tears flowing.

"It's Matilda. She bad sick. I got to talk to Mr. David. I need him to call a doctor for me."

"That ain't gone do no good. Dr. Washington ain't got no phone."

What did Penny think? That Cal had gone silly?

"I been looking for Dr. Washington two days," Cal said. "Left messages, but he ain't come, and nobody know where he at."

Penny put her hands on her hips and raised her eyebrows in disbelief. "You mean you want Mr. David to call Dr. Arnold?"

California nodded. "I wouldn't ask, but she real bad off. I'm 'fraid she gone die." The tears flowed again, and California pulled the kerchief off her head and blew her nose. Her face burned with embarrassment, but she didn't know what else to do.

Penny's face softened. She bit her lip in reluctance, showing her fear of angering Mr. David with an interruption. Thank heavens Miss Lavinia called her in.

Through the door, Miss Lavinia's voice revealed her slight irritation. "What's the commotion in there?" Penny's and Mr. David's voices were muffled, impossible to make out. Cal breathed a sigh of relief. At least he wasn't yelling at Penny. A chair scraped against the floor, and more than two footsteps approached the door.

Miss Lavinia glided in wearing her beaded blue dress. She always dressed for supper like she was going to a party. Her poufy gray-blond hair framed her face like a halo. California hoped she'd be an angel of mercy tonight.

"California, what's wrong?"

"I need your help, Miss Lavinia." Cal stood as she spoke. "Or Mr. David's help. My sister Matilda's real bad sick. Can you call Dr. Arnold for me? Please?"

Miss Lavinia stepped back a pace and asked why Cal didn't call Dr. Washington. Cal wanted to slap her lights on. *She know better than to think I ain't tried that.* Stuffing down her exasperation, Cal relayed what she'd just told Penny a few minutes before. "Tilda can't hardly breathe. She all gurgly like she got water in her chest, and she starting to turn blue."

Miss Lavinia's face contorted like she'd just seen a dead animal on the road. "Blue?"

"How can a black woman turn blue?" Penny asked.

"I can't explain it, but she blue in the lips and fingers. She can't breathe, Miss Lavinia. Please call Dr. Arnold." California leaned forward, her palms together as if in prayer.

Miss Lavinia put her hand on her forehead. Cal knew what Miss Lavinia was thinking, but she hoped her heart was bigger than her concern about what other people would think.

"If you call Dr. Arnold, he'll come. He won't do it for me, but he'll do it for you." Inside, Cal prayed her heart out, hoping Miss Lavinia would remember her own worries when Miss Bea Dot had the flu last spring. That flu was nothing like this one, but that didn't stop Miss Lavinia from calling the doctor every day.

"Why didn't you ask Ben to call earlier on your behalf?"

Penny put her hands on her hips. "Hmph!"

Was Miss Lavinia sick herself? Mr. Ben didn't even call the doctor for his own wife.

"He fired me, Miss Lavinia."

"What? Why did he do that?"

"Cause he Mr. Ben," Penny said, her chest puffed up like she was ready for a fight.

"When Tilda got sick, I asked him could I stay home and tend her," Cal explained. "He told me not to come back."

"My Lord in heaven. That man . . ." Miss Lavinia shook her head again. She stepped into the hallway to the telephone. With her back to California and Penny, she picked up the phone and spoke into it. "Yes, 32A please. Yes, Dr. Arnold . . . Yes, I know it's his home."

Miss Lavinia eyed California with knotted eyebrows. She bit her lower lip. Then she turned away again. California could tell what she was thinking, that the operator would listen in on the phone call and know she was asking the doctor to see about a black woman.

"Hello, Dr. Arnold. This is Mrs. David Barksdale . . . No, I'm not sick. David's fine too. I'm calling for Bea Dot's girl, Cal . . . Yes, I know . . . But Dr. Washington is nowhere to be found, and Cal's sister is having trouble breathing . . ."

Miss Lavinia listened for a long time and nodded every few seconds. Sometimes she said, "I see."

He must be blessing her out, Cal thought.

Miss Lavinia stiffened her back. "But what will I do if I don't have Matilda to help me at my Women's War Guild Monday?"

Bless her heart. California's eyes watered at Miss Lavinia's lie. Tilda had never worked for her, but by asking the question, Miss Lavinia suggested the doctor's call would be for her as much as for the sick woman. Dr. Arnold might be able to say no to Cal, but he'd have a harder time saying no to Miss Lavinia Barksdale.

"Yes, I'll tell her." Miss Lavinia nodded more. "Thank you, Doctor." She hung up the earpiece and turned toward California, her face showing little promise.

"What he say?" Cal almost stepped up and clutched Miss Lavinia's arm. Penny stood close by, wadding her apron in her hands.

"He'll be there first thing in the morning." Miss Lavinia sighed and stepped away from the phone and back into the kitchen.

California's heart fell to her feet. She was so shocked she had to force herself to speak. "Tomorrow's too late."

Then the tears did come, and Penny took California by the shoulders.

Miss Lavinia touched California's arm as well. "He knows Matilda needs help. It's just that he's already got a list of patients to see tonight, all with influenza. Apparently, it's more serious than I'd realized. I'm lucky to have caught him at home. He was on his way out again."

California didn't feel lucky at all. She blew her nose in her kerchief again.

"He says fluid is building up in her lungs," Miss Lavinia continued. "You should sit her up and pound on her back. Maybe she'll bring some of it up."

California nodded helplessly. How could Matilda cough if she couldn't breathe?

"He says to keep her room well ventilated," Miss Lavinia said. "He'll be there as soon as he can tomorrow."

California nodded again, feeling like she'd just killed her own sister.

"Penny, please wrap up some leftover dinner for Cal to take home," Miss Lavinia told her maid.

Penny nodded and shuffled to the stove.

Miss Lavinia told California not to worry, that everything would be fine. How did she know that? Her sister wasn't in bed gasping for breath. Penny returned with a cloth-covered basket and handed it to California, but Cal couldn't say anything in return.

"Be sure to eat dinner," Miss Lavinia said. "You'll need your strength to nurse Matilda until the doctor arrives."

California eyed the basket like it was a bucket of worms.

"It's too dark and windy for you to walk home," Miss Lavinia continued. "Penny, run out to the carriage house and ask Hap to drive Cal home in Mr. Barksdale's motorcar."

Penny wrapped her shawl over her head and ran outside. California gave Miss Lavinia a hoarse thank you. Then Miss Lavinia left to finish her supper.

California sat numbly the whole ride home, feeling as though God had abandoned her. When Hap pulled up to Matilda's house, California got out without saying a word. Not until she was inside did she realize she'd left the dinner basket in the car.

Chapter 12

A Model T chugged past Will's wagon, churning orange dust over the dry country road. The driver, decked out in goggles and a driving cap, waved a leather-gloved hand as he sped by. The horse rotated his ears, then turned his head slowly, as if taking uninterested notice of a strange, bothersome beast. He continued his slow pace toward the crossing.

"He's going nowhere fast, isn't he, Buster?" Will shook his head and curled his lip. People looked silly in their special driving clothes, especially the goggles. If they didn't go so fast, they'd have no need for the thick, bug-eyed glasses. The car had to have been speeding at least twenty-five miles an hour. Those kinds of daredevils were the same ones Will saw stuck in muddy ditches, their rubber tires spinning in the air, the drivers scratching their heads in confusion. Buster had helped pull two or three motorcars out of ditches already, and some folks in town had suggested Will start a business just for that purpose. But he couldn't face a job like that. Not after what happened at Belleau Wood.

He rubbed bleary eyes, stretching and yawning in his seat. The nightmare had returned last night, for the first time since Bea Dot and Netta had come to stay. He awoke in the darkness in a tangle of blankets and couldn't shake the image of the distraught, pale woman with curly red hair, holding up her arms in defense as Will steered the ambulance straight toward her.

He shook his head fiercely. *Stop it, Dunaway.* He rubbed one eye, then the other, with the back of his hand. No need to relive the terror.

At the sound of an engine behind him, Will pulled the reins to the right, guiding Buster to the edge of the road to let the driver pass. To Will's surprise, the engine slowed, and a dusty truck pulled alongside the wagon. Harley, the undertaker's assistant, waved for Will to stop.

"What are you doing out here, Harley?"

"I heard you were back in town today." Harley squinted at Will in the midday sun. "I tried to catch you at Richardson's store, but I was too late."

Will leaned forward, elbows on knees, letting the reins go slack. "I need to get back to the crossing as soon as I can," he replied. "Some folks waiting for supplies." Fortunately, he was finally able to load and unload them without any pain in his side.

"Weren't you just in town a couple of days ago?"

"Yep." Will nodded. "Already running low on some goods. Richardson and I are arranging some standing orders. Maybe he can make some deliveries too, so I won't have to go back and forth so much." Will frowned slightly. "Did you drive all the way out here to ask about that?"

A breeze blew up, and Will turned his jacket collar up around his neck. Buster sniffed the ground and nibbled on a few blades of grass.

Harley shook his head, turning in his seat to face Will better. He fiddled with the gearshift as he spoke. "Pritchett's overwhelmed, what with this flu and all. His suppliers are too. We've got a list of clients who need to schedule funerals, but we don't have coffins for them."

The truck shuddered as its engine idled. Will waited a second for Harley to continue. Then his eyes widened as he caught Harley's point. He shivered. Did the temperature just drop? "You want me to build coffins?"

"Could you?" Harley almost pleaded with him. "You were the first person we thought of since . . . well . . . you don't have any family in town. Most everybody else has a sick one to tend to."

The reference to no family simultaneously tugged at Will and buoyed him. He stiffened his back as another breeze brushed by. Usually his friends and neighbors felt sorry for him—annoyingly sorry—because his father was dead and his mother had moved away. For the first time, someone saw his solitude as a benefit instead of a burden—if one could call the ability to build coffins an advantage.

"Well, I've got Miss Netta and her cousin out at the crossing," he said, wondering if he could look after the women and help Pritchett at the same time. He turned the reins over in his hands, and when Harley said nothing, Will continued. "Maybe I can help you out." How could he refuse?

"Thank you." Harley smiled. "I'll tell Pritchett you'll be along this afternoon."

"Make it tomorrow," Will replied. "I still have to unload these goods and take care of some other business."

Will watched Harley turn the truck around, just to make sure he didn't back it into the ditch. Then he watched the red dust cloud up behind the truck as it drove away.

Will slapped Buster's behind lightly with the reins, and the horse pulled the wagon onto the road to travel the last mile to the crossing. His memories of last night's dream receded to make room for present concerns. How would he manage building coffins and running the store? Could he ask Bea Dot to help out even more? He hated taking advantage of her willingness to pitch in. Then again, she did seem to enjoy the work more for herself than for him. He liked that. His requests for assistance always made her beam, and those beautiful grins always made his insides swim like minnows circling a bait pail. He smiled at the thought of Bea Dot humming behind the counter, dutifully keeping track of all the sales.

Then he checked himself. *Damn it, Dunaway, stop it.* Ralph and Netta had encouraged him to seek out a young lady's company. Just his luck that the first woman he'd taken a liking to was married.

Knit two, knit two together, knit two, slip . . . No, that wasn't right. Netta pulled her stitches out again. She'd pulled out three rows in the past hour.

Purl two, purl two together . . .

She put her needles in her lap and wiggled her fat fingers, their tips tingling at each movement. Her swelling worsened each day, further hampering her knitting and writing, the two tasks she had to do most. When she wasn't working on the layette, she composed her daily page to Ralph, praying for him constantly. She also prayed the telephone would ring and Ralph would tell her to come home.

She shifted in her rocker—she just barely fit in it now—as the back door opened. Bea Dot entered with a large basket on her hip, her cheeks pink from the October breeze. Her dark brown curls had sprung from their pins, and she swiped them away from her face with a raw, cracked hand. "I must look like Medusa," she said. "The wind is picking up out there."

"Well, I look like Jack should chop me down from a beanstalk." Netta chuckled and waited for a contradiction that didn't come. Stung by Bea Dot's silence, she picked up her knitting again.

"I've gotten my sleeves wet doing the laundry," Bea Dot said after a short pause. "And my hands are blocks of ice. I'm going to stand by the stove." And with that, she went into the kitchen.

Oh, no thank you, Bea Dot, Netta grumbled in her head. *I don't need anything, but it's so thoughtful of you to ask.* Netta closed her eyes and inhaled deeply, chastising herself for her grumpiness, which grew with her girth. In her discomfort, Netta often let Bea Dot's poor housekeeping skills irritate her. Repeatedly, she'd had to check her surly attitude and remind herself that her cousin was trying her best at doing the laundry and minding the kitchen. Still, Netta assured herself she'd never again complain about Lola's work.

When she stood to stretch her back, her large middle shifted on its own. She put her hand on her side and felt a little lump—was it a foot or a hand?—roll under her skin and across her torso. "How big will you be when you're born?" she asked her child, whom she'd taken to calling Little Ralph. The baby's recent activity made her think it was a boy. "I hope you'll fit into these clothes I made for you."

Voices from the kitchen interrupted her thoughts. Will must be home. Her heart thumped in her chest, but she told it to stop, daring not to get her hopes up. She'd received no other telephone calls, no letters, nothing, since she spoke to Ralph three days ago. She waddled into the kitchen to hear whether Will had news from town, willing herself not to be disappointed if he didn't.

"Where's Netta?" he asked. She found him holding a plate of last night's ham while Bea Dot stood by warming her hands at the stove. Netta shook her head in disbelief, wondering how Bea Dot could stand there and let Will make his own lunch.

"Will, you're home sooner than we expected," she said, shuffling to the table and resting her hands on one of its straight-backed chairs. These days, sitting was no more comfortable than standing. "Are you hungry?" She lilted her voice, a signal that Bea Dot should offer to make him a plate. But Bea Dot only turned to face Netta, warming her backside. Giving up on her cousin, Netta reached for the plate of ham. "Let me make you some lunch."

"No, no." Will pulled the plate away before Netta could touch

it. "I'm making sandwiches. Have a seat. You'll eat one, won't you?"
He cut thick slices of ham, and Bea Dot went to the cupboard
and pulled out three cups, which she filled with water. At least her
cousin had the wherewithal to do that.

"How were things in Pineview?" Netta asked tentatively, unsure
whether she really wanted news. She eased herself into a chair.

"About the same," Will said, now slicing the bread. "I didn't see
Ralph, but I didn't stay in town long—just picked up my order and
came straight home." He gave her an apologetic look.

Netta lifted her eyebrows and nodded. Why should the report
be any different?

"I do need to talk to you about something," he said, placing
a plate in front of her. The chunk of ham between thick slices of
bread resembled a tongue poking out of a fat man's mouth. Netta
missed Lola's cooking.

Will and Bea Dot joined her at the table. Will bit into his
sandwich, but Bea Dot picked up a piece of bread and spread butter on it and ate her ham with a knife and fork. Netta did the same.

"What do you need to tell us?" Bea Dot asked.

Will swallowed, then spoke. "I talked to Harley this morning."
He turned to Bea Dot. "That's the undertaker's man." To both of
them he continued, "He says Pritchett is overwhelmed with work.
Evidently his supplier hasn't kept up with demand, and he can't
conduct funerals without making coffins."

The morsel of ham Netta had eaten turned to stone in her
stomach. She put down her knife and fork. "Just how many coffins
does he need?"

"I don't know a number," Will replied gravely, "but it must be
a lot if he sent Harley out for me."

The idea of that many people dying was almost too much to
comprehend.

"And he wants you to build them?" Bea Dot asked.

No, Bea Dot, Netta thought, *Pritchett wants Will to sell him a box of nails.*

"Yes." Will turned a table knife in his hand, gazing at it as if it were a puzzling new tool.

After a pause, Bea Dot asked, "How long will you be gone?"

"A few days, I think. Depends on how fast I can work." He faced Bea Dot. "I hope you won't mind helping me out at the store."

Netta couldn't help noticing that Will wouldn't meet her own eyes. She knew he was trying not to alarm her, but what he didn't seem to realize was the more he didn't say, the more nervous she became. Fear and disappointment gripped her, and she searched for words. Fortunately, Bea Dot found them for her. "Are you the only person who can help?"

Will gave her a puzzled frown.

"I mean," Bea Dot continued carefully, "does this Mr. Harley know that Netta and I are here? Does he know Netta is so close to her time?"

"He knows you're here." Will nodded and finally eyed Netta with a considerate smile. "But I didn't offer particulars about Miss Netta's condition."

How irksome. He was about to leave her in the pine forest with no way to get to town. Protecting her privacy was the least of her concerns at the moment. Her heart pounded so hard she was sure Bea Dot and Will could see her chest thumping.

"While I hate to be an obstacle to Mr. Pritchett's needs," she said, "I must say I'd feel terribly insecure without you here." She patted her forehead with the rough rag she used as a napkin. Suddenly the room was too warm.

"How will we get Netta to Pineview when the baby comes?" Bea Dot asked. "You'll have your wagon in town."

Will frowned at Bea Dot as if she'd asked him to untie a Gordian knot. "Miss Bea Dot, I doubt Ralph intended for you two to return to Pineview for the birth."

"What?" Bea Dot asked.

Netta's jaw dropped as her muscles tensed in alarm. "What do you mean?"

"What I mean is"—Will raised his hands in defense—"I don't think Ralph has thought that far ahead. No one expected influenza to be this serious." He laid his palms on the table. "But I've given it some thought, and I think I have a solution." He turned to Bea Dot. "I'll need you to come with me for a while." To Netta, he said, "I'll have her back before you know it."

Netta's chin wrinkled as a lump clogged her throat. She willed her tears to stay put. How could this be happening? After all the trials she'd endured, how could she face having her first and likely only baby in the back room of a country store? Now was no time for risks. She must have Ralph's help. As Will and Bea Dot rose from the table, they left Netta in the kitchen, still biting her lip to keep from crying.

Damn this influenza.

Sniffing and wiping an errant tear with her sleeve, Netta cleared the dishes and put away the ham and bread before escaping to the back porch, where she let the tears flow freely. She already knew Will's plan, that Eliza Taylor could deliver the baby. Well, that wouldn't do. Netta put her hands on her hips in silent determination. So what if Eliza had delivered all of her children at home? She hadn't suffered three miscarriages. This baby should be born under Ralph's care.

The back door opened, and Bea Dot emerged wearing a riding shirt and pants that hung loosely on her petite frame. She looked like a little girl playing dress up. Bea Dot smiled self-consciously as she tugged at her clothes. "They belonged to Will's mother," she said, pushing the shirt's cuff off her knuckles and up to her wrist. She had rolled the pants up to shorten them. "I suppose he got his height from her."

Netta turned her face away, almost sickened by Bea Dot's silly smile. She knew her cousin had grown fond of Will, but now was hardly the time to act like a schoolgirl. The cousins stood side by side, gazing over the water. To the left of the porch, the laundry billowed in the breeze, the sheets and shirts snapping in the wind.

"I'll bring that laundry in when I get back," Bea Dot said quietly.

Netta stared at the water, refusing to respond to such a trivial remark. Who could think of laundry anymore? After a few seconds, Bea Dot spoke again.

"Netta, I can tell you're nervous. I am too, but I think we must trust Will that we'll be all right."

"I suppose so, considering I have no choice in the matter." Aggravation got the best of her. As dependable as Will was, some problems he couldn't fix.

"I'm . . . I'm just as concerned as you are, but I doubt Will would put us in harm's way."

Exasperated, Netta turned sharply on Bea Dot, whose eyes widened in surprise. "We are already in harm's way, dear cousin. We have been ever since this flu came to Pineview." Her voice cracked as it escalated, and she raised her arms to each side as she spoke. "My husband is especially in harm's way. So please do not speak to me as if I'm a child."

"On the contrary, Netta, I am trying to look at this situation like a practical adult, which is far from what I see you doing." Bea Dot's stern voice also revealed an attempt to keep its volume in check. "Do you think I'm not scared of what might happen? If you give birth out here, guess who gets to deliver it?" She pointed her finger at her chest. "Me. I certainly do not relish the thought of that possibility."

"You have no idea what it's like to be in this predicament." Netta held her palm to her chest, then leaned in closer, so close that she could see the flecks of gold in Bea Dot's brown eyes. "I've lost three babies already." She held up as many fingers. "Three. And now that this one's survived this long, I shouldn't bear it out here in the middle of nowhere while my husband's tending other people's wives and children." She clinched her fists in frustration. "But there's not one thing I can do about that."

Bea Dot stiffened as she stepped back. She didn't frown, but anger flashed in her eyes. Netta braced herself for Bea Dot's petulant temper, but surprisingly, Bea Dot replied with cool reserve. "No, I don't know what that's like. But I'll tell you what I do know." Bea Dot pointed to Netta's middle. "I know that your baby has done nothing but thrive and grow since you arrived here. And in spite of your good health, you've done nothing but worry about a possible disaster. If the worst thing that happens is you deliver a healthy child at Dunaway's Crossing, then you have much to be thankful for. I'm sorry you lost three babies, Netta, but at least those babies weren't beaten out of you the way mine was."

That last remark slapped Netta with shame. She'd forgotten what little she knew about her cousin's miscarriage.

"Will has to take me somewhere," Bea Dot said calmly. "We won't be long."

"Bea Dot, wait," Netta stammered. "I'm . . ."

But Bea Dot had already turned her back on Netta and gone inside.

Chapter 13

Bea Dot pushed the door closed a little too hard as she left Netta on the porch calling after her. Invoking Ben's abuse had been a low blow, especially considering Bea Dot's miscarriage had been a relief. But she'd had enough of Netta's incessant worry. People were dying in town, and Netta could only think of herself. Sometimes one had to play the cards she was dealt. Bea Dot had learned that lesson the hard way.

What the cousins needed now was time apart. Bea Dot crossed the store and took a wool coat off a hook by the front door. She slipped it on before stepping outside, and it swallowed her whole. Clutching it close, she walked around the building and found Will in the barn strapping a bit between Buster's teeth. The barn smelled of hay, and golden dust floated in the sun peeking through the barn's wooden slats.

Still shaken from her argument, she watched Will silently as he tended his horse. Moments ago, she'd appreciated a chance for an outing, not only for the relief of tension and change of scenery, but for the change of company as well. She'd grown to like Will more than she had expected, and she'd anticipated enjoying some time alone with him. But now she wasn't even curious about where she was going. She just wanted to go away, even for just a short while. She tugged at the waistband of her pants and wished they were a bit smaller.

When Will buckled the bridle, he turned to her. "Ready?"

"Where's the saddle?"

"We can't both fit in it," Will said. "We'll ride bareback."

"But then how will I get on him?" She perused the barn for a box or stool to stand on.

Will lunged like a fencer while still holding Buster's reins. "Grab his mane and step on my knee."

Bea Dot hesitated at first, but then approached Will. Placing her little boot on his thigh, she flushed at the inappropriate intimacy with him, the same way she had when he lifted her at the Pineview depot. While she liked the feeling, she couldn't help thinking Ben would have beaten her senseless over such a gesture. However, she quickly extinguished thoughts of her husband, refusing to mar her afternoon with unpleasant memories. She pushed herself off the ground, then swung her other leg over Buster's back. The horse huffed a quick breath, as if she weighed a ton.

Will handed her the reins. Then, in one swift movement, he jumped and swung his long leg over Buster's hind end, situating himself behind Bea Dot, who was surprised at how he made such a maneuver seem so easy. As he reached around her and took the reins, Bea Dot's pulse quickened slightly, an automatic reaction reminiscent of earlier times in more hostile embraces. But again she shook off the trepidation, willing herself to focus on the present instead of the past. Will sucked his teeth, signaling Buster to walk, and the horse lumbered out of the barn, into the sunlight, and around the west side of the lake.

A crisp breeze whipped through the pine needles. Bea Dot breathed in the scent of mud and wet grass as they rode along the lakefront. The woodsy smell and the sun on her face helped lift the heaviness in her chest. Although she didn't forget her spat with Netta, it seemed less severe than it had a short while before.

As she rode, Will's breath tickled her ear and the back of her neck. Seated in front with his arms encircling her, she relaxed, once her gut reminded her that Will was different from other men in her life. Now comfortable with their closeness, she wondered if Will liked it. Once Buster carried them into the shade of the pine woods, the temperature dropped, but Will's body warmed her back, and she wished she could face him. They rode along a few minutes before he broke the silence.

"I'm sorry Miss Netta's angry with you." His voice revealed his awkward regret. "It's my fault."

"Don't be." Bea Dot sighed. "We're in an impossible situation. You have to do what you have to do." A pause, and then, "I'm sorry you heard our quarrel." She reddened at the memory of her last words. Oh, if she could only take them back!

"Don't worry. I made plenty of noise in the barn, so I didn't hear what you said."

Oh, please, please be telling the truth, she prayed silently.

In a few minutes they had steered up a hill and approached a two-story clapboard house with a front porch. To the side, a garden grew greens and other fall vegetables. A boy of about fifteen chopped wood underneath a sweet gum tree in the yard. When he saw Bea Dot and Will approach, he ran in the front door.

A man and woman came to the porch and waved. Bea Dot recognized the man as the giant who visited the store the day before. Like the boy, he wore a pair of bib overalls and a worn plaid shirt. The woman, about Netta's height but rounder, wore a plain blue dress that almost reached the floor. With her dark-blond hair pulled back into a tight bun, she resembled pictures of Bea Dot's grandmother. But the old-fashioned dress and hairstyle couldn't mask the woman's pretty face. After dismounting and helping Bea Dot down, Will introduced Bea Dot to her neighbors.

"Bea Dot Ferguson, I'd like you to meet Thaddeus and Eliza Taylor."

"We met the other day," Thaddeus said with a toothy smile.

"Yes, and I'm pleased to meet you, Mrs. Taylor," Bea Dot said before smoothing her hands down the front of her trousers. Suddenly, she remembered she was dressed in ill-fitting clothes and that her fingernails resembled a farmer's rather than a lady's. She hated to shake hands with these new acquaintances.

"Bea Dot is Netta Coolidge's cousin visiting from Savannah," Will said to Eliza. "She's here to help Netta until the baby comes. They're staying at the crossing now—because of the flu in town."

"Oh, I see." Eliza's face brightened with understanding. "That's a far cry from sleeping in town, ain't it?" Her voice had the same twang as her husband's.

"Yes, it is," Bea Dot replied shyly.

"But smart," Thaddeus added. "I hear the flu's spreading like head lice."

"Thaddeus!" Eliza reddened at her husband's grotesque remark. She turned to Bea Dot. "How is Netta?"

"She's doing fine," Bea Dot replied, her modesty relaxing a bit.

"Now you can meet our baby boy," Thaddeus reported proudly. "Eliza, why don't you take Miss Ferguson inside to see him?"

Eliza took Bea Dot's arm and led her up the front steps into a modest but comfortable home. The front door opened into the parlor, and a door in the back wall opened into the kitchen. A fireplace burned on the left wall just beside the stairs, and close to the hearth was a cradle. The boy Bea Dot had seen in the yard sat in a rocking chair next to it.

"This here's Terrence," Eliza said, gesturing to her older son. "Terrence, say hello to Miss Ferguson."

Bea Dot ignored Eliza's error, and the boy stood up, skinny and gangly. He shyly said hello and seemed not to know what to do with his hands.

"Terrence, I got a pot of water boiling. Go on in the kitchen and take it off for me."

Terrence nodded and left the room. Eliza gestured to the rocking chair Terrence had just vacated. "Come sit here. I'll get little Troy for you."

"How many children do you have?" Bea Dot asked.

"Well, my oldest, Tommy, he's working up in Macon. Then Terrence out there's fifteen. My third boy, Ted, died of scarlet fever a couple of years ago, God bless him. And this"—Eliza cradled her baby in her arms and brought him to Bea Dot—"is Troy." She placed the infant in Bea Dot's arms.

Bea Dot tensed at first, having never held a baby. When Eliza beamed with pride, Bea Dot smiled awkwardly, hoping her expression looked genuine. She peered into the baby's blue eyes. What should she say to someone who couldn't understand or reply? Awkwardly, she muttered, "Hello, Troy."

"I'll go make us a pot of tea," Eliza said before leaving the room.

Troy squirmed a bit at being moved from his cradle, and Bea Dot's pulse quickened with nervousness. *Please don't cry*, she prayed. She rocked her chair and shook her elbow gently to soothe him. Troy relaxed, and she did with him.

"Oh, you're a natural." Eliza returned with a tray holding a teapot and two cups. "You're gone be a good helper to Netta when her baby comes."

"I haven't been around babies very much." Bea Dot spoke apologetically, yet she couldn't take her eyes off Troy, who yawned before settling into the crook of her arm. He was a cute little thing.

"Oh, babies are easy," Eliza said. "They don't take no special training to take care of."

"Maybe not," Bea Dot replied tentatively. She tucked her finger under the fat of Troy's chin, and he squirmed again, like a snail prodded with a stick. He balled his fist when he moved, and she couldn't help being drawn in by him. If her own baby had lived, would she have been attached to it at all? She turned her face up to Eliza. "But what about bringing them into this world? I admit, Mrs. Taylor—"

"Please, call me Eliza."

"Eliza. I must admit I'm afraid Netta's baby will come while we're still at the crossing. Ralph won't allow us to come back to town because of influenza."

"I don't blame him." Eliza tilted her head and pressed her lips.

"But what if Netta goes into labor? What will we do?"

"Babies will come. They don't care if we're ready," Eliza said. She had set the teapot on the hutch and was pouring two cups. "When I had Tommy, I dreamed up all kinds of problems to fret over, all for naught. All my babies come into the world just fine." Eliza brought a cup of tea for Bea Dot, and she placed it on the table next to the rocking chair. "And being in town wouldn't have made no difference. If I'd a had a doctor, he would of just sat there and told me to push. I figured that out all on my own."

"You mean you delivered your children by yourself? Ralph didn't do it?"

Eliza laughed. "Honey, Ralph ain't been in town but a few years. Before that, Pineview didn't have no doctor. We ain't had a choice with our first three boys, and by the time Troy come along, well, Thaddeus and I was old hands at bringing children."

Bea Dot tried to laugh along with Eliza, but all she could muster was a nervous chuckle. Eliza made the task seem so simple. "And all you do is sit there and say 'push'?"

"Oh, well." Eliza dismissively flapped her hand in front of her. "You'll want to have lots of hot water ready and plenty of rags.

But they's mostly for cleaning up the baby afterward. If you think about it, Netta's the one gone be doing all the work."

"I suppose . . ." Bea Dot still wasn't so sure.

"Listen, you got any questions, you just call on me," Eliza said. "I'm happy to help."

Eliza's offer would have satisfied Bea Dot if she'd known what questions to ask. She wished Eliza had an instruction manual.

Eliza pulled an armchair from the other side of the room and placed it next to Bea Dot's. "I'm glad Will brought you with him today," she said, changing the subject. "It's good to see him take an interest in the ladies again."

"Oh, no." Bea Dot blushed. "Will and I aren't . . . courting. I think he brought me here specifically to meet you and Troy."

The baby awakened and uttered a tiny yap. Bea Dot rocked again and cooed at him. His blue eyes fixed on the light of the fire. Maybe babies weren't as tricky as she'd thought. This one seemed easy enough.

Eliza smiled and nodded as if she didn't quite believe Bea Dot. "Well, I ain't seen that look on his face in a long time, not since he come home from France."

"Oh," Bea Dot said awkwardly, turning her eyes from Troy to Eliza. "I didn't realize. He hasn't said much about his experience over there."

"The only good thing about it was it was so short." Eliza leaned forward emphatically in her chair. "He wasn't in battle but one day."

Bea Dot nodded. "Netta told me he was injured."

"Yes, but I think if he had his druthers, he'd a been shot through the heart than get hurt the way he did."

"What do you mean?"

"Mmm." Eliza took a sip of tea. "Of course he ain't told you about it. It takes him a while to open up. You see, he got hurt taking other wounded soldiers out of the line of fire."

Bea Dot's heart skipped a beat at the thought of Will in death's way. "What happened?"

"He was at Belleau Wood, and he was driving the ambulance from the front line to a bombed-out farmhouse they was using as a medical shelter. Will lost control of the ambulance."

"Oh, heavens!" Bea Dot gasped.

"I don't know all the details, but he punctured his side and broke his arm real bad. The soldiers in the ambulance died."

Bea Dot covered her mouth with her hand, imagining Will's devastation from the accident. And he'd never said a word. Her heart ached in sympathy, knowing the pain of keeping horrible memories locked away.

Eliza nodded. "And you see all the work he does for us country folk. He don't have to deliver mail or keep a phone at the crossing, but he does. He ain't told me outright, but I think he wants to make up for what happened to them soldiers."

"But he didn't kill them. It was an accident."

"You know that, and I know that, but Will ain't never been able to forgive himself." Eliza shook her head in pity.

"Eliza, I won't mention our conversation to Will." Bea Dot's heart ached for him. "I'm sure he'll divulge this information if he ever wants to. But I thank you for telling me this story. It helps me to understand him more."

Eliza smiled at her new friend. "Let's bring Troy outside so Will can see him."

Bea Dot stood with the baby and followed Eliza out to the porch. The women found Will and Thaddeus on the front steps.

"Be on the lookout for beavers," Will was saying. "They'll dam up that creek, and before you know it, your field is flooded."

"I was afraid a that," Thaddeus said. "I'll keep my eye on it."

"Somebody came out to see you," Eliza sang to Will.

Bea Dot held the crook of her arm out to offer Will a better view.

"Well, will you look at him?" Will smiled at the tiny child. "That's a handsome boy, Thaddeus." He looped his finger under Troy's hand, and it dwarfed the infant's tiny grip. "Hey, there, little fella." He brushed his finger along Troy's soft cheek. "You're going to grow big and strong like your daddy, aren't you?"

Bea Dot smiled at Will, whose green eyes softened as they gazed at the infant.

"Why don't you let Will hold him?" Eliza said.

"Oh, of course." Bea Dot gently handed Troy over to Will, who knew exactly how to support a baby's head. He seemed much more comfortable than she was.

Will wrapped Troy's blanket tightly around him to keep him warm against the October chill. Then he swayed gently back and forth as he gazed at the little bundle. "You're a good looking little boy, Troy. Yes, you are."

"Look at you," Bea Dot said before she'd thought about it. "You'll be a good father one day."

He nodded. "One day."

He handed Troy to Eliza, who held the baby up to her shoulder. Then he turned to Bea Dot. "We should be going. Netta will be wondering about us."

"It was a pleasure to see you again, Thaddeus, and Eliza." Bea Dot smiled at her hosts. "I'm so glad to meet you. I hope we can talk again soon." She meant that. Something told her she should press her neighbor for more information about childbirth.

"Thank you, Miss Bea Dot," Thaddeus replied. "That's mighty kind of you. You're welcome to come out any time you need anything. And Will says he'll be gone a while. I'll be sure to check on you every day. If I can't come, I'll send Terrence."

"And don't you worry about Netta's baby," Eliza jumped in. "I can help deliver it if you need me. Everything's gone be just fine."

Bea Dot thanked Eliza for her offer and hoped she was right. She'd feel more relieved once the baby was born and well.

After saying their good-byes, Will helped Bea Dot up onto Buster's back, and the horse rode them into the pine wood. Will hardly had to manage the animal.

"He seems to know his way home," Bea Dot said.

"He ought to," Will replied. "He's ridden these paths hundreds of times."

"Did you grow up around here? You seem to know Thaddeus's property pretty well."

"Yep." Will shifted the reins from one hand to another. "What did you think of Eliza and Thaddeus?"

"They're nice people."

"I'm glad you liked them. If you ever need them for anything, just follow this path. It's not even half a mile."

"You've known them a long time?"

"Mm hmm. I grew up with Tommy, their oldest boy."

"Eliza says he's in Macon?"

"That's right."

"Does he have a job there?"

"Mm hmm. At the brick works."

The two remained quiet for a few minutes. Ahead, a light from the clearing appeared at the edge of the woods. Just through the trees, the lake water flickered in the afternoon sunlight. Will found a gap in the brush and turned Buster to the bank for a drink. He dropped the reins as Buster lowered his muzzle to the water. Will slid off Buster's back, then held his hand out for Bea Dot, who took it and eased herself to the ground beside him.

"Won't Netta be wondering about us?" she asked.

He tied Buster's reins to a branch, then turned to face the

woods, his hands in his back pockets. "We'll only be a few minutes. The horse could use a drink, and Netta could probably use a few more minutes of quiet time." He pointed into the woods, which sloped up a slight hill. "See that cabin back there?"

Bea Dot peered into the pine trees. In the shadows she finally made out the dark structure. "Oh, yes. I wouldn't have noticed it if you hadn't pointed it out."

"My grandfather built that cabin years ago. It's just an abandoned shack now, but sometimes I go there when I have thinking to do. Sometimes it does the soul good to get away, don't you think?"

Bea Dot's heart stopped for a moment. Did he know why she had come to Pineview? "Yes," she said cautiously. "I suppose it does." After a pause, she asked, "So you own all this land around the lake?"

He shook his head. "No, but my father used to. He lost it when he got sick. Now Thaddeus Taylor owns it."

Bea Dot nodded. So that was how Will knew the lay of the land so well.

"Pardon me for saying so," she said, "but Thaddeus Taylor doesn't strike me as a man wealthy enough to buy so much acreage."

"No, I see what you mean," Will replied. "Thaddeus worked for our family for years. He might have known more about farming than my father did. But when Pop died, Ma made a deal with him. If Thaddeus would pay the taxes on the land, she would give it to him—all but fifty acres of my choice. Once she settled Pop's estate, she gave me half of what was left, then took the rest and moved to Thomasville to live with my sister and her family."

"So you chose the property at the crossroads."

Will nodded. "It already had a building, and it had lakefront. It was perfect for a store, but I had to postpone my plans a bit."

"The war?"

"Yes."

They stood quietly side by side for a few moments. As a slight breeze picked up behind them, a dark curl tickled Bea Dot's cheek, and the pine needles whispered all around them. Attempting to lighten the mood, Bea Dot suggested, "Let's take a look at that cabin."

Taking her hand, Will led her up the hill and through the pine trees, holding down thorny vines and pushing back low branches to clear a pathway. Bea Dot smiled at him each time he cleared the way for her, and even though Will seemed unaware that he held her hand the whole time, she hoped he wouldn't let go. When they reached the cabin, he pushed open the creaky door, and a flapping brown blur startled Bea Dot as it rushed through the doorway. She screamed and leapt at Will, who exhaled a frightened laugh. Her heart pounded against his chest, and he held her close to him until the fear subsided.

"What was that?"

"A barn owl," Will replied. When he looked down at her with those green eyes, a flock of barn owls took flight in her stomach. "Don't worry, we've scared it much more than it scared you."

"Of course we did," Bea Dot laughed awkwardly. Red-faced, she stepped away from him and rubbed her sweaty palms on the fronts of her pants. "Let's go in."

She followed him into the blackness, then stood still while her eyes adjusted to the dark. Will pushed open the shutters, and the sunlight revealed an old crate in the corner and a pile of yellowed newspapers. The interior was about the same size as Ralph's camp house. A black pipe hung from the roof, a remnant of an absent wood stove.

"There's nothing in here," she said, surprised that anyone would want to spend time there.

"Well, I don't really come here for picnics or tea parties," Will said. "But sometimes I'll come out here and whittle a stick and think."

Bea Dot nodded, thinking about her bathtub in Savannah. Will came here to whittle for the same reasons she enjoyed a long soak in hot water.

As the two walked back down the hill, Will led the way again, but chatted with Bea Dot each time he held back a branch for her. "You and Netta are as close as sisters," he said. "I take it you don't have any of your own?"

Bea Dot shook her head and stooped under a Virginia creeper he held up for her. "My mother died just after I was born," she said, a little surprised at having done so. She hardly spoke of her mother. The brown pine-straw crunched under her feet.

"That's a shame," Will said. "So your father raised you?" He pushed back a low pine branch.

"You could say that," she said, slipping past it. "Actually, my maid, California, brought me up—with Netta's help later on. My father never got over my mother's death." Why was she divulging so much personal information? Something comforting about Will made her feel at ease discussing her family. Maybe it was because she knew he'd suffered his own tragedy.

"Is he still in Savannah?"

"No," Bea Dot explained, stepping out of the woods and across the dirt path, over to Buster. She rubbed her hand along his warm back and his withers shivered at her touch. "He died seven or eight months ago."

"Bless your heart," Will said. He took a step and stood behind her. "Was he sick?"

Bea Dot paused before answering, keeping her eyes on the horse. "I suppose he was sick in the head. He killed himself."

After a pause, Will said, "I'm sorry. I shouldn't have pried."

"No need to apologize," she said, looking up at his sympathetic gaze. Then, trying to change the mood, she said, "But we should be going before Netta thinks we've gotten lost."

He untied Buster's reins and handed them to Bea Dot, then helped her onto the horse's back for the trip home. Back on the path, Buster started his slow walk toward the crossing. The barn would be just ahead. As Will held the reins in front of her, Bea Dot silently wished the horse would walk slower so she could enjoy a few more minutes of the security of Will's arms around her. After seeing Will handle a baby, she felt silly at feeling on edge in his arms before.

"Will," she said, "I know you introduced me to Eliza to ease my mind about Netta's condition." She frowned and bit her lip as she considered her next sentence. "And I thank you for that, but . . ." She exhaled as she struggled to find the next words. "I still have misgivings about staying at the crossing alone with her. Netta doesn't want Eliza delivering her baby."

Will stiffened behind her, and for several yards, the only sound was the clop of Buster's hooves on the dirt path.

"I'm afraid," she continued uncertainly.

He exhaled, his breath brushing her right ear and cheek. "So am I."

Her heart sank. So much for words of confidence.

"How soon do you have to leave?"

From the corner of her eye, Bea Dot saw Will raise his arm to his hat as he looked at the sky. "Sun'll be going down soon," he replied. "I suppose I'll spend the night at home and head to town first thing in the morning."

She pulled the corner of her mouth into her cheek, sorry that he'd have to leave so soon. He'd just gotten home.

As Buster neared the clearing, he picked up his pace and startled Bea Dot, who unwittingly clutched the first thing she could get her hand on. At the touch of his firm muscles through the fabric of his pants, she realized she was holding onto his thighs, and she burned again with humiliation as she grasped the horse's mane. What must he think of her now?

"I'm sorry about that," Will said, pulling slightly on the reins to keep the horse at a smooth walk. "He must be ready to get back to his stall."

A few minutes later, he steered the animal into the barn, and Buster came to a stop in front of a bale of hay. As the horse munched on the straw, Will swung his leg behind him and slid to the ground, then tied his reins to a wooden post. When he held out his arms to help Bea Dot dismount, she slid clumsily off Buster's back. When she landed on the ground, her legs, sore from so much horseback riding, buckled under her.

"Whoa," Will said as he took her by the waist and pulled her up.

She blushed with a combination of embarrassment at his touch and excitement at his closeness.

"Are you all right?" he asked.

"Yes, I think so," she said. "I'm just not accustomed to riding that way." She wasn't accustomed to anything about today: his interest in her, his concern for her safety, his efforts to help her and Netta. Mostly, she was unaccustomed to feeling such a combination of emotions around a man. Instead of revulsion or fear, she felt charged, yet timid. She lifted her chin to see his green eyes. His hat had fallen off, and a lock of brown hair had lopped onto his forehead like a stubborn apostrophe. She had her hand on his shoulders, and though she knew she should move them, she couldn't bring herself to step back. Will's eyes acted on her like an elixir.

His smile faded, and he drew her closer to him. Her heart raced with excitement. In her nervousness, she hesitated, but then she reached around his neck. He lowered his face to hers and kissed her once gently, but then again with more emphasis. His kiss was not the clumsy, drunken, wet slather of Ben's mouth. Instead, Will gave her a soft, warm kiss, one that allowed her to return it. She inhaled the hay and leather in his skin and felt the soft scratch of whiskers on her lip. Eventually, she let her fingers wander into the back of his hair, and when he pulled her against him, she felt the same energy she had when they'd ridden horseback. For a few moments, all her trepidation vanished, and she lost herself in his embrace.

"Bea Dot, are you back?"

At Netta's intrusion, she pushed away from him, and pressed her wet lips onto the cuff of her shirt. Buster huffed and shifted his weight behind her. Thank goodness the animal blocked them from Netta's view.

"We've just returned, Miss Netta," Will replied hoarsely as he quickly untied the reins from the post. He led Buster into his stall, and Bea Dot turned to see Netta's silhouette in the doorway of the barn. Though she couldn't make out Netta's face, she couldn't help worrying that Netta had seen her kissing Will. Or was Bea Dot simply feeling guilty?

"I'm glad you're back," Netta said. "I've been trying to mind the store for you, but I can't say I know what I'm doing."

Bea Dot quickly walked out of the barn, eyes down, brushing past Netta and jogging into the house.

"I'm sure you've done a fine job," she heard Will tell Netta. But that was all she heard before she rushed inside and closed the back door behind her. She leaned with her backside on the doorknob, her heart racing, her hairline beginning to perspire.

"Bea Dot Ferguson," she asked herself, "what can of worms have you opened up now?"

Chapter 14

"Doctor'll be here soon, Tilda. Hang on for me—just a little while longer."

California wondered whether Matilda heard her. Boiling with fever, her sister had been talking nonsense for the past two days—when she talked at all. Usually Matilda lay on the bed in the front room of her salt-box house struggling for air, gurgling as if her lungs were fishbowls.

California removed the rag from Matilda's forehead, then dunked it in a bucket of cold water. She wrung out the cloth and placed it back on Matilda's head before wringing out a second one to rub down her arms and legs.

She'd done everything Dr. Arnold had told her—giving Matilda lots of water when she could drink it and keeping her cool with alcohol rubs, at least until she ran out of alcohol. But nothing brought the fever down. California cringed at her sister's every breath, which sounded as if she were sucking air through a wet sponge. More frightening, though, was her skin, now all gray, as if her body were decomposing before it died. *Please, Lord, let her survive the night.* California wished she had pressured Dr. Arnold for more care.

"Don't you got no medicine to give her?" she'd asked.

"I wish I did, Cal," he'd replied, putting his stethoscope in his black bag. The circles under his eyes matched the gray fabric of his vest. "None of my elixirs work on this flu. It's a stubborn thing, fierce too. Matilda's best chance is for you to keep her temperature down. If she gets worse, send your nieces for Dr. Washington."

But Dr. Washington was dead—succumbed to flu two days ago.

Matilda needed a hospital, but California couldn't get her sister admitted. Her only hope was to fetch Dr. Arnold. She alternated her worried gaze from the street to the bed, then back. She knew the hospital was swamped with patients. All of Savannah was down with flu, and the white folks got Dr. Arnold's attention first. Still, she had to hope there was something else he could try. But how could she get word to him? Where was the closest telephone? And should she leave her sister to use it? What if Matilda died while she was gone?

For the fiftieth time that day, California opened the door to her little white house and peered down the muddy street, hoping to see a motorcar rumbling toward her. But the potholed street was empty. Not even one person was hunched up against the chill, face covered with the gauze mask now required of everyone venturing out of doors. Cal saw few neighbors lately. Those not down with flu had departed with their white employers to keep house or mind children on Tybee Island, hoping the fresh air would protect them.

"Auntie? Auntie Cal?"

"Coming, baby." Her nieces lay in the next room, having caught the flu from their mother. California closed the front door, picked up the bucket next to Matilda's bed, and carried it into the children's room. Sweat dampened her forehead, in spite of the October chill. Her head ached too, right behind her eyes. She knew she needed rest, but she didn't dare go to sleep.

Poor babies. Lying side by side, they looked weak as newborn kittens. Their fever came on fast. Inez had just complained of a headache the previous night, and Agnes's had started that morning. By noon, both were coughing to beat all, and they took to bed without eating any of the greens California had cooked. She couldn't even get them to sip on some pot liquor.

She laid her palm on Inez's forehead and whispered another plea to heaven, hoping her prayers hadn't worn out her welcome with God. She couldn't help it. Inez's hot skin could melt an icebox. Agnes's too. She put one rag on each girl's head, but she had to rub them down also. How would she do that? She surveyed the room, then pulled open a bureau drawer, where she found her sister's Sunday petticoat. She plunged it into the cold water and wrung it out before rubbing down Inez's arms, then Agnes's.

The room smelled of sickness and sweat, both hers and the girls'. It smelled of kerosene from the lamps and old, cooked turnip greens, still sitting in the pot on the stove. Who had time to wash dishes?

California's eyes burned with fatigue, but she ignored her body's yearning for sleep, forcing herself to tend her patients. They were all she had in the world. Them and Miss Bea Dot.

"My head hurt something awful," Inez said.

"I know, baby doll. This cold cloth will help."

Would it really?

She rubbed sweat from her forehead and neck before plunging the petticoat back into the water, which stung her raw, cracked knuckles. She'd lit no fire in the stove, trying to keep her patients cool, but the room still grew warmer. What else could she do? Kissing both girls on the forehead felt like kissing a loaf of bread right out of the oven.

"I'll be right back. Just gone check your mama."

The bucket grew heavier every time she carried it from one room to the next. Her back ached from leaning and lugging water. Shuffling to the front room, she ran into the doorsill and sloshed water on the floor and in her boots. Paying it no mind, she kept moving. "I wear a rut in this floor toting this thing back and forth."

A knock shot joy to her heart.

"Hallelujah," she said, eyes to the ceiling. She put the bucket down in the middle of the floor and huffed on aching feet to the door. "Coming."

On the stoop, Penny hugged her crocheted wrap around her shoulders. Her breath puffed out in clouds of steam from the sides of her gauze mask, and her eyes brimmed with worry. She held out a cloth-covered plate. "You all right, Cal?" she asked. "Ain't seen you all week. Miss Lavinia send you some biscuits."

"Penny, go get Dr. Arnold," Cal replied, ignoring the biscuits. "I need him fast." She looked past Penny into the street. The sun had already set, and everything had turned black and dark blue, except for the yellow balls of light from the streetlamps.

"Dr. Arnold?" Penny's eyes widened over her mask. "He been at the hospital the past two or three days straight. Miss Lavinia say he up to his ears in sick folk."

"He already been here once." California felt a stone growing in her gut. "He got to come back. Now Inez and Agnes sick too."

Penny placed the plate of biscuits on the stoop, then stepped into the street—right into a puddle.

"I need Dr. Arnold to put Tilda in the hospital. Maybe Inez and Agnes with her." California leaned on the doorframe. All that talking left her winded, and her head pounded.

"Don't think you oughta count on that, Cal," Penny said sadly. "Even some a the white folks being turned away on the hospital front steps."

Fear gripped California so tightly now, she almost couldn't breathe. "I can't lose Tilda and the girls, Penny."

Penny shook her head in sympathy, but she didn't seem to understand what California was telling her. So Cal stepped out into the damp and clutched Penny's arm. "You the only person come by in two days. You got to talk to Dr. Arnold for me."

"He ain't gone listen to me." Penny tried to pull away, but Cal kept her grip.

"I can't go myself because I can't leave my girls. Please, Penny. Talk to him. Or stay here while I go fetch him."

Penny arched her spine backward, as if California were exhaling poison. Finally, she wrenched free of Cal's grip. "I'll see what I can do."

California's fear dropped away then, and the relief made her light-headed. "Thank you."

Leaving Penny in the street, she went back into the house, leaving the biscuits on the stoop for stray cats to find. Matilda lay still in her bed, and California relaxed somewhat, seeing her sister sleeping soundly. But after a second she realized why. The gurgling had stopped. California rushed to her sister's bedside and laid her hand on Matilda's chest. Nothing. No heartbeat, no rising and falling of trembling breath. Matilda was gone. California dropped to her knees and wailed, sobbing so hard that she fell to her side and lay on the floor like a baby, hating herself for talking to Penny so long, hating Dr. Washington for dying, hating Dr. Arnold for being white, hating the influenza for robbing her of her beloved sister.

She cried and moaned, making her throat raw, provoking a cough. She curled on the floor, coughs interrupting her sobs, until a moment when she paused to take in some air, and a puny voice called to her.

"Auntie."

California pushed herself onto her hands and knees, then made herself stand. Her weeping had made her head pound heavier, but she forced herself to shuffle into the other room.

"Coming."

Chapter 15

Netta shuffled on socked feet to the kitchen and absently reached into the cupboard for a teacup. Startled by a tickle on the top of her hand, she yanked the cup out and found a spiderweb spreading over her knuckles and onto the cup's lip. Shuddering in disgust, she said, "Leave it to a bachelor to store dishes in a dirty cabinet."

She pumped water into a teapot, then heated it on the stove. Next, she filled a bucket halfway with cold water and waited for the teapot to boil. If she had known about the cobwebs, she'd have never eaten from Will's dishes. Why hadn't Bea Dot noticed?

Probably because she crowded her head with thoughts of Will Dunaway. Just yesterday Netta had gone looking for her cousin and found her in Will's back storage room sniffing his pillow. Oh, she'd tried to lie her way out of the embarrassing situation, saying "I came in here for more coffee, and I thought I smelled something rotten." Bea Dot had always been transparent.

Lately, she'd become quite the little merchant as well as a postmistress, now that the mailman, in Will's absence, left a bag of letters at the storefront each day. Bea Dot dutifully sorted envelopes and handed out letters to the neighboring farmers who came to pick them up. Still, Netta couldn't help wondering if the store had been owned by a toothless old man, would Bea Dot have been as enthusiastic about minding it?

Netta removed the dishes, cutlery, and pots from the cupboard and laid them out on the table. She found dead bugs on some, and cobwebs stuck to others. Mrs. Dunaway would have been horrified to see the state of Will's kitchenware. When the teapot sang, Netta poured the hot water into the bucket of cold water before adding soap powder. Then she plunged an old rag into the suds and began scrubbing. She'd been at it fifteen minutes when Bea Dot found her.

"Netta, what in the world are you doing?"

What does it look like I'm doing, teaching Sunday school? Netta held up her rag for Bea Dot to see. "Look at the dirt on this rag," she said. "Will's drawers and cupboards have cobwebs in them. I can't believe we eat off the dishes in there."

She returned to her cleaning while Bea Dot watched with mouth agape, as if she'd never seen soap and water before. Of course, lately she'd been so immersed in her storekeeping that she'd all but abandoned housework. It was all Netta could do to get Bea Dot to wash the supper dishes or do the laundry.

"Are you feeling all right?" Bea Dot asked.

"Of course," Netta said. What a silly question. A wisp of hair tickled her forehead, so she pushed it back with her wrist.

"Aren't you cold? Where are your shoes?"

Netta stopped her scrubbing and eyed her feet. She hadn't seen her anklebones in weeks. "I can't get my shoes on," she replied. "My feet are too fat." She held up her hand. "Look at my fingers." She curled them into claws and said, "I can hardly bend them. They tingle just from doing that."

She plunged the rag into the bucket again and went back to her scrubbing. The cabinet's interior smelled like dust and soap.

"Are you sure you should be working so hard?"

With her head inside the cupboard, Netta couldn't help rolling her eyes and screwing up her face. Who else was going to clean this mess? She ignored the question and continued her attack on the compartment's interior.

"Are you angry about something?"

Netta stopped, sighed, and pulled her head out of the cabinet. Bea Dot's question reminded her of the many times Ralph checked the irritable bite of her. The discomfort of her pregnancy hardly helped matters.

"No, dear. I'm not angry," she replied in a softer tone. "Just uncomfortable. I'm sorry I took it out on you."

"If you'd like, I can bring your rocker into the kitchen, where it's warmer."

Netta shook her head and swished the rag in the water to rinse off the dirt; then she wrung it out again. "I can't fit into that chair anymore," she said. "Besides, I can't sit still while this kitchen is a filthy mess."

Bea Dot's eyebrows came together, and Netta understood the look of confusion. She couldn't explain her behavior either. All she knew was that she had a compulsion to clean up the wreck of a kitchen.

A bell rang in the store, and Bea Dot turned her head toward the doorway, calling, "Be right there."

"That was a good idea to hang a bell on the front door," Netta said. "Better go tend to your customer." Just as Bea Dot turned to go, Netta called out, "When you're finished, though, I could use some help with this floor. It's a pitiful sight."

Of course, Bea Dot met that request with a shake of her head and a chuckle before she went back into the store. "Good afternoon, can I help you?"

Netta returned to her work and listened to Bea Dot chatting with customers. She always made such a production of how busy she was with the mail, the telephone, and her "inventory," as she liked to call it. She could call it inventory all day long, but her interest in commerce lay in one particular item, which at the moment was building coffins in Pineview.

Netta couldn't shake her concern about Bea Dot's fondness for Will. Not that she resented the friendship. Of all people, Bea Dot deserved a man who respected her and loved her. If Ben Ferguson didn't exist, Bea Dot and Will would make a good pair.

But Ben did exist. And that complicated matters.

True, she had invited Bea Dot to Pineview for a respite from Ben's hostility, but she hadn't intended her cousin to fall for someone else. What would Ben do if he found out? Netta chewed her lip as she considered the possibilities. She'd have to talk to Bea Dot about her attraction to Will—before he returned to the crossing.

Netta finished scrubbing the cabinet and started on a drawer, wishing Will had at least lined it with paper. With her fingernail she scraped out the dirt in the corners.

Bea Dot entered again, this time holding a newspaper. "Netta, could you help me? Mr. Ellis Floyd is here with his *Macon Telegraph*, and I'm trying to find some paraffin for Mr. Anderson. Can you read to Mr. Floyd please?"

Netta examined her loaded kitchen table and sighed. *Why of course, Bea Dot. I was just sitting around waiting for something to do.* She inhaled deeply as she searched for her patience. She gestured toward her soiled apron and worn stockings and she replied, "I'm hardly prepared to receive guests."

"Oh, please, Netta," Bea Dot persisted. "You can stand behind the counter so he won't see your feet."

Netta opened her mouth in protest, but Bea Dot stopped her, holding up her palm. "I know, I know. I made the deal with him to read the articles in exchange for the paper, but I don't think I'm the only one around here who pores over the news when it comes."

Netta's shoulders slumped. "Oh, all right. Tell him I'll be there in a minute."

Bea Dot smiled and returned to the store. Netta plunked the balled rag into the water, which splashed up and left a gray splotch on her apron. She followed Bea Dot into the store and stood behind the counter, though her face burned with shame about her looks. Mr. Floyd's pale blue eyes watered from the outside chill, and his cheeks and nose glowed a bright pink, although Netta believed the weather accounted for their color less so than his homemade alcohol. He handed his newspaper to Netta with a shy greeting and word of thanks. Netta unfolded it and browsed the front-page stories. From the back room, Bea Dot's voice floated in as she spoke to Mr. Anderson.

"Let's see, Mr. Floyd. What's happening in the world today? Oh, this article says that President Wilson telegraphed the Democratic convention delegates meeting in Macon this week."

Mr. Floyd nodded with a quiet "Hmm." Apparently he wasn't much interested in politics.

"And in this article," Netta continued, "there's a report about a woman named Jeannette Rankin, who's running for US Senate."

"Why that's ridiculous." Mr. Floyd lifted his chin and his eyes glowed like the blue of a gaslight flame. "First women want to vote. Now they even want to run for office?" He slapped his palm on the store counter. "This world's going straight to hell on a runaway train. You know last week, the paper said that down in Waycross, they let women vote in city elections."

"I do declare," Netta muttered. She wished Bea Dot would finish up with Mr. Anderson. The cupboard was waiting. "Here's some news of the war," she said, pointing to another article. "This is good news too. It says that Arab and British forces have captured Damascus from the Turks. Arabia has been liberated under the leadership of an officer T. E. Lawrence. The British now refer to him as Lawrence of Arabia."

"Enough of that." Mr. Floyd's breath smelled like tobacco. "What does it say about the flu?"

Bea Dot and Mr. Anderson returned from the storage room. "As soon as I speak to Mr. Dunaway again, I'll ask him to restock on paraffin," she told him. She handed him his mail and called a good-bye to him as he left. Then she turned to Netta and Mr. Floyd. "Any news about influenza? Is it subsiding at all?"

"There's an article here." Netta had opened the paper's wide pages. "Odd how they put it on page five." The headline read, "Spanish Influenza Crosses State." She skimmed the article before summarizing it for Mr. Floyd. "In Macon, two hundred fifty new cases have been reported this week."

"How far away is Macon?" Bea Dot asked as she absently shuffled envelopes from the mailbag.

"I'd say about fifty miles," Netta replied. She looked to Mr. Floyd for confirmation, and he nodded his white-haired head.

Bea Dot chewed her lip as Netta scanned the rest of the article. "It says that flu masks are now in use in Macon, but that Atlanta has taken even stronger measures. 'The state capital reports only eight deaths this week,' it says, 'with one hundred five new cases reported. As a precautionary measure, the Atlanta city council has declared all public gatherings closed for the next two months.'" Netta lifted her eyes and alternated her gaze from Bea Dot to Mr. Floyd and back. "That includes libraries, churches, and theaters. It also says that streetcars are to keep all windows open except in rainy weather."

"My heavens," Bea Dot murmured with her hand to her chest. "Well, Atlanta's a big city. If only eight people have died, that's good, isn't it?"

Netta shook her head slowly, unable to see how eight deaths could possibly be considered good news. Besides, the article was several days old. No telling how many people had died since it was published. Her thoughts, as usual, turned to Ralph working tirelessly to keep Pineview alive. She prayed silently, probably for the hundredth time, for Ralph's wellness. Then she sighed.

"I'm sorry, but this talk of the flu has me a bit troubled. Would you mind if I stopped?" Netta folded the paper before placing it on the countertop.

Mr. Floyd patted her fat hand and smiled for the first time since she'd begun reading. Brown stains had settled at the crevices of his teeth. "You've been kind to read to me, Mrs. Coolidge. If you could just tell me what Mutt and Jeff are up to, I'll leave you two ladies alone and be on my way."

Bea Dot took the paper from Netta and said, "I'll do that, Mr. Floyd. Netta, thank you for your help. Why don't you go back and rest?"

Netta said her good-byes to Mr. Floyd and returned to the kitchen. The pots, pans, and dishes taunted her from the tabletop. Reading the paper had drained her energy, and she no longer cared for cleaning Will's cupboards. Still, she had to finish what she started, so she went back to sorting and replacing the dishes. Once she'd finished with the plates and cups, she straightened her back and rubbed it. Then she sat in a chair and rubbed her feet.

Bea Dot's voice startled her. "I'm sure we have something in here you can use."

At once Bea Dot stood at the table with Terrence Taylor behind her, holding a string of wet, dripping fish.

"Oh, my gracious, Bea Dot." Her facing went blazing hot as she stood. "You should have warned me. I look a fright. Excuse me, Terrence." She lumbered out of the kitchen, bumping into the table and making the cutlery clink as she did so. From behind the bedroom door, she heard Bea Dot's and Terrence's voices.

"This'll do," he said. "I'll clean these fish on the dock and bring 'em back to you. I won't take but a minute."

"Thank you, Terrence," Bea Dot replied.

Netta waited for the door to open and close. Instead, Terrence's comment turned up the flame behind her cheeks. "You know what, Miss Bea Dot?" he asked. "My mama done the same thing before she had her baby."

"What do you mean?" Bea Dot replied.

"All this scrubbing and sorting and what not," Terrence explained. "She done the same thing just a day or two before little Troy come along. You think Miss Netta's baby's coming?"

"I don't know, but we'll find out soon enough."

Netta heard in Bea Dot's voice the same touch of worry she felt in her own chest. She sat on the bed, and her round stomach moved, like a puppy trying to crawl out of a burlap sack. Netta rubbed over the moving lumps as she spoke to her unborn infant. "Please, baby, just stay put a little while longer."

Bea Dot had turned over in her cramped bed at least twenty times in the last hour, but she couldn't sleep. Disturbing her more than Netta's light snoring was the voice of Terrence Taylor's innocent question, "You think Miss Netta's baby's coming?"

Oh, dear Lord, she hoped he was wrong.

But fear of Netta's delivery was only one problem weighing on her mind. Will had been gone almost a week, and her inventory was running low. Not only did she not have paraffin for Mr. Anderson, but she had also run out of cane syrup and baking soda. Others requested goods that had never been on the shelves—Lux soap, rubbing alcohol, Vaseline. As the epidemic grew worse in town, people in the country relied more heavily on Will's store. Will hadn't left instructions, so she didn't know what to do with the short supply, but she had a feeling demand would continue to increase.

Giving up on sleep, she sat up and stared out the window at the lake shimmering in the full moonlight. She wished Will would come home, though she dared not utter that thought aloud. Netta already cut her eyes at the slightest mention of him, as if every utterance of his name were a declaration of undying love. Although she understood Netta's concern, how could she not bring up Will Dunaway when she was living in his house and minding his store?

What a pickle her life had turned out to be. All she knew of her mother was the constant despondence she saw in her father. She longed for a home of her own with real love and a happy household. But thanks to her father's drunken despair, she'd been forced to make one desperate decision that pushed her storybook ending far out of reach. She leaned her elbow on the windowsill and rested her head on her fist. If only she could wish on one of those stars outside and reverse the clock.

A low growl interrupted her reverie, and Bea Dot smiled, thinking of how embarrassed Netta would be to learn she'd begun to snore. At another growl, this one louder, Bea Dot frowned and straightened her spine. That wasn't Netta. Then several growls sounded outside, and Bea Dot's heart sped. "Netta, are you awake?"

Netta rolled in her bed, a blanket-covered mountain in the darkness, before resuming her rhythmic breathing. Bea Dot sat wide-eyed, staring out the window, wondering what lurked on the other side of the pane. Two sharp growls made her jump and yelp, and Netta awoke.

"Bea Dot? Is that you? Are you all right?" She sat up and rubbed her eyes.

"There's something outside."

Netta yawned and stretched. "Maybe you were just dreaming."

"No, I heard something." Bea Dot shook her head sharply. "Growling. There's something out there."

They both sat mute for a few moments before the noise occurred again. "What was that?" Bea Dot asked.

"Sounds like animals," Netta said. "Look out the window."

"I already have." What if the animals saw her? Could they jump at the window? She peered through the glass again, this time squinting, as if that would illuminate the pine trees outside. "I don't see anything," she said at first, but then she gasped as something shifted in the shadows. "Wait. There it is."

The growling recommenced, this time continuously, as Bea Dot crouched in front of the window, her hands on the sill.

"What is it?" Netta asked nervously.

"It's hard to tell." Bea Dot watched the movement in the darkness. "All I see is shadows. Maybe it's two animals of some kind. Looks like they're fighting over something." She turned her face to Netta, who looked angelic with the moon shining on her pale face and blond hair.

"Are they raccoons?" Netta asked.

"Is that what raccoons sound like?" Bea Dot shrugged. "I've never heard them." She bent as she put her face closer to the window. The cold from the glass radiated onto her cheeks.

"Oh, for heavens sake, let me see." Netta rose and joined Bea Dot at the window. "I think those are raccoons." She wrapped her quilt around her more tightly and went to the back door.

"Where are you going?" Bea Dot asked. Was she crazy going outside with wild beasts in the yard?

"Out on the porch. Maybe I can see them better out there."

"It's cold out there," Bea Dot protested.

"I won't be long." She opened the door carefully and tiptoed out.

Bea Dot sat quietly for a moment, but fear got the best of her. Preferring company outside to being alone inside, she gathered up her blanket and joined Netta on the porch, watching the two animals. Netta's blond hair curled over the quilt around her shoulders. The growling had subsided somewhat, and the creatures kept their heads to the ground. Maybe they were digging a hole.

"Can you see them?" Netta whispered, her eyes locked on the pair of animals.

Bea Dot nodded. They watched silently for a moment until a larger figure raced across the grass and with a yowl pounced on the two smaller ones. One of them galumphed toward the woods, but the larger beast held the other smaller one down, shaking its head from side to side as it growled. Heart racing, Bea Dot clutched Netta's elbow and pulled her back into the house. Then she slammed the door and rested her back against it, sure that her heart pounded clear through her rib cage and onto the door panel. The thumping in her ears echoed in her skull. Once she had calmed herself, she realized that the growling had stopped.

Netta peeked out the window. "They're gone."

"What was that?" Bea Dot asked.

"I think it was a wildcat."

"You mean a panther?"

"Not the kind you read about in *The Jungle Book*," Netta explained, "but similar. I've heard Ralph call them bobcats before."

Bea Dot's jaw dropped, and she stared at Netta wide-eyed, like a six-year-old witnessing a circus act. "I had no idea wildcats lived in Georgia." She turned her eyes back to the darkness outside. "So there were two little ones and a big one?"

"No," Netta explained in the exasperated voice of a more knowledgeable big sister. "The smaller ones were raccoons, but the big one was a bobcat."

Netta's voice irked Bea Dot. Since when did she become such an expert on wildlife? Still, Bea Dot was more concerned about the animals outside. She shuddered under her blanket. "So the bobcat ate one of the raccoons?"

"Yes," Netta said as she returned to her bed.

Bea Dot climbed back into her bed and rubbed her numb toes under the covers. "I wonder what the raccoons were doing, though. That's the first time we've seen them since we've been here." She pondered them as her feet warmed. "They looked like they were eating something."

After a pause, Netta asked, "What did you do with the scraps after we ate those fish?"

"I tossed them in the woods behind the house." Bea Dot pointed at the pine trees visible through the window.

Netta fluffed her pillow and exhaled in the way she always did just before she criticized Bea Dot. "That's what they were eating," she said. "You should have buried them."

Bea Dot rolled her eyes. "Why?"

"Leaving out scraps attracts all kinds of animals, maybe even bears. It's so dangerous. You didn't know that?"

Says Netta the adventure scout, Bea Dot thought. "Well, pardon me, madam, but after dinner I had to wash the dishes and move the laundry in from the line because it wasn't drying out in the cold. Not to mention that I had to put the kitchen back in order because you wore yourself out before you finished your deep-cleaning project."

More than Bea Dot's feet were warm now.

"I wasn't scolding you," Netta said. "I was just saying—"

"I know what you were 'just saying.'" Bea Dot tugged her covers up to her chest and reclined in her small bed. Honestly, why did Netta always have to be such a know-it-all?

Across the room, Netta sighed and reclined against her headboard as well. After a pause, she said, "I hope the cat doesn't come back. Did Will leave a gun here? Maybe you could shoot it."

In spite of her frustration, Bea Dot guffawed at Netta's suggestion.

"What's so funny?"

"The idea of me using a gun," Bea Dot replied. "I can barely hang a sheet on the line by myself, and you're suggesting I shoot and kill a moving bobcat." She laughed again.

"I guess that was a silly idea," Netta said.

"I'd have more luck beating the cat over the head with a gun," Bea Dot continued. Then a thought came to her. "Maybe when Will comes back, he can teach me to shoot."

After a long pause, Bea Dot eyed Netta's dark form sitting upright in the opposite bed, so she knew her cousin was still awake.

"You don't think he's coming back, do you?"

"Well . . ." Netta's voice sounded cautious as a cat. "I do worry about Will being in town, just as I worry about Ralph, but I think he'll be home eventually."

Bea Dot's heart ached at Netta's comment. She uttered quietly, "I worry about him too."

"I know you do, honey," Netta replied. After a pause, she added, "That's what concerns me."

A pang pierced Bea Dot's chest. Even though she already knew the answer, she asked, "What do you mean?"

"Bea Dot, have you developed an attraction to Will?"

Bea Dot exhaled and leaned her head back against the headboard, gazing up into the blackness for a few seconds before replying. No sense in denying it anymore. "I'm afraid I have. I've never appreciated a man as much as I do Will Dunaway."

"But you're married."

"I know that." A touch of annoyance peppered her voice this time. "I never said I would act on that attraction."

"Does Will feel the same way?"

"I don't know," Bea Dot lied, still unsure whether Netta had seen Will kiss her.

"Don't ask," Netta said.

Bea Dot curled her lip in the cold darkness. Who was Netta to lecture on romance? She married the first man who showed her any interest. "I'm not asking for advice, Netta."

"I can't help giving it, though. Nothing good can come of your starting a relationship with another man."

"Oh, really? You don't think so?" Bea Dot couldn't help showing her irritation. How could Netta talk to her as if Bea Dot were unaware of her own husband's temper? Not to mention public scrutiny. Bea Dot was well experienced in avoiding that. "You make it seem like Will and I regularly sneak off to clandestine rendezvous. Nothing of the sort has happened."

"That's true. So far, you haven't seen the need to sneak off."

Now Bea Dot's irritation escalated to outright anger. "And what is that supposed to mean?"

"I mean that I interrupted something in the barn last week. Don't try to deny it. There's no telling what would have happened had I not walked in. He might have gone so far as to kiss you."

Bea Dot exhaled in relief as her face burned, but she bit her tongue.

"I don't mean to insult you, dear." Bea Dot hated when Netta called her *dear*, as if she were an appointed stand-in mother. "But I would hate for Will to get the wrong impression. Much worse, knowing what Ben's capable of, I would hate for him to have any inkling of an infidelity. Just please be careful."

"Nothing happened in the barn." Bea Dot had become an expert liar. "Will and I are both well aware that I'm married. We're friends, that's all. I enjoy working in the store, and he appreciates the help." As she spoke, though, the memory of Eliza Taylor's misunderstanding slapped her. *I ain't seen that look on his face in a long time, not since he come home from France.* Maybe she and Will were too transparent after all.

Bea Dot played blindly with a loose thread on her bedspread, chewing on her lip as she mulled over her own ambivalence. More than anything she wanted Will to return home safely, but maybe it was better that he remain in town. But how could she think that? The longer he stayed in Pineview, the greater his chance of catching influenza.

Netta's voice intruded on her thoughts. "Bea Dot, you know you're welcome to stay in our home as long as you'd like, but have you given any thought about what you'll do when you return to Savannah?"

"Well, no . . . I haven't." Actually, she'd enjoyed the opportunity not to think of her husband much at all. The last thought she wanted to entertain was the possibility of returning to him. Bea Dot twisted the loose thread around her finger, tightening it to stop the circulation to her fingertip. After a few seconds, she released the thread and felt the blood rush toward her fingernail.

"When is he expecting you home?"

Bea Dot hesitated before answering. "Two weeks ago."

"Two weeks ago? And you haven't written him? Does he even know you are here?"

Bea Dot shook her head in the dark.

"Does he?"

"No."

"Good Lord, he must be mad as the devil," Netta muttered.

"He was mad at me when I left, so you see? Nothing's changed."

"When I invited you to Pineview," Netta explained, "I thought you needed the time away from Ben to figure out what to do. This epidemic has certainly botched things up, but you still need to consider how you're going to contend with your marriage."

"Netta," Bea Dot sighed in frustration, "I don't even know what that means."

"It means you have some decisions to make," her cousin replied. "Do you want to divorce Ben? If so, my father could help you with that. But then you know you'd have to leave Savannah. Where would you go afterward?"

"Couldn't I come here?"

"You're always welcome in my home, dear. But people in Pineview already know who you are. They won't be as congenial to a divorced woman. And if you take up with Will, they might extend that cold shoulder to him."

Bea Dot tugged at the thread until it snapped. "Do you really think his friends would do that to him?"

"It's a possibility," Netta said. "Of course, Ralph and I wouldn't. I doubt the Taylors would. But I don't know about anyone else. You should think about how that would affect his business."

After all she'd seen Will do for the sake of helping others, Bea Dot could hardly fathom the notion of Will's friends turning on him. Pineview, what little she'd seen of it, seemed like such a friendly place. But then again, Mr. Floyd had gotten his shorts tangled over the idea of women voting. What would he say about a divorced woman?

"Are you awake?" Netta asked.

"Yes, just thinking."

"Bea Dot, I can't tell you what to do."

Now there was a first.

"All I'm saying," Netta continued, "is you need to finish your business in Savannah before you start up something new. Does that make sense?"

Bea Dot nodded, although Netta likely couldn't see her.

"Meanwhile, I think you should notify Ben of your whereabouts and your situation. He's likely to assume you've run off with another man."

Bea Dot shook her head and chuckled wryly at her cousin, who had no idea that such an assumption was what brought her to Pineview in the first place.

"What's so funny?"

"Go to sleep, Netta."

Bea Dot slipped down under her covers and turned onto her side, but sleep didn't come to her. Instead, she peered out the window, watching the early-morning sky turn from black to gray to white to pale blue.

Chapter 16

"D ammit!"

Pain bit through Will's thumb as he shook his hand for relief.

"Hit yourself again? How many times is that today?"

Will ignored the hoarse voice across the shed. Couldn't remember the fellow's name anyway. Ever since Harley had given this chap that special oil to rub down with, Will preferred to keep his distance. He felt like he was working alongside a salami sandwich. The two hardly spoke to each other except to say "Can you hand me that plane?" or "You finished with the saw?" For that matter, Will couldn't recall what his associate looked like behind his gauze mask. With his own face covered by a ratty blue bandana, Will resembled a crabby bank robber.

"Need a break?" the other fellow asked.

"I'm fine." Will bent and straightened the fingers on his left hand, then inspected his thumbnail, already turning gray. It would be black by nightfall. That made two bruised knuckles, one blood blister, and a black thumbnail.

All because of Bea Dot Ferguson.

Images of her pestered him like a gnat. That talcum-powder scent, her black curls tickling his cheek when they rode to the

Taylors' house, her small body pressed against his. He sighed as he rubbed his forehead and tired eyes. He'd fallen for her.

Two sides of him debated in the lecture hall of his heart. One side urged him to keep his distance. Although her marriage was the main factor to keep them apart, something about that union was lopsided. Bea Dot never wrote home, never mentioned her husband. If she came to Pineview to get away from him, she took no steps to make the arrangement permanent. Something wasn't right. Did he really want to latch onto her mysterious problems? Didn't he have enough to worry about?

But then the rebuttal began, and this side of him invoked the same evidence to turn the argument on its head. If she never wrote home or talked about him, she must not miss him. She'd mentioned no plans to return to Savannah. Maybe if she knew how Will felt, she'd take those necessary steps to sever her marriage.

Will shook his head as he reached for the box of nails. He always stopped the debate at that point. Why would Bea Dot go through the scandal of a divorce for someone like him? She was money, tea parties, fine clothes. Her refined background was no match for a country tradesman plagued with war wounds and nightmares. He stuck four nails between his lips, then lay a plank on the upturned side of the pine box. Holding a nail point down on the coffin's edge, he lightly tapped it into the wood before pounding it fully to the flat surface—this time moving his hand out of the way.

Still, there was that kiss. She'd been as much a part of it as he. Had she really fallen for him too? Or was she simply swept up in the moment?

He drove the other three nails into the coffin, then turned it on its bottom. But when he did so, no open side faced up. After turning the box two more times, he cursed himself again. He'd nailed the coffin shut.

Thoughts of Bea Dot infiltrated his brain like enemy spies

sneaking into home territory. Every time his mind conjured her image, he'd make a mistake with his work, and usually he hurt himself.

He reached for the crowbar.

"Got any nails, Dunaway?"

Will passed a handful over to his associate, who worked at a faster pace.

"Thanks," he said from behind a sawdust-covered mask before returning to his side of the dimly lit shed behind Pritchett's funeral parlor.

Day in and day out, the two men had been measuring, sawing, and hammering. Having spent the entire week with the fellow, Will supposed he could have tried to get to know him, but he was more concerned with finishing his work and getting back to his store. And Bea Dot.

He wrenched one side off the coffin, nails poking from its edges like Scylla's teeth. The job's end seemed nowhere in sight. Each time Harley picked up another load of coffins, he asked for more, as if he'd hired Will to build peach crates.

"Got any I can take away, fellas?" Harley stood in the doorway, the afternoon sun silhouetting his stocky figure.

Will pounded his fist lightly on the top of the box in from of him. "Just finishing up this one." He pointed with his throbbing thumb behind him. "Got another in the corner."

"How about you, Randall?"

Randall. That was his name.

"Give me ten minutes and you can have this one," he said. Then he cocked his head to the right. "Plus those two over yonder."

Harley nodded and made his way toward Will's workspace, squinting over the dingy mask covering his nose and mouth. He pulled two leather gloves out of his coat pocket and slipped them over his hands. Will helped him lift the coffin off the sawhorses. Together they carried it to Pritchett's wagon and slid it onto the bed.

"Before it gets dark," Harley said, his mask puffing in and out with his words, "could you bring any finished boxes to the funeral parlor?"

Will's chest tightened as he pressed his lips in objection. Harley knew Will couldn't return to the crossing if he exposed himself to influenza.

"Now, Harley—"

"I know." Harley held up his hand to silence Will. "We had an agreement. But can you help me out this once? I've got to bury some folks this afternoon, and I won't be back before sundown. With these recent thefts—"

"What thefts?" Will frowned and cocked his head.

"You didn't hear? Last night somebody stole the coffins from Pritchett's back porch. Now he has to lock them up inside before he closes for the day."

"That beats all I've ever heard." Will shook his head in disbelief. "Our men give their lives protecting us from heathen Turks and Germans. What's the point if we're going to be so uncivilized at home as to steal coffins?"

"Yeah, I know. It's terrible," Harley said quickly, and, Will thought, a little impatiently. "So can you bring the coffins to the funeral parlor for me?"

Will sighed and stomped to shake the sawdust off the tops of his boots. He'd developed a light sweat working in the shed. Now the cold breeze dried the perspiration on his neck and forehead, making him shiver. Sure, Pritchett needed his help. But Bea Dot needed him too. He couldn't leave the women alone at the crossing any longer.

"Tell you what," he said, meeting Harley's red-rimmed eyes. "I'll work through the night. Then in the morning, you can come get what I've made before I leave town."

Harley's eyes widened. "What do you mean? Are you quitting?"

Will shook his head. "Just taking a break. I have to see about my business. I've been gone almost a full week."

Harley turned his face to the sky and exhaled. "How long will you be gone?"

Will shrugged. He'd just come up with the idea. He hadn't figured out the whole plan.

"What are we supposed to do, Will? People are still dying." Harley's voice took on an annoyed edge, as if he were stifling anger.

"You'll have to rely on Randall in there until I can get back." Why did he say that? He'd rather not come back.

Harley huffed and kicked at the dirt. Will felt a little sorry for him, but not enough to put off going home any longer.

"Look," Will said, softening his voice to alleviate Harley's frustration. "I'll try to phone the crossing tomorrow. Maybe Bea Dot can give me a supply list so I can stock up now. That'll save me some time, and I can get back here sooner."

Harley didn't reply, just sighed and gazed into the distance. He must have been mighty put out, and that irked Will. So far, nobody had offered to pay for his work or even bothered to thank him for donating a week of his time. At least in the army he'd earned a paycheck. Will gave Harley a moment to respond, but when he didn't, Will continued. "I'll do my best to build you a load of coffins tonight."

Will left Harley standing outside the shed, puffs of breath clouding around the gauze mask like a muzzled dragon.

➤➤ ➥➥

"Wake up, Dunaway."

Something shoved Will onto his right side, and straws of hay pricked his cheeks and neck. He shook the cobwebs out of his heavy head and opened his weighted eyelids to find Randall standing over him, hands on hips, flecks of sawdust clinging to his wool coat and oily neck. Randall prodded Will a second time with his heavy brown boot.

"I thought you wanted to sleep only an hour."

Will rubbed his face with cold, rough hands. "What time is it?"

"Almost eleven. I've brought back the new load of lumber. Are you staying after all?"

Will shook his head as he slowly came to his feet, his hips and back chastising him for sleeping seated on a brick floor while his head rested at an angle on a bale of hay. His pallet at the crossing was a feather bed next to this prickly pillow. Will leaned on a saw-horse and rubbed his sore back.

"I need to see about my store," he said. "Once I know everything's all right, I'll come back to help if you still need me."

"We'll need you."

Will's chest ached at the truth, and he nodded. Randall walked over to the water bucket and drew out the ladle. He brought it over to Will, who drank greedily, in spite of the cold. The chill ran down his throat and into his empty stomach.

"Thanks." He handed the ladle back to Randall.

"I told Harley how you worked all night until you were out of lumber."

Will nodded.

Randall continued, "I took those last few coffins over to him just now. They ought to get him through today. Harley says if you could be back by tomorrow, he'd be much obliged."

Will felt certain Harley had never used the words *much obliged.* He searched the hay bale for his hat. "Maybe he should find a couple more men to help out."

"He's trying," Randall replied. "So far, you and I are the only men strong enough for the work who don't have the flu."

From between the hay bale and the wall, Will plucked his hat, now halfway flattened. He brushed the dust off and put it on. "Tell Harley I'll be back when I can."

As he turned to go, Randall called out to him, "You're covered with hay. You might want to shake out your coat. And your hair."

Out in the daylight, Will squinted hard in the midmorning sun. A strong cold breeze pushed against him as he made his way toward the livery to get Buster and his wagon. The wind slapped him awake as it burned his cheeks. He pulled his hat far onto his head so it wouldn't blow away.

The livery, dark as Pritchett's shed, smelled of urine and manure. Why hadn't the stalls been cleaned yet? And where was the stable hand? One of only three horses in the barn, Buster was easy to find. He lifted his muzzle in greeting. Will was relieved to find a feed bucket in his horse's stall.

By the time he'd harnessed Buster and hooked him up to the wagon, the stable hand still hadn't returned, so Will stepped into the small office at the end of the building to leave payment for his board. In the corner of the small room, on a rickety cot, the livery owner lay motionless, staring openmouthed at the ceiling. His skin, dark gray, horrified Will, who instinctively tucked his nose into his elbow as he stumbled backward out of the room. This body was more gruesome than those of the dead at Belleau Wood. Will looked up at the sound of running feet. The masked stable hand had returned. Harley, also wearing gauze over his mouth, followed several yards behind the boy.

Will lowered his arm and gazed at Harley. "I just talked to him last night."

Harley nodded somberly. His face shone with a fresh coat of oil. "Sometimes it takes them that fast." He picked up a horse blanket from a nearby bench and handed it to the stable hand. "Cover him up," he said. Then he turned to Will. "If you're leaving, you'd do me a favor if you'd go now and get back fast." Without waiting for a reply, he stepped to the door of the small office. But then he stopped and turned again. "Cover your face."

Will nodded blankly, pulling the tattered bandana from his pocket and tying it around his head. As he walked back into the sunlight to his wagon, fatigue and cold numbed him. His brain told him he should be traumatized by finding a corpse in the livery, but his body refused to react, instead converting to that shielded mode it developed during the short time as an ambulance driver. He'd learned quickly that if he didn't insulate himself from the horror, it would drive him insane.

He climbed atop his wagon and drove to the mercantile, where he bought coffee, sugar, flour, and other goods he felt sure would be in short supply at the crossing. After loading his wagon, he was just about to steer it through town, when a man's voice stopped him. "Dunaway!"

Will turned to find the stationmaster running toward him waving an envelope. He stopped just short of the wagon, then grabbed his knees to catch his breath. Finally, he stood straight and held up the envelope. "You headed to the crossing?"

"I am."

"Got a telegram here for Mrs. Ben Ferguson."

Will winced at the mention of Bea Dot's married name.

"That's Miss Netta's cousin, isn't it? Could you take it to her?"

Without replying, Will held out his hand and took the small yellow envelope. He stuffed it into his coat pocket as he watched the stationmaster turn and jog back to the depot.

As Will steered Buster down the empty street, he counted the bows adorning the door of almost every home and business. Pritchett had started a color-coding system. Two or three white ribbons signified the deaths of children while a handful of gray ribbons told the deaths of the elderly. Most ribbons—the black ones—signified the deaths of adults his age or a bit older, those who should have had the greatest chance of survival. It was a wicked foe, this flu. No matter how horrific the events in France, at least over there Will could see his enemy. An invisible menace, influenza turned the human body into a battlefield, a trench warfare among veins and organs, wiping out victims before they knew they'd been attacked.

Cold wind burned Will's eyes, while his breath behind the bandana moistened his nose, mouth, and chin. As he drove down Pineview's main residential street, he saw a familiar figure in the distance. Turning Buster up the Coolidges' drive, Will approached the house with the large front porch, where Ralph Coolidge sat slumped on the front steps, his coat collar turned up around his neck, his elbows on his knees. A gauze mask hung under his chin. In one hand, he held a half-eaten sandwich.

As the wagon neared the house, Ralph raised his head. Dark circles underscored his weary eyes, and his cheekbones, more prominent than they were three weeks ago, gave him an angular expression. He must have lost ten pounds. From his wagon seat Will noticed his friend lacked even the energy to finish his lunch. It was a miracle Pineview's only doctor hadn't fallen ill himself. Will just hoped he wouldn't collapse of exhaustion. Will didn't dismount, knowing Ralph would object.

"I heard you were in town," Ralph muttered.

Will nodded. "For a few days helping out. I'm on my way to the crossing now."

"Don't think that's a good idea," Ralph replied, though Will knew the doctor hadn't the energy to stop him.

"I've kept myself isolated," Will replied.

Ralph sighed and nodded, then rubbed his eyes with his spare thumb and forefinger. "How is she?"

"Just fine when I left her. She's getting uncomfortable, but otherwise healthy. Any message you want me to give her?"

"Just give her my love." Ralph stared at his dusty shoes. "Tell her I miss her, you know, all those things women want to hear." He looked up at Will, his face pale as paste. "Spare her the details of what you've seen in town. You know how she worries."

Will knew.

"Any relief?" Will asked.

"Wish I could say so, but every time someone dies in the hospital or in here"—Ralph pointed to the house behind him—"another patient takes the empty spot."

"What do you mean 'in here'?"

"Hospital's full. We're using my house as overflow, and we're still out of beds."

Will's gut tightened in alarm. Netta would have kittens if she knew her home were a hospital annex. "Can't you bring some more doctors in to help?"

Ralph held his sandwich-free palm up. "I've been begging for days. The state medical board says there are no doctors to spare. They're either at war or overwhelmed with their own flu patients. My nurses are either sick or overtired."

Will knew the feeling. "You're not showing symptoms yourself, are you?"

Ralph shook his head and rubbed his fingers through his dirty hair. Will wondered when Ralph had bathed last. Or slept.

"Why haven't you caught it yet?" he asked.

"Hard to say," Ralph replied. "Maybe I have a stronger constitution."

He certainly didn't look like it.

"But I wonder if it has anything to do with the flu I had last spring."

Will leaned forward in his seat, resting his elbows on his knees. "You were sick last spring?"

"Yeah, while you were away. Several folks had flu last March. Typical kind, though, not what we have now. I had it. Bradley at the pharmacy had it. So did Harley. None of us are sick now. Can't help wondering."

"Harley's trying to get everybody to rub down with salad dressing."

Ralph huffed a short laugh. "Thieves' oil," he said. "Some people swear by it."

"What do you think?" Will asked.

Ralph shrugged. "Can't hurt. Might help."

Will took up the reins again. "You look like hell."

Ralph raised one eyebrow. "You seen a mirror lately?" He tossed his half-eaten sandwich into the bushes, then stood slowly and stretched his back. "Look after Netta for me, Will. I wish I could deliver the baby, but chances are slim."

"The Taylors are checking on her daily," Will said, straightening his spine to stretch it. "Eliza can help Bea Dot. We'll phone you if we need to."

"Thank you. I'd best get back to work." He turned and climbed the steps slowly, his back hunched, as if he were a convicted felon on his way to sentencing. Before he could enter the house, a voice called from across the yard.

"Doc Coolidge!"

Will and Ralph turned in the direction of the voice. Netta's maid, Lola, ran across the yard, her dingy apron flapping over her frayed skirt and worn boots. "I need your help," she said as she approached. "My Jim Henry, he mighty sick, Doc. I need you to come see him."

Ralph sighed heavily and descended his front steps. Before turning his wagon around, Will watched Ralph put his hands on Lola's shoulders as he listened to her tearful plea.

Chapter 17

Netta paced around the kitchen table, one hand at her lower back, the other arm scooped around her round middle, the baby's weight pulling at her torso like a ten-pound sack of flour under her skin. Rest came only in spurts these days. Walking settled the baby but fatigued Netta, who could hardly stay on her feet more than a few minutes at a time. If only she could go back to town, she'd welcome the baby. But with no word from Ralph and each day drawing nearer her due date, her fear escalated that she'd give birth at the crossing.

She stopped at the end of the table, leaned on it with her left hand, and rubbed her back with her right. Then she turned to face the table and placed both hands on its top, gaining some relief. Sighing, she bent all the way over, resting her forehead on the smooth pine. The baby was still. The throb in her back ceased. She breathed in the scent of pepper and grain.

I might just fall asleep right here, she thought.

At the sound of wood scraping against wood, she called lethargically, "I'm so glad you closed the store today, Bea Dot. No worries about people seeing the circus fat lady."

Netta frowned at the following silence. Then her heart sped at the fading thump, then subsequent crescendo of heavy footsteps, clomps too heavy for Bea Dot's shoes. How did someone get in the locked door?

Netta crept on stockinged feet to the doorway leading into the store and peered around the telephone stand, but saw no one. Frowning, she called again. "Bea Dot?"

From behind the dry-goods shelf appeared a tall man in a dirty wool coat, a blue bandana around his face. His red-rimmed eyes frightened her more than his size, and Netta screamed, her heart pounding like a cleaver on a chopping block.

"Get out!" she screamed, backing away. "I have an axe in the kitchen! My husband is just out back!"

The man held his palms up and walked toward her.

Muscles tensed, Netta backed into the kitchen until her backside bumped against the table. She patted its top behind her with searching fingers. Where was the kitchen knife?

"Netta, it's all right," a familiar voice said. The man reached behind his head and untied the bandana, revealing a filthy, scruffy Will Dunaway with a moss of whiskers on his cheeks and chin and two hammocks of dark circles under his eyes. When he removed his hat, brown locks jutted from his head in all directions, as if they'd never met a comb. And was that hay poking out of it?

Netta slumped into a kitchen chair, one hand on her still-pounding heart, the other on her belly. "Have mercy, I almost dropped this baby right here!"

"I'm sorry to scare you," he said, coming into the kitchen. "I forgot I was wearing this bandana." He kneeled in front of her. "Are you all right?"

She nodded, taking a deep breath, trying to slow her heartbeat. "I will be. Give me a moment."

"Let me make you some tea," he said, stepping to the wood stove. He picked up a cup, then scanned the cupboard and table.

"Don't worry, Will. We've run out of tea, but I don't want any."

He scooped some water out of the bucket on the counter and brought it to her. She took it and thanked him, even though she wasn't thirsty. As he crossed over to sit in the other chair, Netta caught a whiff of him and immediately covered her nose with her palm. He smelled just like Jim Henry after a summer day trimming hedges.

"I was just bringing in the supplies from town," he said.

"Did you see Ralph?" she asked, her heart accelerating again at the thought of her husband. "Is he all right?"

Will nodded, resting his elbows on the table. "Yes, I saw him just before I left town. He's tired, but well."

Netta sighed with relief. "Did he send me a letter? Any message?"

"No letter." Will lifted his eyebrows slightly as he replied. "He's too busy to sit down and write, but he sends you his love, and he asked how you're feeling. He's mighty sorry he can't be with you right now."

Netta slumped back in her chair, an ache spreading in her chest as if a hole were forming. Of course Ralph was too busy to write, but she couldn't help feeling neglected, having never been away from her husband so long. Impending childbirth made the distance seem even greater.

Will continued, "Where's Bea Dot?"

"She's gone to the Taylors' house," Netta explained, "to see if she could borrow some eggs."

This time Will slumped in his chair. "I shouldn't have stayed away so long. You ladies must be out of everything. I won't let that happen again." He rose to browse the cupboard, finding it almost empty.

A pang of regret shot through Netta. Here was Will bringing her supplies, and she'd greeted him with screams and a complaint about no tea. "We've been able to manage," she said. "Terrence comes by once a day. He's been a great help." After a pause, she added, "You look exhausted."

He nodded. "I worked through the night so I could come home today." He ran his grubby hand through the brown mop on his head. "I'm going to finish unloading the wagon and put Buster in the barn. Then I'll get some sleep."

Still supporting her unborn child, Netta stood. "Do you know what will help you rest more?" she asked. "A nice bath. I'll put some water on the stove and then let you have the kitchen."

"Thank you, but don't worry about the water. I'll take care of it myself."

Will shuffled back to his storage room, his shoulders slumped, as if walking in his sleep. Flecks of sawdust released their grip from his wool coat and fluttered to the floor. He disappeared into the small, dark room like a sequestered monk. Shame enveloped Netta again. All the while she'd been at the crossing, her thoughts had revolved solely around her pregnancy, her husband, her problems. Since she and Bea Dot moved in, Will had slept on a mat on the floor. Now that he needed a bath, he would have to wait until she got out of the way.

Finally, she realized what Bea Dot had understood from the beginning. True, Bea Dot had grown too fond of Will, but maybe that fondness had grown from a desire to give back. *I'll just have to change my tune*, Netta resolved.

At the sound of the front door closing, Netta peered through the window. Will led his horse to the barn. *Might as well start changing now*, she thought as she stepped onto the back porch. The October air relieved the heat in her cheeks. Finding the washtub in the corner, she clutched its rope handle and dragged it indoors into the kitchen and put a large pot of water on the stove to heat. Then she went into the bedroom, shutting the kitchen door to give Will privacy when he returned.

She'd rested on her bed several minutes before realizing her baby wasn't kicking. She chuckled. Maybe all it needed was a good scare. Relishing the inner calm, she reached for her knitting needles and worked with clumsy, tingly hands.

Will awoke to the sound of shuffled footsteps, followed by a man's voice. Through the window, the southern yellow pines swayed in a slight breeze against a bright blue sky. The shadows on their trunks revealed he'd slept until afternoon. The late October chill penetrated his wool blanket.

Netta's voice slipped under the storage-room door. "Schools will remain closed until further notice . . ." Will smiled. She was reading the newspaper to Mr. Floyd. Will rose and dipped a rag into his bucket of cold water. Shivering, he washed his face, then dipped his comb in the water and winced as he dragged it through his tangled hair. By the time he'd made himself presentable and entered the store, it was empty. He shuffled into the kitchen, finding Netta at the wash pan with a bunch of collard greens, her shoulders stooped as if the leafy greens were made of lead. At the sound of his steps, she turned her head.

"Good morning," she said, her tired face pink from exertion. "I'm glad you rested." She wiped her nose on her apron before returning to the collards.

"The hot bath helped," he said with gratitude. "And it felt good to shave again." He rubbed his fingers over his jaw; then he shivered. "It's chilly in here." He moved to the wood stove, and finding the wood box empty, opened the stove's door. "Why haven't you lit a fire? Where's Bea Dot?"

"She's out gathering pinecones and sticks. We're out of kindling, and we didn't want to wake you."

Will's heart plunged into his stomach. "I'm sorry, Netta. I should have cut some for you last night."

"No apologies," Netta said, waving her hand. "I'm actually fine." She patted her stomach. "This baby keeps me warm. Bea Dot will be back in a few minutes. We knew she could get a flame going with pinecones."

In spite of Netta's good nature, Will blushed with embarrassment. He should have come home earlier. "I'll get this fire going in just a few minutes."

He went out the back door and split several logs from the woodpile, reminding himself to sharpen the dull axe. Then he carried in an armload of kindling and lit a fire in the stove to warm the kitchen. Next, he returned to the chopping block to split enough logs to fill the wood box. Back inside, he filled a pot with water for Netta and placed it on the stove so she could boil the greens.

"Thank you, sir," Netta said as she placed the rinsed collards into the pot. "This baby has grown so much that he gets in the way of everything I do. I feel like a clumsy old bear."

Will smiled and opened the icebox, finding a ham hock on a plate. He pulled it out and held it out to Netta. "Will you need this?"

"Yes," she said, smiling. She put the ham in the pot with the greens. "Now we just need this water to boil." She wiped her hands on a towel before taking a seat at the table. "I hope you like collards."

"I like any meal someone cooks for me," Will said, smiling. He sat at the table and faced her. "I'm on my own so much that I'm used to grabbing a bite here and there."

Netta nodded and lifted her eyebrows slightly, as if something were bothering her. "I know our presence has been inconvenient for you. I want you to know how much I appreciate your hospitality."

"Not at all, Netta." Her concern surprised him. "It's good you and Bea Dot are here, especially when I'm in town. I don't know what I would have done without the help in the store. I heard you reading the paper to Mr. Floyd. That's mighty nice of you to do that."

Netta smiled and blushed. "We're happy to do whatever we can."

Then her face lit up with an idea. "Have you thought about hiring a clerk to mind the store for you?"

"To tell you the truth, I haven't." He straightened in his chair as he considered the idea. "Of course, the store was only open a week or so before the influenza broke out, and now all of middle Georgia's topsy-turvy." He scratched his chin as he thought. A clerk would allow him to keep the store open regularly, even if he was on a mail route or getting supplies in town. "You know, Bea Dot's been a good clerk, hasn't she?" He smiled, liking the idea of her working long term at the crossing.

"Yes, and she does enjoy this work," Netta said with some hesitation in her voice. "But I don't know what long-term decisions she's made—if any. She hasn't said whether she plans to return to Savannah."

Will sighed as he rested his back on the wooden chair's slats. The thought of Bea Dot's other life left a lump of clay in his gut. Then a shock of memory jolted him straight in his chair. "Bea Dot got a telegram from Savannah yesterday, and I forgot to give it to her." Almost knocking his chair over as he rose, he rushed to the storage room and grabbed his coat with the telegram in its pocket. He pushed his fists through the sleeves as he walked back through the store and into the kitchen. "Excuse me, Netta. I'm going to find her."

Bea Dot shivered and pulled her coat collar tight around her neck. Though the afternoon sun still shone overhead, it hardly penetrated the shade of the pine woods. After walking almost an hour, she still couldn't chase away the chill from her bones. She hefted the burlap bag, half-full of pinecones and sticks, over her shoulder. As she plodded over the moist pinestraw-covered ground, briars tugged at her skirt and coat hem. She picked up a pinecone here and there, disappointed to find only a few, and most of them soggy from recent rains. The sticks she'd put in the bag poked at her shoulder.

So that she wouldn't lose her way, she kept the lake's edge in sight, intending to follow it back to the store. She'd walked only a short distance farther when she found Will's grandparents' abandoned cabin. Her heart ached as she recalled the last time she saw him, and it pounded heavily at the memory of his arms around her. She loosened her grip on her collar as she made her way toward the slightly ajar cabin door.

Pushing it wide open, she peered inside, her eyes adjusting slowly to the darkness. The one-room structure smelled earthy and damp, the air inside slightly cooler than outdoors. She stepped in, treading lightly to avoid tripping. Her foot found an old wooden crate, which she absently shoved aside with her heel. A rustle in the darkness sent a chill up her spine until she remembered the barn owl that had frightened her on her last visit. Smiling at the memory of her girlish screams, she shook off the creepy crawl in her backbone as she turned to exit the cabin.

At a slight tapping, she stopped. Had she really heard it, or did her mind play tricks on her? After a moment of silence, the tapping arose again, slowly, methodically, like a lazy dog's footsteps. But wouldn't a dog have barked?

A growl froze her. That was no dog. Where had she heard that noise before? Then a yowl jarred her memory of the bobcat she and Netta watched through the window several nights ago. At a second yowl, Bea Dot turned and stooped, feeling for the crate she'd shoved with her foot. Fortunately, she found it close by and heaved it toward the noise before turning to bolt from the cabin, her skin tingling with the electricity of fear.

As she lunged at the door, she tripped on the cabin's threshold and fell facedown in the pinestraw. Pressing her palms into the briars, she pushed herself up, and turned just as the cat leapt through the doorway. It landed on her chest, sinking its claws in her shoulders as it screeched at her with rotten breath. Operating on pure instinct, Bea Dot pulled her knees under the cat and managed to push it off her with her feet. It howled as it hit the cabin's side, and in the moment it took to right itself, Bea Dot jumped to her feet to flee.

But the cat pounced after Bea Dot had taken only two or three steps. With a deafening feline growl, the animal clung to her back, pushing Bea Dot to the ground. Pain pierced her shoulders.

She squeezed her eyes shut and fisted her hands, pressing the briars farther into her skin as she attempted to rise to her hands and knees. All the while she braced for a bite, but instead of bearing the puncture of teeth or claws, she heard a screech as the cat's weight lifted off her back. Another squall, this one weaker, was followed by silence, then a thud, and Bea Dot opened her eyes to find Will Dunaway clutching a bloody knife and stepping over the furry mound.

She pushed herself up to her knees and shakily tried to stand. Will bounded to her side, dropped the knife, and helped her up. "Are you all right?" Panic shook his voice. Without waiting for a reply, he turned her around, checking her back and neck for bite marks. She felt his hand rub her coat where the cat had ripped it.

"Lord," he whispered before turning her to face him again. "I've got to get you back to the house. It didn't bite you, did it?"

Still shocked, Bea Dot shook her head, her shoulders burning where the cat's claws dug into her skin through her coat. She opened her shaking hands, revealing the thorns stuck in her palms, but she could hardly pull them out with her entire body quaking so violently.

"No, let me do that," Will said, pulling a bandana from his back pants pocket. Gently, he pulled out one thorn, then another. Bea Dot winced each time he did so, but when he was finished, he pressed the bandana against one palm and then closed the other hand on top of it, pressing both hands inside his.

Bea Dot stared at the blood underneath his fingernails and in the wrinkles of his knuckles.

"You're going to be all right," he said, before pushing a curl away from her face and behind her ear.

As she gazed into his worried green eyes, the shaking subsided a bit, but then her chin quivered, and just as the tears poured down her cheeks, her knees gave way. Will caught her and pulled her to him with one arm around her waist and the other cradling her head as she rested it against his chest. She gripped the back of his coat as she released the shock, the fear, and the relief of his arrival. He held her several minutes, waiting out Bea Dot's catharsis. She looked up into his eyes and said, "I have never been so glad to see you."

As if on cue, their mouths found each other, and upon that connection, Bea Dot's fear and shock gave way to the warmth of his lips against hers. She stood on her toes and reached her arms over his shoulders, crossing them behind his neck. She was aware only of him, of his strong arms around her, his fingers in her hair, his scent of woods and leather and soap, his clean-shaven skin, and his pulse throbbing against her finger, which rested just under his jaw. When he pulled away for a quick breath, she reached up farther and pulled him to her again, unwilling to part from him just yet. Just as instinctively as the kiss began, it ended with him gazing down at her, letting her commit those irresistible green eyes to memory.

"You have perfect timing," she said.

He huffed a small, shy laugh and examined his shoes for a second before pulling her to him again.

"I've missed you," he whispered into the top of her head. He kissed her there before checking her hands to see if the bleeding had stopped. He kissed her palm, then picked up his knife, wiped the blood on his pants, and said, "Wait here just a second."

He walked to the water's edge and rinsed off his knife and hands, drying them with his bandana. Then he put the knife back in his boot. After returning to her, he took a quick look around before asking, "What were you using to carry your pinecones?"

Pointing to the cabin, Bea Dot said, "A burlap bag. It's in there."

Will went inside, stooping just at the door to pick up Bea Dot's sack. Outside, he held it by its bottom and shook out the soggy sticks and pinecones. Then he stuffed the bobcat in the bag and hefted the load over his shoulder.

"You're going to keep that thing?" Bea Dot asked, bewildered.

"Dinner," he replied.

Bea Dot's jaw dropped as her eyebrows disappeared under her dark curls.

Will chuckled before explaining, "I'm just teasing you. I thought Thaddeus Taylor might want the hide."

"Oh," Bea Dot said, exhaling with relief.

"I'll leave it here if you don't want me to bring it," he offered.

"No," she said. "I don't mind."

"Can you walk home?"

"Of course," she said, and the two set off toward the house. *Home*, he'd said. She liked the sound of that word.

Chapter 18

With a frustrated sigh, Bea Dot rolled over in her small bed, knowing she'd be awake to see the sun rise. Though exhausted, her back and shoulders, achy from the bobcat attack and burning from the claw marks, refused to give her a moment's rest.

But her soreness paled in comparison to her troubling thoughts. How many times in her mind had she relived that kiss? Just the thought of it sent Bea Dot's heart thumping like a stick on a picket fence. Ben's sloppy, drunken kisses repulsed her, made her wonder why her friends ever dreamed of marriage. How strange that the one man who had kissed her soberly left her feeling intoxicated. And like whiskey, having more of him complicated her already-muddled life. She'd certainly opened a can of crawly worms, but good heavens, that kiss might have been worth it.

Could she possibly leave Ben for Will? She'd heard of wives divorcing their husbands, but those women hailed from New York or Chicago. The papers always portrayed them as amoral harlots, selfishly abandoning their families. Divorces were taboo in the South, even in Atlanta. If she moved to Pineview with Will, she'd be an outcast, likely even damaging Netta and Ralph's reputation.

Of course, in Savannah, news of a divorce from Ben would spread faster than influenza. What's more, she wouldn't put it past Ben to spread the truth—or what he believed to be the truth—about her failed pregnancy. If she left Ben, how would the scandal affect Aunt Lavinia and Uncle David?

Sighing, Bea Dot had to agree with Netta's advice. Although she wished she could ignore her marital strife indefinitely, she couldn't continue a romantic liaison with Will until she'd settled matters at home.

She shook her head, refusing to get ahead of herself. She and Will had only kissed twice. Their romance was too new for contemplating marriage. *Get some sleep*, she told herself before punching her pillow and lying back down.

Across the room, Netta sighed and rolled over. Within seconds her snoring resumed. Bea Dot rolled her eyes in the darkness. Another reason she'd never get to sleep. Pushing herself to a sitting position, she winced as the scratches on her shoulders tore at her, as if the cat had left its claws inside her skin. She reached behind her and dabbed her fingertips on the sticky lines of her wounds. She must be bleeding again.

Quietly slipping out of her bed, Bea Dot padded out of the bedroom and into the kitchen, where she lit a kerosene lamp before adding more wood to the stove. She put a pot of water on to heat while she found a clean rag and the rest of the bandages.

Netta's snores rumbled softly in the other room as Bea Dot stood before the stove, waiting for the water to heat, all the while still thinking of Will. He might feel as conflicted as she did. When he had brought her back to the house, he had treated her as he usually did, like Netta Coolidge's visiting cousin. And knowing Netta's concerns about her fondness for Will, Bea Dot hoped her own charade was just as convincing. When she'd politely thanked Will for his heroism, she'd had to combat her urge to embrace him one more time. Will had told Netta the story of the bobcat, and he assured her that it had not bitten, only scratched Bea Dot's shoulders and back. Most of the cuts on her hands and face came from the briars and twigs when she tripped and fell. After the explanation, he'd left Bea Dot's care to Netta, going outside to sharpen the axe and split logs.

Bea Dot dipped her finger in the water. Hot, but not boiling. Just right. She unbuttoned her nightgown, carefully removing her arms from the sleeves without pulling on her wounds. She stood naked from the waist up as she untied her bandages and then dipped the rag in the water. Extending her arm over the opposite shoulder as she had in the bed, she tried to dab the angry claw mark. When she examined the wet rag, it showed a few spots of blood, but she couldn't tell how much good her process was doing.

"Let me help you."

Bea Dot flinched at Will's soft voice behind her and instinctively raised her arms to cover her bare breasts, even though her back was to him. Her first visceral reaction was defensive alarm—her usual stance when Ben approached. Embarrassment warmed her now more than the stove, but to replace her nightgown, she'd have to drop her arms. As his light steps neared, she kept her back to him, listening the same way she'd listened cautiously to the tapping of the bobcat's claws on the cabin floor. But then Will placed his hands gently on her shoulders and ran them down her arms. He reached around and held out his palm. "Hand me the rag," he whispered.

Chin tucked into her chest, she quickly dropped the cloth into his hand, then recrossed her arms against her front. Her heart pounded like a scared rabbit's. When he stepped away, she turned her head to see him open a cupboard and pull out a glass bottle. He blotted some of its contents on the rag before saying, "This is going to sting a bit."

The tonic roused the wound with a sharp sting, making Bea Dot gasp and draw her hand to her mouth. Biting her lip, she struggled not to voice her pain. The wound throbbed as the medicine did its work. Will tossed the rag on the table and put his warm hands back on Bea Dot's arms.

"I'm sorry that hurt you," he murmured. "Are you all right?"

She nodded and exhaled slowly, realizing she'd tensed herself unnecessarily. Will was not Ben.

Will laid a soft kiss just above the offending wound. "It'll feel much better in a few minutes."

Bea Dot breathed in deeply, this time not from the pain, but from the exhilaration of feeling his lips against her bare skin. He kissed her softly on the back of her neck, then on its side, then just behind her ear. "Is this all right?" he asked.

She relaxed more, her heart swelling at being asked permission, but her nerves pulsating with exhilaration. When he nibbled at her earlobe, he reached around her torso and cupped her breast. She felt guarded at first, but only momentarily. Desire for Will subdued her hesitation, and she turned to face him. He put her face in his hands and bent to kiss her deeply, urgently, as if he'd never have the chance to do so again.

He pressed her against him, accidentally brushing his hand against the wound he'd so carefully tended. To Bea Dot's surprise, instead of smarting, the claw mark felt numb from the medication. With relief, Bea Dot ran her fingers through Will's hair and held the back of his head as she caressed his lips with her own.

At a grumble from the next room, Will pulled away from her, just far enough that she could look into his eyes. Their depths revealed a wildness, a hunger, she'd never before seen.

"What's that?" he whispered.

"Netta," she explained. "We might wake her."

In one swift motion, Will lifted Bea Dot in his arms. "Take the light," he told her, and she grasped the handle of the kerosene lamp with one hand while she wrapped her other arm around his neck. As

Will carried her into his storage room, the sleeves of her nightgown dangled beneath her. The room smelled of gunpowder, pepper, and leather. Burying her face under his jaw, she took in his earthy scent.

Will first carried Bea Dot to the far wall, where she hung the lantern on a hook. After crossing to his pallet, he knelt and laid her there. The lamplight flickered over her pale skin.

"Are you cold?" he asked.

Bea Dot nodded, her nerves rendering her speechless. Both eager to and afraid of lying with a man, she wondered what she should do. Until now, sex was something done to her. Would it be the same when done with her?

Will must have noticed her tension because he stroked her cheek with his forefinger. "Your skin is like silk," he whispered. He nuzzled her neck, and she relaxed at the sound of his inhalation. Straightening, he put his finger under her chin and lifted her gaze to his. "Don't worry." He must have read her mind. "I won't hurt you. If you want me to stop, just say the word."

She nodded, still cautious, but grateful for his sensitivity. But in spite of her trepidation, stopping was the last thing Bea Dot wanted.

He pulled her nightgown over her hips and legs and tossed it behind them as he gazed at her body. "My stars, you are so beautiful."

Bea Dot's mouth twitched into a weak smile. No one had ever spoken to her that way before. She began to shiver, partly from cold but mostly from nerves. She stiffened at this intimate stage fright.

He unbuttoned his shirt, then lay next to her. Though she loved the sensation of his skin against hers, she felt lost. What should she do now? Her lips found his, and to her relief, he grasped her hand and pulled her arm around his bare waist as he maneuvered over her. Fear and uncertainty combined with her pent-up affection for him, and a new sensation—an urgency of sorts—swelled within her.

Will raised himself on his elbows and looked down into her eyes. She knew the intensity in them mirrored her own. "I can't believe I'm finally lying here with you," he whispered to her. "All the while I was in Pineview, I couldn't get you out of my mind."

Bea Dot's heart soared at his words, his feelings alleviating her fear. She smiled and combed her fingers through the hair on his chest. "I've missed you too," she whispered. After a pause, she added, "I think I want to do this. You'll think I'm silly, but I don't really know . . ."

How could she articulate her trepidation?

"We'll go slow," he said. Then he rolled to his side and unfastened his belt and pants. Bea Dot helped tug them over his legs, which fascinated her with their lean muscles.

For the next few minutes he lay next to her, holding her, caressing her, until her skittishness subsided.

"Do you want to keep going?" he asked.

She nodded, and he rolled on top of her, easing himself into her. The pleasure of the erotic experience blended perfectly with her adoration for him. Finally, she understood the joy of making love.

Afterward, she lay tucked in the crook of his arm, her head on his chest, tracing the lines of his muscles with her index finger. His lean body intrigued her. She'd had no idea a man's physique could be so alluring. As her hand surveyed his rib cage, it found a long dimple in the skin. She examined it manually until she realized she'd found a scar. Will's hand covered hers and squeezed it gently.

"Did I hurt you?" she asked.

He shook his head silently, but she knew the sensitivity she'd found ran deeper than flesh.

"The war?"

Will nodded, then uttered a quiet "Yes."

Bea Dot didn't pry, fully understanding the need to lock some memories away to move beyond them. Instead, she kissed him sweetly on the lips and said, "I'm glad you're home and here with me."

Will turned to face her. He lifted her hand to his face and kissed her palm, still punctured from briars. "Then be with me always."

Her insides flipped. She hadn't expected a proposal. She bit her lip as she stroked his tousled hair, wanting nothing more than to stay with him in this moment. But a pang of reluctance held her back as she remembered all the questions she'd mulled over earlier. Did they have to make this decision now? Unsure how to reply, she reached her face toward his and kissed him, breathing in the scent of him, trying to commit it to memory.

He returned the kiss at first but then pulled away and regarded her solemnly. "Is that how you're going to answer me? With a kiss?"

Bea Dot tried to make light of the question, raising her eyebrows as she spoke. "Don't you like it?"

"Very much. I hope to get more, but I don't know if a kiss means yes or no."

Now Bea Dot pressed her lips in ambivalence. As she grasped for the right words, Will continued.

"Do you love me, Bea Dot? Or do you just want me?"

"How could you ask that?" Her eyes widened in surprise. If he only knew what a huge leap of trust she'd just taken, he wouldn't question her feelings.

"Because you haven't said one way or the other. I love you. I'm sure of it. But if you don't feel the same way, it's best you tell me now."

"Of course I love you, Will. I wish I could marry you tomorrow, but I'm already someone else's wife." And that was only part of the problem.

"I know," he replied, still holding her hand, stroking her fingers with his thumb. "But you don't have children, so maybe your husband would agree to a divorce."

"I wish it were that easy." Bea Dot sighed and sat up, drawing her knees to her chest. She shivered in the chilly darkness. "But it's more complicated than that. There's . . . there's so much you don't know." What if he found out about her past? Would he still feel the same way? Would she be able to keep the truth from him for the rest of her life?

Will draped a blanket over her back, then rubbed his palm over the scratchy fabric. "The day you came to Pineview . . . ," he began. After a pause, he added, "He'd hurt you, hadn't he?"

Was she that transparent? Her face burned with shame. She wrapped her arms around her knees and placed her forehead on her kneecaps.

Will kept his head close to hers as he spoke. "Netta constantly asks about Ralph. You've never uttered a word about your husband. It's not hard to put two and two together."

With her face still to her knees, she held her palm up, tacitly asking Will to drop the subject. Instead, he took her hand in his and kissed it.

"All I'm saying is that if you've come this far from him, we might as well make that final step."

"That's easy for you to say," Bea Dot replied, finally looking at Will. "You just don't know—" How could she tell him without saying too much?

"Is it money? I can't give you the big house and fine clothes he does, but we wouldn't have to live here at the crossing. We could have a nice house in town."

"Of course not," she replied sharply. "I'd rather be here than there. It's just that I'm afraid."

"Of what?"

"Of everything. Who knows what he'll do if I ask for a divorce?" Ben's violence was one thing. But his scheming temper was another. Surely during divorce proceedings, Ben would paint her as a promiscuous woman. If Will learned of her illegitimate child, she could lose him. And then she'd have nowhere to go.

"I just jumped in between you and a bobcat," he smiled teasingly. "If I can take that, what's to be afraid of?"

She pulled in the corner of her lip and gave him a sober stare, not in the mood for jokes.

"Listen," he continued more earnestly, "I'm by your side. Whatever happens, I'll go through it with you."

She nodded, still uncertain. Will's proposal sent her mind whirling. In the past few hours, she'd fought off a wild animal, fallen in love, and enjoyed the greatest sensual pleasure of her life. Now she was contemplating a venture into the lion's den. The day had been too much for her. All of a sudden she needed to be alone. She fumbled around in the dim light until she found her nightgown, which she slipped over her head. As she stood, Will propped himself on his elbows and gazed at her sadly.

"Are you leaving?"

"I don't want Netta to know I've been with you. Not yet anyway."

"You still haven't answered my question."

She knelt beside him and pressed her face into his neck. "I know. Give me some time?"

Will sighed. "I have no choice, do I?"

She shook her head and kissed him. "I'll see you in the morning."

Chapter 19

Will yawned and stretched on his lumpy pallet. For the first time since returning from France, he'd slept soundly all night. Just one more way Bea Dot was good for him. Although he understood her hesitation, he hoped to convince her to ask her husband for a divorce.

He rose and rinsed his face, the chilly water in the washbasin shocking him awake. After brushing his teeth and combing his hair, he dressed and took his coat off the nail before going into the kitchen.

He found Netta sitting at the table, a half-eaten biscuit on a plate in front of her. She looked up at him with eyes underscored with dark circles. Pregnancy had rounded her face so that even her nose looked swollen. Though he would never say so aloud, it was probably better that Ralph couldn't see her.

"Good morning," he said. He hung his coat on the back of a chair.

"Good morning," she replied quietly. "Would you like breakfast?"

"I'll make it, but thank you," he replied. He opened the pie safe and pulled out a biscuit and the honey. Then he dipped out a cup of water from the bucket. "Would you like me to brew some coffee?"

"No, thank you, Will," she replied, concentrating on her biscuit.

"It's no trouble."

"Truly, I'm fine." Netta waved her hand in refusal.

"Maybe Bea Dot would like some," he said, picking up the coffee pot.

"She's not up yet," Netta said.

"Oh? She's still asleep?"

"She was up late last night," Netta said. After a pause, she added, "As you know."

As he put the coffee pot down, his face and neck burned with embarrassment, then irritation. What gave Netta Coolidge the right to comment on what he did in his own house? Still, he bit his tongue as he sat at the table and spooned honey on his biscuit. The two sat in silence a few moments before Netta continued.

"Will, I know you're fond of Bea Dot, but she's a married woman."

Will forced himself not to roll his eyes. "Yes, I know that."

"What are your intentions, then?"

"Isn't that something her father should ask?"

"Perhaps, but I'm the closest thing to that," Netta said bluntly, "so you get to deal with me."

"I've asked her to marry me," Will said, looking straight into Netta's eyes.

"Oh." She raised her eyebrows. "Then do you want her to divorce her husband?"

"We discussed it."

"What did she say?"

"She wants to think about it."

"So she's reluctant to break away from Ben."

"I think Bea Dot should say for herself how she feels," Will said. He stared at the honey glistening on the biscuit. He took a bite of it and forced it down along with his resentment of the conversation.

Netta put her pudgy hand on top of Will's and patted it. "I know you mean the best. You always do. But I don't think you've thought this matter through. Bea Dot can't simply divorce her husband and move to Pineview."

Annoyed, Will huffed a breath, then said, "I know it won't be simple. But it's what we have to do if we want to be together."

"That's the problem, though," Netta continued, leaning as far forward as she could over her mountainous middle. "If she went home and asked for a divorce, with Ben's volatile temper, he'd likely punish her for it."

"But I would be there to protect her," Will persisted. Didn't he have this same conversation last night? "I wouldn't let him hurt her."

"I'm sure you wouldn't," Netta replied, nodding. "But there's more to that marriage that you don't know."

"So I'm told." Will laughed cynically as he shook his head.

"Did you know that Bea Dot was pregnant?" she asked.

Will straightened at that information. "She's pregnant?"

"Not now." Netta shook her head. "She was. Just before she came here."

Will frowned. "What happened?"

"Ben killed the baby."

"He what?" How could anyone do that to his own child?

"He hit her and knocked her down, and I don't know what else. But she lost her baby as a result of his temper." Netta had picked apart her biscuit into a pile of crumbs. She stared at her fat hands and frowned as she spoke. "If that man's rage is fierce enough to kill an unborn child, there's no telling what he might do to Bea Dot if she tries to leave him. And while I admire your valor in wanting to protect her, I question whether you could stop him."

Will shook his head in disbelief. "You're right. I didn't know that." After a pause, he added, "But that's even more reason for Bea Dot to leave him. She'd be crazy to go back to that monster."

"I agree," Netta said, "which is why she's here, but you need to know her situation is complicated. Her father died shortly before she married. Within a year, she was with child and then lost it. Bea Dot seemed unaffected by her father's death, and she hasn't even mourned the death of her baby. I think so much tragedy at once has been too much for her. She needs time to close one door before she opens another. Does that make sense?"

Will sighed and put his head in his hands, his elbows resting on the table. "I suppose so," he muttered. Then he lifted his eyes to hers. "What should we do? We love each other. But even if she refuses me, she shouldn't go back to that man."

"You're right," Netta said, palms on the table. "I can try to reason with her again. My father could help her work out a divorce. And although I'm no lawyer, I'm sure the process will go more smoothly if she were not romantically involved with another man—especially the man whose home she's living in."

Will took a swallow of water to cool his resentment and buy a few seconds before responding. Trying to squelch the irritation in his voice, he said, "I've hardly been here, Netta. You make us sound as if we're living as man and wife."

"I know the truth," she explained, "but Ben's attorney will paint a sordid picture if he finds out about you and Bea Dot. And he will find out. But a bitter divorce isn't the half of it. If Ben finds out about you and Bea Dot, he might come after her. I lost my cousin once, Will. I don't want to go through that again."

Will leaned back in his hard-backed chair and stared at the ceiling, wondering at the complication of something that should be so simple. He and Netta sat in silence for a few heartbeats until she spoke up.

"Maybe Bea Dot and I should stay at the camp house."

Will couldn't help laughing at that suggestion. "You know as well as I do that's the last place you should be."

Actually, he found her proposal annoying. On the surface she might have been suggesting a solution, but he doubted the sincerity of her offer. As much as she fretted about having her baby at the crossing, there was no way she could be willing to move to Ralph's one-room shack.

The telephone rang and Will silently thanked the caller for interrupting the conversation. He stepped into the next room and lifted the earpiece from the receiver. "Dunaway's Crossing."

"Will? That you?" Harley's tired voice sounded tinny through the line.

"Yeah, Harley, it's me."

"We still need your help. Soon as you can get back, I'd appreciate it."

Will's insides turned heavy. He leaned on the wall with one hand as he held the receiver in the other. "I just got here," he replied.

"I know, but Randall can't hardly keep up with the workload. I've been trying to pitch in, but I got to go back and forth transporting bo—the deceased."

"All right," Will answered with defeat in his voice. "I'll see what I can do."

"Can you get here today?" Harley persisted.

"I said I'll see what I can do." Will placed the earpiece on the receiver and stared at the phone. The last thing he wanted was to leave again. But if Pineview needed him and Bea Dot needed her distance, then maybe he should go back to town.

He returned to the kitchen to find Netta washing the breakfast dishes. She turned to face him, a dishrag in her hand. "I was thinking while you were on the phone," she said. "Maybe Bea Dot and I could stay with the Taylors. I know it would be an imposition, but we'll need Eliza's help anyway."

Will's frustration softened at Netta's proposal. This was the first time he'd heard her express any acceptance of giving birth without Ralph. That had to have been a hard offer to make. He took the rag from her and dried the last dish.

"No need for that," he said. "I have to go back to town. You two stay here. That way, Bea Dot can mind the store for me."

"Is it worse than the papers say?" she asked, her eyebrows knotted.

"I'll find out when I get there." He put the dish back in the cupboard, then reached for his coat. He slid his hand into the pocket, expecting to find his bandana. Instead, his fingers found the small envelope the stationmaster had given him. He pulled it out and held it up. "I meant to give this to Bea Dot yesterday afternoon. What with the bobcat and all, it slipped my mind. Would you give it to her?"

Netta took the telegram from him. "Of course."

"I'll stay in Pineview as long as Harley needs me. When I come back, I'll stay at the camp house."

"Now, Will," Netta protested, "that's not what I meant. I wasn't trying to run you out of your own home."

He held up his hand to stop her. "I know, I know. Still I think it's best." Will cared less about propriety than Netta did, but if Bea Dot needed her distance, he'd give it to her.

Netta sighed and rubbed her eyes before turning them to his. "I'll try to convince Bea Dot to contact my father. Maybe he can speak to Ben on her behalf."

"Thank you," Will replied. "I'll talk to the Taylors, let them know you're on your own again. And if you run low on anything, please phone the operator in town. Get word to me, and I'll have supplies sent out to you. I won't have you ladies going without."

Netta assured him she would follow his instructions, and he left the kitchen. With aching heart, he gathered a few belongings from his storage room before walking out to the barn and hitching Buster to his wagon. Then he drove it onto the dirt road and steered toward Pineview.

❧ ❧

Two fifteen.

Bea Dot bolted upright in the bed after reading the time on the small clock on her bedside table. She couldn't remember when she'd ever slept so late; then again, she had watched the sun rise and light the sky. She hadn't expected to sleep at all, so this late slumber was a welcome surprise.

As she stood and stretched, the skin on her shoulders ripped at her. The medicine's effect had worn off. Carefully, she dressed, washed her face, and pinned her hair. She took more time than usual this morning, eager to see Will on the other side of the door.

In the night as she lay awake revisiting her encounter with him, she'd had to pinch herself multiple times to make sure she wasn't dreaming. So that was why all the women in Savannah swooned over those dime novels. Her only regret was that she'd turned Will down when he'd proposed. Well, she didn't really turn him down, but she didn't accept. And he'd looked so heartbroken. She'd let her fear of Ben, fear of her past, keep her from grasping what she wanted. But during the night, she'd wondered how California would advise her, even imagining Cal's own words: *You got a kind, strong, handsome man that love you. Child, don't you let him get away.*

She'd kept her vile secret from everybody. And now she knew Will had his too. They could simply keep their pasts private. Even if Ben divulged the truth—what he thought was the truth—about her pregnancy, she'd simply explain what Netta had concluded, that Ben had taken advantage of her, so she had to marry him. If Netta believed that, Will would believe it too. Still, she hoped the subject would never come up.

Today she would find a private moment to talk to Will and make plans for the future. She smiled at herself in the mirror before stepping into the warm kitchen, which was empty, but Netta's voice drifted in from the adjacent store. She must have been helping a customer. *Bless her heart*, Bea Dot thought, *minding the store so I could sleep.* Netta had a soft spot after all.

As she approached the cast-iron stove to pour a cup of tea, she spied a yellow envelope leaning against a saltshaker on the table. Her name was typed on it. Sensing it was from Ben, she opened it carefully, as if a snake might jump out:

1918 OCTOBER 20 AM 0825

MRS BENJAMIN FERGUSON

PINEVIEW, GA

YOU WERE DUE HOME TWO WEEKS AGO STOP

RETURN IMMEDIATELY STOP =

Irritated, Bea Dot ripped the document into small pieces, then threw them in the stove. How dare he order her home? How could she travel back to Savannah with Netta in her condition and influenza raging across Georgia? Surely he realized how dangerous the trip would be, not only for herself but for Netta as well. But then, Ben never worried about her safety. She'd reply to the telegram explaining her inability to return to Savannah, but she'd have to write Uncle David today to ask how she could go about dissolving her marriage.

Finding no pen or paper in the kitchen, Bea Dot entered the store to write her reply before calling the telegraph office. She found Netta handing over a small stack of mail to Birdie Henderson.

"Well, look who's here. Good morning, sunshine," Netta sang. Though her voice was cheerful, her eyes showed the strain of carrying a tremendous burden. Would that baby ever come?

"Good morning," Bea Dot replied. She turned to Birdie Henderson holding her parcel of envelopes. "Will didn't deliver the mail to you today?"

Netta touched Bea Dot's upper arm with a consoling expression on her face. "Will had to leave, dear. He went back to town."

"Oh?" Bea Dot's heart fell to her feet. "I didn't realize. Why did he go back?"

"Pritchett and Harley needed his help," she said, her hand still on Bea Dot's arm, rubbing it up and down. She cocked her head to one side in what might have been sympathy, but Bea Dot suspected smugness instead.

How could Will leave without saying good-bye? Was he angry because she'd put him off last night? He didn't seem angry when she'd left him. Maybe Netta had convinced him to go. As soon as the notion crossed her mind, she latched on to it, and anger simmered within her. Will would not have just left her unless someone convinced him to. And it was just like Netta to meddle.

"I need some paper and a pen. I must send a telegram home." Trying to hide her disappointment from Mrs. Henderson, she turned to search the workspace behind the counter. She breathed deeply and evenly. How could she talk to him now? How could she reach him to tell him her decision? What if he caught the flu before she could tell him? Damn that Netta!

Spying a notepad and a pen on the back shelf, she scribbled a reply to Ben until she regained her composure: "Influenza makes return impossible. Letter follows." Then she walked to the phone, picked up the earpiece, and turned the crank. No one answered.

"They say the school's closed and the churches have canceled services," Birdie Henderson said. "Good thing we're out in the country. Hope it doesn't spread out here." Then noticing Netta's worried expression, she quickly added, "I'm sure Doc Coolidge has the whole thing under control."

Frowning, Bea Dot put the earpiece on the hook, then picked it up again. After turning the crank a second time, she heard only the repeated buzz of the telephone ringing at the other end.

"What's wrong, Bea Dot?" Netta asked.

"The operator isn't picking up," she said, turning the crank a third time. "I've never known that to happen before."

Birdie Henderson piped up, "Oh, Charlotte's a wonderful operator. Takes her job very seriously."

"She's not there now." Giving up, Bea Dot put the earpiece back on the hook. Her resentment mixed with confusion.

"Maybe a line is down," Netta suggested.

"The line is ringing into the switchboard." Bea Dot shook her head. "So it must be fine. It's just that no one is picking up on the other end." Wonderful. One more obstacle between her and Will.

"That don't sound like Charlotte," Mrs. Henderson said. "Even when she had her baby, she had her oldest daughter, Jilly May, fill in for her."

"Birdie's right," Netta said. "Ever since we've had a phone at home, Charlotte has always been on the line."

"Then why isn't she picking up now?" Bea Dot asked.

The three women gazed at each other, none of them venturing to utter a reply. In an instant, Bea Dot's anger at Netta gave way to a sickening feeling that Charlotte was dead.

Chapter 20

Don't you get uppity with me, Lola. Dr. Coolidge needs all the alcohol you've got. Now."

Lola stifled her anger as the squat nurse frowned over a breath-soaked gauze mask.

"No disrespect, ma'am. I just ain't got any alcohol to give you. I used it up days ago." She swept her arm in a wide arch to display the groaning patients lying on the sofa, on the coffee table, on the heart-pine floors, even on the dining table. "I had one bottle in Miss Netta's medicine closet to use on this houseful of sick folk. Now all I got to use to cool 'em down is cold water compresses."

The nurse narrowed her eyes. "You're lying to me."

Lola's chest pulsed with contempt. Why would she lie? "You welcome to search the house if you like. Doc Coolidge's office too."

A young man rolled onto his side with a gurgling cough.

"I got to tend these patients now." Lola left the nurse and knelt at the coughing man's pallet, lifting his shoulders and back in attempt to ease his labored breathing. She took his hand in hers and inspected his fingers. Blue, as she suspected. This one would be gone by tomorrow morning. Her death toll grew steadily. Three bodies already lay on the screened porch awaiting removal, and she'd not yet had time today to move the ones who had died this morning.

She scratched her nose through the linen napkin, which she'd secured at the back of her head with a clothespin. Then she turned her eyes to the nurse, who glared at her with hands on hips.

"Wait until Dr. Coolidge hears how you've talked to me. He'll turn you out on the street."

"And I'll thank him for the favor," Lola replied under her breath as she grabbed two sofa cushions from a dead man's pallet and placed them under the coughing man's head. "Then I could go home."

The nurse stood over Lola, seething, but after a moment or two, she stepped over the groaning bodies and slammed the front door on the way out.

Lola huffed in exasperation. Normally, she'd be fired for standing up to a white woman. Not that she was working for pay. But flu changed everything. Since Jim Henry died, Lola no longer cared what white folks thought of her. Besides, by the time that nurse returned to the hospital, the boatload of groaning flu patients would make her forget about Doc Coolidge's uppity housekeeper.

A woman groaned behind Lola, so she took the compress off the woman's head and dipped it in a nearby pot of water, squeezed it out, and replaced it over the woman's half-closed eyes. The woman sucked in a couple of breaths, not as labored as the coughing man's, but her fever was mighty high. If she kept the coughing at bay, maybe this patient would pull through.

Lola wiped her brow and eyed the clock on the mantle. Two thirty. She'd been working since seven that morning. Rising from the wood floor with crackling knees, Lola put her hands on her lower back and stretched. Then she stepped carefully between the suffering patients and made her way to the back stoop.

She sat on the top step, pulling from her pocket a can of tobacco, a package of rolling papers, and a box of matches. She fumbled with the paper. Jim Henry had always made rolling a cigarette look so easy, but Lola hadn't mastered the skill. She always used too much tobacco.

After striking a match on the bottom of her shoe, the way she'd seen Jim Henry do a thousand times, Lola held the flame up to the fat cigarette and put it to her lips, as if she were sucking on a dead white man's finger. Taking her first drag, Lola let her shoulders and back relax. If Jim Henry could see her now, he'd take her over his knee and spank her. "You too pretty to take up such a nasty habit," he'd told her. "Don't you ever let me see you smoking."

Well, he wouldn't see her now. He died after two days of influenza. Two days. He'd come home from work with a cough and a headache, and by the next morning, he was delirious with fever. No amount of cold compresses, not even the October breeze through an open window, cooled him off. Nothing relieved the congestion that tormented every breath. Then he'd turned a bluish gray, as if he were rotting from the inside out. Who knew a black man could turn blue? She'd run like a bat out of hell to get Doc Coolidge's help, but by the time she got home, Jim Henry was already dead, a line of bloody saliva running across his blue-brown cheek. They'd been married eleven months.

She should never have left him.

Only an hour after Jim Henry's burial, Dr. Coolidge asked Lola to help care for the patients overflowing from the hospital into his home.

"You've already been exposed," he said. "You can't take the sickness back to your sister's house, so you might as well be my nurse."

He'd been so practical about the request, never uttering any words of condolence for the loss of her husband. So she balked at first. What if her sister fell sick? Her nieces? Who would take care of them? Dr. Coolidge stood his ground, though.

"Is your sister sick?"

"No, sir."

"Your nieces?"

"No."

"Well, if you go back to them, you'll make them sick. You know I'll care for any patient, black or white, who knocks on my door. But right now I need your help here."

Dr. Coolidge had always been kind to Lola and her family, but she couldn't help wondering: How were sick black folk supposed to get to his house to knock on his door? She learned the answer soon enough. They didn't. Doc Coolidge asked her to run the overflow unit—that's what they were calling his home now. So here she was, as usual, taking care of the white folks. But who would take care of her and her family?

Grinding the cigarette stub into the concrete step with her heel, Lola put the smoking goods back in her pocket, stood, and stretched her arms over her head, trying to relieve her aching back. She turned to open the screen door, but children's voices stopped her.

I had a little bird.

Its name was Enza.

I opened the window.

And influenza.

A month ago, that ditty would have sent chills up Lola's spine. Now, all that impressed her was that someone in Pineview was well enough to skip rope. She reached for the door handle, but before she stepped inside, she spied the undertaker's wagon rolling slowly across the yard.

"Finally," she grumbled as she reached into her skirt pocket for her linen napkin. As she pinned it behind her head, she watched

Harley, shiny with that thieves' oil he swore by, pull his wagon up to remove the dead. "I'm glad you're here, Mr. Harley," she called. "We could use the space."

"I'll take 'em off your hands, but first I got to get these three inside."

Lola sighed through the linen napkin and stepped wearily up the back steps. She opened the screen door as Harley brought in the first of the new patients.

"Just put them on the parlor floor, there. Wherever you can find space," she said. She watched him disappear inside the house, then forced herself to follow him.

Chapter 21

Netta spread the quilt over her little bed, then rubbed the small of her back as she stood straight. She'd been aching all morning, but she dared not complain. Bea Dot hadn't spoken to her in two days.

From the next room came the *zumpa, zumpa, zumpa* of Bea Dot's scrubbing on the washboard. From outdoors came the slow *thock . . . thock . . . thock* of Terrence Taylor chopping wood. The house buzzed with activity, yet no one said a word.

After straightening Bea Dot's blanket and fluffing her pillow—maybe that would soften her mood—Netta's toe tangled on something under her bed. She reached down and pulled up Bea Dot's nightgown. Spots of blood on the back glared against the white cotton, signs of her wounds from the bobcat attack. Netta rubbed her thumb against the stain and felt her heart swell for her cousin. She'd invited Bea Dot to visit to rescue her from any future harm. Some protection. Netta took the nightgown into the kitchen.

"I found this under your bed," she said, holding the garment out.

Bea Dot took it silently and placed it in the small pile of dirty laundry before resuming the up, down, up, down rhythm of the washboard. She might have been taking vengeance out on Netta's housedress.

"You're going to scrub the blue out of that frock," Netta joked.

Bea Dot sill ignored her, instead wringing out the garment and setting it aside for a rinse. Sighing, Netta reached out and gripped Bea Dot's elbow. "How long are you going to give me the cold shoulder?"

Bea Dot jerked her arm from Netta's grasp and picked up the nightgown, which she plunged into the soapy water.

Netta sighed and rubbed her back again. She pulled out a chair and sat at the table next to the wash bucket. "How many times do I have to say I'm sorry?" she asked. After several *zumpa zumpas*, she persisted. "I know I shouldn't have minded your business, but I was afraid for you. And Will."

Bea Dot glared as she plunked the nightgown into the soapy water, splashing onto the tabletop and Netta's sleeve. "When are you going to realize that I am a grown woman and can take care of myself?"

Netta had seen that petulant glare a thousand times over the years. She cocked her head and raised one eyebrow. "Oh, really? Is that how you ended up in Pineview? By taking care of yourself?"

"Oh, shut up, Netta." Bea Dot grabbed the nightgown again and resumed scrubbing.

"Wait. I shouldn't have said that. I'm sorry." Netta held up her hands in surrender. When Bea Dot ignored her apology, Netta raised her voice. "Will you please just give me a chance to explain myself?"

Exhaling heavily, Bea Dot dropped the nightgown into the bucket. With a slant look she said, "Go ahead. Explain."

"Sit down." Netta gestured to the chair opposite her.

Bea Dot dried her hands on her apron and sat, arms folded in front of her. Her knuckles were the color of raspberries. Her eyes could have frozen lava.

Netta swallowed her discomfort, then began. "When I spoke to Will, I didn't ask him to leave. He made that decision on his own." Netta paused for a reaction from Bea Dot. Receiving none, she continued. "I merely wanted him—and you—to think matters through carefully before jumping into a romantic . . . scenario."

"What exactly did you think I hadn't thought through?" Bea Dot asked with steel in her voice.

"Will told me he'd asked you to marry him," Netta said, "that he wanted you to seek a divorce from Ben."

"So?"

"So I think he doesn't realize how complicated that would be. I told him the same thing I've already told you. Pineview is a friendly town, but it can be unforgiving at times."

When Bea Dot huffed and looked away, Netta persisted. "But that's not the worst thing that worries me," she said. Maybe it was best not to divulge that she'd told Will about Bea Dot's miscarriage. She proceeded carefully. "Let's say you went to Savannah and asked Ben for a divorce. What might he do to you? I know you don't like to think about it, but you must recognize that he killed your child. His own child."

Bea Dot turned her face to the ceiling and shook her head.

"Listen to me, cousin. If he did that because you forgot to make him lunch, what might he do to you when you ask for a divorce? And what would he do to Will? I think it's gallant of Will to offer to protect you from Ben, but I wonder if he could. True, his war wounds have healed, but I wonder if he's strong enough to take on someone of Ben's size and temper."

"He managed a wildcat with no problem," Bea Dot jabbed, her face still full of contempt.

"True," Netta conceded. At least Bea Dot was talking to her. She put her palms flat on the table. "We may have different parents, but in every other way you're my sister. And Will is a dear friend. I don't want either of you to get hurt."

Bea Dot's eyes warmed slightly as she replied, "But, Netta, don't you think I've already thought of that? Yes, Will asked me to marry him, but I didn't give him an answer. I needed to think all those matters through."

Netta's face heated. Will had told her that.

"In fact," Bea Dot continued, "before I knew he left, I was planning to talk to him about what we'd have to do to seek a divorce. I had a letter to Uncle David all written out in my head."

"I didn't know that," Netta said quietly as she put her head in her hands. Her insides squeezed her in remorse. She'd really put her foot in it this time.

"If you had bothered to ask me," Bea Dot said, "you would have known. Instead, you went behind my back, and now Will's gone, and I didn't even have a chance to say good-bye." Her voice shook at those last words, so she inhaled slowly, as if to steady herself. "He's back in that flu-infested town, and now I'm truly afraid."

Netta reached across the table and clutched Bea Dot's chapped hand.

"We haven't gotten an operator on the telephone line since Will left," Bea Dot said, staring past Netta's face and at the opposite wall, as if she were talking more to herself instead of her cousin. "If the town hasn't replaced her, that must mean they've got no one else to do it, which means more people are sick. If that's the case, there's only a matter of time before Will gets the flu too."

Netta's gut clenched as she realized Bea Dot had silently nurtured her fears for two days.

"He could die in town." Bea Dot's eyes watered. "And I don't know what I'd do if I didn't get to see him again to tell him how I feel about him."

At that remark, Netta's eyes burned with sympathetic tears. She squeezed her cousin's hand. "I know the feeling. I've been living with it for the past several weeks."

Bea Dot finally met Netta's gaze, and her shoulders relaxed, perhaps opening a door to reconciliation.

"It seems we have more in common than we realized," Netta said, venturing a smile. "I was wrong to pry into your business, dear. I was thinking of the Bea Dot I used to know, the one who rushed into a wedding with Ben, and—"

"I had my reasons," Bea Dot interjected.

"I'm sure you did. Forgive me?"

Bea Dot sighed. "All right."

Relieved, Netta pulled her hand away from Bea Dot's and picked up her wrung-out blue dress. Her back had stiffened from sitting in the hard chair, and she walked to the pump to relieve the tension. As she rinsed the dress, she said, "Of course your fear is understandable, but it's also probably good that you're no longer in the same house with Will. I mean, you don't want to end up with another baby before you figure out—"

"Oh, honestly, Netta!"

Netta held up one hand in resignation. "All right, all right. I'll shut my mouth, but do know how hard it is to bite my tongue. It's just that I love you."

"Well," Bea Dot said, standing and tightening her apron, "you're about to love me to the brink of insanity."

Netta grinned at Bea Dot's remark, and seeing Bea Dot try to stifle a smile, Netta poked at her cousin until her lips curled up and she snickered. A ton of guilt fell away from Netta's shoulders as Bea Dot's anger subsided.

The back door opened, bringing with it a rush of cool air that cleared the room. Terrence entered carrying an armload of kindling, which he placed in the wood box. Shavings and bits of bark clung to the sleeves of his plaid flannel shirt.

"I split a bunch of logs out there for you, Miss Netta," he said. "They oughta get you through the next few days. I also brung over a chunk of fat lighter I found in the woods. I split that up to small pieces for you too." He stepped outside the back door and returned with a small bucket of dark-brown sticks. Netta loved their piney scent, which quickly spread through the kitchen.

"Thank you, Terrence. You've been a great help today."

He blushed and smiled. "Need anything else?"

"No, but does your mother need anything from the store? You're welcome to take anything you like."

Terrence shook his head and thanked her. "I'll just be going now. I'll tell my mama there ain't no news yet. Me or my pa will stop by tomorrow to check on you."

As he reached for the doorknob, Bea Dot stopped him. "Before you go, I was wondering, has your family heard any news from town, maybe any information about the telephone operator?"

Terrence furrowed his brow and stuck his hand in his back pants pocket, replying, "Pa heard she caught the influenza."

Bea Dot pressed her hand to her chest, and Netta leaned on the countertop. Her back muscles tightened at that news, and her stomach compressed into a tight ball.

"Do you know when anyone will take her place?" Bea Dot asked carefully. "We'll need to call in when Miss Netta's baby comes."

"I wish I could tell you, Miss Bea Dot," Terrence said, raising his eyebrows and shaking his head sadly. "Ain't nobody else in town can work that switchboard. Miss Charlotte's whole family is sick."

Bea Dot straightened her back and lifted her chin. Netta could tell she was putting up a brave front.

"I'm sorry to hear that," Bea Dot said. "Thank you, Terrence."

"Yes, ma'am," he replied before he stepped out the door.

The two women waved weakly as he shut the door behind him. Then they faced each other. Netta wondered if the nervousness in her eyes mirrored what she saw in Bea Dot's. But neither woman spoke, and Netta supposed Bea Dot was just as reluctant as she was to articulate her fear.

Netta rubbed her back again and frowned. Why were her muscles so tight today? Then she jumped at a tickle on the inside of her leg and warmth in her undergarments. Her face widened in shock and embarrassment. "Oh, my soul and body! I think I've wet myself!"

Immediately, heat flamed her face as she realized she'd admitted aloud her humiliating mistake. She put her hands to her hot cheeks and said, "I don't know what's come over me. I feel like I've lost complete control of my body. I didn't even realize I had to . . . go."

Bea Dot came to her side and put her hand on her arm. "It's all right. I'm sure this happens to all expectant women this late in their terms. Besides," she said lightly, pointing to the wash bucket, "you picked the right time. Go change, and I'll clean your clothes."

Netta still burned with shame. "I think I should go to the outhouse first."

She stepped outdoors and let the October breeze cool her flushed cheeks. She walked as fast as her heavy legs could take her to the privy. How could she have let such a thing happen, as if she were a three-year-old child? At least Terrence had already gone home. Oh, what a horror if she'd made her mistake with him in the room! She blushed all over again at the thought. She had just reached the outhouse door and had her finger on the hook when the muscles around her torso squeezed her like a corset. Then a warm wetness gushed between her legs and down to her stockings. Was she losing the baby? *Oh, no, please God, no, no, no, no, no.* Her heart sped like a locomotive as she lifted her skirt to look for blood, and the odor of pickle juice wafted up. Her legs weren't bloody, just

193

soaked. Excitement and terror seized her at once, and she turned to hurry back into the house. "Bea Dot!" she called as she lumbered toward the back door. "Bea Dot!"

Her cousin came to the steps, frowning. "What's wrong?"

Netta reached the house and gripped her cousin's elbow. "My water just broke."

Chapter 22

That night lasted a moment and a lifetime. As Bea Dot sat through the afternoon and into the night holding Netta's hand, wiping the sweat from her brow, telling her cousin everything would be all right, she cursed under her breath. She cursed the influenza. She cursed the operator for catching the flu. She cursed Ralph Coolidge for isolating his wife in the country and for leaving her in the care of a frightened, naïve newlywed who had no idea how to bake a loaf of bread, much less bring a life into the world.

On occasional visits to the Taylor farm, she'd picked up bits of information here and there: have lots of towels ready, wash her hands often, clean the baby's mouth and nose immediately. But now with the moment upon her, Bea Dot flooded her brain with questions she'd never known to ask.

How long after the water breaks should the baby arrive?

What if the baby doesn't crown? Should Netta push anyway?

Should she feed Netta to keep up her strength? Was it safe to give her water?

From Eliza's instructions, Bea Dot had conjured images in her head, but this labor was not turning out the way she'd imagined. For one thing, she expected to have time to run to the

Taylors' house to get Eliza. But Netta begged Bea Dot not to go. "I'm afraid," she said with a shaky voice. "What if something goes wrong while you're gone?"

What if something goes wrong while I'm here? Bea Dot asked herself. More frightening than a complication was a complication *without Eliza*, the only person around who knew what to expect. Bea Dot pleaded with Netta, but her cousin gripped her hand and insisted that she remain at her bedside.

Then once the pains grew closer together, time raced by, and Bea Dot worked up and down, back and forth, like a ball on a tennis court. First Netta needed a sip of water. Then she needed to sit up. She needed to lie down. She needed Bea Dot to rub her back and comfort her. She needed Bea Dot to wipe the sweat from her forehead. Although Bea Dot tried to hide her fear and exhaustion, she knew Netta saw it in her eyes.

All she could do was pray for sunrise. Terrence usually dropped by during the morning.

Netta's eyes and mouth pinched as another contraction seized her. She clutched her quilt into bunches as she endured the pain, then panted with relief when the contraction subsided. Bea Dot sat helpless, holding her cousin's hand and cooing encouragement: "You're doing fine, Netta. Any time now, Netta."

Useless words. Were the situation reversed, Bea Dot would have socked Netta by now.

Netta pushed. She pushed more. She pushed for hours, it seemed, until she had no more strength. After the tears and the strain, her face looked like it had been stung by bees. Bea Dot wanted to reach inside, pull the baby out, and end her cousin's agony. Instead, all she could do was wait and be encouraging.

But when the baby crowned, Bea Dot momentarily forgot her fear, replacing it with excitement and joy at the first glance of her new little cousin. At last the ordeal would end. Ralph, Eliza, Will—they had all been right. Everything would turn out just fine. Finally, the baby ripped its way into the world, tearing its mother with its tiny, gigantic body, then wailing with a ferocity that belied its size.

She was a little girl, strong and healthy, who gave Bea Dot only seconds to clean her up, wrap her in a piece of torn sheet, and hand her to her exhausted mother before returning to work. No instruction would have prepared Bea Dot for the trauma. Eliza had said Netta would bleed, but so much? She plied Netta's womb with compresses as Eliza had instructed, but Netta bled through them, the panels of ripped sheet no match for the life flowing out of Netta's body.

She'd have to reuse them. Bea Dot applied one set of compresses and took the others to her tub of water on the stove, washing the pieces of linen and draping them over chair backs to dry. The fire's heat on the wet fabric emitted a pungent steam, which Bea Dot had no choice but to ignore.

How could a person bleed so much? Terrified by the red-soaked compresses, Bea Dot forced a bright countenance for Netta's sake. "You're doing fine, Netta, just fine." How many times had she said that? "I'll be right back with more towels."

"Bea Dot, help me sit up. I want to nurse my baby."

She pulled Netta into a sitting position. Before stacking the pillows behind her cousin, she removed the pillowcases to use as compresses. She put one pillow in Netta's lap as a prop, fearing her cousin was too weak to hold the baby on her own. Once the baby took hold of the breast, Netta relaxed slightly, and Bea Dot hustled to Will's storage room to search for anything she could use as a compress.

She yanked the sheets off his pallet and found a towel or two. She searched his shelves and reluctantly pulled out his more tattered-looking shirts. But if Netta's bleeding didn't subside, these few articles would do her little good.

On the way back to the bedroom, Bea Dot stopped at the telephone and tried with desperate hope to reach an operator. No answer. She thumped her forehead on the wall next to the phone and berated herself. She should have never allowed herself and Netta to be stuck in this god-awful predicament in the first place. She should have taken Netta to Savannah, where Aunt Lavinia could look after her. Why didn't she think of that before?

Oh, please Eliza, Terrence, anybody. Somebody please come and help.

Crossing into the bedroom, Bea Dot spied her trunk—the one Will had so easily loaded onto his wagon, carried into the camp house, and to his store. That was an age ago. She tore open the lid and pulled out petticoats, chemises, blouses, anything absorbent. There in the bottom lay a flannel receiving blanket she'd brought for Netta as a gift. She'd forgotten all about it. She took the baby from Netta's weak, shaking arms and exchanged the child's torn sheet of a blanket for the new flannel one. Then she laid the baby next to her mother and went back to stanching Netta's bleeding.

Through the night she toiled, soaking with red her favorite blouse, her war crinoline, the tunic she'd bought in Atlanta, all of which meant nothing to her except the chance to keep the life from seeping out of her cousin.

She lost track of time until the sun peeked over the pine trees. As Netta grew quieter and weaker, Bea Dot tried to convince herself her cousin's pallor was only the pale daylight on her face. The bleeding had slowed, thank goodness. Netta had stopped talking a couple of hours ago, lying still and watching Bea Dot work. The baby lay quietly cradled between its mother's arm and her torso, as if knowing not to be of any trouble.

Her head and arms resting on the edge of the mattress, her mind cloudy with fatigue, Bea Dot sat on the hard wooden floor next to the soiled bed. For a second she thought she was dreaming the sound of footsteps. But she forced her eyes open and turned her face toward the door. Terrence Taylor, with a basket of collard greens in his hand, stared slack jawed at the bloody rags piled on the floor.

Bea Dot raised her head. "Go get your mother."

Will's upper arms throbbed from hours of hammering, and his head pounded with fatigue. After a sixteen-hour stretch of making coffins, he'd run out of lumber, so he trudged out of Pritchett's shed in search of food and a place to wash up.

In the light of the streetlamps, his wristwatch read six forty-five. Options were scarce during the evening. Pineview's one restaurant, with only one waitress still working, closed after lunch. The mercantile closed at six, but Will knocked on the door, hoping to find the clerk still inside. No such luck. After peering through the glass into the dark store, Will turned and surveyed Pineview's empty main street.

On a normal day, he'd knock on a friend's door—likely Ralph Coolidge's—and pay a visit. Almost certainly he'd be invited in for supper. But nothing was normal about today or the past month. Will could think of no Pineview household unaffected by influenza.

The only person definitely working at this hour was Pritchett, who had repeatedly offered him meals. However, determined not to pass influenza on to Bea Dot and Netta, Will had sworn not to cross Pritchett's threshold. His chest ached at the thought of Bea Dot's dark, curly hair and her coffee-brown eyes. Their one night together convinced him that she loved him as much as he loved her, in spite of her ambivalence. As soon as the epidemic ended, he planned to sit down with her and figure out a way for them to marry.

But Will's stomach growled like a trapped bear. To be any good tomorrow, he had to eat. He turned around and retraced his steps to the funeral home. He'd go in this one time, vowing from now on to plan ahead for meals. Fatigue burned his eyes as he trudged up Pritchett's front steps and knocked. In a few seconds, Harley, coated with oil and smelling of vinegar, opened the door and welcomed Will in.

"Pritchett's already gone back downstairs," Harley explained, leading Will to the back of the house. "He's preparing one last body before calling it a night." Catching a whiff of death and chemicals, Will held a grubby hand over his nose as they passed the stairway to the cellar.

Harley led him to the kitchen, where Will washed his hands at the sink. Harley dished up a bowl of stew for Will and put a slice of bread on a plate. Will jumped into the food like a stray dog. Harley sat across from him with a cup of coffee.

"It's a good thing you stopped by this evening," he said, spooning sugar into his cup. "I've been talking to Pritchett, and I think I have him convinced to stop this marathon coffin production."

Will looked up from his stew, his eyebrows elevated with hope. His heart picked up its pace. "Is the flu subsiding already?"

But Harley shook his head. "No, no," he said. "Actually, it's the other way around. The sick are dying so fast we can't schedule the funerals. We've started doing two, sometimes three, at a time."

That explained the recent pressure to pick up the pace of Will's carpentry.

"I got the mayor's support," Harley continued, "and he also spoke to Pritchett this afternoon. Tomorrow the city council will pass an ordinance forbidding individual and small group funerals."

"Small group funerals?" To Will, the phrase made death even more gruesome.

Harley nodded. "I know it sounds strange, but it's a temporary ordinance to require all deceased to be buried in mass graves. It's the only way we can handle the workload and prevent the spread of disease."

Will's appetite vanished. Harley's explanation provoked nightmarish images of the trenches on the western front. Packed with the terrified, sick, and injured, they may as well have been mass graves. He shuddered before pushing the memory to the back of his mind, and he sat back in his chair, eyes to the ceiling.

"I know what you're thinking," Harley continued. "I don't like it any more than you do, but it's the only way. Pritchett's about to fall over with exhaustion."

Will knew the feeling.

"So the good news, if you can call it that, is that you've hammered your last pine box." Harley slurped his coffee. "Now we just need a few more fellows to help us dig."

Surprise sparked in Will's chest. "Us?"

"You, me, and Randall." Harley pointed his thumb toward the shed behind the house, where Will and Randall had been working for the past two weeks.

Will shook his head slowly. He'd never signed up for graveyard duty, and he resented Harley's assumption that he'd be willing to handle scores of deceased flu victims.

"Now, before you start making excuses—" Pounding at the front door interrupted Harley's argument, much to Will's relief. When Harley left the room to answer, Will rose from the table and searched Pritchett's cabinets. He could use a drink.

The sound of a familiar voice caught his attention. "Looking for Will Dunaway. You know where I can find him?"

"I'm here, Thaddeus," Will called as he passed through the hallway into the parlor. "Don't come in. Let's talk on the porch."

Will's mood elevated somewhat. Netta must have had her baby. About time for some happy news. As he stepped outside and pulled the door shut behind him, he smiled as he greeted his friend.

"Well, what is it? A boy or a girl?"

Thaddeus took an awkward step back, as if surprised by Will's question. "Well, um, it's a girl, I think. I . . . I don't recall that I asked."

Thaddeus's face looked bewildered. Ashen, almost. Maybe from the dim light through the window.

"You didn't ask? That's the first thing Ralph will want to know." Will chuckled nervously. As a father, Thaddeus should have known that. But he dared not ask what was wrong.

"I already talked to Ralph," he said. "But I ain't here just 'cause of the baby."

Will frowned and put his hands on his hips, staring at his boots and dreading anything Thaddeus might utter next.

"Netta's dead."

Chapter 23

The ride to town was a horrid déjà vu. Bea Dot had not ridden through Pineview since the day she arrived, the day she met Will. Now she was returning, this time seated next to Thaddeus Taylor in his truck. And this time, instead of transporting a trunk of clothes, they carried more solemn cargo. For days she'd longed to see Will again, but not this way. She clung to her seat as she bumped along the dirt road, thinking that if she let go, she'd lose what was left of her sanity.

In the nightmare of the last day and a half, Bea Dot stood numbly by as the Taylor family dealt with the aftermath of Bea Dot's botched delivery. Although Eliza and Terrence had tried to comfort her, she'd felt lost, numb, useless. Guilty. She'd let Ralph down. She'd let Netta down, and now Netta was dead. She couldn't help Thaddeus and Eliza clean Netta's body. All she could do was sit at the kitchen table and gaze at the newborn child who lay with baby Troy in a laundry basket.

Now she bumped along in a farmer's truck, with her dear, dead cousin in the back, lying in a pine box Thaddeus nailed together three hours ago. She had lost count of how many times she cried herself to exhaustion. When she thought she'd run out of tears, her eyes watered again, as they did now with Thaddeus at the steering wheel beside her.

"I sure wish I had some words to make you feel better, Miss Bea Dot," Thaddeus said gently, keeping his eyes on the road. "All I can say is I sure am sorry."

"Thank you, Thaddeus," she said before blowing her swollen nose, raw from constant swipes of the handkerchief. "There's really nothing more to say. I just don't know how I can face Ralph." She stared out the window and watched the pine trees pass by.

"Now you ain't blaming yourself, are you? 'Cause there ain't no call for that. You did everything you could to help Miss Netta. Sometimes these things happen."

Thaddeus may have been right, but why did "these things" have to happen to her? She caught herself. They didn't happen to her. They happened to Netta. Her eyes watered again.

After several miles, the truck drove into Pineview. Every building, every street looked the same as it did the first time she passed through town, the only difference being the ribbons on the doors in black, white, and gray. Here and there on a light pole, a public notice, its corners flapping in the cold breeze, warned citizens to go home if they were coughing or felt headaches. Every other store window bore a sign informing customers, "Closed due to flu." Still, the sleepy Georgia town had not entirely shut down. A few masked people walked the streets, perhaps on their way to post a letter, buy medicine, or pick up a newspaper. Life did go on, in its limited way, in spite of the dreadful sickness that befell many Pineview citizens, and in spite of the tragedy in the Coolidge family.

The truck chugged down Pineview's main street, then turned a corner, where it approached another, larger wagon, this one loaded not only with pine boxes, but also with a number of odd, long bundles wrapped in sheets. The wagon resembled Will Dunaway's, but the driver wearing a gauze mask was stockier, heavier than Will. Thaddeus steered the truck slowly behind the wagon, so Bea Dot stared into her lap, refusing to acknowledge the heartbreaking cargo ahead of her.

Around a curve, the cemetery appeared. Thaddeus and Bea Dot followed the wagon through the gate and passed the long-established family plots with obelisks and angel statues, the occasional marble tree stump bearing the insignia of the Woodmen of the World. One plot bore the name of Coolidge, but the truck continued to the back of the cemetery, where the larger wagon pulled up to a long pit. Two dirty men wearing bandanas over their faces leaned on the handles of shovels. Bea Dot's jaw dropped in horror, and she grabbed Thaddeus's arm to alert him they had driven to the wrong place.

"I know how this looks, Miss Bea Dot," he said, trying to placate her. "But it's the only way. They ain't got enough time or manpower to dig individual graves."

Bea Dot gaped at Thaddeus in disbelief. "But Netta didn't die of flu." Somehow the thought of her cousin buried in the mass grave convicted her of a crime she didn't commit.

"I know." Thaddeus frowned and nodded. "But it don't matter how somebody died. It's the number of dead that's the problem."

The truck rolled to a stop, and Thaddeus engaged the brake as a haggard Ralph approached the truck. A white gauze mask dangled by its strings under his chin. He stopped two or three yards away.

"Hello, Bea Dot," he said with sandpaper in his voice. Except for the dark circles under his eyes, his skin was ghostly, his eyes bloodshot. He'd lost weight since she'd last seen him, and his dingy shirt hung off his hunched shoulders. The burden of influenza and his wife's death physically pressed down on him.

Bea Dot struggled for comforting words. "I'm sorry for your loss" seemed trite and inappropriate, especially considering she was the cause of that loss. She climbed out of the truck, still searching for words as she stood on shaky legs. All she could muster was a feeble "Ralph, I'm so sorry."

She burst into tears, resting her elbow on the truck window and laying her head on her arm. Her shoulders shook so hard that Thaddeus stepped up behind her and put his hands on them to settle her.

Ralph remained where he was. "I'm surprised to see you here. You shouldn't be in town," he said.

"I told her not to come," Thaddeus said, "but she wouldn't have it no other way."

Bea Dot wiped her face with her hands, then dried them on her pants—Will's mother's pants, the only garment not stained with Netta's blood. She faced Ralph, her cheeks burning with shame, and said, "I hate myself for letting this happen."

He shook his head sadly. "Don't blame yourself. It's my fault. I should have listened to her when she said she needed me. There's nothing you could have done."

Now tears fell from both their eyes. Bea Dot stepped toward Ralph to offer a comforting embrace, but he backed away and held up his hand.

Thinking he was too upset for a hug, Bea Dot nodded and mustered a smile. "You have a beautiful baby girl."

He nodded, unable to speak through his tears.

"She's with Eliza now," Bea Dot told him, "and she's doing just fine. I can't wait for you to see her."

Ralph pulled a handkerchief from his pocket and blew his nose. Poor Ralph. How heartbreaking it must be to lose his wife in childbirth and not even get to meet the child. Finally, Ralph found his voice. "Thank you, Bea Dot, for all you've done for Netta and the baby. I hate to ask you for more, but I'm still contagious. Can you and Eliza mind the baby until the flu breaks?"

"Of course," she replied warmly. "I'd be honored."

Ralph smiled weakly, again too choked up to speak.

"I know it's not my decision," Bea Dot said, "but would it be all right to name the baby after Netta?"

"Yes, that's perfect. Thank you." Ralph inhaled deeply, then let out a long, slow breath as he slid his handkerchief back into his pocket.

A minister approached, stopping a couple of yards away from Ralph, and said, "We should begin."

From his distance, Ralph introduced the minister to Bea Dot. "Reverend Sikes has agreed to say a few words for us."

"I know it's not the kind of memorial we'd prefer," the reverend added, "but the gesture is the same in the eyes of the Lord. Shall we get started?"

Reverend Sikes led Bea Dot to the mass grave, and Ralph followed them several paces behind. Thaddeus followed slowly in the truck to bring Netta's coffin closer to the pit.

From the corner of her eye, Bea Dot noticed a gravedigger peering at her from over his bandana. Then she recognized the green eyes, and her heart jumped. She took one step in his direction, but he silently shook his head. Disappointed, she followed the reverend to a spot at the pit across from Will. He stood with slumped shoulders, and even in this brisk fall air, his forehead glistened with perspiration. He rubbed the back of his neck, rested his forehead on the handle of his shovel, then stood again as the minister began the ceremony.

After a short speech about the sanctity of motherhood and a prayer blessing Netta's soul, Will and another masked man stepped to the edge of the grave and used ropes to lower Netta's coffin to the bottom. When they finished, Will caught Bea Dot's eye and put his hand to his heart. Tears spilled down her cheeks as she did the same. All she wanted was to rush to him and bury herself in his embrace. Though nothing would alleviate her grief, his arms would have strengthened her. She wished she could comfort him as well. All that wood work and then today's grave digging had clearly worn him out.

Will turned and followed the other two men to the wagon. Ralph joined them. In pairs they lifted the remaining coffins, then the bundled bodies, and laid them in the dirt. Fear seized Bea Dot as she realized why Will had kept her from approaching him. Her heart pounded as she considered the danger of helping bury dozens of flu victims. She offered a silent prayer begging for Will's safety. If she lost him as well as Netta, she might as well die herself.

Thaddeus gently took her elbow and guided her to the truck. She walked numbly to the door and sat like a lump in the passenger seat, dull with fatigue from the last thirty-six hours. Thaddeus got in behind the steering wheel.

"Miss Bea Dot?" he said gently.

Bea Dot lifted her heavy head in response, too tired to utter a word.

"Anybody told Miss Netta's parents yet?"

In her confusion and grief, she'd forgotten about Aunt Lavinia and Uncle David. She'd let them down too. How would she ever be able to look them in the eye? She shook her head wearily, almost certain Ralph hadn't sent word to Savannah.

"Eliza wrote down a message," he said, pulling a slip of paper out of his coat pocket. "We'll stop by the telegraph office before we go home." He pulled a pencil out of his pocket and held it out to her. "Will you please write down Miss Netta's parents' names?"

Bea Dot took the pencil and paper and scribbled the information for Thaddeus. Before handing it back to him, she read the bad news bound for Savannah:

NETTA DIED IN CHILDBIRTH STOP

SO SORRY FOR YOUR LOSS STOP

LETTER FOLLOWS STOP =

Bea Dot wished the world would stop.

Chapter 24

L ola tossed the soiled linen napkin, dingy and moist from her breath and sweat, into the dining room fireplace. No point in wearing it now, what with sick folk coughing into her eyes and spitting up bloody froth onto her hands. By this point, she would either get the flu or she wouldn't.

Next to the hearth, a two-hundred-pound sawmill worker lay motionless, his lips and fingers the color of a thundercloud. Lola felt his neck for a pulse. Nothing. Sighing, she stood and grabbed both his feet and tugged on them. She'd have to put her back into dragging this one out to the back porch.

She'd only pulled him a couple of feet when a motion in the corner of her eye caught her attention. Through the window she spied Doc Coolidge dragging himself up the front steps. *He look like he just walk through the gates a hell,* Lola thought as the doctor entered through his front door. The poor man had just buried his wife. Now here he was, back to work like he'd just finished his lunch break. *Wonder if he even seen that baby yet. Probably not.*

Doc Coolidge stepped over the patients lying on the parlor floor and walked straight down the hallway like a sleepwalker, not even acknowledging Lola's presence. She dropped the dead man's feet and followed the doctor into his and Miss Netta's bedroom. Three sick women lay on his bed, and four lay on the floor, but he ignored them as he went to Miss Netta's bureau and opened her jewelry box on top. When he picked up his wife's strand of pearls and rolled them between his thumb and forefinger, Lola asked, "You looking for something, Doc?"

Finally, he turned to face her with despondent, swollen eyes. Then he burst into tears like a little boy who'd just lost his lollipop.

Sighing heavily, Lola took his arm and let him lean on her—he was about to collapse on top of all the suffering women. With nowhere to let him sit, Lola led the doctor to the bathroom, where she seated him on the toilet. Still clutching his wife's pearls, he put his elbows on his knees and wept while Lola rubbed her palm across his shoulders. She even spilled a few tears herself over her mistress's death, but after about five minutes, she left him alone. She had a dead man to drag to the porch, and sick folk needed her attention. Besides, that few minutes of comfort was more sympathy than Doc Coolidge had shown her when she lost her Jim Henry.

She worked up a little sweat dragging that body out, but she finally got it to the porch and laid it next to the others. Holding her hand over her nose, she said to nobody, "These bodies starting to smell."

She peered across the yard, hoping to see Oily Harley's wagon. Instead a lone, long-legged boy loped down the road toward the black section of town. She recognized him as Quilly Jackson, the first black face she'd seen in weeks. She stepped onto the back steps and hollered for him to come to the fence.

He came toward her a few steps, but when he saw Lola approaching, he stopped, and Lola recognized his fear of getting too close to her. She halted in the middle of the yard and called to him.

"You seen my mama lately? Or my sisters?" She rubbed her arms and stomped her feet to chase away the chill.

He nodded with a slight frown, as if he weren't sure of his answers.

"How they doing?" Lola asked. "They all right?"

Quilly dug the toe of his shabby boot in the road, as if the dirt would answer the question for him. At his hesitation, Lola felt queasy.

"You can tell me, Quilly," she called. "It's all right." It really wasn't. She dreaded bad news, but at the same time she just had to know, much in the same way she always felt compelled to stick her tongue against an aching tooth.

"Well," he said, reluctant to meet her gaze, "you mama 'n' daddy's fine, but Julia done come down with flu."

Lola's chest tightened, and her chin wrinkled and shook, but she breathed in deeply, trying not to cry. "How long ago?" she asked. "She started coughing real bad yet?" If she wasn't coughing up that thick spit-up, maybe she'd pull through.

"Don't know much more 'n that, Miss Lola," he said. "My mama say to stay away from there."

His mama was right about that, but Lola's heart sank when Quilly ran along his way. How many other black folk had taken sick, and who was taking care of them? Was Oily Harley collecting their dead too? With slumped shoulders, Lola returned to the house. She searched the kitchen cabinets for something to eat. She'd already been through all the bread and meat, and although she regretted using up Miss Netta's food, she had no choice since Doc Coolidge rarely thought to send over supplies. And with Miss Charlotte and her family lying in the dining room, Lola could no longer use Miss Netta's phone to call the mercantile for grocery deliveries.

Lola found a package of soda crackers and a tin of raisins in the cupboard. They'd have to do. She ate enough to make her stomach stop growling; then she washed them down with water. Good thing flu patients were too sick to eat. They would have starved to death. As it was, Lola was simply babysitting them until they died. Only a handful recovered.

As she brushed the soda-cracker crumbs off her fingers, she spied Doc Coolidge through the kitchen door. He came out of the bathroom and stepped over the sick people in the hallway. Some moaned, some coughed, some rattled as they sucked in air. All were too sick to notice his presence, and he simply passed over them like they were logs.

Lola met him in the parlor. "I sure could use an extra pair a hands over here, Doc, if you could send someone over from the hospital."

He ignored her and slowly grasped the front doorknob.

"Well, could you at least send over some bottles a rubbing alcohol so I can keep these fevers down? Doc, you listening to me?"

Still no response. Instead, he slowly pulled the door open and shuffled out. Today was the first time he'd come over since sticking Lola in his house, and he hadn't looked at one patient.

Lola hated him for it, but she also knew how he felt, losing his wife and all. Poor Miss Netta. She'd tried four times to have a baby, and now that one of them lived, she died. God sure had a strange sense of humor.

She shut the door that Doc Coolidge left wide open and turned back to her house full of patients, no longer worrying about whether somebody spit up on Miss Netta's sofa. She wouldn't be using it anymore. After returning to the kitchen, Lola poured water into a bucket for her next round of cold-water compresses. It was half-full when she glanced out the window and noticed Oily Harley driving his wagon down the path he'd worn across the lawn and through Miss Netta's flowerbed. She watched him pull all the way up to the house, trudge onto the back porch, and carry the corpses one by one to the back of the wagon. Knowing he'd ask her to help him carry the bodies, she waited until they were all loaded before she stepped out to greet him.

"Glad you here, Mr. Harley," she said, "I starting to run outa room on this porch."

He didn't reply from behind his gauze mask, just stepped to the end of the wagon bed and leaned in to pull something out.

Lola continued. "We short on everything here, Mr. Harley. I wonder could you please have some food and rubbing alcohol sent over here as soon as you can?"

"I'll see what I can do for you, Lola," he grunted.

She didn't put much stock in that answer, but it was her best hope for some relief.

Harley pushed his arms under a man's legs and torso and lifted him off the wagon bed. Then he carried the patient toward the back door. "I got one more patient for you, though."

Lola sucked her teeth with resentment. All these white men brought her more and more work. "We really need your help," Doc Coolidge had said. But how could she help anybody if she didn't have the supplies she needed?

Harley carried the man up the steps, and Lola held the screen door wide to let him pass. "Just bring him in the dining room," she said. "I got a free spot on the floor next to the hearth."

Harley carried the man into the house and laid him in the spot just vacated by the sawmill worker. Lola knelt next to her new patient and felt his forehead to see how high his fever was. That's when she noticed the patient's face. Staring deliriously through her were the glassy green eyes of Will Dunaway.

Chapter 25

Somewhere in the distance a baby cried. Bea Dot opened her eyes and found herself lying on a single bed under a homemade quilt. She inhaled deeply and stretched as she scanned the room. Next to the door stood another single bed with Will Dunaway's old wool coat, the one she'd been wearing, on top. On the floor next to the bed sat her shoes.

Again a baby cried, and instantly she remembered where she was. The Taylors' house. Thaddeus had brought her here after Netta's burial yesterday. Bea Dot's throat tightened and her chest ached at the memory of that horrible day in Pineview. When they'd returned to the country at dusk, she'd been so drained that Thaddeus carried her into the house. She didn't remember being put to bed. When she pulled the quilt off, she saw she was still wearing the riding pants she'd worn to town.

She rose, stretched again, and peered out the window, October's frost emanating from the glass and onto her cheeks and nose. The sun, low in the bright blue sky, cast long shadows from the pine trees across the grass behind the house. She couldn't tell if it was early morning or late afternoon. How long had she been asleep?

Padding on bare feet downstairs, Bea Dot found Eliza at the

fireplace with two infants. Baby Netta lay in Eliza's arms, suckling at her breast. Troy, a couple months older, lay on a quilt on his back, kicking his little leg over his torso in attempt to roll over. Eliza smiled with delight as she watched her son's exertions. Bea Dot smiled sadly too, realizing all the milestones Netta would never see her baby reach.

"Good morning," Eliza said with a smile. "You was mighty tired. You been asleep almost twenty-four hours. You hungry?"

Bea Dot's stomach grumbled at Eliza's question, and she nodded. "Yes, a little."

The infant at Eliza's breast had drifted off to sleep, so Eliza laid her in a bureau drawer lined with baby blankets. She picked up Troy and carried him into the kitchen, where she put together a plate of biscuits, ham, and honey with one hand while using the other to hold Troy on one hip. While Bea Dot ate, Eliza played patty-cake with Troy, then put three pots of water on the stove, all the while chattering about mundane topics, such as this year's cotton crop, the recent drop in temperature, and her new bathroom that Thaddeus had built onto the house last spring. Bea Dot listened as she ate, grateful that Eliza monopolized the conversation, as if she knew not to remind Bea Dot of the turmoil of the past two days. While Bea Dot cleaned her plate in the dishpan, Eliza stepped out of the room momentarily and returned without her baby.

"Now, you need a bath," she announced, and she picked up two pots of hot water and instructed Bea Dot to pick up the third.

Bea Dot followed Eliza into her bathroom, a tiny space that included a pump, which spilled out into a white enamel tub. She supposed the bench on the opposite wall was for sitting and undressing.

"It ain't a real bathroom, least not yet," Eliza explained, pouring the boiling water into the tub. "I ain't got a toilet in here, and until we get electric service out this way, we have to heat our hot water on the stove." She took Bea Dot's pot and dumped that water in too.

"But it's a treat to have a private room to take my bath, especially with all these men in the house." She then pumped cold water into the tub and after testing the temperature, said, "Now get them clothes off so I can wash them. I'll bring you some soap and something to wear."

Bea Dot shed the riding pants and shirt she'd worn for the past three days and lowered herself into the warm water, her back to the door. While this tub was a far cry from her luxurious private bath at home, she relished the ability to stretch out her legs instead of hunching over in a washtub in the kitchen at the crossing.

The door opened again, and Eliza entered. "Here's a dress," she said, placing the clean clothes on the bench. "Good Lord a mercy, look at your back."

Bea Dot reached behind her shoulder, feeling the scabbed scratches. The attack seemed like ages ago, not just a few days. Her jaw tightened with reluctance to relive the bobcat episode for Eliza.

"Will come by here a few days ago, on his way into town. Left a bobcat carcass with Thaddeus. Said we might want the pelt." Eliza reached out and gingerly touched the healing flesh. "I didn't realize that cat done gone after you."

Bea Dot remembered Will stuffing the dead cat into the burlap bag, but she had forgotten about it after that. She drew her knees to her chest and hugged them, recalling the evening that had distracted her from her wounds—the one good memory she could retreat to.

"We got it in the barn right now," Eliza continued. "Thaddeus gone treat it so we can make a hat, maybe line the collar of my coat. Wouldn't that be fancy?" She didn't even wait for an answer. "Well, I'll give you some privacy," she said, handing Bea Dot a cake of soap. She picked up Bea Dot's dirty clothes. "I'll start washing these." For a moment, Bea Dot enjoyed a recollection of the days when California drew her bath and picked up her laundry. She missed Cal. Then Eliza interrupted her reverie. "Holler if you need anything," she said before pulling the door closed.

Bea Dot leaned her back against the tub's hard surface and felt the steam drift over her face before scrubbing herself with Eliza's homemade soap. She let her toes turn to prunes before drying off and putting on Eliza's housedress, which was a little big, the hem reaching almost to her feet.

Back in the parlor, she found Eliza standing over the bureau where she'd laid baby Netta earlier. After pinning a fresh diaper on the child and dropping the soiled one in a bucket of borax, she held the infant out to Bea Dot. "Come see your new little cousin."

Bea Dot took little Netta in her arms and padded gently to the rocking chair in front of the fireplace. The infant yawned and stretched, then opened her little blue eyes and gazed upward at Bea Dot. Though she knew the baby's vision was blurry, Bea Dot still felt as though the child were considering her with skepticism, as if wondering, *Will you be able to take good care of me?* Bea Dot wondered the same thing. Eventually, little Netta turned her gaze toward the fire, and she lay there staring at the flickering light. Bea Dot examined the baby's small hands, then reached under the blanket to inspect her tiny toes. Finally, she lowered her head to the infant's and inhaled deeply before kissing it.

The front door opened with a gust of fall air, and in walked Terrence. Over his shoulder he carried her trunk. Looking at the floor, he muttered, "Me and Pop was cleaning up over at the crossing."

Bea Dot's heart ached as she imagined having to clean the aftermath of Netta's gruesome demise.

"We seen this trunk with your name on it, so we brung it home for you." Soot smudged his face, and he smelled of smoke. He'd probably burned almost every piece of fabric in Will's small bedroom. "You want me to go put it in your room?"

"Thank you, Terrence," she replied with a frog in her throat. As he hefted the trunk up the stairs with ease, he reminded her of Will and the way he lifted that same trunk the day she first met him. A few minutes later, she carried baby Netta up to her room and laid the infant on the bed, a pillow on each side of her. Then Bea Dot kneeled in front of the trunk and opened it, expecting it to be empty, but instead finding a pair of stockings, a chemise, and the wool hobble skirt she'd worn on the train from Savannah. She lifted it out of the trunk and laid it on her lap, fingering the raveled fibers from the rip Will made down its front. Soreness spread in her gut, as if someone had kicked her for putting off Will's proposal. She'd let her uncertainty drive him away, and now she didn't know whether she'd see him again. If she did, she promised herself she'd tell him she loved him. Whatever it took, she'd find a way to leave Ben and be with Will.

A mewl from the bed trumpeted to a loud squall, and Bea Dot picked up little Netta, who now emitted a sour odor. Bea Dot carried the angry baby downstairs and found Eliza, who taught her how to change a soiled diaper.

From that point, Bea Dot and Eliza teamed up to manage the household and tend Troy and little Netta. Working at the crossing had been a challenge, but adding children on top of the responsibility gave Bea Dot new respect for motherhood. She'd never realized how time-consuming were the tasks of bathing babies, changing diapers, washing and drying dirty linens, and lulling infants to sleep. On top of that, several times a day, Eliza had to interrupt her chores to nurse both children. Bea Dot regretted her inability to help in that respect, but she tried other ways to pick up the slack. Often, Eliza sat with a baby at her breast, giving instructions while Bea Dot baked corn bread, washed turnip greens, cleaned out the fireplace, or mopped the kitchen floor. Though it drained her, Bea Dot welcomed the work, for any time that familiar ache in her chest emerged when she thought about her deceased cousin, a baby would cry, as if to say, "Don't think about her. Think about me instead." At night she craved her bed, but she dared not mention fatigue, for she knew it was Eliza who wakened in the darkness to feed two babies.

Bea Dot quickly noticed with surprise how much she loved her cousin's child. She'd never loved anyone, not even Will, the way she loved this baby. If my own baby had lived, she asked herself repeatedly, would I have loved it this much? Each time, she shook the question out of her head. Considering how that baby was conceived, it was best for all that she never learn the answer. Still, she finally understood Netta's protectiveness of her unborn child, and Bea Dot's own love for this little girl helped alleviate some grief.

On her third day at the Taylor home, Bea Dot hung laundry on the line while Nettie—as she'd started calling her little cousin—slept. In the distance, Thaddeus and Terrence slowly made their way along the rows of the back field. Thaddeus was eager to bring the cotton in now that October had ended. Even though the sky was a brilliant blue, and the laundry billowed in the cool breeze, Thaddeus had warned, "November always comes with rain."

At the rumble of an engine and the crushing sound of tires, Bea Dot turned to peer down the drive to the house. A shiny black Model T emerged from the pine trees. She shaded her eyes with her hand, trying to make out the driver, but the sun reflected off the windshield and blinded her. The car pulled all the way to the clothesline before stopping, and out of it came a squat man with hair parted in the middle and slicked back on either side. His trim mustache covered his upper lip, and his short body resembled a cylinder in a black suit. Was this the Pritchett fellow from town? Her heart sped at the anticipation of bad news.

As he approached her, she asked, "May I help you?"

"Yes, ma'am," he said, his voice whiny and nasal. "I've been looking for Mrs. Benjamin Ferguson."

"I'm Mrs. Ferguson," she replied. His use of Ben's name poked a wasp nest in her gut.

"Mrs. Ferguson, my name is Kermit Bonner, and I'm a private investigator from Macon. I work for your husband."

"For my husband?" What would Ben need with an investigator?

"Yes, ma'am," he said, scratching his lip at the corner of his mustache. "Your husband has been mighty worried about you. He says you came to Pineview at the end of September with intent to stay two weeks. He hasn't heard from you since."

Bea Dot reddened and exhaled with embarrassment. "I'm sorry to have troubled you so, Mr. Bonner. Obviously, the influenza epidemic has upset the entire state. My cousin, Netta Coolidge, and I had to retreat to the country to avoid contagion while she awaited the arrival of her baby. I couldn't leave as expected."

Bonner nodded as he pulled a tablet from his inside coat pocket. He flipped a few pages before pausing to scan his notes. "Mrs. Coolidge has already delivered her baby, hasn't she? And she has since died?"

Bea Dot stiffened at the tone of his voice. The wasps hummed inside her. She wanted to swat him. "Yes, that's correct."

"My condolences for your loss," he mumbled before continuing his questions. "So isn't it safe to say that your responsibilities have ended?"

"No, it is not safe to say that," Bea Dot answered, trying to suppress irritation in her voice. "My cousin's husband, Dr. Ralph Coolidge, is in town treating the sick. He asked me to take care of the baby until the flu subsides and he can take custody of the child." How dare he speak as if her care for Nettie was an assignment or a job?

"According to your husband, you have not communicated any of these complications to him."

"I tried, but as you probably already know, the telephone operator has come down with flu. I could not reach the telegraph office from the crossing. It's all a big misunderstanding, really. Please tell my husband that I am well and he should not worry. I'll write a letter to that effect if you would like to deliver it to him. Mail service has been affected by this epidemic as well."

"Yes," he said, scratching at his mustache again. "The mail carrier in this area is a Will Dunaway, isn't that correct?"

"Yes, sir."

"And at the time of your cousin's death, were you then residing at the home of Will Dunaway?"

Bea Dot twisted the pillowcase she was holding and shifted her weight to one foot. Bonner made her and Netta's evacuation sound so seedy. "Yes, that is correct as well."

"And when did you inform your husband that you were living with another man?"

Now her wasps swarmed, and she threw the pillowcase in the laundry basket as she raised her voice. "You, sir, are out of line. I'll thank you to leave at once."

"I have an obligation to my client, Mrs. Ferguson," Bonner said calmly. "Since you have not communicated your whereabouts to your husband, he has hired me to do so. My information tells me that you have been living at a place called Dunaway's Crossing with its owner, and that is what I have reported to Mr. Ferguson."

"I don't know where you got your information," Bea Dot said, her chest pounding with fury, "but you are jumping to the wrong conclusion, and I insist that you contact my husband immediately and correct your report."

"Perhaps you should return and clear the air yourself. Mr. Ferguson has hired me to accompany you back to Savannah."

Bea Dot gripped the post of the clothesline. Her anger combined with fear of leaving Nettie, Will, all she'd grown to love in rural Georgia. She straightened her back and hoped her cool voice belied her internal turmoil. "I cannot return to Savannah immediately. As I told you, I must care for my cousin's baby."

"Can't you leave her in the care of this fine family?" he asked, turning to survey the house and property of the Taylors. Bea Dot seethed at the sarcasm in his voice.

"No." Bea Dot was getting nowhere with this stranger, and she would go nowhere with him either. "You should leave, Mr. Bonner."

"Not without you, I won't." He put his face in hers. He had cabbage on his breath.

"Mister, I believe Miss Bea Dot asked you to leave my farm."

Bea Dot exhaled and relaxed at Thaddeus's voice behind her. Bonner scanned Thaddeus's large frame, and Bea Dot slipped out from between the two men.

"I have been hired to accompany Mrs. Ferguson back to her husband," Bonner said, this time with a squeak.

Thaddeus paused for a second, before spitting on the ground next to Bonner's shoe. In a cool, steady voice, he said, "And I heard Mrs. Ferguson tell you she ain't going. Now you want to get yourself off this farm, or do you need some help?"

Bonner backed away. Ignoring Thaddeus, he turned his gaze to Bea Dot. "You haven't seen the last of me," he said. He opened the door of his car and put one foot on the sideboard. Before getting behind the wheel, he said, "Think about this, Mrs. Ferguson." He pointed at her as he spoke. "You ought to go back right now to your husband and your life in Savannah. If you have any designs to carry on with that gravedigger Dunaway, you might be wasting your time."

"I don't know what you're talking about," Bea Dot said, her face and neck burning.

"Well, just know this." He sat in the driver's seat and shut the door, then leaned out the window as he spoke. "Your Mr. Dunaway went to Coolidge's house two days ago, sick with the flu."

Chapter 26

Bea Dot marched off the wooded path onto the dirt road leading to Pineview. Surveying her surroundings, she tried to remember which direction Thaddeus took when he drove her to town for Netta's burial. In the distance, she spied a crossroads. It must be the crossing. From that spot she would know the way to town.

A gust of wind pushed her along the road, and she pulled the old wool coat collar up to her jawline. Good thing she'd worn her pants this morning, but she wished she had a scarf. It would probably be dark before she got to Pineview, but nothing could keep her from getting to Will. She would never forgive herself if he died before she could promise herself to him.

An engine's rumble grew louder behind her, and in a moment, Thaddeus's truck bounced along her side. He pulled to a stop and rested his elbow on the window. "What the hell are you doing all the way out here? Eliza's worried sick about you."

"I've got to get to Pineview," she replied, and she resumed her walk toward the crossing.

Thaddeus rolled in first gear alongside her. "I done told you I'd go in the morning to ask after him."

Bea Dot shook her head as she walked, keeping her eyes straight ahead. "That could be too late. I've got to tell him something."

"It'll be dark 'fore long. Get in the truck, Miss Bea Dot. Let me take you home."

Bea Dot stopped walking and faced him again. He jerked his truck to a stop.

"Thaddeus, I'm going to town. If you won't take me, I'll understand, but I'm going with or without your help."

He shook his head, then rested his forehead on the steering wheel, mumbling something about stubborn women. After a moment, he sighed and said, "All right, dammit. Get in."

She crossed over to the passenger side of the truck and took her second trip to town with Thaddeus. She gazed out her window as she chewed on her thumbnail, wondering if central Georgia had a square foot of land without a pine tree growing on it. For the first mile, Thaddeus silently steered next to her. She knew his mind churned with resentment about driving her to town, but if Will was going to die of influenza, at least he would know how she felt about him.

Eventually, Thaddeus broke the silence. "That Bonner fellow's right, ain't he?"

Bea Dot continued chewing on her nail, and her thumb burned where she'd bitten down to the quick.

"Me and Eliza thought you wasn't married," he went on after a short pause. "Will think the same thing?"

"No," she said. "He knows about my husband."

Thaddeus raised his eyebrows and pulled back the corner of his mouth. "He carrying a torch for you too? 'Cause if he ain't, you might as well let him alone."

Bea Dot sighed and turned her face to Thaddeus. She couldn't blame him for being concerned about his friend. "He wants to marry me."

He sucked his teeth, then said, "Mm, mm. You in a real pickle." They rode in silence the rest of the trip.

Will wanted a table. On the floor, he had to shift his position to avoid being hit by Lola's dripping water bucket, or even worse, someone else's spittle. One time he was too slow and caught some drops of urine. No telling what got on him while he slept. The slick, grimy floor smelled of rot. He had to get out of the filth.

Unfortunately, every movement brought on debilitating pain. His head ached even worse than a moonshine hangover, and his fever made him shiver and sweat simultaneously. His skin hurt constantly, and the occasional cold rag Lola plopped on his head brought no relief. Why did she even bother with it?

Maybe because she had no choice? He'd caught snatches of her conversations with Harley and heard the phrases "need alcohol" and "out of food." Once she'd raised her voice: "You tell Doc Coolidge I leaving if he don't get me no supplies." She didn't leave, so Will assumed she got her supplies.

Good for Lola.

Still, she took her frustration out on her patients. Understanding the resentment of being forced to volunteer, he tried not to irritate her. But today was different. When the woman died on the dining room sideboard, he watched Lola push her body onto the floor, then drag her by the feet out of the room. If he could get onto that table, he could see out the window—and stay dry. The next time Lola passed by, Will clutched the hem of her skirt.

She scowled at him and asked, "What you want?"

He tried to ask for help, but when he inhaled to speak, he provoked a fit of coughs that he thought would make his lungs explode. Lola stooped and pushed his torso up to a seated position until the coughs subsided. When she tried to ease him back to the floor, Will shook his head and pointed to the sideboard.

"I can't lift you up there, Mr. Will," she said sharply. "You got to wait 'til Mr. Harley come back."

Refusing her refusal, he pulled himself up to his hands and knees, even though his head and chest punished him for it.

Lola stood with crossed arms, cocking her head to one side as she watched. "Oh, so you gone try to do it yourself? I gotta see this."

Pressing his hand against the side of the fireplace, he lifted himself to kneeling before resting for a few seconds. After a couple of brutal coughs, he grasped the mantle and pulled himself to his feet. Immediately, he swayed with dizziness, and his legs gave way, but Lola caught him under his arm with her shoulder.

"Oh, all right," she complained. "You so bent on getting up there, come on. But if I can't get you on top of it, you gone have to settle for lying under it."

Leaning on Lola's shoulder, Will slowly shuffled between other sick citizens of Pineview, most of them delirious with fever. He panted with exertion, as if he were hiking across Georgia, and a sharp pain radiated across his chest and back, but he forced himself to creep the eight remaining feet to the sideboard. Upon reaching it, he coughed heavily, then waited for the dizziness to subside, Lola holding her arm around his waist. Fortunately, the tabletop came just to his hip, so he could easily sit on it, then recline with Lola lifting his feet and legs. His lungs rattled with each shallow breath.

"You satisfied now?" Lola asked caustically. "You need anything else? Fresh linens? Shrimp cocktail?"

Responding out loud would hurt too much, so Will shook his head and ventured a grateful smile. Lola huffed away without noticing his expression, and he drifted off to a fitful sleep. Fragmented dreams peppered his slumber with images of trenches, coffins, Bea Dot, a mailbag, a bobcat, Bea Dot, an ambulance, a red-haired woman, a mass grave, Bea Dot, his box wagon, Bea Dot.

He woke once to find a blanket covering him and a pillow under his head. He awoke later and spied the blanket on the floor. Not daring to ask Lola to retrieve it, he drifted off to another shivering sleep. A captain in Belleau Wood shone a lantern in his face, making him squint and cover his eyes with his hands. Then he awoke to find the morning sun shining through the window on him.

Lola approached him, smelling of chemical and vomit. She felt his forehead, then wiped off his face and arms with a cold cloth before examining his fingernails. He'd seen her do that often and wondered why. Then she put one hand on her hip as she regarded him with one raised eyebrow.

"You got the last half bottle a alcohol, Mr. Will. Look like you just might walk outa here."

When she walked away, Will surveyed the dining room. Several spaces on the floor had cleared out, and through the doorway he noticed a new patient lying on the sofa. He turned his head slowly toward the window, trying not to exacerbate the ache, which had dulled overnight. In the front yard, brown dogwood leaves clung to their branches against a stiff breeze, eventually giving way and fluttering to the ground. One or two held fast in spite of the wind. Moments later, his box wagon pulled into the yard, Harley at the reins, rolling across the grass and through the rosebushes before disappearing around the corner of the house. The wagon's bed was empty. A short while later, it reappeared with bodies lying in the back, the morbid pile bouncing slightly as the wagon drove over the bumpy yard. Will counted six pairs of feet before another fit of coughing ignited his lungs.

When the truck rolled into Pineview, Thaddeus turned it down a road Bea Dot had never seen before. After a short distance, he stopped in front of a two-story brick building with wide front steps. Over the double front door, a sign read, "Shine Bunn Memorial Hospital." Two men in gauze masks stood guard by the entrance.

Bea Dot leapt out of the truck, taking the steps two at a time. Ignoring the guards, she reached for the door handle, but one guard grasped her arm and said, "Ma'am, you can't go in there."

"It's all right," she lied. "I'm Dr. Coolidge's sister-in-law. I'm taking care of his baby, and I need to see him."

The guard shook his head sternly, his authoritative eyes focused on hers. His grip hardened slightly. "No, ma'am. City ordinance. The hospital is quarantined. No one goes in who ain't got the flu."

Bea Dot ripped her arm out of the guard's grasp. "You don't understand," she persisted. "I must see Wi—I mean Dr. Coolidge. It's important." She paused, then added, "Life or death."

The second man had taken position next to the first, with hands on hips. His gauze mask puffed when he spoke. "Everything in this hospital is life or death, ma'am. You can't go in."

Thaddeus had climbed the steps and joined the cluster by the door. "Miss Bea Dot, let's go."

"No, I came all the way here. I have to see him." Her voice wavered, and she inhaled deeply, willing herself to control her temper. She turned to the first guard again. "I'll give you twenty dollars to let me in."

Thaddeus shook his head. "Oh, good Lord."

"Ma'am, I don't want to arrest you, but I'm about to have to," the first guard said, scowling behind his mask.

"You'll have to carry me off these steps," she persisted, her voice rising an octave, "because I'm not leaving." She stomped her foot for emphasis, realizing too late her childish behavior.

"Suit yourself," the first guard said, and he picked Bea Dot up by the waist.

"No need for that, Pete," Thaddeus interjected. "I'll take her."

The guard lowered her just as the front door burst open. Ralph Coolidge emerged with a stethoscope around his neck and a white towel in his hands. His cheekbones jutted from his face, and above his gauze mask, his sunken eyes looked like a dead man's.

"What in hell is going on out here?" He spied Bea Dot, and his jaw dropped. Hands on hips, he demanded, "Bea Dot, what are you doing here?" After a beat, his expression changed from surprise to frown. "Is the baby all right?"

"The baby's fine, Ralph," Thaddeus said. "No need to worry."

"Then what are you doing in town?" Ralph said to Bea Dot. "Why aren't you at home minding her?"

"Ralph, I just want to see Will for a minute. I have to tell him something. Please. I'll keep my distance. I just have to see him." Her heart pounded with desperation.

Ralph shook his head slowly and relaxed his stance. He waved the two guards away as he spoke to Bea Dot. "He's not even here. He's over at my house with the overflow patients."

Bea Dot started to descend the steps, but Ralph grabbed her arm to stop her. "Don't you dare go over there."

"But Ralph—"

"Don't." He turned his eyes to Thaddeus. "Take her back to your house, and don't let her come to town again until I send for her." To Bea Dot, he softened his voice and said, "You promised to care for my baby. She's all I've got left. If you go in this hospital"— he pointed his thumb toward the door—"or in my house, you'll expose yourself to influenza and take it back to the Taylors' home. I'll not have you making yourself or any of their family sick. Especially not my daughter. Do you understand me?"

Bea Dot nodded and took a step back, burning with shame at the risk she posed for the Taylors. Still, she'd come all this distance to see Will. There must be a way. Maybe she could convince Thaddeus to let her slip a note under the door of Ralph's house.

"It's been a devastating week for all of us," Ralph continued, "but you must be strong. The flu is subsiding a bit, and if we can keep it contained to this hospital and my house, we just might stand a chance."

Bea Dot stared at her shoes, embarrassed at having caused a scene, but still trying to think of a way to get a message to Will, maybe get a glimpse of him.

Ralph turned to enter the hospital, but Bea Dot stopped him. "Ralph, can you at least tell me how Will is?"

He ran his hand through his dirty hair before answering. "I haven't heard from Lola, but I haven't seen him in the back of Harley's wagon either. That's a good sign."

He disappeared into the hospital.

Dejected, Bea Dot descended the front steps with Thaddeus, who opened the truck door for her. "Do you think we could find this Harley person and ask him if he knows anything about Will?" she asked.

"That won't be necessary, Mrs. Ferguson," a familiar whiny voice came from behind her. She inched up her shoulders in irritation.

She turned to face Kermit Bonner, still scratching his lip above his mustache. In his other hand, he held a small yellow envelope.

"I think you should come with me," he said.

"Mister, I done told you to let Miss Bea Dot alone," Thaddeus said, his voice rumbling.

Bonner held up his palm to silence Thaddeus and said to Bea Dot, "Perhaps you should read this telegram before making your decision."

Bea Dot took the envelope from his pale hand and stepped to the back of the truck before opening it. Her nerves jittered as she unfolded the paper. The afternoon sun, just touching the distant treetops, made the page glow.

RETURN TO SAVANNAH IMMEDIATELY OR I WILL REVEAL THE
TRUTH ABOUT YOU AND YOUR FATHER STOP =

Bea Dot's legs buckled, and she gripped the truck's side for support. How did he know? She thought he'd suspected adultery, but he knew the real truth. But she'd told no one. She'd been so careful all this time to keep that horrible secret. How was it that Ben was threatening to use it against her?

Will couldn't know the truth. If he ever found out, he'd despise her. She put her hand to her eyes for a few minutes before sighing in resignation. Then she returned to the two men. Thaddeus cocked his head with a curious frown. Bonner gloated beside him.

"You all right, Miss Bea Dot?" Thaddeus asked.

"Please apologize to Eliza for me," she replied, "but I must return to Savannah right away."

Chapter 27

Bea Dot stepped inside the doorway of her home and let her eyes adjust to the darkness. She felt as though she were stepping back in time. The house smelled dusty and stale, as if it had been shut tight for the last two months. Had Ben been away too?

After several seconds, she felt her way to a window and opened the shutter, letting the moon and streetlights illuminate her foyer. She had no bag to unpack, just Will's old woolen coat, which she had put on at the Taylors' house. That seemed like weeks ago.

Bonner stood just inside the door, his arms extended downward, his hands clasped like a prison warden. A short, cylindrical prison warden.

"Your job is over now, Mr. Bonner," Bea Dot said. She'd hardly spoken a word to him on the train. She moved to the door as a gesture for him to leave. "Good-bye."

He stood his ground. "I'm paid to deliver you to Mr. Ferguson, ma'am. Looks like he's not home. I'll just wait for him."

Irritation simmered in Bea Dot's chest. She took a deep breath before speaking. "Well, I am home, and I must wash up and change. I can't invite you to stay. You'll have to wait for my husband on the porch."

Bonner nodded shortly and stepped outside. After shutting the door and turning the bolt, Bea Dot made her way through the house, lighting the lamps and surveying the home that was no longer hers. In the parlor, the dining room, the kitchen, she found glasses on tables and mantles, some holding an ounce or two of liquor, some empty, as if someone—Ben—had put them there and forgotten about them. Why hadn't California picked them up? Bea Dot found two empty bottles as well, and when she opened the icebox, a few smelly, unidentifiable scraps of food revealed the ice had long ago melted. So the grocer hadn't made deliveries either. Where was California? Or any sign of her? Bea Dot's body hummed with trepidation.

When she stuck her head in Ben's bedroom, the mess took her aback. Dirty clothes draped every stick of furniture, and a box from Ben's tailor, opened with tissue paper sticking out of it, sat on his unmade bed. Another box lay on the floor.

Her foreboding heightened, Bea Dot finally crept through the mausoleum of a house to her room. She found her bed made, her clothes (what was left of them) hanging in the closet, her jewelry box atop her bureau—just as she had left them, save for the thin layer of dust on every horizontal surface. She leaned in the doorway of her adjacent bathroom and gazed at her tub, remembering how she'd once adored a long soak in it. Now only eight weeks later, she'd give it up, and everything else in this modern home, in favor of a simple life with Will in Pineview. She silently prayed he was still alive.

But how could she return to him with Ben's threat hanging over her head? If she asked for her uncle's help, Ben would surely divulge the truth about her pregnancy. Uncle David and Aunt Lavinia would surely despise her for it, but she could promise to leave Savannah for good in exchange for their assistance. Then Will could be none the wiser. She'd be exchanging their love for Will's— a choice she hated to make, but a better choice than remaining in her failed marriage. Now was the time to act—while Ben was gone.

Her heart racing, she rushed to Ben's room and rifled through his bureau drawers and nightstands, searching for money. She found only a few coins before checking his suit coat pockets and pants. Finally, at the touch of soft, folded paper, Bea Dot's spirits soared. Not bothering to count the bills, she slipped them into her coat pocket, then rushed to the back door to make her getaway. But when she opened it, Ben's stocky frame blocked her way.

"Leaving so soon?" he sneered as he stepped over the threshold.

Before she could reply, he punched her in the gut. Clutching her stomach, she fell backward and winced at the sharp thump of her head on the floor before the room went black.

Her head pounding, Bea Dot opened one eye, then the other, to a view of the aged, slick bricks of the kitchen hearth. Almost instantly, she squinted at the sunlight peeking through the kitchen window. As she pushed herself to a seated position, the mantle clock chimed: seven-thirty. Ben must have dragged her into the kitchen and left her there all night.

Her head hammered as she rose and gripped the back of a kitchen chair. Dizzy, she swayed momentarily before shuffling through the dining room, wanting the comfort of her bed. A dry voice beckoned her from the parlor.

"Good morning, Mrs. Ferguson."

Bea Dot's skin turned cold as she stopped, and she inhaled deeply to quell a bout of nausea.

"Come in here and have a seat. I want to talk to you."

Still dizzy and drowsy, Bea Dot crept into the parlor. Her side ached, and dread hummed in her chest. Ben lounged on the sofa, empty bottles and glasses adorning the side tables like perverse bric-a-brac. However, he was washed, shaved, and dressed for work.

He gestured for her to sit, as if conducting a business meeting. Bea Dot carefully lowered herself into the chair across from him.

"And so the wife returns," he said, drawing a cigarette from his gold case before striking a match to light it. The smoke made Bea Dot queasy, and she held her hand to her nose to mask the odor. "Only four weeks late," he continued, his voice sober and business-like. "So glad I sent Bonner after you. Seems you'd lost your way."

Bea Dot sighed and rested her aching head on her hand. "I tried to contact you . . ."

Ben held up his hand to halt her explanation. "No need. I understand perfectly."

Bea Dot frowned and lifted her head. "You do?"

"Of course," he said. "But I'm not just talking about your venture into the wilds of middle Georgia. I'm talking about our entire marriage. No doubt, you've proven you can't be trusted, but I realize now you could not have turned out any differently, considering your upbringing. What other influence could a drunken father and a deceptive mammy have had on you?"

Bea Dot's jaw tightened. What was he getting at?

"I'm willing to acknowledge my part in the demise of our marriage as well," he continued as Bea Dot listened, perplexed. "After all, I knew of your deception early on, and still, I allowed that black biddy to remain in our home, all the while letting her convince you to spin your web of lies."

At the mention of California, Bea Dot's heartbeat sped with worry and confusion. Where was she?

"But all that will change, now that you're back and she's gone. I've asked Mr. Bonner to stay here indefinitely. While I am at work, you will remain at home under his guardianship. You will only leave the house with me, and over time, perhaps you can repair your image as a respectable lady of Savannah."

Most of Ben's edict passed her by, as concern for California eclipsed his words. Nausea and dizziness escalated with her fear. "Where is Cal? What do you mean she's gone?"

"I'm sure she's rotting in hell," Ben said, snuffing his cigarette in one of the empty whiskey glasses. "After all the damage she's caused this household, that flu was exactly what she deserved."

Bea Dot's stomach lurched, and she bolted from her chair, rushing to the kitchen, barely making it to the sink before she vomited. Gripping the counter's edge, she stood for a moment, waiting for the room to stop spinning before she rinsed her mouth and splashed water on her face. After regaining her composure, she returned to the parlor, her hand to her forehead in attempt to stop the pounding.

"Ben, how could you—"

"Oh, there's no need for histrionics," he interrupted. "It's good riddance, and you know it."

Bea Dot sank into the same chair she'd sat in before, wincing at Ben's condemnation.

"I have to admit, she was a good liar, and she taught you well. You had everyone convinced I was that baby's father, but what neither of you realized, my dear, is that I do know how to read a calendar. You were too far along in your pregnancy for that child to be mine. True, for a while I suspected you'd had a . . . liaison . . . with another man, but I eventually figured out the truth. That California always did talk too loud, and when I heard her tell you—you must have thought I had not come home yet—that the only other person who knew the truth was dead, I put two and two together."

Bea Dot's heart plunged into her stomach at Ben's recollection. The conversation he described occurred right after his first outburst at her, and she'd told Cal she feared he had discovered the truth about her baby. California had grasped both of Bea Dot's forearms and said, "Now you stop that worrying. Me and you's the only ones know the truth. Only other person know the truth put a bullet in his head."

"Of course," Ben said, "when I sent you that telegram and you returned straightaway from Pineview, you confirmed your deceit. By that time, I'd realized you're not the piece of trash I'd originally thought you were. Not exactly. I remembered how naïve you were growing up. You wouldn't have thought of that ruse by yourself. It had to have been that nigger woman put you up to it."

"Stop it, Ben, please." Bea Dot put her elbows on her knees and her head in her hands. For a year now, she'd pushed those dreadful memories deep inside. To bring them to the surface again made her whole body hurt.

"What did he do, rape you?"

"Stop."

"Let's just say he did," Ben said, rising. "The alternative is too disgusting to think about." He walked around her chair and put his hand on the mantle. After a long pause, he exhaled, then said, "Now, I must be off to work. I'm late as it is."

"Wait." Bea Dot lifted her head and tried to ignore the swirling room as she rose to face him. He regarded her with a curious, amused smile. Gripping the back of the chair for support, she said, "I should never have deceived you, and I'm sorry for that."

She expected him to soften at those words, but instead, he stiffened haughtily, as if considering whether to accept a belated apology.

"I think it would be best," she continued, trying to cease the shaking in her voice, "if we declared the marriage a failure. Clearly, no love survives between us. If you divorced me, you could marry someone else to make you happy."

Ben laughed cynically. A slight tic in his cheek warned Bea Dot that she'd lit the pilot light of his rage. Her muscles tensed at the signal, even though she tacitly urged herself to remain calm.

"You're so stupid, Bea Dot," he said. "I won't scandalize my family with a divorce, especially if it confirms you as a two-tim-ing whore. You've already made a fool of me by tricking me into this marriage. I'll not let you make me a bigger fool before all of Savannah." He stepped away from the mantle and pointed his fin-ger at her. Instinctively, she backed away. "Besides, you've made your bed. Now lie in it. And while you're at it, you can make a son. My son this time. My parents are expecting an heir."

The back door opened, and Bonner's frame glided into the hallway before slipping silently into the kitchen. Ben turned at the noise, then returned to Bea Dot. "I'm going to the office. While I'm at work, get this house in shape. It's a wreck." He turned to leave, but then faced her one last time. "But first get out of that cowgirl getup you're wearing and take a bath. You stink."

Bea Dot rubbed her palms down the fronts of her riding pants, wrinkled with wear, as if consoling the garment after Ben's insult. These clothes were her only link to Will. She wouldn't wear them again around Ben, but she refused to get rid of them. She slipped her hands into the pockets of Will's wool coat, and only then did she remember the dollar bills she'd taken from Ben's clothes the night before. Her spirits rose at the touch of them. Once she got a telegram to Will or Ralph, she'd call Uncle David, who could help her find a way out of this mess.

Ben walked out the back door, leaving Bea Dot in the par-lor. Using a tray from the tea cart, she picked up the empty whis-key glasses and carried them into the kitchen. She rinsed the sink, then filled it with warm, soapy water. Her dizziness had subsided, although her head still plagued her. As she silently washed and dried the glasses, Bonner sat at the table reading the newspaper. Bea Dot glanced at him once, but he took no notice of her. The paper's headline read, "Armistice! Hostilities End on Western

Front." A smaller headline to the side read, "Influenza Subsides. Face Mask Ordinance Lifted."

Bea Dot turned back to the sink, glad the war was over, but hardly in the mood to celebrate. She folded her dishtowel, then slipped past Bonner to the hallway and sat at the telephone stand. She asked the operator to connect her to the telegraph office, but as soon as she heard the words "Western Union" on the other end, a fat finger pressed on the receiver, disconnecting her call.

"How dare you?" Bea Dot glared at Bonner, whose cylindrical form stood over her in her small chair.

"Mr. Ferguson says you are not to make or receive any telephone calls," he said plainly.

Bea Dot's anger mixed with despair, which heightened her headache and left her at a loss for words. Instead of making matters worse by retaliating, she pushed past him and retreated to her bedroom. She slammed the door, then gripped the bedpost as a strong wave of dizziness nearly took her off her feet. After steadying herself, she shuffled into her bathroom. The sight of her toilet made her retch again, but afterward, her headache subsided.

She saturated a washcloth with cold water, then went to her bed and laid the cloth on her forehead. Her head swirled with worries about Will, grief over California's death, and anger at her husband, but fatigue eventually took over, and Bea Dot sank into a heavy sleep.

She awoke to knocking. Had the sound been real? Or had she dreamed it? Sunlight streaming through the shutters indicated that hours had passed. It must be late afternoon. Another knock. "Mrs. Ferguson? Are you in there?"

Bea Dot rose slowly. Her head still ached, but the pounding had stopped, and the dizziness subsided. She cracked open the door to find the round Mr. Bonner.

"So sorry to wake you," he said from underneath his mustache, "but Mr. Ferguson phoned. He says you're to be ready for dinner at his parents' house at eight."

Bea Dot studied the man with the tubular frame. Although his weasely eyes and small pointy nose enhanced his irritating demeanor, and even though his craftiness and haughtiness angered her, he was not aggressive. Bonner was not her enemy. Ben was. All she had to do was gain Bonner's trust, or at least his sympathy, and she might be able to slip by him.

"Are you all right, Mrs. Ferguson? Did you hear what I said?"

"Oh, yes," she replied. "I'll be ready."

At the sound of an odd rumble, Bonner patted his stomach. Blushing, he said, "I was wondering, well, Mr. Ferguson told me my meals would be provided during my stay here."

Bea Dot bit her tongue to keep from laughing. Where did he think he was, the DeSoto Hotel?

"Oh, would you like something to eat?" she replied flippantly. "Where are my manners? Please follow me." She hadn't eaten since she left Pineview, and she was hungry. But she didn't dare tell him that. Instead, she glided past him and led him to the kitchen, where she pretended to search her empty cupboards. "Let's see," she said as she looked. "I've been away for a while." She turned to look at him with a raised eyebrow. "As you know." Continuing to open cabinets, she said, "I'm afraid I don't have much." She pulled out a small canister and shook it and heard a faint brushing sound. "I do have a few grits. I could cook them for you. I have no butter for them, though."

Bonner stiffened, then said, "Mr. Ferguson and I agreed on a fee that included board and three full meals a day."

"Then I suggest you take this matter up with Mr. Ferguson," Bea Dot said with hand on hip, leaning on the countertop. "But you have sealed no contract with me. What's more, I can assure you that Mr. Ferguson gave no thought to your needs, only his."

"We had an agreement." Bonner shifted his weight. His whiny voice grated on Bea Dot's nerves.

"My husband has hired you to ensure that I stay locked up in this house with no access to my friends or family. In short, you're a private prison guard," she said. She paused to let him process the information. Then she asked, "Does he sound like someone who cares whether you eat a solid lunch?"

Bonner stammered, but offered no response.

"For now I can offer you a bowl of grits," Bea Dot continued, shaking the canister again, "but if you'll let me use my telephone, I can order food and a block of ice. I can have the milk delivery reinstated, and I just might be able to have it done in time for you to have supper." She omitted the fact that she hardly knew how to cook.

"That's not what Mr. Ferguson said . . ."

"We've already established that, but fine." Bea Dot placed the canister on the table. "Grits it'll be. But first I must bathe and change my clothes. I must look a sight. I've been wearing this outfit since Pineview."

She moved toward the kitchen door, but Bonner stopped her.

"All right," he said. "Make the calls. Do what you need to do."

Internally, Bea Dot beamed at her success, but she kept a straight face as she made her way to the telephone stand. As she placed orders, first with the grocer, then the iceman, then the dairy, she extended her conversations, hoping Bonner, who stood over her monitoring every call, would become bored and go back to his newspaper. But she'd expected too much too soon. She'd have to sneak in a call to the telegraph office later. Maybe tomorrow.

Chapter 28

Will inhaled fresh air—it felt so good to breathe normally again—and slowly ascended the three cinder-block steps of the small, weathered house. Lola, along with most other black residents of Pineview, lived on the north end of town in a section many Pineviewans called Boar's Head. Will never understood where the name came from.

He rested a second on the top step before knocking. As he waited for a response, he took in the worn, warped boards, brownish gray from decades without paint. A scrawny woman, about as old as the house, shuffled to the door and met Will's eyes without a word.

"Is Lola home? I'd like to speak to her, please."

The woman lifted one eyebrow, then turned her back on Will, calling into the darkness of the house. "Sista! You got comp'ny!" The volume of her screechy bird voice surprised Will. She shuffled her skinny, stooped form away from the door, leaving him to wait alone.

Lola appeared wearing a pink calico dress and a flour-sack apron splattered with grease. A red rag wrapped around her head. Although her eyes appeared less tired than they did the last time he'd seen her, they revealed uncertainty or maybe skepticism. He knew that look from his short time in France—the permanent countenance of someone who'd witnessed a horror most people could never imagine.

"Mr. Will, I surprised to see you here." Lola wiped her hands on her apron. "Come in, will you?" Her flat voice belied her reluctant hospitality.

"No, thank you," he said, quickly pulling his hands out of his coat pockets and folding them behind his back. "I'll only be a minute. I just wanted to thank you for tending me while I was sick."

Lola's stiff spine softened, and she tilted her head to one side.

"I would have thanked you earlier," he continued, "but you left Ralph's house so quickly. I'm sure you were eager to see your family."

"I 'preciate that, Mr. Will. I knew you would pull through. You had a strength about you. I ain't seen that in many patients, but you had it. Glad you all right now."

Will nodded and an awkward pause hung over them like a bad smell.

"I'm sorry to hear about your sister," he said, staring at his shoes.

"Thank you," she replied, putting her hand to her chest. "She in a better place now." After another awkward silence, Lola broke it. "I s'pose you going back out to the crossing."

"Yes."

"When you gone get yourself an automobile like all the other white folks?" Lola tilted her head toward Will's horse and wagon. "Make all that mail carrying a lot easier. And faster."

"Buster's got a long way to go before he's done." Will smiled sheepishly.

"You an old soul, ain't you, Mr. Will? Don't take to change like the other folks do."

Will shook his head and smiled faintly. He felt a camaraderie with Lola, a kinship he felt with no one else in Pineview. Somehow he knew she'd understand what he'd never been able to articulate to anyone else. "Lola, after what I went through in France, I don't belong behind the wheel of a motorcar."

"Maybe so," she replied, "but you done survived the Great War. Then you come home and survived the worst disease this town ever seen. Now I don't know 'bout you, but seems to me somebody up there want you around delivering the mail. Could get a heap more done in a motorcar."

"Food for thought," he said, unconvinced. He stepped down one step, paused, then turned to speak again. "But wouldn't that same principle apply to you?"

"What you mean?" She put her hand on her hip and frowned, but her voice revealed no anger.

"I hear you quit working for Dr. Coolidge," he said. "He needs you more than ever now that Netta's gone."

Lola huffed. "I done give him enough a my time. And my hide. All those weeks slaving away at his house. All for nothing. Didn't get paid one dime."

"True," Will said. "But how much do you think Ralph got paid for doing the same work at the hospital? All those nights he spent there with no time off? And those nurses? They worked the same hours as you. I don't think one of them had a chance to punch in a time card."

Lola stood silent.

"You were all in the same boat," he continued. "And Pineview would be in ruins if it weren't for you. We all owe you a debt of gratitude."

Lola's stature softened, but her frown remained. She leaned on the doorjamb and folded her arms in front of her. "What's that got to do with me working for Doc Coolidge?"

"Netta always wanted you to mind her baby," Will said. "I'm sure Ralph would consider it an honor if you did that."

"Hmph."

"Didn't he pay you a fair wage before the influenza hit?"

"Yeah."

"I'm sure he'd do it again if he had the chance."

Lola raised her chin and eyed Will for a beat before replying. "Heard he hired some woman from Atlanta."

"But he'd rather have you."

Lola sighed and gazed out into the distance. Will offered a weak smile and shrugged. He'd tried.

"Well," he said, "I just wanted to thank you for taking care of me, Lola. I won't take up any more of your time." He descended the last two steps, but just as he'd picked up Buster's reins, Lola called to him.

"If I was to work for Doc Coolidge," she said, "I'd need a horse. I been on my feet enough. Don't intend to walk to work no more."

"Okay." Will scratched his head, confused.

"You decide to get yourself a motorcar, you sell me that horse, and I can ride it to work."

Will grinned. "So you'll do it?"

"Didn't say that," she replied. "But I got to work somewhere. I'll buy that horse from you. For a decent price anyhow."

"Lola, if I ever decide to buy a car, you'll be the first to know."

Buster came to a stop at the crossing. Harley sat next to Will on the bench, his own horse tied to the back of the wagon.

"You feeling all right? You've been quiet for the past fifteen minutes," Harley said. He'd finally washed all the oil off his skin.

"I don't have all my strength back," Will said, "but I'm fine. I'm just a little tired."

They climbed down, and as they unloaded supplies and moved them indoors, Harley insisted on carrying the heavier crates. "Need help unpacking them?" he asked.

"Thank you, but no," Will said. "I'm not going to do that right now."

So Harley said his good-byes and untethered his horse. Will watched him ride away before unhitching Buster and taking him to the barn. Patting his horse on the neck, he said, "Been a long time since you stayed in your own stall."

Back inside, Will surveyed his store, then his small home. The floor had been scrubbed clean since Netta's death, and one bed frame sat empty of a mattress. The corner looked desolate without Bea Dot's trunk filling it. Of course, she would have taken it to the Taylors' house. He'd have been in a world of hurt if they hadn't stepped in to help Netta and Bea Dot. He didn't know how he'd ever thank them enough.

Throughout the house and store, little things reminded him of Bea Dot. The bottle of medicine still sat on the kitchen counter. When he went to the storage closet to roll up his pallet, he remembered the last night he'd spent on it with her. Even when he opened his ledger book, he found Bea Dot's handwriting. His chest ached from missing her, but his body hummed in anticipation of seeing her again.

He pried open a can of sardines and ate them quickly for lunch. Then he cleaned his teeth before setting off bareback on Buster toward the Taylors' farm.

Riding up the wooded path along the lake, he passed his grandparents' old cabin, where he'd killed the bobcat. Then he rode into a clearing and along the edge of a cotton field, where hired hands picked and stuffed the fluffy white fibers into their croker sacks.

As he approached the Taylors' house, a Model T in the yard told him Ralph Coolidge had arrived. When he knocked on the door, Terrence let him in and immediately left to help Thaddeus in the field. Will entered to find Ralph awkwardly holding his baby daughter. Eliza stood over him, baby Troy on her hip, giving instructions.

"Her neck's a lot stronger now, but you still got to support her head. And make sure you keep her wrapped up tight. She likes that."

"Eliza, I'm starting to think you don't trust me with her," Ralph teased.

"I have to admit, I'm gone miss this little angel," she said. "I ain't never had a daughter. It sure was nice to have a little girl in the house."

"I thank you again for minding her for me," Ralph said. "And I might call on you from time to time for advice."

"You're welcome to any time," she replied, "but Lola will know what to do. She's a natural with the young'ns."

"Actually, I've hired a nurse from Atlanta to help me," Ralph explained. "She arrives later this afternoon."

"But I thought Netta always wanted Lola to be her baby nurse," Will said.

"She did, but these days Lola doesn't want anything to do with me," Ralph said. "I can understand how she feels, with her sister dying and Lola being stuck in my house. It couldn't be helped, but she has to aim her resentment somewhere. Might as well be me." Ralph sighed and tickled Nettie's chin. She reached up and grasped his finger with her tiny fist.

"Try to talk to her one more time," Will suggested. "Maybe she's softened up a bit."

"I doubt it, but I'll give it a shot," Ralph said.

Will surveyed the room, but saw no evidence of the one person he came to see. "Eliza, where's Bea Dot?"

She broke her gaze on the baby and turned surprised eyes to Will. "Nobody told you?"

"Told me what?"

"She went back to Savannah," she said, shifting Troy to the other hip. "A few days ago."

Not wanting to jump to conclusions, Will tried to squelch the alarm in his gut. He turned questioning eyes to Ralph. "Why did she do that?"

"The last time I saw her was when she found out you were sick," Ralph said. "She thought you were in the hospital, and she wanted to see you." He shifted his eyes to Eliza as if expecting her to fill in the gaps of the story.

"Thaddeus took her to town that day," she said. "And he come home later saying that Bonner fellow gave her a telegram and then Bea Dot said she had to leave right away. Thaddeus tried to stop her, but she insisted on going."

"And she left the baby with you?" Will asked. That didn't sound like something Bea Dot would do. Who was that Bonner fellow?

Eliza nodded. "I don't think she had no choice, Will. She loved this young'n. She wouldn't just leave if it wasn't important."

Will's heartbeat sped now, fear for Bea Dot welling up in his chest. Her swift departure had something to do with her husband, he was sure. "She must be in trouble. We have to go get her."

Ralph shook his head slowly, a sad frown forming across his brow. Eliza chewed on her lower lip and jiggled her baby in her arms.

"I don't think you should, Will," Ralph said. "She went on her own accord, and she's a married woman. Maybe it's best that you leave well enough alone."

Electricity coursed through Will's veins at the mention of Bea Dot's marriage. "You don't understand," he said. "Her husband is a monster. That's why she came here in the first place."

"I knew she was having some troubles . . . ," Ralph said.

"Troubles my foot. He nearly killed her." Will's tone elevated at the thought. "We've got to get to her before it's too late."

Chapter 29

While a chicken roasted in the oven, Bea Dot filled her tub and washed the kitchen smell off her skin. Although she had her kitchen in order, for the past two days she'd walked a tightrope in her own home, bristling under Bonner's supervision and avoiding Ben's ire. Even in her private bath, she felt wound up like a toy.

She'd just managed to dry and put on her robe when Ben opened her bedroom door without knocking. "What's taking you so long?" he complained, pulling his watch out of his vest pocket. "We have to leave in ten minutes." Then he was gone again.

Bea Dot breathed deeply, trying to calm herself. *Just get through tonight*, she encouraged herself. *Don't do anything to make him angry. Then you can work on Bonner again tomorrow.*

She rifled through her closet, half-empty since she departed for Pineview, for something suitable to wear to an armistice celebration at the Wesleyan Club. In the back, she found the midnight-blue dress from her trousseau. The sleek lines of the bodice added an inch or two of height to her petite frame, and the beaded embroidery on the front panels dressed up the garment for a formal occasion. With matching stockings and shoes, Bea Dot almost resembled the girl she'd been a year ago before she married. She felt like a decade had passed since then.

The door burst open again, and Ben glared this time. "Let's go."

"Just one second," Bea Dot said as she took her wrap off its hanger. Opening her bureau drawer, she pulled out a drawstring purse and a pair of gloves, which she stuffed into it. Lastly, she opened her jewelry box and selected an ornate glass brooch, a gift from Aunt Lavinia. She pinned it to her shoulder, securing her wrap, as Ben nagged her to move along.

As they departed through the back door, Bea Dot glanced through the kitchen door and saw Bonner peeking into the oven at his supper. She wanted to tell him to give the bird fifteen more minutes, but Ben pushed her into the cold darkness toward his new touring car. In his hurry, he stumbled into Bea Dot, who hit her shoulder on the car door. The brooch cracked against the metal, and Ben clutched her arm, growling, "If you've scratched that paint, I'll slap you silly."

"I'm . . . I'm sure it's all right," she stammered before getting into the car. Her entire body hummed with trepidation, and she fought to calm her nerves as he cranked the engine and settled into the driver's seat. Maybe by morning he would have forgotten the scratch.

Weaving erratically around Savannah's squares, Ben blew the car horn at pedestrians daring to cross a street. Bea Dot's skin crawled at the eerie sight of people gathering in the squares to celebrate victory. Most shook hands and kissed cheeks, barefaced after weeks of wearing gauze masks. Still others maintained the cautionary measure and kept their mouths and noses covered. Ben had driven the touring car around two squares when he took an unexpected left turn.

"Where are we going?" Bea Dot asked. "I thought we were having supper at the club."

"We are," Ben replied, "but I have to mail a letter first."

"Now?"

"Yes, now," he said coolly. "I thought it best, considering your behavior the last two days."

"What are you talking about?" Bea Dot asked, frowning in confusion.

"It seems that you are determined to defy me, in spite of my specific instructions," Ben said, lowering the pitch of his voice, as if talking business with associates. "I know about your attempts to make telephone calls."

Bea Dot huffed in exasperation, on the verge of objecting to Ben's complaint, but then she caught herself and paused. No need to fuel his temper. "That's true. I did try to place a call to Aunt Lavinia," Bea Dot lied, "because I didn't realize that wasn't allowed. Mr. Bonner stopped me."

"That was not the only time you used the telephone," Ben said with a grimace.

"That's correct," she continued. "And I'm sure Mr. Bonner explained that he monitored me the entire time I placed my orders." Bea Dot's shoulders and back tensed with her efforts to remain calm and placate Ben. She felt as if she sat next to a rattle-snake, coaxing it not to strike.

Ben's frown loosened, which suggested his acceptance of her reason.

"You must let me phone the grocer, Ben," Bea Dot said gently. "Unless you want to accompany me to the store every other day."

Ben lifted an eyebrow as he glanced at her. Bea Dot wished she knew what his expression meant, but he said nothing more. Instead, he swerved the car to the side of the street next to the post office. After engaging the brake, he pulled an envelope from his inside coat pocket. He held it up, but in the darkness, Bea Dot couldn't make out the address.

"I don't believe you, my dear," he said. "I know you weren't call-ing your aunt; you were trying to reach the telegraph office, likely in attempt to reach that Dunaway fellow Bonner told me about. So I'm taking this precaution." He stepped out of the car and dropped the letter in the mailbox next to the post office door.

"I don't understand," she said when Ben returned to the driver's seat. A bed of ants had erupted inside her, and she clasped her hands together, trying not to let him agitate her.

"At first I wrote a letter to that Dunaway," Ben explained. "Then I figured there'd be no point of that. He's likely dead by now."

Bea Dot's throat tightened at the thought.

"Instead, I penned a letter to those people you were staying with, the Taylors," Ben said with a sneer.

Bea Dot felt the blood plummet from her face.

"In my letter, I've told them all about your past. I've informed them of the kind of person my wife really is."

"You didn't." Bea Dot felt as though he'd knocked the wind out of her. How much of the truth did he tell? And how much did he exaggerate? Her face burned with a combination of fear, shame, and defeat.

"I've apologized for any inconvenience you may have caused them to this point, and I warned them not to have any other contact with you. What's more, I've asked them to inform others of your tendency to lie and cheat. After all, I wouldn't want you to try to take advantage of anyone else the way you did me."

Ben put the car in gear and pulled it back onto the street. Bea Dot forced herself to breathe evenly, her face turned toward the window. Willing herself not to cry, she racked her brain for ways to return to that mailbox, to reach into it and pull Ben's letter out. With all her effort she hid her emotions, but never had she hated anyone as much as she hated Ben at that moment.

When the car reached the exclusive Wesleyan Club, white-gloved valets opened doors for Bea Dot and Ben, and Savannah's elite filed into the redbrick building in their tuxes and party dresses. Ben sauntered around to her side of the car and holding his arm out, said, "Smile, my dear. It's a party."

Numbly, Bea Dot followed him up the front steps. In the crowded ballroom, people shook hands, kissed, and hugged with a freedom Bea Dot had not witnessed in two months, as if armistice had wiped away any risk of contagion. She approached her mother-in-law and greeted her, forcing a weak smile. "Good evening, Mother Ferguson. How nice to see you."

Ben's mother kissed the air next to Bea Dot's cheek, then said, "So glad you came, my dear. All of Savannah's been wondering where Ben's wife ran off to."

Bea Dot ignored the slight and nodded.

Fingering the brooch on Bea Dot's shoulder, Mrs. Ferguson added, "My, what an interesting piece of costume jewelry. Did you find it up in, where is it? Pine Wood?"

"No, it was a gift," Bea Dot answered.

"Oh," Ben's mother cooed. "Well, I wouldn't know where to buy such things. I only wear true gemstones."

"Bea Dot, you're home!"

Bea Dot's heart soared at the sound of the familiar voice. She turned to find Aunt Lavinia, dressed in black and looking frail, the burden of grief poorly hidden behind her smile. She held her arms out to her niece, and Bea Dot fell into them with loving relief.

"Oh, Aunt Lavinia," Bea Dot moaned into her aunt's shoulder. As she fought tears, her throat contracted, keeping her from uttering more. But what else was there to say?

Aunt Lavinia pulled Bea Dot to arm's length and studied her with a loving tear at the corner of her eye. "I heard you'd returned," she said. "I wish you had come to visit me, but I understand why. Darling, I don't blame you."

Bea Dot put her hand to her mouth and fought her tears. Once she'd overcome the emotion, she said, "Oh, Aunt Lavinia, the first thing I wanted to do was come see you. But I couldn't. It's Ben. He's—"

"There you are, darling," Ben's voice resounded behind her. She felt the tight grip of his hand just above her elbow. "I thought you'd snuck away from me. Good evening, Mrs. Barksdale."

Aunt Lavinia tilted her head as she gazed at her niece. Bea Dot hoped her aunt would sense her tension. Lavinia then turned her eyes to Ben as she replied, "Thank you, Ben, and same to you."

"I was just going to escort my wife to the dinner table," he said with false joviality. "Do excuse us, please."

"Oh, dear, how sweet of you to wear the brooch I gave you. But I'm afraid it's broken." Aunt Lavinia fingered the piece on Bea Dot's shoulder. "Come. We'll go to the powder room and repair it." She took Bea Dot's other arm and tried to pull her away from Ben, but he tightened his grip on her.

"No need, Mrs. Barksdale," Ben said with a tight smile. "We're walking that direction. I'll escort her. Excuse us, please."

He pulled Bea Dot away from her aunt, and as they made their way through the crowd toward the powder room, Bea Dot looked over her shoulder and caught a glimpse of her aunt with a worried frown. Then Uncle David appeared at Aunt Lavinia's side, and she said something to him, still frowning, while pointing in Bea Dot's direction.

"Don't stray from me again," Ben murmured in her ear. His breath already reeked of whiskey. Then he called to his friend with a smile, "Roger! Good to see you, my man!"

Bea Dot waved to Roger before speaking. "What about the powder room?"

"I'll be just outside the door," he said. "Hurry. I don't want to stand here all night."

Bea Dot nodded, then slipped through the door. Immediately,

her muscles relaxed as she seated herself at the vanity. She removed the brooch from her shoulder and dropped it in her drawstring bag, then sat quietly on the cushioned stool and put her head in her hands. Relieved by the short respite from Ben, she still wondered how she would ever endure this evening. And even if she did, what then? In the past fifteen minutes, Ben had destroyed any chance she might have for an ordinary life. Now, added to the agonizing uncertainty about Will was the shame that he, if alive, would learn her disgusting secret. Bea Dot raised her head and stared blankly at her reflection. Was there any point in trying to get away?

An opening door washed in the noise of the party, interrupting her thoughts. A woman about Netta's age entered and sat before a mirror across the room. In her own looking glass, Bea Dot watched the woman dab the dew of perspiration from her upper lip and forehead.

"A crowded room gets mighty warm, doesn't it?" Bea Dot asked.

"Yes, it certainly does." The woman fiddled with her handkerchief without looking up. Then she coughed so severely, Bea Dot feared the woman would damage her throat. The woman covered her mouth with her hanky and coughed again, this time retching also.

Bea Dot bristled at the noise. "Can I get someone to help you?" she offered. "A friend or relative?"

"Thank you, but no," the woman said, rubbing her temples. "My husband is just outside. I think I'll ask him to take me home."

Good idea, Bea Dot thought. As the woman exited the powder room, Bea Dot wished her well, then shuddered at how close she sat to sickness. As she rose to leave, she stopped at the sight of the woman's handkerchief, crumpled atop the opposite vanity. She first recoiled from it, but upon second thought she sat on the woman's stool and stared at the lacy white fabric, its center soiled with the woman's sputum. She'd had a temperature, a headache, a cough—every ailment pointed to influenza.

The hanky teased her. It could be her key to escape from Ben. But did she have the nerve to use it? She shook her head with shame, rose, and stepped to the door. But before she pulled it open, she lunged back to the vanity and opened wide the mouth of her drawstring purse. She retrieved the brooch, which she used to sweep the soiled handkerchief into the bag. Then she dropped the brooch back in and pulled the strings tight, muttering, "Just in case."

Bea Dot endured the rest of the party in a daze. Ben attached himself to her side and craftily steered her away from conversations with any of her old friends. She'd managed to speak to Aunt Lavinia and Uncle David once, but Ben stood guard, her elbow in one hand, a glass of whiskey in the other. When Aunt Lavinia had invited them to dinner the next week, Ben quickly replied, "Oh, what a shame. We already have prior commitments. Some other time perhaps." Then he'd led her away.

Never one to turn down a drink, Ben insisted they stay until the party's end. When they'd finally returned home, Bea Dot was exhausted, not only from the erratic car ride, but also from her tempest of emotions. She'd hardly been able to mourn California's death, and the worry over Will's health tormented her. But now with Ben's cruel letter on its way to Pineview, she felt spent, defeated, hopeless. She'd almost hoped he'd crash the car and kill them both.

After Ben parked behind the house, Bea Dot entered through the back door and dropped her drawstring purse on the telephone stand in the hallway. Without a word to her husband, she made her way to her bedroom, but Ben caught up to her and grabbed her arm, twisting her around to face him. With a grunt, he pressed his fat, wet lips onto hers and kissed her in that clumsy, besotted manner that had always disgusted her. She tried to shake away from him, but he gripped her tighter, then lost his balance and fell forward, pushing Bea Dot in front of him. She landed on her back on the sofa with Ben on top of her, his face pressed into her neck and his heavy breathing snorting into her ear. She turned her face to avoid the odor of liquor and cigars and pushed against his chest as his hand snaked up her dress and fumbled with her stockings. He was too heavy for her, too drunk to realize she was resisting. Fortunately, alcohol got the best of him, and his hand went still. Within seconds, he was snoring into the pillow behind Bea Dot's neck.

Wrinkling her nose, she wriggled from underneath him and thumped to the floor. Then, leaving him unconscious in the parlor, she tiptoed to her room. At a faint sound across the hall, she turned and peered through the shadows. She heard nothing more, but could have sworn she saw a movement by the guest room door.

"Mr. Bonner?" she asked hoarsely.

Hearing no reply, she slipped into her room and went to bed. She awoke three hours later to her husband's furious bellow. "What the hell is this? What kind of a fool do you think I am?"

What is it this time? she wondered as she tied her robe and opened the bedroom door. At the same time, Mr. Bonner emerged from his bedroom, the tail of his nightshirt overlapping his trousers. Ben, still intoxicated, stood swaying at the telephone stand. He shook his fist, which held Bea Dot's drawstring bag.

"You've been using the telephone!" he screamed. Then he railed at Bonner. "I told you to keep an eye on her!"

"Ben, no," Bea Dot said calmly, trying to dispel his temper. "We've all been asleep. You fell asleep on the sofa, and we've been in our rooms." Her heart pounded, not so much at his fury, but at the notion that her husband might be not only brutal but also insane.

"Liar," he said. "Who did you call? Someone back in that podunk town, I'm sure." He sprayed saliva as he spoke, and a drop of spit clung to his lower lip as he ripped open the drawstring. "What do you have in here? A secret telephone number? An address?"

"I left the bag on the telephone stand when we came home tonight. Didn't you see me?" Her neck and shoulder muscles contracted at the strain of trying to calm him.

"The operator." Bonner stepped forward, his palms facing forward in submission. "I'll ask if any calls have been made from this number tonight." He went to the hallway, and Bea Dot listened as he picked up the earpiece. "Hello, operator . . . yes, I know it's late . . ."

Still suspicious and seething, Ben plunged his fat hand into her bag, ripping its seams as he did so. He pulled out the soiled handkerchief and tossed it onto the floor. Then he plunged his hand back into the bag.

"Dammit!" he yelled, yanking his hand away with Bea Dot's broken brooch puncturing the heel of his palm so deeply that it was embedded into his hand. He tugged the brooch away from his skin and hurled it across the room. He picked up the handkerchief and wiped away the blood. "You meant for me to do that," he growled through gritted teeth.

"No," Bea Dot said quietly, almost hopelessly, as she knew he would not believe her.

Still huffing like an angry bull, he stepped toward her, his fierce eyes still focused on hers. Bonner stepped between them, facing Ben.

"The operator says no telephone calls have come from this number tonight," he said. "It's all been a misunderstanding."

Ben paused, then, still frowning, backed away a step. Bea Dot exhaled and put her hand to her chest. Never would she have thought she'd be thankful for Bonner's intervention.

"Mrs. Ferguson, you should go back to bed. It's very late. Mr. Ferguson, if you'll allow me, I'll help you dress your hand. That's a nasty wound." Bonner took Ben by the elbow and eased him down the hall away from Bea Dot. Relieved to have weathered Ben's storm, she turned to go back to bed. Suddenly, she lurched forward, as the heel of Ben's boot shoved her backside. She fell against her doorframe, hitting her chin and biting her lip.

"Mrs. Ferguson!" Bonner rushed to her side and took her arm as she put her hand to her mouth.

"Leave her alone," Ben boomed, and Bonner immediately stepped back. Bea Dot listened for their footsteps to disappear before she moved again.

Back in her room, she checked the clock before returning to bed. It was a quarter after three. As she reclined on her pillows, she sighed and laid her arm over her forehead. Her shoulders pinched at her, and an ache radiated up her neck and to the back of her head. She tried to will the tension away, but at the same time, she knew it would return at each encounter with Ben. How would she ever manage a way out of this mess when she constantly tiptoed around him? She'd have to sleep—or pretend to sleep—well into the morning after Ben left for work. Maybe during his absence she could manipulate Bonner into opening a window of escape.

When she opened her eyes, the clock showed 8:00 a.m. She listened intently, hoping Ben was out of the house. Hearing nothing, she rose and bathed before dressing for the day. She put on a spring dress with long sleeves, entirely inappropriate for November, but since she'd ruined most of her clothes in Pineview, she had little else to wear. She wrapped a crocheted shawl around her shoulders for warmth.

As she stepped to her bedroom door, she spied a slip of paper on the floor. A smile spread across her face as she read it:

Dear Mrs. Ferguson,
After leaving a letter of resignation with your husband, I
depart. When he hired me, I mistakenly believed his dispar-
aging descriptions of you, but recent events convince me of my

error. I cannot in good conscience work for a violent man. As I suspect he will remain asleep for some time, I strongly recommend that you take yourself to a friend or relative who can offer you a safe place to stay. I wish you well.

Kermit Bonner

Bea Dot leapt to her closet and retrieved her satchel, putting in it only Will's mother's riding pants and shirt, plus the small stash of money she'd taken from Ben's pocket a few days prior. If she hurried, she could dash out the door before Ben awoke. Quickly, she fastened the latch on the bag, but with her hand on the bedroom door, she halted at Ben's booming voice.

"Bonner!"

Her pulse quickening, Bea Dot slid her satchel under the bed, then steeled herself before greeting her husband.

"Bonner!" he called again, obviously not yet aware of his employee's departure. Well, she wouldn't be the bearer of the news. Let him discover that on his own.

Bea Dot stepped into the hallway and followed her husband's voice into the parlor, where she found him dressed for work but looking haggard with red-rimmed eyes. He rubbed his forehead with a bandaged hand.

"What's the commotion about?" Bea Dot asked, feigning ignorance.

"Where's Bonner?" he asked.

"I have no idea," she lied. "Have you checked his room?"

"Of course I checked his room, you idiot." Ben glared at her. "I've checked all over the house."

Bea Dot doubted that but said nothing.

Ben plopped on the sofa and put his head in his hands.

"Are you all right?" she asked. "You look awful."

"My head's killing me," he groaned. "That cheap liquor at the club."

Bea Dot nodded, lifting the corner of her mouth. True to form, Ben blamed his hangover on the alcohol, not his drinking it.

"Have you taken any medicine?"

"Of course I have," he snapped back.

Bea Dot backed away slowly at his hostility. Her back tensing again, she spoke softly. The sooner she could get him off to work, the sooner she could leave herself. "Let me cook you some breakfast. That might make you feel better before you go to work."

"I can't go to the office until I find Bonner," he said, standing, clenching his fists.

"He may be in the bathroom," Bea Dot suggested. "Did you check the yard? Maybe he had to go outside for something." She wished Bonner had delayed his departure an hour or two. At least that way both of them could have left unnoticed. She moved to the kitchen, hoping Ben would forget Bonner for a moment. He followed her as far as the breakfast table, but as she took the skillet out of the cabinet, he asked, "What's this?"

She turned to find him holding an envelope, which he'd taken off the mantle. Anticipating his rage, she slipped toward the door as he tore the envelope open. As he read the letter of resignation, his breathing intensified, and Bea Dot braced for his fury, hoping Bonner's letter omitted any mention of last night's outburst. Upon finishing the letter, Ben crumpled it in his hand, and Bea Dot gripped the doorsill as she watched sweat form on his forehead.

"That son of a bitch," he growled as he threw the ball of paper at her. "Left in the middle of the night." He pounded his fist on the table, then turned his glare to her. "You had something to do with this, didn't you?"

"Of course not," she said. She picked up Bonner's wadded-up note and read it. Fortunately, he'd simply told Ben that for personal reasons he had to rush back home to Macon.

The telephone rang. Ben ignored it, his shoulders rising and falling as he seethed. It rang two more times before Bea Dot spoke. "Am I allowed to answer that?"

"Shut up," he snapped before moving to the phone.

Bea Dot rolled her neck to relieve the stress. She felt like she'd been in an arena with an angry bull. Listening to his side of the conversation, she deduced Ben's father had called inquiring why he was late.

"I know . . . I know . . . ," Ben said. "I'll be there for the meeting, don't worry."

Bea Dot's spirits lifted. He had no choice now but to leave the house, and she could go to Aunt Lavinia's.

He returned to the kitchen, grumbling. When he kicked over a chair, Bea Dot forced herself to breathe evenly so Ben wouldn't notice her amusement. Stifling a smile, she said, "Let me make you some eggs before you go."

"I told you to shut your mouth!" he screamed, picking up the bud vase on the kitchen table. He hurled it at her, but missed, and the porcelain shattered on the wall next to the door.

As the shards of porcelain fell to the floor, Bea Dot's tension snapped, and her fear disappeared. Instantly, she saw a two-year-old before her. For that matter, Ben's attitude and behaviors had always been puerile. She had allowed a man to control her when he obviously had no control over himself. With that discovery, she finally recognized what she wished she'd seen when Bonner introduced himself.

She didn't need Bonner's departure to open the door to her release. She could have walked out any time. What would Bonner have done? Tackled her on the street? She doubted it. He hadn't even the courage to resign to Ben's face, but instead left in the cover of darkness, leaving Bea Dot to face Ben's ire alone. Why, even when he'd forced her to come home, he'd done it with Ben's threatening letter, not with his own force.

Of course, Ben was a greater obstacle, but he'd already ensured her friends in Pineview would despise her. What did she have to lose? Although Ben glared at her with sweat at his hairline, for once she didn't shrink in fear. Instead, she laughed. She couldn't help it.

"What's so funny?" Ben screamed like a petulant brat, but the strain on his vocal chords provoked a fit of coughs that doubled him over.

This time Bea Dot did back away, her fear returning, but for a different reason. Ben's headache was no hangover. Quickly she turned her back on her husband and rushed to her room for her satchel. She had to get out immediately.

Once his coughs subsided, though, Ben followed her and caught up to her at the front door. "Where the hell do you think you're going?"

"Aunt Lavinia's house," she said as she reached for the doorknob.

"Oh, no you don't." He snatched her satchel away and tossed it behind him, where it landed on the floor with a thud. "You must be crazy thinking you can just walk away from here. Get back in that kitchen."

"No."

Ben gripped her arm and slung her toward the interior of the house. "You'll do what I say or you'll be sorry."

"I'm already sorry," she replied. Energy rushed through her veins, and her whole body shook at the newness of confronting her abuser. "You were right. I was wrong to mislead you, and I'm sorry I married you. We've both been miserable."

He backed away a step at her newfound confidence.

"But I am not afraid of you anymore," she continued. "You have taken everything away from me. You took my child, not that

I wanted it, but you killed it. You've cut me off from my only living relatives, and you've destroyed any chance of happiness with the one man who actually loved me."

At that remark, Ben's glare returned, and with it the tic in his cheek. But she continued.

"You are so angry that you want to make me as unhappy as you are. Well, I won't let you do that anymore." She picked up her bag and strode toward the front door, unsure whether he'd let her pass or not.

He didn't. Instead, he grabbed her at the collar and pushed her back to the wall, just next to the front door. There he pinned her, his face to hers. Bea Dot turned her face away as he panted putrid breath in her face, his fingers wrapping around her throat.

"I could snap your neck in a heartbeat."

"Then do it," she replied with a shaky voice. She closed her eyes, praying her hunch was right, that Ben wouldn't kill her. If he did, he'd have no one left to punish. His pause lasted an eon, but then his fingers tightened, and pressure built in her face as the room went dark. But then she heard a bang, and Ben's hands flew away. As she sucked in air, her vision cleared. Two men tumbled on the floor, then broke apart.

"What the hell?" Ben shook his head as he pushed himself to a seated position. Then he coughed violently.

Will Dunaway rose quickly and rushed to Bea Dot's side. He was thinner than before, paler too, but he was alive, and she couldn't have been happier to see anyone. He frowned at her in concern. "Are you all right?"

She nodded.

"Let's go now," he said, taking her hand and pulling her toward the door. "Your aunt Lavinia's waiting."

Recovered from his coughing spell, Ben lunged and grabbed the back of Will's collar, pulling him close. Then he drew back and punched Will's rib cage, sending him crumpling to the floor and gasping for breath.

"No!" Bea Dot cried as she fell to his side. She tried to help him up, but Ben gripped her waist to pull her away from him. Fighting back, she yelled, "Let go of me, you monster!" She managed to slip out of his hands for a moment, but Ben came back, this time with more force. As he pulled her up, she clutched at Will's legs, resisting Ben's strength, as her fingers searched the top of his boots. Just as they found what they were looking for, Ben yanked her from the floor and turned her to face him. Gripping the front of her dress with one hand, he drew back his other to slap her, but stopped short when Bea Dot pointed Will's hunting knife at his neck.

"Let go of me this instant," Bea Dot said, her voice low like a bobcat's growl.

Ben hesitated, so Bea Dot pressed the knifepoint into his neck, just enough to draw a speck of blood. "I'll kill you if you don't."

He stood with his back to the wide open front door. Bea Dot locked eyes on him, not daring to turn to check on Will, but she heard raspy breath and movement behind her. She hoped he could stand.

Ben's expression transformed from anger to surprise to utter confusion, and even though he loosened his grip on her, he didn't let go. She pressed the knife at his neck and narrowed her eyes, refusing to break her gaze.

Aunt Lavinia's voice sliced through the tension.

"What in the world is happening here?" she asked as she stepped into the door. Her eyes widened when she saw the knife, but she checked her surprise instantly and turned to Bea Dot. "Darling, put that knife away before you hurt someone," she said, touching Bea Dot's forearm. "Where did you get this thing? Does it belong to Mr. Dunaway?" Gently she pulled Bea Dot's arm away from Ben until it was extended to her side.

Hunched and bleeding from the mouth, Will stepped forward and took the knife from Bea Dot's hand. Aunt Lavinia slid between Bea Dot and Ben, and though she kept her eyes on him, she spoke to her niece. "Gather your things, dear. I think you should come home with me."

Bea Dot backed away slowly, then turned to Will for reassurance. When he nodded, she picked up her satchel, then stood at his side. He took it from her, before putting his arm over her shoulders. Aunt Lavinia maintained her gaze at Ben, but not with anger or threats. Instead her face was as congenial as if she were greeting a visitor to her house.

"We'll be going now," she said. Then she took Bea Dot's arm and led her toward the front door. Will followed.

Just as they reached the front door, Ben called to her. "If you walk out that door, Mrs. Ferguson, you can be sure all of Savannah will learn your filthy secret."

The exertion provoked another coughing spell.

Bea Dot froze for an instant, then relaxed and faced her husband for the last time. His shoulders shook as he coughed into his bandaged hand. Then she turned her back on him and descended the front steps, flanked by Will and her aunt. She felt lighter than she'd felt in two years.

"Gossip?" Aunt Lavinia asked. "That's what he's holding over you?" She shook her head in amusement. "That won't get him far. That man's got more dirt on him than a ditch digger's shovel."

Chapter 30

Bea Dot's uncle David pulled two cigars from his coat pocket as he descended the club's front steps. After offering one to Will, which Will declined, he stuffed the other in his mouth, stopping on the sidewalk to light it. His pink cheeks undulated as he puffed life into the tobacco.

"Thank you for joining me for lunch today, Will." Mr. Barksdale puffed sweet smoke from his mouth and nostrils as he spoke. He strode in the direction of his Jones Street home.

"The pleasure is all mine, sir," Will replied, almost jogging to keep up with his host. The man had legs longer than a life sentence. "The meal was quite a treat, and I appreciate your loaning me this coat and tie." In truth, Will couldn't wait to loosen the silk noose around his neck.

"Not at all," Mr. Barksdale said. "Least I could do for the man who saved my niece's life."

"Actually, sir, that was Mrs. Barksdale." Will huffed and puffed as the two men walked. "She handled Ben like a snake charmer."

"Ha, ha!" Mr. Barksdale's laugh echoed off the Jones Street homes. "Maybe I should send my wife to Atlanta to meet with the General Assembly!" He laughed again and clapped Will between the shoulder blades, which sent Will into a bout of coughing. Bent over at the waist, Will hacked into the cracks of the brick-paved street.

"Good heavens, boy. Are you all right? I didn't think I'd hit you that hard."

Shaking his head no, Will coughed a few more times before straightening.

"I'm fine," he said gruffly. "Since the influenza, my lungs have cleared, but every now and then they want to give me a little reminder."

"Well, take it easy, son." Mr. Barksdale resumed walking, but slowed his pace. "If anybody deserves a respite, it's you, what with your military service and then this influenza ordeal."

"I should have said so sooner, Mr. Barksdale." Will's face reddened as he walked and talked. "Ralph told me you were instrumental in securing my discharge. I thank you for that."

"No need." Mr. Barksdale waved his hand as if swatting mosquitoes. "With your injury, you would have come home eventually. I just lit a little fire under Senator Holder to speed up the process. Good thing too, if the papers are right. Camp Gordon took a beating during the epidemic. If you had caught the flu there, you might not have survived." He puffed again on his cigar. "Besides, I hear you looked after my Netta and Bea Dot. It's I who should thank you."

They approached the Barksdale home, and Mr. Barksdale stopped at the front walk. He dropped his cigar to the sidewalk and ground it with his heel. Pointing to the house, he said, "If I know my wife, she is still holding Bea Dot captive with women's talk."

"They have much catching up to do," Will said. He would love to be a fly on the wall when Bea Dot told her aunt about the bobcat attack.

"I have some business to attend to," Mr. Barksdale continued. "You might be able to help me with it. How about you and I give the women more time to themselves?"

"Whatever you say, sir."

"We'll take my car." Mr. Barksdale pointed to the carriage house behind his home. Inside sat a black automobile, its headlamps peering through the open double doors like round eyes. "Chevrolet Series H," Mr. Barksdale boasted. "They call it the Royal Mail. It's the only one in Savannah." He sauntered toward the carriage house, and Will followed. "All my friends drive Model Ts, so I went with something different. What do you drive?"

"Well, sir . . ." Will struggled for an answer. Although friends constantly urged him to purchase an automobile, Mr. Barksdale was the first to assume he'd already done so. In fact, the only person who hadn't pushed him to drive a car was Bea Dot. "I still use my horse and wagon. It suits me fine."

"You have a mail route, in addition to your trading post, correct?"

"Yes, sir."

"And you manage to fit in all that work with a horse and wagon?"

"So far, sir. Of course, Bea Dot has been a big help."

Mr. Barksdale cocked his head and studied Will for a moment. Will didn't know what felt more confining, his necktie or Mr. Barksdale's gaze.

"Will, have you ever fallen off a horse?"

"Yes, sir."

"Yet you still ride one, correct?"

"Yes, sir." He got Mr. Barksdale's implication, but the man didn't understand the difference between his analogy and what had happened at Belleau Wood. He inhaled deeply to squelch his resentment.

"Don't let that war define you, son." Mr. Barksdale stepped closer to Will and put a hand on his shoulder. Its warmth seeped through the wool of Will's suit jacket. "I can't begin to understand the hell you endured over there, but you've got a rich life ahead of you. Don't carry those burdens along the way."

Easier said than done, Will thought, but he responded with a polite "Yes, sir." Resentment gave way to ambivalence. Will had always hated the way people told him what to do and how to feel. However, Mr. Barksdale's advice was different. In one breath he'd acknowledged the horrors of war, yet in the next he'd made it sound so simple to overcome.

"Let's take a ride, shall we? You turn the crank, and I'll set the spark control lever." After firing the engine, Will settled in the passenger seat, his stomach a bucket of crickets. He eyed the gearshift warily as Mr. Barksdale shifted the gears and moved the car forward. Perhaps the open air helped, but Will found the ride surprisingly more comfortable than he anticipated. Not until the motorcar reached the corner of Jones and Whitaker did Will wonder where he was going.

"What business am I helping you with today, sir?"

"Not a meeting you'll relish," Mr. Barksdale said. "I need you to go with me to talk to Ben Ferguson."

Loathing washed over Will, and he turned the corner of his mouth in disgust.

"I'm not hot in the pants to talk to him myself," Mr. Barksdale explained. "But for Bea Dot's sake, I must. I'll not have him causing her any more trouble—not for her or my family."

"What do you intend to tell him?"

"I mean to convince him that he should give Bea Dot a quiet divorce." Mr. Barksdale's face had turned from a stern countenance to a scowl. Will understood the expression. The thought of Ben Ferguson easily provoked it. "If I must, I'll tell him that if he resists I'll charge him with attempted murder. I want you there as a witness."

"I see." The crickets in Will's stomach jumped again as he doubted Ben would take Mr. Barksdale's suggestion easily.

"This situation between him and Bea Dot might get uglier before it gets better," Mr. Barksdale said, "but I've got to give it a try."

Will nodded, and the two rode in silence the remaining few minutes as the Chevrolet bumped along the few blocks of Whitaker Street to the Ferguson home. Will eyed the pastel-colored porches adorned with gingerbread, and he wondered at Bea Dot's ability to leave such refinement and feel at home in his country trading post.

The Chevrolet slowed, and Mr. Barksdale pulled it to the side of the street in front of Bea Dot's house. Will gazed at the wide brick steps leading up to the front porch and heavy oak door. This house was an unfamiliar part of Bea Dot—one he didn't care to know.

"Let's go in," Mr. Barksdale said, holding the passenger door open. Will hadn't noticed him getting out of the car.

Slowly Will got out himself, and the two approached the front steps, but a strange sight halted Will, and he grabbed Mr. Barksdale's arm.

"Why is the front door open?" he asked, the back of his neck prickling with suspicion.

Mr. Barksdale waved away Will's question. "Everybody knows Ben likes his whiskey. He probably left it that way."

"At two in the afternoon?"

"Wouldn't surprise me." Mr. Barksdale loped up the walk and ascended the front steps, and Will followed. After knocking twice on the door, Mr. Barksdale called in. "Ben? David Barksdale here. I need to talk to you."

After pausing for a response, Mr. Barksdale pushed the door open, and Will followed him into the foyer where he'd recently wrestled Bea Dot's louse of a husband.

"Ben? Are you here?" He stepped farther into the house.

"Maybe he's not home," Will suggested.

"Let's just look and see. I'd rather not come back here again." He crept through the foyer and into the dining room, with Will close behind. They peered into the parlor and then the kitchen, but found no one.

"I don't think he's here," Will persisted, discomfort swelling within him. What would Ben do if he came home and found him and Mr. Barksdale snooping around?

Mr. Barksdale stepped into the back hall and then stopped short.

"Oh, good God!" he exclaimed as he buried his nose in his elbow.

Will rushed to his side and peered over the man's shoulder. On the floor next to an overturned telephone stand lay Ben Ferguson, gray in the face and struggling for breath. A pink line of sputum ran from the corner of his mouth and over his pudgy, bluing cheek. He smelled of sweat and urine. The candlestick telephone lay just out of reach, its earpiece disconnected from the receiver. Ben weakly lifted his hand in Will's direction.

"Get out of here. Now." Will grabbed Mr. Barksdale by the elbow and pulled him back into the kitchen. "He's got influenza."

The two men locked eyes for a beat. Then Mr. Barksdale stammered, "We . . . we must call a doctor."

He stepped toward the hallway, but Will stopped him again.

"Don't use this phone," he warned. "Go next door and call a doctor from there."

"What about you?" Mr. Barksdale asked.

"I've already had it," Will said. "If Ralph Coolidge is right, then I can't get it again."

Mr. Barksdale stood motionless, staring at Ben's deathly face.

"Go," Will said. *Before I change my mind.*

Mr. Barksdale ran out the back door, and Will turned his attention to Ben, who curled into a ball as a coughing spell turned him into a hacking, choking mess. Will turned his back until the fit subsided. Then, removing his suit jacket, he stepped over Ben and stooped at his feet, covering them with the coat. Then he grabbed Ben's ankles and tugged, pulling him into the adjoining bedroom.

Littered with whiskey bottles and soiled towels, the room reeked with the same sour odor. Bed linens lay crumpled in a pile on the floor. As Will tugged Ben toward the bed, he knocked the sick man's head against the door frame. He couldn't help feeling a touch of satisfaction from the thump.

He stopped to rest once Ben lay on the floor next to the bed. Then he stooped and grabbed him under the arms, lifting Ben's torso to heave him up to the mattress. But then he stopped himself, remembering the days he lay lingering on Ralph Coolidge's floor, delirious with fever and clenching with the excruciating pain of each breath. A memory flashed through his mind of Bea Dot, her back against the wall, struggling against Ben's choking grasp. Will released his grip, and Ben dropped to the floor with a groan.

"I can't leave you here to die," he said. "But I'll be damned before I make you comfortable."

He stepped over the ailing drunkard and went to the kitchen, where he found a cake of soap in the window over the sink. He scrubbed his hands thoroughly, not so much to protect himself from contagion, but to wash any residue of Ben Ferguson from his body. Retching coughs sounded from the bedroom, and Will wandered into the front of the house to escape the disgusting noise. Mr. Barksdale and a doctor appeared at the front door just as Will reached it. Flustered, the white-haired, red-eyed doctor skipped any introductions.

"Where is he?"

"Back in the bedroom." Will pointed his thumb behind him, and the physician rushed around him toward his patient.

"Thought we'd seen the last cases . . ." The doctor's voice trailed away as he disappeared into the back of the house.

Mr. Barksdale stood at the threshold, breathing heavily.

"I just ran to his house," he explained. "He lives just a couple of blocks away."

Will nodded, then stepped onto the porch with Mr. Barksdale. He sat on the top step and rested his elbows on his knees, his face in his hands.

"Call me the devil," Will said to his feet, "but I hope we were too late to save him."

Mr. Barksdale sighed and joined Will on the step. He put a hand on Will's shoulder, but said nothing. After a few minutes of silence, Will turned his gaze to Bea Dot's uncle.

"Earlier, you said Ben likes his whiskey, as if everyone in town knows he's a drunk."

Mr. Barksdale nodded sadly, his forearms resting on his knees. He gazed at Forsyth Park across the street for a few seconds before answering.

"No boy needed a sibling as much as that one," he said. "His parents made sure he never wanted for anything, never had to work for anything. Officially, he's employed at his father's shipping firm, but he spends most of his time at the club paying the tab for anyone who will drink with him. He's always been an arrogant, spoiled son of a bitch. Not a drop of responsibility."

Nothing Mr. Barksdale said surprised Will. The few minutes he'd spent with Ben Ferguson gave just the impression Bea Dot's uncle described. The only thing he couldn't understand was how Bea Dot ended up as his bride.

"How long has Bea Dot been married to him?"

"Not a year yet," Mr. Barksdale said sadly, still staring at the park. "About ten months. We never understood it. She's such a sweet, beautiful girl. Lavinia always said Bea Dot could have any man she wanted."

"And that's who she wanted?" Will asked.

"She insisted on marrying Ben. Right away too. Wouldn't let her aunt plan a wedding. In fact, she and Netta argued about it, and that's why Netta didn't come to the ceremony."

"Oh." Will hadn't realized Bea Dot and Netta had fought. No wonder their time at the crossing was so strained.

"I thought she might be worried about money," Mr. Barksdale continued. "My brother—her father—had just recently passed." He paused for a moment, then continued. "But I told her I'd always take care of her." His brow creased as he spoke, and Will nodded, now realizing the enormous sorrow the Barksdale family had endured over the last year. "We knew about his drinking. If we'd known how . . . brutal . . . he was, we'd never have stood for it."

Mr. Barksdale buried his face in his hands, and Will put a consoling hand on the man's back, fully understanding the heaviness of feeling responsible for another's tragedy.

Chapter 31

"A unt Lavinia? Where are you?"

"In here, dear."

Bea Dot followed the voice to the parlor, where she found her aunt seated on the divan, reading a magazine.

"This article says that we should substitute the word 'parlor' for 'living room,'" she said with a puzzled look on her face. "I think that sounds right odd, don't you?"

"How do I look?"

Aunt Lavinia raised her face, and Bea Dot turned, allowing her aunt a full view of her borrowed clothes. Aunt Lavinia clasped her hands over her chest and smiled warmly. "I think those will do just fine for now. They're a little outdated, and I was afraid they'd be long. But I'm sure they're warmer than the frock you had on yesterday."

Bea Dot ran her hand down the front of Netta's old wool skirt. Aunt Lavinia had found it and the narrow-waisted shirt in Netta's former armoire. The outfit was out of fashion, but not as much as Aunt Lavinia's 1899 hairstyle. Besides, Bea Dot valued the clothes for sentimental reasons.

"If you'd like, I'll ask Penny to alter them for you," Aunt Lavinia offered. "They might be more comfortable until you get some clothes of your own."

Bea Dot doubted she would have new clothes any time soon. All the money she had was the small pack of bills she took from Ben's pocket. Even that wouldn't last long.

"Where's Will?" Bea Dot asked, noticing the quiet in the house.

"He went with your uncle David," Aunt Lavinia answered, marking her place in the magazine, then laying it on the table. "Some errands they had to attend to. They should be back soon." She patted the divan seat. "Come sit with me. We still haven't had a chance to visit."

As much as Bea Dot appreciated her aunt's love and help, she dreaded this tête-à-tête. She'd let Aunt Lavinia down, but she had to face the music. "Aunt Lavinia—"

"Darling, I can't tell you how grateful I am to you," her aunt interrupted. "Thank you for all you did for Netta. I'm sure you were a great comfort to her, especially at the end." Lavinia's voice quaked on her last two words, and Bea Dot's throat constricted as well.

"How can you be so gracious?" Bea Dot asked. "I've failed you and Ralph. Netta would probably still be here today if I'd insisted on a doctor's care."

Aunt Lavinia clutched Bea Dot's hand and leaned toward her niece. "What doctor's care?" she asked. "There was no way Ralph could have delivered the baby. You were all in an impossible situation. Of course, my heart is broken at the loss of my child, and a grandchild to boot, but it's a comfort to know that you were with Netta at her last moments. She loved you so much."

The tears pooling in Aunt Lavinia's eyes intensified the blue of her irises. Bea Dot's heart swelled with relief and gratitude, but then she registered Aunt Lavinia's last sentence and frowned. "What did you mean, 'and a grandchild to boot'?"

This time Aunt Lavinia wrinkled her forehead. "Why, just that, dear. I'll never know my grandbaby, and I'll never have another. Maybe one day you'll have a little one for me to dote on."

"But Aunt Lavinia, the baby didn't die," Bea Dot said, shaking her head. "Netta had a little girl. She's named after her mother."

"Really?" Aunt Lavinia drew her hand to her mouth. This time tears of joy spilled onto her cheeks. "I have a granddaughter?"

"I'm so sorry for the confusion," Bea Dot said. "I thought Ralph had explained."

Aunt Lavinia shook her head, then pulled a handkerchief from her sleeve and blew her nose. "We haven't spoken," she said. "We got a short letter from him. He was so distraught, and so over-whelmed with the influenza." She inhaled deeply and stared out the window as she recalled the horrible day of Netta's death. "Reading it broke my heart to bits. I was crushed to learn of my baby's death, but also terribly worried for Ralph and for you. We tried to phone, but we couldn't get through."

"I never learned what happened to Pineview's operator, but I think she died." Bea Dot's heart ached at the thought of her aunt and uncle's worry, and she punched a fist into her lap. "I should have written. I should have done something to get word to you. I'm so sorry."

Aunt Lavinia stopped her niece by putting a finger to Bea Dot's lips. "Not one more apology. You just made me a very happy woman. We'll have to go to Pineview soon to meet the baby. I'll ask Penny to cook us a special dinner tonight. We should celebrate."

She leaned forward and wrapped her arms around Bea Dot, who relaxed in the warmth of her aunt's embrace. She rested her cheek on her aunt's shoulder and took in the scent of lemon verbena. She sighed at the comfort of Aunt Lavinia's palm rubbing her back. "You and Uncle David have always been so good to me."

"Now it's my turn to feel guilty," her aunt said, pulling away, then standing and stepping to the fireplace. "I should have done more. I should have taken you out of Ben's house the minute I suspected any hostility." She shook her head as she stared through the painting over the mantle. "When you insisted on the marriage, we all figured you must love him, so I told myself that you'd be in no danger as long as California was looking after you." She shook her head and smiled derisively. "What a fool I was."

"She was looking after me," Bea Dot said. "Her heart was always in the right place, but looking back I realize I should never have let her talk me into marrying Ben."

"That's why you married him?" Aunt Lavinia turned to face her niece, her eyebrows a slight V on her forehead. "Why would she want you to do that?"

Bea Dot stared at her hands balled in her lap. The heat of her cheeks spread down her neck and between her shoulder blades, but the rest of her shivered with shame. Still, while reluctance nagged at her, a stronger internal force reminded her that Aunt Lavinia had put her own safety at risk by stepping in on Ben's fury. If her aunt was willing to jeopardize her own life, Bea Dot at least owed her the truth. So she told her everything. "I needed a husband, a father for the baby I was carrying."

And with that simple admission, an internal gate opened, allowing her to lay her whole life on the table.

"It's no secret my father never got over my mother's death. She must have been a remarkable woman to affect him so. I wish I'd known her."

"She was a beautiful lady with a heart of gold," Aunt Lavinia said softly.

"You'll have to tell me about her," Bea Dot replied, "because I know almost nothing except that I look like her, and for that reason, Father always resented me. Each birthday was a day of mourning at our house, and as I grew older and looked more like her, Father's resentment turned to contempt, which he exacerbated with heavy drinking. Soon, he hardly said a word to me except 'Leave me alone' or 'Hand me that bottle.'"

Aunt Lavinia came to the divan and knelt, taking Bea Dot's hands and drawing them to her own chest. "Darling, we knew how brokenhearted he was. That's why we included you so much in our lives. You know how much we've always loved you, don't you?"

"Of course I do," Bea Dot said. "You and California have always tried to fill my mother's shoes. Perhaps Father depended too much on you for that, but every time he looked at me, he saw my mother looking back."

"But I don't understand what that has to do with your decision to marry Ben Ferguson," Aunt Lavinia said. "You said you needed a father for your child." The pitch of her voice elevated as she uttered the terrible thought. "Did Ben force himself on you?"

"Not Ben," Bea Dot whispered. "My father."

Aunt Lavinia gasped, and Bea Dot closed her eyes as she recalled that dreadful night just over a year ago, when Charles Barksdale stumbled home drunk after an evening of cards at the club and found Bea Dot in the kitchen, wearing her nightgown and pouring a glass of milk before bed. In his confusion, he called her by her mother's name and said how much he'd missed her and how happy he was she was home. When Bea Dot tried to correct him, he'd embraced her, kissing her full on the lips before she could wrench free. She rushed to get away from him, making it only to the parlor, where he caught her by the arm, threw her on the sofa, and raped her. Only after it was over, when he realized she was sobbing, did he come to his senses and understand his horrific act. California entered as he rushed out of the room and up the stairs. Bea Dot sought refuge in California's arms until both women flinched at the crack of a gunshot.

Bea Dot finally looked her aunt in the eye. Tears streaked Aunt Lavinia's face, which was struck with shock and sorrow. "My God," she whispered. "We thought he was drunk and depressed. We had no idea that—" She couldn't finish her sentence, but sobbed into her hands. She put her head into Bea Dot's lap as she cried, and Bea Dot stroked her grayish-blond hair. Eventually Aunt Lavinia looked up, her bright blue eyes lined with red. "We had no idea."

Choking up now, Bea Dot pressed her lips to squelch her own weeping. She nodded at her aunt, then composed herself. "That was the plan," she explained. "I couldn't tell you, Netta, or anybody else. I was so ashamed. I hated that even Cal knew, even though she kept my secret when I discovered I was pregnant."

"Oh, my dear," Aunt Lavinia moaned.

"That was just before Ben asked me to dance at the Hibernian gala. He'd been vying for my attention for weeks. I couldn't stand his snobbery, but Cal saw him as a way out of my predicament, and she convinced me to encourage him. I didn't know what else to do, so I listened to her."

"So that's why you rushed the wedding," Aunt Lavinia sighed, tears dried now. "And because of that wedding, you and Netta fought and didn't speak for months."

"Exactly. I couldn't explain to her the reason I married Ben. At the time, I thought her disapproval of my husband was better than her knowing the truth. I feared everyone would despise me."

"How could we despise you? You'd done nothing wrong. We would have helped you."

"I didn't realize that then. Anyway, Ben solved the problem for me. The baby died. Then I was stuck with him."

Aunt Lavinia rose from the floor and sat next to Bea Dot again. "Well, it's a mixed blessing. And as a result, you reunited with Netta."

"Yes, there is that. But as it turned out, Ben discovered the truth months ago, and he's been holding it over my head all this time. He's so angry with me, and I can't blame him, but now he's sworn to spread this information all over Savannah. I'll be a pariah once he's finished with me."

"I can assure you that won't happen." Uncle David's voice resounded in the room.

Bea Dot turned to find her uncle's broad, six-foot frame just inside the doorway. In his navy suit with white hair and steel-gray eyes, Uncle David could command attention just by standing there. No wonder jurors always found in favor of his clients. Will followed her uncle into the parlor, his wide-brimmed hat in hand. He walked directly to her, a grave expression on his face, and Bea Dot covered her face with her hands. She hadn't intended Will or Uncle David to hear her story. She wanted to crawl under the divan. But when Will stood behind her and placed his hands on her shoulders, she felt a little relief. Maybe he wasn't disgusted with her after all.

"When did you get home, dear?" Aunt Lavinia asked. She rose and greeted her husband with a kiss on the cheek, which she had to offer on tiptoe. "We didn't hear you come in."

"Just now," he said, putting his hand on her upper arm. "I'm sorry to interrupt your visit, dear, but I must speak to Bea Dot."

Bea Dot's heart galloped, but she maintained an air of composure, now accustomed to receiving bad news. "Have you talked to Ben?" she asked. "I imagine he bears nothing but contempt for me."

She felt Will's fingers tighten on her shoulders as Uncle David approached the divan and sat next to her, his mouth a thin line. "Ben is dead."

Bea Dot's heart skipped a beat. Had she heard correctly? The news struck her speechless. All she could do was gaze at her uncle's gray eyes.

"He came down with influenza," her uncle explained. "It progressed very quickly. By the time Dr. Arnold arrived this morning, it was too late. He died about an hour ago."

Bea Dot shifted her gaze to Aunt Lavinia, who stood wide-eyed at the door, her hand over her mouth. She turned to face Will, who responded with a solemn nod.

"Look at me, Bea Dot," Uncle David commanded. When she did, he peered closely at her as he spoke. "Do you feel all right? Any headaches or fever?"

She shook her head.

"Are you sure? You must tell us if you feel at all unwell."

"No," Bea Dot said numbly, still trying to absorb the news. "I feel fine." A pause, and then, "Perfectly fine."

"It's very important that we find Ben's will as soon as possible," Uncle David continued. "Given the circumstances, I wouldn't put it past Ben's parents to try to keep you from inheriting what's rightfully yours."

Bea Dot smiled at Uncle David's desire to protect her, but this time it was her turn to reassure him. "I don't know where Ben's will is, or even if he has one," she explained. "But it doesn't matter. I don't deserve anything of his, and I don't want it."

"I disagree with you about deserving it," her uncle said, "and I'll advocate for you however I can. You can depend on that."

"Thank you."

Will leaned forward so that he could meet her eyes. "You know I'm on your side too."

Bea Dot clutched his hand on her shoulder and squeezed it with appreciation.

"David, let us go into the other room so these two can talk," Lavinia said. "I have some good news to tell you as well."

"We could certainly use more of that," Uncle David said as he rose and joined his wife. "Bea Dot, we'll talk more about this later."

Bea Dot nodded, then watched her aunt and uncle leave the room, imagining her aunt's glee at telling her husband about their grandchild. Will came around the divan and sat in the place Uncle David had just vacated. "Really. How do you feel? This time, I'm not asking about your health."

She couldn't answer right away, unsure of how to pinpoint her emotions. She picked at the cuff of her sleeve as she frowned in contemplation. "It's hard to say," she finally answered. "Relieved, perhaps? Purged? Mostly overwhelmed. So much has happened in the last few days. Just after I learned California died, I learned you were alive. I awoke this morning wondering if I'd be able to get a divorce. Now I'm a widow. In my mind, I know the worst is over, but at the same time, I don't feel like celebrating. Does that make sense?"

Will took both her hands in his warm, comforting palms. "It makes perfect sense. In fact, it reminds me of how I felt when I returned from France—awfully glad to be home, but crushed at the reason for being there."

Bea Dot squeezed his fingers as she smiled at him. Will had never spoken to her of his wartime experience. Even now, his deliberately cryptic words revealed that this admission was a big step for him, and that his trust in her had grown. She didn't push for more details. One day, he'd share them with her. He sat with her in silence for a few minutes before Bea Dot suggested they join Uncle David and Aunt Lavinia.

"One more thing." Will stopped her as she shifted to rise. "I know this is the worst time to bring this up, but I'll have to return to Pineview tomorrow."

"Oh?" With her own life a whirlwind, Bea Dot hadn't thought about Will's leaving.

"I must get back to the crossing. I've been away far too long. But I want to remind you that I've asked you to marry me. You haven't given me an answer, and I don't expect you to give me one now. But the offer still stands, and I hope with all my heart that you'll eventually join me in Pineview."

Bea Dot reached out and put her hands to Will's cheeks, smiling at the thought of how lucky she was to have him in her life. "Nothing would make me happier."

Epilogue

"Why must we have this conversation again, Uncle David? My mind is made up." Bea Dot latched, then unlatched the leather handbag in her lap, spending her frustration through her fingers instead of her voice. "After installing a nice headstone for California and her family, I want to give the rest of the money to charity."

Uncle David sighed, then leaned forward in the train seat facing Bea Dot, holding his head in his gray-gloved hands. He shook it slowly, before raising his face to hers. She could see the exasperation in his eyes.

"You can give the money to charity, dear. I'm not opposed to that." He held his palms up to her as he spoke. "But why must you give it all away? Why not use some of it to invest in a house for you and Will when you marry?"

"Will already has a place," she explained for the hundredth time.

"A country store?" Aunt Lavinia chimed in next to her. "That's no place to raise a family."

"Let's not put the cart before the horse," Bea Dot said to both of them. "Besides, you don't know Will the way I do. He would never want to live in a house bought with Ben's money—"

"It was your father's money mostly," Uncle David reminded her, pointing his finger for emphasis.

"Nevertheless," Bea Dot persisted, "Will's not that kind of person. He would much rather use that fortune to help others. I would too."

Uncle David sighed, then leaned back in his seat.

"I told you she wouldn't budge," he said to his wife, who shook her head in defeat as she bundled up her knitting and tucked it away in her satchel.

Bea Dot peered through the window, where the afternoon sun glinted through the limbs of the rapidly passing pine trees. They'd been riding for several hours, but the train had recently left the Hawkinsville station. Pineview was next, and she couldn't wait to arrive, not only to see Ralph, Nettie, and Will again, but also to escape this belabored conversation about how to spend her inheritance.

"If you insist on giving the money away, have you decided on a beneficiary?"

"So many choices," she said, before biting her lip. "I want to get Will's input before making a final decision. I'll let you know soon."

Through the window, pine trees gave way to cotton fields, then the occasional farmhouse. Eventually the train passed the cotton exchange, and she knew the depot was imminent. She clutched Aunt Lavinia's arm. "We're here."

Aunt Lavinia gathered her wrap around her shoulders and put her satchel in her lap. As the train slowed, then came to a stop, Bea Dot rose and stepped back in the aisle to let her aunt deboard first. Aunt Lavinia would have run all the way to Pineview if she could have.

"What a nice little town," Uncle David observed as he stooped to peer out the window. "You'll have to introduce us to all your friends while we're here."

"I don't have many," Bea Dot said, nervous jitters developing in her stomach. "As soon as I arrived last time, Netta and I had to move out to the country. I hardly know a soul in Pineview." *And I doubt I have friends in the country, thanks to Ben's letter,* she thought.

The porter opened the doors of their car, and Aunt Lavinia nearly flew out. When Bea Dot and Uncle David stepped onto the platform, Aunt Lavinia had already found Ralph and greeted him quickly before taking baby Netta from the dark-skinned woman standing next to him. Ralph laughed heartily as Aunt Lavinia cooed and tickled the infant. The woman, whom Bea Dot supposed was the baby's nurse, smiled politely, then stepped back from Ralph and his mother-in-law.

Uncle David shook Ralph's hand, then pulled him close for a hug and manly thump on the back. Then he reached his finger under the baby's chin and said hello. Bea Dot approached Ralph next, smiling warmly.

"Hello, Ralph. It's good to see you again."

"I was never able to welcome you to Pineview the first time," he said. "Thank you for giving me this second chance." Although the strain had faded from Ralph's eyes, gray now streaked his formerly dark hair. He had not yet regained the weight he'd lost.

"Nettie has certainly grown," she said, dying to hold the baby but knowing she must wait for Aunt Lavinia to release the child.

"Yes, she certainly has. She's a blessing."

Aunt Lavinia stepped over to Ralph, declaring how her beautiful granddaughter favored the Barksdale side of the family. Ralph listened patiently, nodding and smiling, as his mother-in-law gushed.

Bea Dot approached the baby's nurse, who stood quietly with hands folded in front of her crisp, white apron. She wore a blue kerchief around her head. She met Bea Dot's eyes but said nothing.

"Hello," Bea Dot said gently, as if approaching a nervous cat. "I'm Bea Dot Ferguson, Mrs. Coolidge's cousin. You must be the baby's nurse."

"Yes, ma'am," the woman said pleasantly enough, but with no real enthusiasm.

"What is your name?" Bea Dot asked.

"Lola, ma'am."

Bea Dot's eyebrows rose at the recognition of Lola's name. "You worked for Mrs. Coolidge before her death, didn't you? And you cared for patients in the Coolidge home during the epidemic?"

"Yes, ma'am." Lola's countenance remained unchanged.

"Then you nursed my fiancée, Will Dunaway," Bea Dot said. "I can't thank you enough for all you did for him. He wouldn't have pulled through without your help."

Lola's shoulders relaxed, and something in her eyes softened. "He done it himself, ma'am. Ain't nobody survived that flu didn't have the strength to pull through."

"Well, I think you sell yourself short," Bea Dot said, cocking her head to the side and smiling. "And I will always be grateful for your assistance." She reached out and touched Lola's upper arm.

"Thank you, ma'am." Lola's eyes crinkled slightly as her lips elevated to a pretty smile. Then she nodded toward the Barksdales and Ralph as the baby began to cry. "I best see 'bout that child. Her grandmama gone jostle her to death."

Bea Dot chuckled as she watched Lola take the baby from a reluctant Aunt Lavinia, when a tall figure striding her way caught her attention.

"There's my bride to be," Will said as he embraced Bea Dot and planted a kiss firmly on her cheek. Then he picked her up and squeezed her as he whispered in her ear, "I'll give you a better kiss when we're alone."

"Can't wait," she whispered back before he put her on her feet.

"Did you have a good trip?" he asked.

"Long, but uneventful," she replied.

"Hello, Will," Aunt Lavinia interrupted them as she reached

up to kiss his cheek. "So good to see you again." Uncle David approached him and shook his hand, making the usual small talk about the train ride.

"Well, look who's finally come back to see us!" Bea Dot turned quickly at the familiar voice behind her. Thaddeus Taylor towered above her, with Eliza next to him, holding a much bigger baby Troy. She wore a familiar brown wool skirt with a gathered hem and slit in the front, where a lacy petticoat peeked out. On her head she wore a smart hat of brown-and-gray-spotted fur.

"Why, Thaddeus! Eliza! I wasn't expecting to see you here." Bea Dot grinned at the Taylors' friendly greeting, though her insides still hummed at the possibility of disapproval, still not knowing exactly what Ben had told them in his letter. "You are so kind to meet us at the station. And Eliza, you look so pretty in that outfit. Have I seen it before?"

"When you left it at my house, I figured you didn't want it no more," Eliza said, blushing and smiling sheepishly.

"That's my skirt?" Bea Dot asked with surprise.

"It's the one got ripped down the front," Eliza explained. "I fixed it up real nice with this petticoat because I needed something fancy enough to wear with this hat Thaddeus made me."

"That there's the bobcat Will killed," Thaddeus said with a proud smile.

Bea Dot stepped back to admire Eliza in her new hat and altered hobble skirt.

"I hope you don't mind me wearing it," Eliza said shyly.

"Of course I don't," Bea Dot said. "I think it's very becoming."

Eliza grinned at the compliment, then smiled at her husband with satisfaction.

"Well, why are we all standing here?" Ralph said to the whole group. "Let's go back to my house and start Thanksgiving a little early. Come, Mr. and Mrs. Barksdale, you can ride in my auto-mobile." He gestured to the porter to follow him with the luggage.

"We'll be along behind you," Will called out to Ralph as the group made their way to the edge of the platform. Bea Dot slowly surveyed the station's surroundings, but all she saw were Ralph's motorcar and the Taylors, who were now getting into Thaddeus's truck. Two or three other passengers got into cars with their loved ones, but where was Will's horse and wagon?

"Are we going to walk to Ralph's house?" Bea Dot asked.

"I have a surprise for you," he said with a wink. "Follow me."

Taking her hand, Will led Bea Dot to the other side of the station, where she found a porter had already placed her trunk in the back of a shiny black flatbed truck. Will walked up to it and opened the passenger's-side door. Dumbstruck, Bea Dot stared at the machine, then forced her eyes away from it to gape at Will.

"Well, what do you think?" he asked.

"I think a pig just flew by," she said. "Either that or hell just froze over. You bought a truck?"

"Yes, ma'am," he said, his back straightening with pride. "After you said you'd marry me, I figured my wife shouldn't ride around town in a wagon. Besides, the first time I picked you up at the station, the wagon proved a bit of a problem."

Bea Dot smiled at the memory.

"Come on," he said. "Get in." He gestured toward the door, and Bea Dot slid into the seat. Will shut the door, then turned the crank before taking the wheel.

"How long have you had it?" she asked.

"A little more than a week," he answered. "Just long enough to get comfortable driving it." He put the car in gear, then pulled away from the depot. "How do you like it?"

"Oh, it's mighty fine," Bea Dot said, rubbing her gloved hand along the leather seat. "Will you take me for a short ride around town before we go to Ralph's?"

"Certainly, madam," Will said in jest. Then he added, "I'd love to have a few minutes alone with you anyway."

Bea Dot's heart warmed at the anticipation of having this man all to herself by New Year's. Still, she lowered her voice and turned to a more serious topic. "Will, I must ask your opinion about something."

"What is it?"

"You know I've decided to donate my inheritance to a charity," she began, examining her fingers as she spoke. When Will frowned at the mention of Ben Ferguson's estate, she continued quickly to get the matter over with. "Well, it just came to me that the money would best be used in the form of scholarships."

This time, Will's eyebrows lifted. "That's a good idea," he said. "Have you chosen a school?"

"Not definitely, but I was thinking, well, have you heard of Spelman Seminary in Atlanta? Or Morehouse College?"

"I think so," Will replied slowly. "Those are schools for black folks, aren't they?"

"Yes. I was thinking of giving Ben's money to them."

Will's laugh came straight from his gut, and its volume made Bea Dot jump at first.

"What's so funny?" she asked.

"The thought of Ben Ferguson turning over in his grave," Will said, brushing a lock of hair off his forehead. "What a perfect ending to his story—giving his money to a couple of black schools. Have you told his parents yet? They'll have kittens."

Bea Dot pulled back one corner of her mouth in disapproval. "This isn't a joke, Will. And donating to those schools has nothing to do with what Ben would think. I truly believe they're the best choice."

"All right then, why are you considering them?" Will turned his truck off the main street and drove Bea Dot toward the primary school.

"The thought just came to me as I was talking to Lola," she said. "I don't know her well, but I would imagine she had very little education. Yet when you and all those other people were sick, Ralph depended on her to care for you. Just think what she could have done if she had been schooled. She probably wouldn't take advantage of a scholarship herself, but I think she would appreciate the gesture of giving others a chance."

Will's voice softened at Bea Dot's explanation. "I hadn't thought of that. You have a good point."

"There's also Cal," she continued. "You didn't know her, but she was the most important person to me for most of my life. She died because a white doctor wouldn't make time for her. If our black folk can't turn to white doctors for help, then they need their own doctors to care for them. Maybe scholarships will help black students get the education they need to serve their own kind. And that would be good for the general public."

Will smiled and took his hand off the gearshift to clutch hers. "Well, sweetheart, you've sold me, but you don't need my opinion. It's your money. You do with it what you think is best."

"Then that's what I'll do," Bea Dot said, resting her head on the back of the seat.

Will had driven the truck around a block of Pineview's residential neighborhood before turning it back onto the street where Ralph lived. As the truck approached Ralph's house, Bea Dot spied his motorcar in the yard alongside Thaddeus's truck.

"I'm so glad Thaddeus and Eliza met us at the depot," Bea Dot said, exhaling with relief. "I've been so worried about them."

"Why's that?" Will asked.

"Oh, you know. I told you how Ben mailed them a letter telling them all about . . . well . . . my past." Bea Dot still hated to think about that dreadful night. "I'll never be sure of what he wrote, but knowing him, he told all. I was so afraid they would turn their backs on me."

"They're not the kind of folks to draw conclusions about a friend based on the words of someone they've never met," Will said. He turned into Ralph's driveway, and the truck bumped along the gravel. "Besides, I'm sure they never read that letter." He pulled the truck beside Thaddeus's and engaged the brake.

"What makes you think that?" Bea Dot asked.

Will got out of the truck and walked around it to open Bea Dot's door. He took her hand as she got out, and placed it under his elbow. Then he smiled mischievously.

"Have you forgotten, my love, that I'm the mailman?"

Acknowledgments

In 2005, I had the honor of meeting and conversing with physician and award-winning author Richard Selzer. As he encouraged my work, he told me that he started writing when he was forty years old. At the time, I was thirty-nine, and I told myself that I'd better get busy.

Ten years later, my first novel has far exceeded my expectations, and it would never have succeeded had it not been for the love, support, and guidance of many people in my life.

I must thank my team at Lake Union Publishing, who not only believed in this book, but also taught me how to work through the editorial process. My editor, Jodi Warshaw, knows how nervous I was about signing on with Lake Union, but she and the rest of the team—Clete Smith, Matthew Patin, Karen Parkin, Patrick Hurley, Nicole Pomeroy, Jessica Poore, Thom Kephart, and Gabriella Van den Heuvel—showed me how smoothly the process can work.

Two beloved writing groups helped me draft, revise, and re-revise this book until it was finally ready to publish. To my Pen and Ink group—Lois Lavrisa, Patricia Mason, and Donna Shea—I extend my deepest thanks as they gave me loving friendship and constructive feedback from the moment Bea Dot first appeared on the page. To my Savannah Scribes writing group—Amy Condon,

Judy Fogarty, Lyn Gregory, Katherine Oxnard, and Tina Kelly—I extend sincerest gratitude. They showed up at book signings, cheered me on, and encouraged me to start another novel. Their influence makes me a better writer, and I am blessed to work with such a smart group of women.

A big salute goes to Tammy Ray and Lori Mallard, who taught me the hard but rewarding work of walking into stores and convincing their owners to schedule book signings. From them I learned the business of being an author.

For their love and support as I wrote, published, and marketed this book, I thank all my extended family, especially my in-laws JoAnne and Bruce Remler and my father and stepmother, Hugh and Barbara Lawson, who attended many of my speaking engagements and encouraged their friends to read *Dunaway's Crossing*. I thank my children, Davis and Lawson, for their patience as I took time away from home to attend writers' workshops and book signings. I extend my heartfelt gratitude to my brother, Harley Lawson, and my sister, Sabra Lawson, for reading my draft when it was still in the three-ring binder. Much appreciation goes to the writer who has been most present in my life: my mother, Skippy Davis. Showing her my manuscript was a difficult but important step because handing it off to her somehow made it real. So when she phoned me one day and said, "This is good," I knew the book was ready.

But most importantly I must thank my most enthusiastic supporter: my husband, Stephen Remler. His love and patience enabled me to juggle the various commitments in my life so that I could always have time for writing. I could not have written a word of this book without him, and no words could express how much that means to me.

About the Novel

Pineview is an actual Georgia town, situated in Wilcox County, just below the Pulaski County line. Although some names of Pineview locations are authentic in this novel, the characterization of the town is an amalgam of details of the Wilcox County and Pulaski County areas. Some names of well-known real people or places have been included in the book to lend the story some historic authenticity. However, characters are fictional and any resemblance to actual people is coincidental.

About the Author

© 2014 Bunny Ware

Nancy Brandon grew up in middle Georgia and graduated from the University of Georgia. She has taught college English for the past twenty-three years in Savannah, where she lives with her husband and two children. This is her first novel.

Follow Nancy Brandon online at http://nancybrandon.com.